More Praise for *The Lions of Fifth Avenue*

"Davis delves into the history of the New York Public Library in this delightful mystery. . . . The characters and story are stellar, but the real star of the show is the library, which Davis evokes beautifully."
—*Publishers Weekly* (starred review)

"*The Lions of Fifth Avenue* is a book written for booklovers."
—*O, The Oprah Magazine*

"Davis gives readers a mystery and a historical novel all in one absorbing tale."
—*Library Journal*

"The magnificent Fiona Davis has written a page-turner for booklovers everywhere! I was on the edge of my seat. . . . This is a story of family ties, their lost dreams, and the redemption that comes from discovering truth."
—Adriana Trigiani, *New York Times* bestselling author of *The Shoemaker's Wife*

"In a compelling novel that's part family saga, part high-stakes heist, and part love story, Fiona Davis creates an intricate and beautiful puzzle that kept me turning page after page as I tried to solve its central mystery along with her characters. A gripping and satisfying story for booklovers the world over."
—Jill Santopolo, *New York Times* bestselling author of *The Light We Lost*

"A captivating ode to the power of books, the bonds of family, and the beauty of finding the strength to be ourselves. . . . This is a novel for all those who believe in the transformative magic of the written word."
—Kristin Harmel, international bestselling author of *The Winemaker's Wife* and *The Room on Rue Amélie*

"[A] masterfully executed story about two women living decades apart, mysterious family secrets, and the quest to stake a place in society and history. Dazzling and evocative, with vibrant settings and unforgettable characters, this novel is perfect for fans of female-driven historical fiction. I loved it."
—Karma Brown, internationally bestselling author of *Recipe for a Perfect Wife*

"In this thrilling, poignant, and utterly irresistible novel, we are immersed in the secrets of the famed New York Public Library and the family whose lives are intertwined with it in 1913 and 1993. At once a breathtaking, page-turning mystery and a deeply personal story of women attempting to forge independent lives, it is, ultimately, a glorious tale of love."

—Sarah-Jane Stratford, author of *Radio Girls* and *Red Letter Days*

"With *The Lions of Fifth Avenue*, author Fiona Davis proves she is the master of the dual timeline! Once again she illuminates another New York City landmark—the New York Public Library—and expertly creates two rich, mysterious worlds, which she deftly braids together into a compelling, page-turning read. This is a novel for all who treasure books." —Renée Rosen, author of *Park Avenue Summer*

"Fiona Davis takes readers on a journey into the heart of one of New York's most venerable landmarks, the New York Public Library, in a story that follows two generations of strong-minded women, both connected to a mysterious series of rare book thefts. This novel is brimming with juicy literary details and fascinating feminist history."

—Whitney Scharer, author of *The Age of Light*

"Davis's latest NYC-set historical novel is grounded in researched detail, transporting readers between the 1910s and the 1990s. Bibliophiles and fans of Naomi Wood and Paula McLain will especially enjoy this glimpse inside the history of the institution and the tireless dedication of those who serve it." —*Booklist*

Praise for *The Chelsea Girls*

"Davis tells a very good story and deserves all the praise she won for her other books set in famous New York landmarks. . . . What finally emerges from the mix of detailed research and solid writing is a tale that is intricate and subtle, unpredictable and exciting."

—*The Washington Post*

"Davis, who has given juicy supporting roles to New York landmarks in *The Masterpiece* and *The Address*, uses Chelsea as a metaphor for the grandeur that was within reach but spirals into a much darker place."

—Associated Press

Praise for *The Masterpiece*

"Fiona Davis has made a name for herself in writing about famous New York City locations, and in *The Masterpiece*, she delivers another unputdownable gem."
—*PopSugar*

"A touch of glamour and a dose of captivating history fill Fiona Davis's latest novel."
—*Southern Living*

Praise for *The Address*

"A delicious tale of love, lies, and madness."
—*People*

"*The Address* is compelling, historically minded fiction with unexpected—and entertaining—twists and turns. . . . The novel delights."
—*Ms.*

Praise for *The Dollhouse*

"*The Dollhouse* is a thrilling peek through a window into another world—one that readers will savor for a long time."
—Associated Press

"An ode to old New York that will have you yelling for more seasons of *Mad Men*."
—*New York Post*

The

LIONS

of

FIFTH
AVENUE

A NOVEL

FIONA DAVIS

DUTTON

DUTTON

An imprint of Penguin Random House LLC
penguinrandomhouse.com

Previously published as a Dutton hardcover in August 2020

First Dutton trade paperback printing, May 2021

Copyright © 2020 by Fiona Davis
Excerpt from *The Spectacular* © 2023 by Fiona Davis

The Library of Congress has cataloged the hardcover edition of this book as follows:

Names: Davis, Fiona, 1966– author.
Title: The Lions of Fifth Avenue: a novel / Fiona Davis.
Description: First edition. | New York: Dutton, [2020] |
Identifiers: LCCN 2019057269 (print) | LCCN 2019057270 (ebook) |
ISBN 9781524744618 (hardcover) | ISBN 9781524744625 (ebook)
Classification: LCC PS3604.A95695 L56 2020 (print) |
LCC PS3604.A95695 (ebook) | DDC 813/.6—dc23
LC record available at https://lccn.loc.gov/2019057269
LC ebook record available at https://lccn.loc.gov/2019057270

Dutton trade paperback ISBN: 9781524744632

Printed in the United States of America
8th Printing

For librarians everywhere

CHAPTER ONE

New York City, 1913

She had to tell Jack.

He wouldn't be pleased.

As Laura Lyons returned from running errands, turning over in her head the various reactions her husband might have to her news, she spotted the beggar perched once again on the first tier of the granite steps that led to her home: seven rooms buried deep inside the palatial New York Public Library. This time, the beggar woman's appearance elicited not pity but a primal fear. It was certainly some kind of ominous sign, one that made Laura's heart beat faster. A woman on the verge of ruin, alone and without any resources. Unloved.

The beggar's black mourning gown was more tattered than it had been last week, fraying at the sleeves and hem, and her face shone with summer sweat. Every few days for the past month, she'd taken up a spot off to one side of the grand entryway under one of the towering stone lions, one of which had been named Leo Astor and the other Leo Lenox, after two of the library's founders, John Jacob Astor and James Lenox. Laura's children had admired them right off, with Harry claiming Lenox as his pet and Pearl doing the same for Astor, neither caring that the sculptures had initially been mocked in the newspapers as a cross between a dachshund and a rabbit. Only last week, Laura had just barely prevented her son from carving his initials into the sinewy rump of Leo Lenox.

The beggar woman shifted, finding what shade she could. The miserable-looking child who typically filled her lap was missing. Laura wondered where he was.

"Money or food, please, miss. Either will do."

Laura reached into her shopping basket and pulled out two apples. One of the library's employees would shoo the beggar away soon enough, and she was glad to have caught her in time, even if the act of offering the poor woman assistance was inspired, at least in part, by a ridiculous, superstitious bargain that existed only in Laura's mind. As if extending a kindness to someone in need would smooth the conversation ahead.

"Thank you, miss." The woman tucked the fruit away in her pockets. "God bless."

Laura hurried up the steps and into Astor Hall, past the dozens of visitors milling about, their voices echoing off the marble steps, the marble floors, the marble walls. Even the decorative bases for the bronze candelabras were made from Carrara stone sliced from the Apuan Alps. The choice kept the building cool on steamy September days like this one, even if in winter it was like walking into an icebox, particularly in the evenings, when the library was closed and the furnaces only lightly fed.

She turned left down the grand South-North Gallery, passing under a series of globed pendants of thick, curved glass that broke up the long lines of the coffered ceiling. About halfway down the hallway, she took a right, then another, before climbing up a narrow set of stairs that led to the mezzanine-level apartment where her family had lived for the past two years.

Their seven private rooms formed a right angle that hugged a corner of one of the library's two inner courtyards, the bedrooms and Jack's study along one side, and the kitchen, dining room, and sitting room along the other. The open area that formed the crux of the right angle, and where the stairway emerged, had become the kids' playroom, where Harry laid out his train tracks in one corner and Pearl parked her doll's pram under the door of the dumbwaiter. When they first moved in, Jack had had to give them a stern warning when they were caught poking their heads inside the dark shaft, but soon enough the family had settled in and adjusted to their new surroundings.

The director of the library—Jack's boss—had pointed out during their orientation how the classical architecture of the building followed a progression from hard materials to soft, starting with the stone entrance hall before yielding to the wood paneling of the interior rooms. Laura had done her part to stay true to the continuum, softening the hard floors with a mishmash of Oriental rugs and hanging thick drapes over the giant windows. On the fireplace mantel, she'd framed the newspaper article about their unusual living arrangements, which had been written the year they moved in.

She called out the children's names as she headed to the kitchen, and the sound of their heavy stomping behind her brought a smile to her face.

"Harry lost another tooth." Pearl dashed in first, her eyes flashing with glee from scooping the news out from under her brother.

Laura would have thought living in a library would turn them into a couple of bookworms, but Pearl wanted nothing to do with stories unless they involved ghosts or animals. Harry was different, although he preferred not to read himself but rather to be read to, particularly from his worn copy of *Maritime Heroes for Boys*. Earlier that summer, when Jack quoted a line from one of Shakespeare's sonnets into Laura's ear in a silly falsetto while she washed the dishes, Harry had demanded to know what it meant. At his bedtime, Laura had taken down the volume from the bookcase and read some of the poems aloud to him. Harry interrupted to ask questions about the more ribald phrases, which Laura dodged as best she could. Later, when she and Jack were lying next to each other in bed, they laughed quietly about their son's natural—and thoroughly innocent—ear for the smuttier bits.

Where Pearl could be bossy, Harry was sweet, if sometimes dim when it came to the vagaries of human nature. When Laura dropped off the children at the school on Forty-Second and Second Avenue for the first time two years ago, Pearl had taken a moment to analyze the groups of schoolgirls arrayed around the playground, figuring out the best approach, while Harry had recklessly stumbled over to some boys playing marbles, accidentally kicking several with his foot in the process, which resulted in a hard shove and a quick rejection.

Harry, at eleven, was older by four years, but Pearl was wiser, faster. Laura and Jack had discarded the original name they'd picked for their daughter—Beatrice—after she showed up with a white frost of fine hair covering her head, more like a little old lady than a baby girl. Her eyes weren't the vivid blue of Laura's but more a gray, and her features and coloring gave her an ethereal appearance. "Pearl," Laura had said, and Jack had agreed, tears in his eyes. "Pearl."

The last school year had been tough for Harry, who, unlike his sister, never brought friends home to play or got invited to birthday parties. Laura hoped this year would be different and he'd gain some confidence, especially since, if everything went according to plan, she wouldn't be around as much.

Pearl ushered her brother into the kitchen. "Show her the tooth, Harry."

He opened his palm, where a baby tooth sat like a rare jewel. Laura took it and held it to the light. "It's a beauty, let's see your gap."

He smiled wide, showing off the space where one of his canines had been. "It didn't hurt at all, I was playing with it with my tongue, and suddenly, pop, it was gone."

"You're lucky you didn't choke on it," said Pearl. "I know a girl who did and she died."

"Pearl, that's not true." Harry looked up at Laura for confirmation.

"You don't have to worry about that." Laura pocketed the tooth in her apron. "Now go get cleaned up before your father comes home."

She cut up the roast beef and potatoes from the other night, glad to not have to turn on the stove in this heat, and was slicing apples for dessert just as Jack came in.

Jack yanked at his tie and looked wildly around the tiny room. "I don't have time for dinner, the payroll still needs to be done."

This wasn't the right time for her news. She gave him a quick kiss, then turned and slid the letter that she'd left out on the worktable back into the pocket of her apron.

"Of course you have time for dinner, it's still early."

But she knew what he meant. He meant that if he skipped dinner, he would have time to do both the payroll and work on his manuscript. The book he'd started several years ago and was so close to finally completing.

"Can I take it into my study?" He shifted the payroll file to his left hand and grabbed a slice of apple. "I can do the numbers for payroll and eat at the same time."

His beseeching eyes reminded her of their son's. She made a plate and carried it into the extra bedroom, where he'd pushed one of the library desks up against the window. It was all out of proportion to the room, like a huge wooden barge squeezed into a tiny boathouse.

He was already working his way down the rows of the ledger, filling in each one with the name, position, and monthly salary of the eighty people under his employ at the New York Public Library. She looked over his shoulder at the list: attendants, porters, elevator runners, carpenters, steam fitters, electricians, stack runners, janitors, coal passers. And at the very top, Jack Lyons, superintendent.

When he'd been offered the job, back when they still lived at the Meadows, Laura had been reluctant to return to the city. Reluctant to give up the sunshine and fresh air that living sixty miles north of New York provided the children, as well as the kind community of fellow workers who lived within the perimeter of the ramshackle estate where Jack oversaw the grounds. The decision to move out to the country in the first place hadn't been her idea, either, but the position had offered them an escape of sorts: a way for Laura to avoid the worst of her father's wrath and disapproval at being an expecting bride. Together, she and Jack had decided to forgo the city lights for a quieter life, where Jack diligently oversaw the estate during the day and wrote at night. Every winter, Harry and Pearl marched out to sled down the big hill behind the owners' mansion after the first snowfall, and every spring, they picked daffodils from their cottage garden and presented them to Laura as if they were made of spun gold.

But then the wealthy old couple who owned the estate died, and their grown children decided to sell off the land, sending the employees packing.

Laura, Jack, and the children had moved into the library just before it opened to the public. Laura's view of the giant oak tree outside the caretaker's cottage window had been replaced with the harsh whiteness of twelve-inch-thick blocks of marble. Not a speck of green to be seen. The walnut paneling in the salon and the modern kitchen had appealed to her at first, as did the idea of living within the walls of the most beautiful building in Manhattan, but the isolation had eventually worn her down. While the library had lived up to its founders' expectations as the largest marble building in the world, an inspired example of classical design that took sixteen years to complete, Laura hadn't realized how remote their lives inside the white fortress would be. There were no neighbors to wave hello to each morning, as there had been at the brownstone where she grew up, nor picnics down by the river with the other families, as at the Meadows. Instead, just an endless parade of anonymous visitors who came in to see if the building lived up to its reputation for grandeur and beauty (the answer was always a resounding yes), or those who simply wanted to pull up a chair in the Main Reading Room.

Jack swaggered about the building as if it were his own castle, which, in some ways, it was. He knew all the secrets, every nook and cranny. He bragged about the place to the children so often that they easily parroted back his statistics: thousands of visitors a day, eighty-eight miles of stacks holding one million books.

And in the very middle of it all, their small family, tucked behind a hidden stairway.

She couldn't wait any longer. Once he started in on his manuscript, her interruption would be even less welcome. She thought of the beggar woman squinting in the harsh sunlight, one bare hand lifted. That would never be her.

Slowly, she withdrew the envelope from her pocket and slid the letter out, the only noise the scratch of Jack's fountain pen.

"I heard back," she finally said.

He placed his pen down on the desk without looking up. "Is that right?"

She waited.

"And?"

"I've been accepted."

The Main Reading Room on the third floor was the best place for a good late-night cry. Laura had discovered this soon after they'd moved in. She'd always been easily moved to tears, and the vastness of the space, with its fifty-foot ceilings adorned with puffy clouds, was as close as she could get to the fields behind the upstate cottage where she'd retreat when her emotions overcame her. During the day, the room's gleaming tables, punctuated with desk lamps, were flanked by the curved backs of patrons, reading or making notes with the quiet scratch of a pen. Laura often imagined what it would look like if all their thoughts became visible, the enormous cavern above their heads suddenly crammed with words and phrases, floating in the expanse like bubbles.

Tonight, though, the room was the repository for only her own wretched musings.

She cried not for herself but for how upset Jack had been to not be able to grant her that one wish: to go to Columbia Journalism School. They simply couldn't afford it. He had such a pleasant face—open and quick to smile—that to see him distraught made her twice as disappointed in herself for bringing him pain.

When she'd first brought up the idea with Jack earlier that year, he'd approached it with his usual meticulousness. Together, they'd made a list of advantages and disadvantages, and decided that it would be feasible only if she received a full scholarship. Which she had not. As a matter of fact, she hadn't even been accepted, only wait-listed. Until today.

She hadn't considered the idea of going back to school until several months ago, when the assistant director of the library, Dr. Anderson, had heard her joke about her life raising children within the library's walls and suggested she write a piece on the subject for the employees' monthly newsletter. She'd dashed off a silly article about the difficulty of keeping Pearl and Harry quiet during the day, especially in the summer, when they weren't in school, and how she'd come up with the idea of a ten-minute "stomp" every evening, after the patrons had drained into the streets and the administrative offices had emptied. At her signal, the three of them would leap about the hallways, dancing and singing, Harry running laps and Pearl practicing her yodel, bringing the night watchman sprinting to the second floor to find out what on earth was going on. He'd stood there, panting, hands on his knees, and Laura had worried he might collapse from the fright. After that first time, though, he'd gotten used to the idea, sometimes even joining in, offering up a yowl that echoed down the stairwells and probably frightened the rats rooting around in the basement.

Once Dr. Anderson took over as director, he'd insisted Laura write a monthly column called "Life Between the Stacks," which she dutifully tapped out on Jack's typewriter while he was at work. Soon after, she'd seen an announcement in the newspaper about a school of journalism being started at Columbia University, open to both men and women. Upon inquiring, she discovered that students who already held a bachelor's degree could take just one year of courses. One year. Eighty-five dollars a term. A grand sum, considering Jack's salary. But still, just two terms. It would be over before they knew it, and then she could get a job at a newspaper and bring in her own salary. After her discussion with Jack, she'd asked Dr. Anderson for a recommendation and been delighted when he'd agreed to provide one.

Laura had learned that she'd been placed on the waiting list a few weeks after she'd mailed in her application. Then, today, she'd learned the good news. A place had opened up and was hers, if she wanted it. But Jack didn't seem to see it the same way.

"I wish we could afford it so you could go, but maybe this is for the best," he'd said back in the apartment. "Even if we could, what about the children?"

She'd been expecting the question. "They're old enough to take care of themselves. If there's ever a problem, you're right here in the building."

"Why not keep doing what you're doing, Laura?" asked Jack. "Dr. Anderson said just the other day that you've got a lovely way with a phrase in the newsletters."

"Because it doesn't pay. I want to help so you don't feel the full burden of our life on you."

"We always land on our feet. What burden are you talking about?"

She couldn't mention the beggar; he wouldn't understand. That she feared if something happened to Jack, she'd also end up on the steps, ragged and dirty, begging for money. She'd seen her parents' lavish lifestyle curtailed after several financial struggles, although they refused to speak of them, as if by ignoring the problem, it would disappear. Which it had, in a way. Every few months, Laura noticed another empty space in their Madison Avenue town house where an antique bureau had been sold off, or a too-bright square in the wallpaper where a severe portrait had once hung.

The latest issue of *McCall's* had included an editorial about the restlessness growing among modern women, of the need to have some power over their lives. She experienced that restlessness in her bones every day. To live in a building that spilled over with books and knowledge, with its shelves of maps and newspapers from around the world, yet to feel so utterly stifled, was torture.

"I want a passion, like you have for your manuscript." Maybe he'd understand it if she put it that way.

"Look, Laura, I'll be done with the manuscript by next year. If we wait until then, we can use the advance for your tuition. It's the least I could do, after everything you've done for me."

She slumped into his lap and put her head on his shoulder. "We can't do that, silly," she whispered. "The advance is for you to quit this work and write full-time. But you see, if I've graduated by then and have a position, you'd be able to quit no matter what."

She could see she'd said the wrong thing by the way he blinked twice. That was how well they knew each other, after eleven years as man and wife. They'd met when she'd been in New York City in between terms at Vassar, at a party where she'd worried she'd talked too loudly and brashly about the meaning of a Poe poem. She was still getting used to being the youngest in the room and no longer the smartest. Laura had whizzed through high school in three years and been accepted to college at sixteen, urged on by her mother to take hold of every opportunity. But Laura's time spent back in the city, among greater minds than her own, had brought her quickly down to earth. Embarrassed after her Poe soliloquy at the party, she'd retreated to the kitchen to help wash up. Jack had joined her, drying the champagne coupes, both of them stifling a laugh after the hostess breezed by and warned them to be careful to not break the stems.

"Do be careful," Jack had said with an affected accent after she left. "They're quite delicate, you know." He held one up to the light to check for spots, his enormous hand like a bear's paw. At which point the glass had fumbled away from him, landing in the sink in a pile of icelike shards.

They'd stared at each other in shock before doubling over with laughter. Later that evening he'd called her beautiful, and he didn't seem to mind that her thick, dark eyebrows made her look sanctimonious (or so said her father) or that her hair was an unruly mess (her father again).

She caught Jack glancing at his typewriter. He was eager to get back to work, to use up every possible minute before he fell into bed at midnight, exhausted.

"We can ask my parents, maybe." She knew it wasn't really an option but wanted to encourage him to consider it from all angles.

He stiffened. Mentioning her parents had been another mistake. He'd spent the past decade trying to prove himself as a good husband and father. "No. We don't go to them."

"Right. Sorry."

Jack opened the letter and read it. "It's eighty-five dollars a term, plus twenty dollars for books." He placed it back down on the desk and lightly wrapped his arms around her. "It's out of our reach. Besides, you'll be older than the other students. By ages."

She swatted at him, although the words stung more than she let on. "I'm only twenty-nine. Don't look a day over twenty, they tell me."

"Twenty-one at the most."

"It's only for a year. Quicker than any other type of degree. What if we scrimp?"

But she knew their finances as well as he did. How strange to be barely managing month to month while living in such architectural splendor. The kids were growing so fast, they needed new clothes every other day, it seemed. Pearl had come down with a terrible influenza in January, and the doctors' bills had almost done them in. She was fine now, thank goodness, but they were still catching up. The timing couldn't be worse.

He took her chin in his hand and gave her a kiss. "I'm sorry I can't give you the world."

"Not yet, but soon." She put as much cheer into her voice as she could muster and left him to his work.

After washing and drying the dinner dishes, she'd checked on the children—Harry was fast asleep and Pearl was in her room playing dress-up with her doll—before stealing out of the apartment and up a flight of stairs to the Main Reading Room to nurse her injury in private. Her father had warned her that if she went against his wishes and married Jack, her life would drastically change. He'd been right about that, but not in the way he'd envisioned. She loved watching as the children grew taller, faster, and funnier every day, and she was lucky to be sharing her life with the man who knew her best.

But still. Time was going by so quickly, and she wanted to do more, be more. The daily chores, the sameness, weighed her down like stones in her pockets. Every day, there was yet another dinner to cook, yet another sock to mend.

She took a handkerchief from her sleeve and wiped her eyes, enjoying the stillness of the space, the dark quiet.

A sound up on the walkway that ran the length of the room above the shelves made her jump. A door opened, and there stood Dr. Anderson, squinting over the railing.

"Mrs. Lyons, is that you?"

She prayed her red eyes wouldn't be noticeable in the darkened room. Rays of moonlight streamed through the giant casement windows, but not enough to see well by.

"Certainly is, Dr. Anderson." She had no reason to be here at this hour, and she struggled to come up with an excuse before settling on the truth. "I like the quiet, sometimes."

"Me, too. I was just finishing up and wanted to enjoy a smoke. Have you been up here yet?"

"No, sir."

He motioned for her to take the door beneath him, sandwiched in between the shelves. It led to a spiral staircase that spilled onto the bronze-railed walkway, where she joined him. "Come this way." She followed him through yet another door, this one implanted in the marble slabs between the second and third windows. Inside, a couple of steps led into a tiny, narrow passageway, hardly big enough to fit three people. Before them stood a door with a small, barred window. As he opened it wide, she gasped and stepped forward.

They stood in the night air on a balcony high above Bryant Park, looking west across the city. The full moon had brightened the neighboring buildings, while directly below, the trees cast moon shadows along the walkways, as if it were midday.

"I always wondered about these balconies," she said. "They seem so far away when viewed from the park below."

"Rumor has it they were meant to eventually be walkways, for an extension of the building that was never realized, but I have a feeling the architects simply liked the way they looked." He took a drag on his cigarette. When she first met him, she'd been cowed by his high forehead and puffy lower lip—he reminded her of the portraits of French aristocrats from the seventeenth century—but his encouragement with the newsletter columns had softened her initial impression, and his recommendation letter had been nothing less than glowing.

"Any news from Columbia?"

She'd hoped he'd forgotten about it, as she'd first mentioned it way back in the spring when she applied. No such luck. "Yes."

"Do tell."

"I was wait-listed at first, but I recently learned that I was accepted."

"Well, congratulations on that achievement. Jack must be very proud."

"He is. But I think I'll wait to go anyway. Now's not the time."

"Is it the expense?"

If she said yes, it would seem like she thought Jack's salary was unfair, which was far from the truth. In her confusion to find the right response, her face became hot. She blushed furiously under Dr. Anderson's close scrutiny. "No, not at all," she stammered. "The children need me. I'll try again next year, when they're a little older."

"So you had me write that letter for naught?"

His tone cut to the quick. He was not pleased.

"No, that's not it at all," she quickly assured him. "Circumstances changed, you see."

He put out his cigarette and held the door open for her to retreat back inside. As they walked through the Main Reading Room and into the adjoining Catalog Room, they spoke of the heat wave gripping the city and other mundane matters before she retreated to the apartment to put Pearl to bed.

Three days later, Jack dashed into the apartment to fetch her as she was in the middle of drying the children's clothes, her arm worn out from cranking wet undershirts through the wringer.

"Dr. Anderson wants to see both of us," Jack said, his face pale. "Right now, his secretary said."

Her stomach lurched as she followed him down the hall. Had she shared too much with Dr. Anderson the other night? He'd seemed curt, perhaps angry that she'd asked for a recommendation but not followed through. What had she done?

CHAPTER TWO

New York City, 1993

Sadie Donovan leaned against the stone lion named Patience
and waited for the line of tourists entering the library to sub-
side. The March sun was bright, offering a tease of warmth, but
the intermittent gusts of wind made it clear that a temperamental
spring was still firmly in charge. The chilly air irritated her, as
did the crowds storming the building. They came in wave after
wave, first taking photos of the two marble lions that flanked the
steps—the one across the way was called Fortitude, the names
conferred in the 1930s by Mayor LaGuardia as a reflection on
Depression-era virtues—then around the revolving door that deposited them into the foyer like widgets in an assembly line. From
there, they'd wander aimlessly, running their greasy hands over
the polished walls and jamming up in the entrance to the Reading
Room on the top floor as they stared up at the painted ceiling, fish
mouths agape.

She almost wished the architects hadn't put so much fuss behind their design for the building. This ought to be a place for scholars, where the maps and books and artifacts took precedence, not the scrollwork or chandeliers. If it were up to her, she'd allow the gawkers limited access, say seven A.M. to nine A.M. every other Wednesday. If the tourists wanted a museum, they could go to the Met uptown and be pests there. Not on her turf.

Finally, the crowd eased and she headed inside, maneuvering up the stairs to the northeast corner of the library's top floor, through the heavy wooden door marked BERG COLLECTION. While the Reading Room down the hall offered a vast expanse of desks and chairs under rows of massive windows, the Berg had no windows and only a couple of large tables. Yet it offered its own quiet sense of majesty, with fluted Corinthian columns flanking Austrian oak panels. Glass cabinets showed off valuable editions and manuscripts by Thackeray, Dickens, and Whitman, generously donated by the brothers Henry and Albert Berg back in the forties. The room felt intimate, safe.

As she walked into the back-office space, her colleague Claude looked up from his desk.

"Any sign?" she asked.

"No." His phone rang and he turned away. Sadie settled in, placing her purse in the drawer of her desk. On the other side of the room, a dozen interoffice envelopes sat piled up on their boss's desk. Sadie supposed she might as well start her day going through them so the administration of running the Berg Collection wouldn't fall behind.

Yesterday, Marlene Jenkinson, the Berg's curator and Sadie's mentor, hadn't shown up for work as expected from the weeklong trip to New England she'd taken with her husband. When there was no sign of her early that afternoon, Sadie and Claude had approached the director of the library, Dr. Hooper, and been told to carry on with their work—he'd fill them in soon. Sadie had continued working on the master sheet of the Berg Collection's highlights for an upcoming exhibit, entitled *Evergreen*, while Claude had been one room over, in the exhibit hall, going over the floor plan with the carpenters.

It wasn't like Marlene to extend her trip and not tell them, to leave them in the lurch like this. The exhibit was an opportunity for the Berg to shine. It would attract international attention, and they'd all been working doggedly ever since it was announced, spending weekends down in the stacks, going through the rare books and taking inventory.

Over the past four years, Marlene had proved a kind and generous advisor and friend to Sadie. Surely, if something were wrong, Marlene would have reached out and let her know. The mystery around her absence, followed by Dr. Hooper's curt dismissal, worried Sadie. She considered airing her concerns out loud to Claude after he hung up the phone, but thought better of it. They'd been circling each other with caution the past couple of months, now that their "relationship" or whatever it was called was over, and she didn't want to show any vulnerability in front of him.

Sadie had always preferred books to people. In high school, she'd eaten her lunch in the library to avoid the confusing maze of social rules in the cafeteria. She'd befriended one of the librarians, who, Sadie's senior year, urged her to get a degree in library sciences at Rutgers, where Sadie aced every class. After eight years working at the university's library, she landed a job at the New York Public Library and moved into an apartment in New York's Murray Hill neighborhood, not far from the town house where she'd been raised. It was perfect, with soaring ceilings, a fireplace, and a narrow stairway that led to a generous sleeping loft. The first night, she hugged herself with happiness, hardly believing that this was her life.

It was at the New York Public Library that she truly began to shine, manning her station at the reference desk in the Catalog Room next to the old pneumatic tubes that still carried the book requests down to the stacks far below. The questions came fast and furious, and she loved the more difficult ones.

How much horse manure was dumped on the streets in 1880? Sadie scoured the Department of Sanitation's books from that year and found the answer: approximately one hundred thousand tons.

When did the Statue of Liberty turn green? Digging through the library's archives, she came upon letters that described the landmark, looked up artists' renderings, and compared postcards of the statue over the decades, before pinpointing 1920 as the year it had weathered enough to turn completely green.

The crazier the request, the more fun. Here at the library, she was the queen of the inquiry, and her colleagues envied her talents. Sadie's skittishness around strangers, her worry that she was somehow lacking, disappeared at work. Because books didn't play games. Facts didn't play games.

Then she was promoted to the Berg Collection. While the library's vast holdings included several rare book and map collections, the Berg was Sadie's favorite. It wasn't like the Reading Room, where anyone with a library card could request a book. At the Berg, scholars and researchers were closely vetted. To gain access, they had to describe their research topic, summarize their research to date, and submit a reason for requesting whatever item it was they wanted to see. Which meant the inquiries were more challenging than the general ones down the hall, and also more satisfying. Even if she had to put up with a preening Claude repeatedly tossing his hair out of his eyes like a horse in the dressage ring, it was the perfect job.

None of the envelopes on Marlene's desk were time sensitive, so Sadie closed them back up and placed them in the in-box. Where could she be?

The phone at her desk rang, and she rushed to pick it up.

"Sadie, I need you to do me a favor." She recognized the voice as Dr. Hooper's. "Marlene was supposed to give a tour for our new board members today. Can you take over? I'd completely forgotten and they're already here. Then I'll need to see you and Claude in my office at two thirty."

"Of course. Where shall I meet the board members?"

"The Trustees Room. They're waiting."

The tour group consisted of a tall man with a neatly trimmed beard named Mr. Jones-Ebbing, and a married couple called the Smiths.

Sadie led the trio through the halls, pointing out all her favorite spots: the painted ceiling of a cloudy sky above the back stairwell, the Edward Laning murals depicting the history of the written word in the rotunda, and the view of the foyer from the second-floor balcony. Then down to the stacks, where the library's millions of volumes were housed. "If the shelves were laid end to end, they would measure over eighty miles," she said.

Mrs. Smith let out a small "Oh, my."

"This particular branch of the New York Public Library is a research library, not a circulating one," said Sadie. "That means we don't lend the books out, they must be consulted on-site. Furthermore, the stacks are not for browsing, they are closed off to the general public. Instead, a patron consults the card catalog and puts in a request, and then the book or books are sent to the Reading Room. The retrieval process hasn't changed much in all the time the library has been open to the public, since 1911."

The stacks consisted of seven tiers that rose from the basement level to just below the Reading Room. They reminded Sadie of an ant colony, with library pages dashing up stairs and down the narrow aisles, locating one book among millions within minutes along the steel shelves. She pointed out the conveyer system that carried books up to the patrons waiting in the Reading Room, as well as the dumbwaiter used for oversized works.

Mr. Jones-Ebbing ran his fingers along the spines of the books beside him.

"Don't touch." She smiled in an attempt to soften the command. These were the people who supported the library with their large donations. Marlene was quite good at coddling the VIPs. Sadie really needed to work on that.

Mr. Jones-Ebbing withdrew his hand and grinned, thankfully not in the least offended. "I just love the feel, and smell, of old books. Can't help myself."

"I'm the same way."

The group emerged into the newly constructed storage area that extended deep under Bryant Park. Sadie proudly reeled off the statistics. "The temperature is kept to sixty-five degrees with forty percent humidity, in order to best preserve the books. There's even another level below this one."

She showed how the bookshelves could be moved back and forth with a large wheel, so there was no wasted space. "Near the very back are a couple of small escape hatches—in case of fire—that exit onto the west side of Bryant Park." She was surprised to catch Mrs. Smith raise her eyebrows at her husband, unimpressed, as if they were touring a seedy warehouse.

"I prefer the old part of the library better," said Mrs. Smith.

"We had to expand to accommodate all the books. Although we currently use only one story of the two that were excavated, together they'll accommodate up to 3.2 million books and half a million reels of microfilm, effectively doubling our storage capacity."

Polite nodding. They were bored. She was boring them. Sadie racked her brain for something interesting to show them, something unexpected.

"We'll cut this short and go upstairs. Follow me."

They took the elevator back up to the third floor, to the Berg Collection, where Sadie led them over to one of the enclosed bookcases. She pointed through the glass door at the bottom shelf.

Mr. and Mrs. Smith leaned down to stare. "Is that a cat's paw stuck on the end of a knife?" asked the wife.

Sadie removed a white glove from her pocket and fitted it onto her left hand. She fiddled with the lock on the case and, once it was opened, slipped her gloved fingers carefully beneath the cat-paw letter opener and lifted it out, placing it on one of the tables reserved for researchers. The paw was about four inches long, easily recognizable as that of a gray-and-black tabby. The inscription read, *C.D. In memory of Bob 1882.*

"This is what Charles Dickens used to open letters," explained Sadie.

"Is it real?" asked Mrs. Smith, scrunching her turned-up nose. Maybe this had been a mistake.

"Yes," said Sadie. "The cat, called Bob, was so beloved by Charles Dickens that he had his paw put on a letter opener after he died."

"That's disgusting."

Sadie stumbled through the explanation as Mr. Jones-Ebbing slid his finger lightly along the sharp end of the blade; she barely stopped herself from giving his knuckles a good rap. "It's an important artifact, one that tells us a lot about Charles Dickens and the time period he lived in. Back then, taxidermy was all the rage. People made hats out of birds, inkwells out of horses' hoofs. By doing this, Dickens could still touch the fur of his beloved pet every day."

What else to show them? Sadie replaced the letter opener and looked around. "Over here is a walking stick that belonged to the essayist and writer Laura Lyons."

"Oh, gosh, I read all about her in some magazine not long ago," said Mrs. Smith, her stridency melting. "It's really hers?"

Finally, a hit. "Yes. She had it with her when she died, in 1941."

Sadie stared down at the stick, as she had many times since she'd begun working there. Sometimes, after hours, when she was alone, she'd take it out and place her bare palm where Laura Lyons's had once been.

"Simply fantastic," said Mrs. Smith.

Mr. Jones-Ebbing broke into her thoughts as they retreated into the hallway. "We were told you're working on the Berg Collection exhibit. Can you give us any hints of what you'll be showing?"

"I won't spoil the surprises, but I can tell you it will be the best that the collection has to offer."

"Cagey, I see," he said, eyes twinkling. "Can you at least share how you and your colleagues go about curating a big exhibit like this one?"

"We sift through the collection and allow the objects that capture our attention and imagination to illuminate the theme. In this case, the exhibit will be called *Evergreen*."

"What does that mean, exactly?" asked Mrs. Smith.

"The focus is on pieces that have retained their value to scholars and historians over time. While the Berg has some fantastic manuscripts and first editions and diaries and such, we would also like to showcase the quirkier pieces—the ones that have a different kind of story to tell."

Mr. Jones-Ebbing leaned in with a mock whisper. "I hope the letter opener makes the cut."

"I'll let you in on a secret: it does. But you can't tell a soul."

He put his fingers to his lips, and they all laughed.

Maybe this wasn't going so badly after all.

"Once we know the objects we want," Sadie said, feeling more at ease now, "we go through them and make sure they're in good shape, figure out how best to highlight them: what page a book should be opened to, what historical context needs to be explained." They'd reached the door to the Trustees Room. By now, all three board members were gathered around her, listening. "We'll consult with top scholars to determine what's the most important thing to mention, what should be revealed. Then there's all the work with the designers on the exhibit room itself, regarding the exhibit cases, the general aesthetic. What color paint on the walls? What typeface for the labels? How will we control the climate inside the cases? We'll also put together the catalog, which needs to be in language that's both suitable for the average reader and accurate."

"Quite a job. I look forward to the opening," said Mr. Jones-Ebbing. "Seems like it's in very capable hands." He smiled down at her. "I'll be sure to tell Dr. Hooper that you impressed us all."

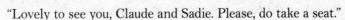

"Lovely to see you, Claude and Sadie. Please, do take a seat."

The director of the library, Humphrey Hooper, MLS, PhD, spoke with a quick, flat cadence, something Sadie had noted when she first met him a decade ago. Originally from Alabama, he'd somehow mastered a vocal inflection that couldn't be pinned to a particular place yet clearly signaled an upper-class upbringing, like Cary Grant in the old movies.

Since that first meeting, Sadie had risen from assistant librarian to librarian to assistant curator of the Berg Collection by learning everything she could about the library, from the genealogy department to the map room to the prints and photograph department, by coming in early and staying late.

Claude, sitting in the chair next to her, had taken a different approach, taking his superiors out to lunch and wooing them with his charm and wit. He wasn't handsome—his eyes bulged out slightly, and his upper lip tended to sweat when he got excited—but he had broad shoulders and a thick head of hair, and most of the female librarians swooned when he paid them the slightest bit of attention. He'd shone his light on Sadie during the library's last Christmas party, kissing her in the back-office area and making her feel breathless and beautiful.

That time of year had always been a dismal one for Sadie. Christmas Eve was when her father had passed away, so even decades later the sight of a pine tree aglow with a riot of primary colors induced in her an anxious melancholy. It also happened to be Christmas Eve when, sick with dread, she'd rifled through her now ex-husband's briefcase and found a bill for a credit card she'd never known about, filled with charges to the Washington Square

Hotel and several Greenwich Village restaurants. All conveniently located near NYU, where Phillip was a tenured math professor. Even though that was six years ago, the holidays still filled her with an ominous apprehension that the world might fall apart at any minute.

So it really was no surprise that with Claude's unexpected kiss, even though his breath smelled like Scotch, Sadie's yuletide clouds of misery had gently evaporated.

He'd been away for a week after that, during which time she'd let her imagination run wild, thinking of them together, wandering around the city, roaming from bookstore to bookstore. After he'd returned, they'd gone out to lunch together and sometimes dinner, where he held her a little too long when they said goodbye out on the street. At work, he'd made sweet overtures, like sharing a magazine article on the new Tennyson biography, or passing along the *Times* crossword once he had finished the paper.

But then, one morning, she'd turned the corner near the administrative offices and spotted him deep in conversation with one of the young pages who worked in the stacks. The girl had thrown back her head and laughed—a high-pitched, ludicrous sound like she was being strangled with sleigh bells—and something in Sadie had shut down, hard. The ups and downs of heartbreak were not for her, no way, not after what she'd already been through with Phillip.

That same day, deep in the stacks of the Berg Collection, Sadie had come across an intriguing title she didn't remember seeing before: a first edition of *Surviving Spinsterhood: The Joys of Living Alone*, published in 1896, by Abigail Duckworth. She plucked the thin volume from the Berg's caged shelves and began reading, turning her back so any passing pages couldn't see what was in her hand. She'd flown through it, delighted at the timeless advice for successfully maintaining independence as a woman, chock-full of pithy chapter headings like "Solitary Refinement" and "Pleasures of a Single Bed." For decades, women had lived happily, easily, without a man. That was good enough for her.

Claude had made overtures after that and been rebuffed at every turn. If he brought her the crossword, she'd say she'd already finished it. Articles? Read them. These days, she and Claude had maintained a respectful, if chilly, distance, and whenever loneliness threatened, she'd pluck the book off the shelf and turn to a random page for a quick dose of witty inspiration.

In Dr. Hooper's office, she smoothed down the voluminous skirt of her dress, hoping Dr. Hooper didn't find her outfit too frivolous for someone who'd just given a tour to trustees. That morning, she'd chosen a marigold-colored fifties shirtdress with thin orange stripes, admiring the way the full skirt fell away from her hips. It had been one of her most recent finds at the Antique Boutique thrift store, downtown on Broadway. But today, under the harsh lights of the director's office, the yellow zinged brightly. Perhaps too brightly.

She'd gotten used to the various reactions to her daily ensembles, ranging from a surprised "How lovely" to "Well, that's an interesting outfit." Sure, her tastes were a far cry from the current craze for Doc Martens and oversized suits, but eventually they'd come back into style and she'd have the last laugh. In the meantime, she liked the idea of wearing a piece of history, whether it was a tailored 1930s suit, only slightly faded, or the fifties frock she wore today.

Dr. Hooper consulted his notes. "We've had to do some reshuffling. Marlene, as you know, unexpectedly extended her vacation. Permanently, it turns out."

"What?" Sadie and Claude spoke at the same time.

"She reached out to me yesterday to let me know that she's taken the job of chief of collections at the Boston Library."

Sadie sat back, stunned. That explained the unexpected good-bye hug that Marlene gave her the Friday before she left for vacation. As well as her extra-detailed instructions for while she was gone. The decision to take the job, in charge of all the collections at the third-largest library in the country, must have been very difficult. Yet it was a big step up, and Sadie just wished Marlene could have felt comfortable confiding in her. But that wouldn't have been professional, and Marlene was nothing but professional.

"She was poached?" asked Claude.

Dr. Hooper harrumphed. "Yes. She gave her resignation yesterday and apologized for the short notice but said that it couldn't be helped. She added that she was certain the two of you could take on the mantle. I hope she's right. This is terrible timing, with the Berg Collection exhibit to open in May. We're in a bind."

If Marlene was no longer in charge, the logical next choice would be either Claude or Sadie. Sadie had been at the library longer, but Claude had more years in the Berg Collection. It was a toss-up.

"What can we do to help, Dr. Hooper?" asked Claude.

"There's no time to look for an outside hire, so I've talked with the board of directors and we've decided that we'd like Sadie to take the helm. For now."

The director wanted Sadie to become curator of the Berg Collection, one of the most esteemed literary collections in America.

Right when they'd be mounting a major exhibition that would be written about in all the newspapers.

"I'm sorry, but why Sadie?" Claude was not amused. "I've been working closely with Marlene this past year, day after day. I know what she wants to include."

"Right," said Dr. Hooper. "Luckily, we have the final list, so there are no decisions to be made there, as much as we appreciate all your hard work, of course. Sadie's been at the library longer and, we hope, will bring her comprehensive knowledge to bear as we get the exhibit up and running. That means long hours, lots of research and writing, but we believe you both will rise to the occasion."

"Of course." Sadie tried to contain her joy. What she really wanted to do was leap to her feet and jump up and down, the way her six-year-old niece, Valentina, did when she won at Connect Four. But that wouldn't do at all. "I'll get right on it."

"Thank you. I want to be clear, this is on a trial basis. I'll make another, more permanent decision after the exhibit is up and running." He shifted to address Claude. "Claude, I can't tell you how much we appreciate all of the hard work you've done. And will continue to do."

What an opportunity. The job went way beyond her current role as a chronicler of old books and literary paraphernalia. As the face of the exhibit, she'd be able to share with the world her love of these historical objects and the emotions they represented to her. She might even get offered the job for good, as the permanent curator of the Berg.

For the next twenty minutes, Dr. Hooper went through the list of exhibit items one by one, in alphabetical order, asking for a progress report. All went smoothly, until he reached the L's. "I noticed that the Laura Lyons walking stick is on the list of exhibit items," he said.

In the past five years, there had been a reawakening in interest around Laura Lyons, as her essays were reexamined by feminist scholars and cited for their forward thinking. The few details of the writer's reclusive life were being mined for clues, which made the walking stick a perfect choice.

But Sadie stiffened as Dr. Hooper continued. "Since she lived here at one point in her life, I want one of you to go through the library's archives, see if you can find anything about her that we've missed. I'd like to include more than the walking stick. An essay, some original piece of her work, a letter, something that would attract a lot of attention."

"I'll do that," offered Claude.

"No. I'll do it." Sadie didn't care that she was being rude. "I studied her work in college and so have a background that will be useful. Of course, all her private letters and manuscripts were destroyed right after her death. So I'd be surprised if we found anything of interest."

"In any event, let me know what you discover."

She avoided meeting Dr. Hooper's eyes as she assured him she would.

CHAPTER THREE

New York City, 1913

Laura and Jack waited outside Dr. Anderson's office on the second floor like schoolchildren caught cheating in class. She could hear the chimes of the grandfather clock on the other side of the wall, one of the many refined pieces on display. Dr. Anderson trusted only Jack to wind it each week; no one else was allowed to even touch it. It was as if the clock were the library's heart, ticking away, and Jack its surgeon.

"Do you have any idea what this is about?" he whispered.

She didn't mention her encounter with Dr. Anderson in the Main Reading Room a few days back. Certainly, she hadn't said anything untoward. But maybe he'd been more upset than she'd realized to learn that she was turning down Columbia after he had done her the favor of his recommendation. If they were turned out, they'd have absolutely nowhere to go, and no savings.

Jack had grown up on a thriving orange tree farm in California, attending a private school where he studied Latin and French, literature and philosophy, before throwing away a full scholarship to Stanford and heading to the East Coast with a friend. He wasn't ready for college, he told his disappointed mother, and might never be. There was more to life, he believed. Plus, Jack wanted to write.

Through connections, he and his mate Billy broke in with a crowd of wealthy young men and women who fancied themselves budding literary giants. Among them, Jack was certainly the most serious about his craft. The rest of the group devoted the majority of their energy to throwing parties for artistic types, like the one where Jack and Laura had met. But Jack had imagined writing a novel contrasting city with country life that would take the world by storm. He was so close to finishing it, he'd said repeatedly the past several months. Any day now, it would be ready to be submitted. Sometimes she wondered what would have happened if they hadn't met. He might have already been a shining star in the publishing world, probably on his second or third book. Not winding Dr. Anderson's clock week after week.

Dr. Anderson appeared and ushered them inside. He didn't gesture for them to take a seat. "Mr. and Mrs. Lyons, come in. This won't take long."

Oh no.

He picked up a thin envelope on his desk and held it out. Jack lifted his hand, but Dr. Anderson shook his head. "This is for your wife."

Laura took it, looking from one man to the other.

"I have good news," Dr. Anderson said. "I was able to secure a scholarship for Mrs. Lyons at the Columbia Journalism School for the first term. Just the first, I'm afraid. It was the best I could do."

Jack cleared his throat. "Sir, I'm sorry. You what?"

"I reached out to the bursar, who's an old college chum. Apparently, there was some scholarship money returned by a student who opted not to enroll, and I suggested it be directed your way."

"I have a scholarship?" asked Laura.

"You do. For one term. I wish you the best of luck."

Outside the office, Jack took Laura's arm and led her down to the basement level. Although the official building superintendent's office was on the main floor of the library, he'd also commandeered a small storage space in the basement, to be closer to the rest of the staff. They passed the chief engineer and several porters, all taking off their hats and nodding as Laura went by, as if she were the queen of the place, when it was really a testament to Jack's good standing among them. He was a natural leader who made a point of knowing the name of everyone who worked for him. Finally, they reached his basement office. Laura shut the door and leaned against it as he made his way behind the desk to his chair.

She quashed any outward show of excitement at the news, unsure of how to react, even as her thoughts raced in a loop: She'd gotten a scholarship. She could go after all.

"When did Dr. Anderson find out about our financial issues?" asked Jack. She could tell he was trying to keep his voice even, like she'd heard him do with an employee who'd disappointed him. Resentment rose up at the idea of being treated like a worker instead of a wife.

"He didn't. He'd asked me about my application a few days ago, but I told him I'd decided not to attend because of the children. You remember he wrote a letter of recommendation?"

Jack nodded.

"Well, he wanted an update, and that was that."

"So then he went and arranged a scholarship for you?"

"I don't believe it myself, to be honest. I know he likes my column, and the recommendation was nice, but I never expected something like this."

His nose scrunched up in a way that reminded her of Harry when he was miserable about something. She wished he could be happy for her, at this lovely turn of events. But Dr. Anderson was his boss, and she understood that Jack didn't want his relationship with his superior to become muddied or complicated.

She came around and perched on the edge of his desk, looking down at him and taking his hands in hers. "He did something kind, that was all. I'd like to go, and I'd like to have your support." She reached down and kissed him, feeling his rough beard on her lips. "You realize what this means, don't you?"

He shook his head.

"I can get a job at a newspaper next year and write a glowing review of your new book, saying that you're the next literary sensation. We'll play up the idea that you've been living in the library, scribbling away after hours, a poet who's soaked up the words of the masters and created a masterpiece himself. It's a terrific story."

Jack's smile spread slowly. "May I point out that it's a huge conflict of interest, a wife reviewing her husband? It seems that you need some schooling after all. They teach a course in ethics, I hope?"

Laura had already memorized the list of classes: "Training in Reporting and Interviewing, Editing and Rewriting Copy, History of Journalism, and Elements of Law."

"I suppose the law class will keep you on the straight and narrow. No sensational journalism for my wife."

"Never, my love." She'd done it. Somehow, she'd done it. "Never."

While the journalism school had officially opened its doors the year before, classes had been scattered around the campus until a new building was constructed, just in time for the class of 1914, Laura's year. The five-story Beaux Arts–style journalism building was located just south of the main campus library, and after registration, Laura and a dozen other students were given a quick tour. The spacious entryway reminded her of the prelude to her own home on Fifth Avenue, with a soaring ceiling and marble floors. In one corner, Rodin's bust of Joseph Pulitzer, the founder of both the *New York World* newspaper and the journalism school, glared at all who passed by. While the building had regular classrooms like those at Vassar, it also boasted a "morgue," which held a collection of newspaper clippings dating back to the 1870s, as well as a full-blown replica of a newspaper city room, replete with typewriters, a telephone, and a copy desk.

Laura made her way to a seat in the lecture hall. The opening address by the head of the school, Mr. Talcott Williams, flew by in a blur of pronouncements and a recap of the school's brief history. After, Laura gathered her things and sped to the city room, where her year was meeting under the tutelage of a well-known newspaperman named Professor Wakeman.

"Everyone, please, your attention." Professor Wakeman sported an unruly white mustache and barked out his words like a terrier. "Introduce yourselves, class of 1914."

One by one, they made their way around the room. Several of the men had already worked in journalism for a few years, and exchanged witty repartee with the professor about various editors they'd worked under, sharing chuckles and knowing smiles. The woman sitting beside Laura introduced herself as Gretchen Reynolds, a recent graduate of Barnard, who said her dream was to write for *Ladies' Home Journal* on the subject of fashion. Laura spoke of her desire to study journalism and left it at that, as she was too tongue-tied to go any further. Of the twenty-eight students who comprised the class of 1914, four were women. After the last student spoke, Laura pulled out a notebook and a fountain pen, eager to begin.

But Professor Wakeman had other ideas. "Gather your things, I'm sending you out on your first assignment. Go down to City Hall and listen to Mayor Kline's eleven-o'clock speech. After, get a statement from someone—you decide which official—about how the new mayor is settling into the role."

City Hall. She'd imagined the first week or so would be about the basics of newswriting, not to have to go right out and report so quickly. The thought unnerved her. But she knew where to go, and certainly listening to a speech, getting a quote, and doing a write-up wouldn't be that difficult. She was gathering her things in her satchel when the professor held up one hand.

"Wait a minute, that's only for the men." He glanced over in Gretchen and Laura's direction. "For the women, your assignment is to investigate what's going on at the Women's Hotel in the East Twenties, off of Park."

Laura's mind raced. A scandal at the first women's hotel in New York? One that called for an investigation? Whatever it was, this sounded much juicier than covering city politics.

Professor Wakeman gathered steam. "They've announced that they are no longer serving butter to the hotel guests, as part of a health initiative or something. Write up five hundred words on that. For everyone, the deadline is four o'clock this afternoon. Put your copy inside the vault." He pointed to what looked like a safe on one of the corner tables. "It locks automatically at four. Anything that's not inside will not be accepted."

A couple of students groaned.

"You don't like it? Then you don't deserve to be a journalist. We live on deadlines and cigarettes, remember. This is your first assignment, so make it count."

A steamy rain poured down as Laura, Gretchen, and the other two female students made their way downtown. Outside the hotel, they paused, unsure of what to do next.

Gretchen tried to smooth over the mangled curls of her bangs with one hand, irritability dripping from her like the rain. "This weather is wreaking havoc on my coiffure. Shall we go inside?"

"I suppose we should ask for the manager," Laura suggested, eager to get on with it.

Right then, a couple of young women draped in percale and long strings of pearls exited the hotel. As they waited under the awning for a cab, the other two students broke off and approached them, notebooks open, while Gretchen and Laura headed inside.

With surprising alacrity, they were shown up to the manager's office, where a woman with a long neck sat upright in her chair. "You're reporters?"

"Yes," said Laura. She didn't want to specify where from, not just yet. "We heard about the butter ban and were curious what prompted it."

"We care deeply for the health of our guests, who tend to be on the younger side." She looked over at Gretchen. Laura supposed she was too old to make the cut. "After a year of study, I have concluded that it is not conducive to good health. Same with cotton mattresses."

"I'm sorry?" said Gretchen. "What's wrong with cotton mattresses?"

"They will be switched out for hair mattresses instead. The cotton ones will be burned."

"But why?" asked Laura.

"Hair is healthier."

"Do you mind if I ask where exactly you found this information?"

The manager threw her an irritable glance. "I don't remember, exactly. A magazine article, I think."

"Have you consulted a physician about these two issues, about not eating butter and sleeping on hair mattresses? I mean, to get a professional opinion."

"I don't need to. I can see it with my own eyes, what's good for the girls and what's not."

Laura was about to ask her to be more specific, when Gretchen jumped in. "Do you worry that guests will go elsewhere if they can't get butter on their bread?"

"The parents of the girls are the ones who decide where they will stay, and they understand our concerns. We are the first and oldest women's hotel in New York City, and my guess is the other hotels will soon follow our lead."

What an utter waste of time. Who on earth cared about this subject? The men were downtown talking about the future of the city with the people who decided the future of the city, while Laura was stuck discussing hair mattresses. "Do you eat butter?" she asked.

The manager sniffed. "I do not. I have a very strict diet and follow it religiously, and believe all should do the same."

Laura couldn't help herself. "Can I ask what type of mattress you sleep on at home?"

The woman's eyes gleamed with the pride of the martyr. "I sleep on a mat on the floor, in fact. Much better for one's spine and circulation."

"So why not insist the guests do the same? Cheaper, by far, probably."

Gretchen threw her a look to stop teasing, but it was too late. The manager rose from her chair, the interview over.

"May I ask who you write for?" asked the manager.

Laura and Gretchen exchanged glances. "We're students at the Columbia Journalism School," Laura said.

"So you're not real reporters?"

"Not yet." Laura wished Gretchen would jump in and help out, but the girl remained mute.

"Why are you wasting my time, then?" The woman shooed them out and was still castigating them as they hurried down the hall.

"Well, that was a bust." Gretchen looked about. "I'm going to wait for a couple of guests to leave and interview them. I'll see you back at the school."

Laura walked east, annoyed at the whole ordeal. Ahead of her, she spied a red-haired woman heading to a smaller entrance off to the side of the hotel. "Excuse me," she called out.

The woman stopped, one hand on the door. "Yes?"

"Do you work here? I was hoping I might have a word with the cook." It was worth a shot.

"Sure. Follow me."

She was led down an alley and into a back entrance. The kitchen bustled with waiters pouring in and out from what must be the dining room. They moved with the synchronicity of ice-skaters, twisting their torsos to narrowly avoid colliding, and barking out orders above the din. At the center of the swirling stood a sixtyish woman with frizzy hair and enormous hands, cursing in an Irish brogue.

"I'm here about the butter!" yelled Laura when she got near. "May I ask you some questions?"

"The butter. Gah." The woman wiped her hands on her apron and stepped off to one side. "What do you want to know about the butter?"

"I'm a student journalist at Columbia." Better to be up front about the whole business this time. "I've been asked to write an article on the butter ban."

"You don't have better things to write on?"

"It's really not my decision. At any rate, how are you managing?"

"It's repressive and stupid. Write that down."

Laura already was, as fast as she could.

"The new management has silly ideas that will sink this ship fast."

"Have you had any complaints from the guests?"

"Not yet." The cook pointed in the direction of the stove, where a massive slab of butter sat nearby on a plate. "I have my principles."

"So you're just ignoring the new rule?" This was fantastic. The subject matter itself was deathly boring, but Laura knew she'd stumbled on a conflict worth writing about. The quarrel between kitchen and management would make for a juicy read.

"You bet I'm ignoring the rule," said the cook. "And you can write that down, too. If they don't like it, they can fire me. I won't go in for any nonsense when it comes to the quality of my food. My reputation is at stake."

Back uptown in the city room at the journalism school, Laura banged out an article with five minutes to spare, reading it over once quickly before putting it into the vault. The pressure made her heart beat fast, and the energy in the room—the students all tapping away on their typewriters, knowing that this assignment was crucial in making a good first impression—fueled her nerves even more. But in a good way. This was a challenge, even if the subject matter was a bore. Figuring out which quotes to include and which to summarize, how best to portray the hotel and that manager without seeming judgmental. If this was journalism, she couldn't wait for more.

The next day, they sat through a law class in one of the lecture halls. Unlike her time at Vassar, where Laura was overwhelmed by the social circles within the school, here, as an older, married student she didn't feel the need to hobnob the way the younger set did. She spent two hours scribbling notes as fast as she could, realizing that she'd need to look up some of the cases cited by the professor at home in the library to fill in the missing gaps in her knowledge.

Later in the city room, Professor Wakeman called the students up one by one to go over their articles from the day before. Laura was edgy with anticipation as she took the chair next to his desk and looked over at the paper in his hands, which was filled with red marks. Not a good sign.

"Mrs. Lyons, the assignment was five hundred words. This is five hundred eighty."

"Sorry, Professor, I figured an extra few sentences wouldn't make a difference."

He gave her a sharp look. "You seem to think that you're an *artiste*, and I'm here to disabuse you of that notion. If your editor says five hundred words, you give them that. You are one small part of a giant newspaper, one where every inch counts. So don't tell me that the manager's neck was 'long like a dancer's,' and I don't care what they are wearing. It's about butter."

"Of course." This wasn't like writing a column for Dr. Anderson's newsletter, where her flowery prose was encouraged. She really should've known better, but she'd been trying to show off. "I understand."

"Today, I want you to edit it and fix it. Get to the point."

"I certainly will."

She rose to go.

"But nice work getting the cook to talk. No one else had that. That's a well-reported story. Not well written, mind you. It was painful to read. But the reporting was good. Quite good."

She practically floated back to her seat. Writing more succinctly, more like a journalist, was something she could learn. But her instincts were on target. Professor Wakeman had given her a compliment. For her first assignment.

She couldn't wait to tell Jack.

CHAPTER FOUR

New York City, 1913

"There's been a theft."

Laura looked up from her mending at her husband. One of Pearl's pinafores had lost a button, and Laura's eyes, already tired from reading textbooks, were strained even further by her trying to sew by lamplight. In the week since journalism school had begun, Laura had made an effort to keep up with the housework, although she could tell already it was a losing battle. Dust had settled lightly on the fireplace mantel, and Harry had ripped a pair of trousers this week that she still needed to get around to fixing. Unfortunately, the thrill of attending school only served to make the housework feel more of a bother, requiring precious time that could be spent elsewhere.

"What kind of theft?"

"*Leaves of Grass.* A first edition."

Laura inhaled. She knew that a missing book might be considered by some as fairly inconsequential. After all, there were thousands upon thousands of copies of the poetry collection available in bookstores around the world. But a first edition of one that had gone on to become an American classic meant more than that: It was a piece of history, the closest example of the author's intent. And quite valuable, in the case of Walt Whitman's masterpiece. "Where from?"

"We're trying to figure that out. It looks like it was last requested in the Stuart Room a week or so ago, but I'm afraid we can't be sure exactly when it went missing."

Unlike a lending library, the Fifth Avenue branch did not allow books to be checked out. It was a research library, where tomes and volumes remained on-site at all times, under the watchful eye of the librarians. The purpose was to keep the items safe from loss or damage, yet still allow the public access.

"The library has been overflowing with crowds," Jack explained. "A good thing, certainly, but it means we're not running as tight a ship as we should be. The librarians have assured me and Dr. Anderson they will be stricter with their oversight, and that two will be on shift at all times, so that when one has to retrieve a book, there's another always there to keep watch. It's a terrible, terrible loss."

"What does it look like?" she asked.

"It's got a gilt-decorated green cloth cover, and is quite fragile."

"I'll keep an eye out."

"Thanks, love. They've brought in the library's detective to assist in our search, a man named Edwin Gaillard. We don't want this to become a habit, losing books, so it's all hands on deck. I'm going to take a look around the Stuart Room."

"This late?"

"It's easier when everyone is gone. I don't have to worry about upsetting the patrons or the staff."

She offered to join him in the search.

Jack unlocked the door to the Stuart Room with the heavy set of keys he carried around with him at all times. When they first moved into the library, Harry had liked to shake them and burst into "Jingle Bells."

The Stuart Room wasn't nearly as large as the Main Reading Room, but it had generous dimensions all the same, filled with two rows of polished oak tables and brass lamps, a rectangle of skylight above. This was where scholars could study the more valuable objects in the library's archives, including a Gutenberg Bible from the 1450s and Thomas Jefferson's own copy of the Declaration of Independence. Not to mention a Shakespeare First Folio.

Together, they searched as best they could, the only sound the soft scuffing of books against each other, or the opening of a desk drawer.

As Jack went through the librarian's desk for the second time, Laura looked over his shoulder and gave him a nudge. "You know the librarians were probably up in arms when it was discovered missing. I'm sure they've checked their drawers."

He stood unexpectedly, pulling her close. The lamps had been lowered, but his eyes still picked up the reflection, shining brightly at her. "Cheeky girl. I'd like to check your drawers."

She burst out laughing. "You have got to be kidding. Do you really think a line like that would work on a girl like me?"

"I see, now that you're in graduate school, my lowly sense of humor no longer thrills?"

"To be honest, it works like a charm."

They kissed like they used to, before the kids were born, before they'd wed, when kisses were pleasures to be stolen. This was one aspect of their relationship that hadn't faded with time. He could still touch her in a way that left her gasping out loud, praying that her cries wouldn't wake the children, just as he had when they were first intimate.

If only her family saw in him what she did. That he was a good, solid man. Maybe not a wealthy financier, but a good man nonetheless. Money wasn't everything, although her father would certainly disagree.

She had finally gotten up the courage to introduce him to her parents at a Sunday luncheon, with a full warning to Jack that her father might be difficult. From an early age, he'd pointed out the travails of marrying a poor man, usually in front of her mother, who'd purse her lips and turn away. After the panic of 1896, his admonishments increased. While they'd suffered losses, they certainly weren't poor in the true sense of the word. After all, Laura always had food to eat and a roof over her head, even if that roof was in dire need of fixing. Yet Laura knew better than to point out the water stains creeping along her bedroom ceiling.

After the crisis, Laura's mother had been put on a strict allowance by her father, one that they squabbled over every Sunday evening. He expected a full accounting of how she'd spent the money, and Laura again knew better than to mention the hatboxes and other deliveries that came during the day while her father was at work and were quickly shepherded up to her mother's suite.

The afternoon that Jack met the family, over a meal of fish soup and mutton, Laura was bursting with the happiness of having him by her side, of formalizing their situation. But her father had cut right to the quick.

"What field are you in, Mr. Lyons?" he'd asked without looking up from his soup.

"I plan to be a writer," Jack replied.

"A writer of what?" He put down his spoon and motioned for the maid to collect the first course, even though the rest of them hadn't finished.

"Literature." Jack launched into the idea for his story, and Laura cringed inwardly. When he'd recounted it to her, over a picnic in the park, it had seemed brilliant, inspired. But now she saw it through the lens of her father's judgment, and Jack's fervor came across as boyish exuberance. Her mother, though, stepped in and began asking questions. The two laughed over writers they both disliked and purred over others they adored. Her mother, once again, saved the day.

That evening, they'd first made love, at his apartment in Morningside Heights. She'd been waiting for the moment for what seemed like ages, and now that her parents—or at least one of them—were on board, there was no need to wait any longer. He'd been careful and kind, and even though it hurt like the dickens, before long her body had craved him constantly, each moment they were apart only feeding her appetite more.

Up in the Stuart Room, Jack pulled her into another kiss, lifting her up onto the table and raising her skirts.

"What if someone sees?" Her head dropped back as he ran his hands along the insides of her thighs. Even through her stockings, her skin tingled at his touch.

"The night watchman doesn't come up here until eleven."

"And that means?"

"That means I get to have you right here, right now."

"We ought not to, not when things have gone missing. What if someone comes up and finds us?"

"You worry too much."

Maybe he was right. He breathed gently into her ear before following the line of her neck with a trail of kisses, and eventually the excitement of doing something where they shouldn't overrode her worry. Knowing what they each liked, they came together within minutes. Laura stifled her cries, making the wave of pleasure even greater, and Jack's look of utter happiness after made it all worthwhile.

As long as she didn't get with child again. If that happened, she wouldn't be able to continue with her courses, and she'd be right back where she started. Dependent, caught up in the relentlessness of rearing an infant. Utterly unfulfilled.

Jack noticed her stiffen and pulled her close.

"What is it, my love?"

How could she explain? There was no use. No use at all.

Laura smiled at her husband. "I think we should get back to the children, enough of this silliness."

He took her hand and led her out of the Stuart Room. "How's school going?"

"I wish I were reporting on more interesting subjects. They seem to think the women are incapable of writing about anything other than tea parties and dress-shop openings."

"What did you expect?"

"I know it's what I'm supposed to be interested in. But I'm just not." Not that she didn't enjoy her classes, where they learned how to conduct interviews and scribble down the salient points fast, and where the professors filled them in on the inner workings of the city government, along with rousing, real-life stories about gaining the trust of sources and exposing injustice and greed. She'd also learned how to write headlines—this wasn't her strong suit—and edit copy, which she enjoyed and was good at. "Over the semester, we'll learn about different types of journalism, including editorials, book and play reviews, and will have to go to plays and write what we think. The Elements of Law class is probably the most boring, but I know the subjects of slander and libel are vitally important once a reporter gets out in the field, which I hope to be. One day. When I get to write stories that actually interest me."

"Why do you have to limit yourself to what they expect you to do?"

She looked at him like he was mad. "What, do a story on my own? I don't think they'd like that."

"Well, maybe you'll get more freedom to choose as the weeks go on. If so, you have to jump at the chance." He snapped his fingers, and the sound echoed off the marble, sharp and quick. "Don't be cowed. You're a good, solid writer. Your columns showed that."

"And what about you, how's the book coming along?" She tried not to ask him about it too much, not wanting to pressure him, but she liked the idea that they were both working in the same medium, and hoped she wasn't being presumptuous.

She needn't have worried.

"I've had a burst of inspiration recently." He gestured for her to go ahead of him, up the stairs to their apartment. "I swear it's this building, feeding my brain at every turn."

"You're not too tired at the end of the day?"

"Not a whit." He gave a tug at her skirt. "As I think I've proved by our earlier assignation."

"Oh, you seem just fine to me." Laura batted him away, laughing. "Just fine."

"Today, your assignment is to report and write a piece for our simulated newspaper, the *Blot*."

Professor Wakeman tugged at his mustache and glared around the room at the bleary-eyed students, who'd come in at the ungodly hour of seven in the morning. Laura, who'd been up since five finishing an essay for the law class and then getting the children ready for school, hoped her schedule would work in her favor today, that her alertness would lend her an edge. Just the other day, they'd learned the shocking news that only a third of the original class of students had graduated the prior year, and the idea that all this could be for naught terrified her. It didn't help that the workload had increased every day, much more than any of them had expected. "Don't get complacent," Professor Wakeman had warned. "Last year, I failed the best writer in the class because he misspelled a word—a lesson he'll never forget."

A couple of the professors were wary of the women students in particular, commenting on their attire if their skirts were deemed too short, one even sneaking about the building in the hopes of catching them committing immoral acts with male students. The ridiculousness only served to pull the women in the class closer together. Gretchen had reduced them to tears of laughter the other day by writing an anonymous, perfumed love letter to the most egregious professor and placing it in his mail cubby on the second floor. "That'll give him something to think about," she'd said with a look of glee.

Professor Wakeman carried on. "Your copy is due at two this

afternoon, and by four, our dummy edition will be finalized. Only the best reported and written stories will make the cut, and I will decide which ones land on the front page and which deserve the bin. This will be a good test of the culmination of your skills so far. Good luck."

The men, of course, headed downtown to the criminal courts to cover the latest sensational murder trial ("It would be far too disturbing for you ladies," Professor Wakeman had said), or to the waterfront to investigate a possible strike. The women, meanwhile, had been told to visit the Charity Organization Society and dig around for stories that would tug at the readers' heartstrings. "Crying children with grubby faces, you know what I'm talking about," he'd said. "That's what you must master in order to succeed as women reporters."

Laura lingered outside the organization's headquarters on the Lower East Side, taking notes on the surroundings. Harsh smells assaulted her senses: a rancid mixture of human waste, greasy smoke, and decaying vegetables. She'd read in the newspapers that conditions had improved since the turn of the century, but if so, it couldn't have been by much.

"You. Come. Mother's waiting."

A boy a few years younger than Harry—or maybe he was the same age; it was hard to tell if his thin frame came from malnourishment or youth—tugged at her hand.

She knelt down so she was at the same level as he was. "I'm sorry, I don't understand."

A tear rolled down his face, carving a white line down his dirty cheek. Professor Wakeman would approve of this tyke, she thought with chagrin.

"Mother said to find you and bring you to her. The baby's not eating."

He yanked hard, pulling her over to a tenement across the street. Laura followed, trying to ask questions but to no avail. She looked back at the building where her fellow classmates had disappeared. Perhaps this would make a better story, and she could be of assistance in some way at the same time. The boy's blue eyes reminded her so much of Harry's.

Inside, when he pointed out a dead rat at the bottom of the narrow stairs so that Laura could avoid stepping on it, she shuddered. He looked at her, curious, and continued up the stairs to the third floor. The light grew dimmer as they climbed.

He opened a door and she stepped inside. She'd seen photos of tenement life in the newspapers, of children huddled on mattresses on the floor, coal ovens and cruddy sinks. This apartment wasn't so terrible: the curtains seemed clean, and the dishes and pots had been stacked with care on the open shelves.

A group of children ranging from what seemed to be four to fourteen looked up from their work at a large table in the front room, piled high with black strips that Laura recognized as garters. The mother didn't stand as Laura entered, just wiped her forehead and pointed to one corner, where a baby lay swaddled on a blanket on the floor.

"I put the baby there so she doesn't get stepped on," said the mother.

"I—I'm sorry?"

"She didn't eat last night or this morning. Don't know what's wrong." The woman went back to sewing, and barely raised an elbow toward the child. Her son, the boy who'd fetched Laura, seemed more concerned than his mother, gently lifting the child from the floor and carrying her over. As he did, the baby let out a soft bleat.

"Keep her quiet," ordered the mother. "If my husband wakes up, we'll all be in trouble."

"Too late for that," a man's voice boomed from the kitchen. The husband, a barrel-chested man with thinning hair that stuck straight out from the top of his head, appeared soon after. "Who are you? What are you doing here?"

Should she say she was a student reporter? No, probably not. She needed to get out of there. The baby in the corner looked up at the ceiling, mute and expressionless. She didn't seem to be in pain, but at the same time, the baby lacked vitality, as if she had never been held a moment in her life.

"I'm sorry, there must be a mistake. I'll go."

"No. You disturb my sleep when I just got done with the night shift, I think you owe me something."

"Money?"

"That'll do."

With shaking hands, she opened her satchel.

"In fact, give me that bag. That'll do even better."

The one with her finished essay for the law class, all of her notes, all of her money. "No, I can't."

He stepped toward her with a growl, reaching for the satchel with a hand the size of a baseball mitt, the nails rimmed in black.

She'd made a terrible error. What a stupid idea to come up here alone.

CHAPTER FIVE

New York City, 1993

One afternoon when Sadie was a little girl, walking hand in hand with her mother down Fifth Avenue, they passed by the colossal library. "Like Buckingham Palace," Sadie said, having seen an image of the queen of England's home on the television the night before.

"I lived there, once," her mother had said, her mouth in a tight line. "When I was a little girl like you."

"Buckingham Palace?" Sadie asked, unsure.

"No. The library. In an apartment built deep inside. It was even written up in the newspaper, back when we first moved in." When pressed, though, she'd refused to provide any other details. At the time, Sadie figured her mother was teasing her. After all, who lived in a library?

Soon after Sadie started working there, she'd met Mr. Babenko, a longtime employee and the building's de facto historian, and had been surprised to learn that, yes, there had indeed been an apartment included in the architect's plan, designed specifically for the superintendent and his family. He'd directed her to the mezzanine level, accessible by a private staircase off the first floor. To Sadie's dismay, the area had been converted into storage, full of boxes and janitors' supplies. It was hard to imagine a family of four living there.

She'd spent a Saturday going through old newspapers on microfiche and found a short article written in 1911 about the apartment's inhabitants. A black-and-white photo showed a handsome man with ears that stuck out standing next to a dark-haired woman whose face was blurry. She'd been caught looking down at her children, not at the camera. The children, a boy and a girl, smiled proudly in front of their parents. Sadie recognized her mother by the lightness of her hair and eyes, like she was an angel. The boy, Harry, was Sadie's uncle, who had died before Sadie was born.

Invigorated, Sadie had stopped by the Rare Book Room and requested any superintendent records from the years the family had lived there. After a ten-minute wait, the librarian lugged over two boxes filled with ledgers, letters, invoices, and other paraphernalia. Sadie's grandfather's name, Jack Lyons, was on every one. As she sifted through them, she marveled at how large a job he'd held. It was a bit like running a ship or a small city, keeping the library going. An entire ledger was filled with the monthly payroll, from electricians to porters, all neatly typed out in rows with *Name, Position*, and *Amount*, then a handwritten total at the very bottom. To think her grandfather had written those numbers, so long ago, and here she was working at the very same place. Excited, she'd told her mother and brother what she'd discovered. Her mother had responded by turning up the television volume, drowning her out.

Back then, Laura Lyons's legacy hadn't yet been resurrected. Only in recent years had Sadie's and her brother's checks from the executor of the estate—Laura Lyons's former secretary in London—gradually increased, as their grandmother's collections of essays were reissued. Yet even when the Berg Collection acquired Laura Lyons's walking stick, Sadie hadn't mentioned her connection, knowing that Marlene would be curious and ask questions she wouldn't be able to answer.

Today, with Dr. Hooper's new interest in Laura Lyons, Sadie figured it might be time to acknowledge her family tie as a way to get into his good graces and secure the position of curator permanently. Claude wouldn't think twice if he was in the same position—she had no doubt about that.

First, though, she had some homework to do.

After her shift was over, she requested the administrative records of the library from 1911, hoping there might be some record of the Lyons family there. A starting point, at least. Inside a dozen boxes, Sadie found the usual—letters, files, a few photos of stiff-looking men standing stiffly—but also several newsletters, which had been written for the library staff at the time. The first began with a letter from the director, a Dr. Edwin H. Anderson, followed by several short articles about upgrades or exhibits. The second edition, though, caused her to let out a squeak of glee. Inside was a column written by Mrs. Jack Lyons. The tone was whimsical and airy, about the travails of raising two children in the library, her favorite books of the month, and what she was reading to her children, Harry and Pearl, before bed.

Her grandmother had started off writing puff pieces, a far cry from the serious, feminist essays she was so well-known for. Essays that delved into what true equality between the sexes entailed, and that stressed the importance of women working outside the home, of having a passion beyond children and housework. The newsletters were terrific artifacts on Laura Lyons's early domestic life, and Sadie couldn't wait to share them with Dr. Hooper.

But her excitement was tempered by a letter she found in the last of the boxes, in a file marked CONFIDENTIAL. It contained a letter from a man named Edwin Gaillard, dated May 1914.

> *Dr. Anderson,*
>
> *After a thorough investigation, I'm sorry to admit that I'm still stymied. It's almost as if the thief dropped from the sky, stole the books, and then disappeared. I understand your concern that we will face great difficulty as an institution if this most recent incident becomes known. Mr. and Mrs. Lyons are under watch, and in the meantime, I will do what I can to keep this quiet, per your request.*

Her grandparents had been "under watch," whatever that meant, associated with some kind of book theft. The strange letter curbed Sadie's desire to share her own lineage with Dr. Hooper. Laura Lyons, hailed as a "new feminist icon" in the *New York Review of Books* a few years ago, appeared to have had a shady past, one that was probably better left alone.

Sadie called her brother, Lonnie, from her office.

"I've got some news," said Sadie when he picked up. "Marlene has taken another job, and so for the short term, I'm in charge of the Berg Collection."

She laughed as her brother let out a whoop on the other end of the line. She explained about Marlene's new position in Boston and how she'd been chosen by Dr. Hooper to take over. Temporarily.

Even though they lived a few blocks from each other in Murray Hill, Sadie had made a point of reaching out to Lonnie at least once a week on the telephone since their mother had moved in with him and his wife, LuAnn, a month ago. The move was temporary—once Pearl recovered from a bout of pneumonia, she'd go back to her place in her senior center—but since Lonnie was a doctor and had more than enough room in the four-story town house they'd grown up in, it made sense to keep Pearl close to home. Still, Sadie felt a stab of guilt at how much her brother was juggling these days, and touching base by phone was the least she could do. So Sadie had written the weekly phone call into her Filofax calendar and, every week, crossed it off when completed. Most of the time their calls consisted of Sadie rattling off the mi-nutiae of her job, but sometimes Lonnie recounted one of the more interesting cases at the hospital, and she'd listen closely and ask lots of questions, encouraging him to open up. Their ten-year age difference meant that they had never really bonded as children. Sadie had been a late-in-life surprise for her mother, and when their father passed away, when Sadie was eight, Lonnie was al-ready off at college.

But when LuAnn had entered the picture, Sadie and Lonnie's mutual adoration of her had acted as a sort of sibling bypass op-eration, pulling them closer in spite of their very different person-alities and childhoods.

"I'm proud of you, sis," said Lonnie. "LuAnn will be thrilled. We'll have to celebrate when she's back."

LuAnn traveled extensively for her job as a corporate lawyer. "When does your lovely wife return?"

"Not until Saturday."

Sadie leaned back in her office chair, happy to have the room to herself. Claude had spent the day in a snit, upset about the sudden turn of events, and when he finally left, it was like a noxious cloud evaporating. "Here's the thing, though. Dr. Hooper wants me to find something about Laura Lyons to include in the exhibit."

He listened quietly as she filled him in on the discovery of the newsletters and the disturbing note. "That's crazy. I wonder what it's all about."

"Did Mom ever mention anything about an investigation?"

He laughed. "Mom never mentions anything at all, you know that. That woman's a closed book."

"How's she doing today?"

"Physically better, but mentally still uncertain about things. The hospital stay confused her, and she's still not quite all there. The day nurse just left. She's been asking for you. Hold on a second." His voice became distant. "Valentina, you have to wear a coat, don't be silly."

"Where is she going?" asked Sadie.

"She and Robin are going out for ice cream."

Robin, the new babysitter, had recently taken over looking after Valentina, a role that Sadie had gladly undertaken after she'd been born, right around the time Sadie had divorced Phillip. LuAnn had folded her sister-in-law into her own family, in the hope that caring for the new baby would bring Sadie out of her depression. Indeed, helping to raise Valentina had been Sadie's absolute privilege and joy, but lately, with the exhibition looming, she'd been unable to devote as much time as before. LuAnn said it was a natural progression and that it made sense for Sadie to open up her life now. Six years was a long time to mourn a husband who really wasn't worth mourning. And who wasn't even dead.

"Isn't it late?" Sadie asked Lonnie. "They're going out for ice cream now?"

"It's not that late, and they're not going far."

"How's Robin working out?"

"Robin's great. We really lucked out. Valentina loves her to death."

Sadie felt a prick of jealousy. "Maybe I'll stop by, say hi to Mom before bed."

"Sure thing."

She told him she was on her way.

As Sadie turned the corner to Lonnie's town house, she spotted Valentina's moss-green coat, the one they'd picked out together in the fall, hurtling down the sidewalk toward her. Valentina ran into her arms as Sadie leaned down to hug her. The girl beamed up at her, her blue eyes bright against the whiteness of her skin and hair, a trace of chocolate ice cream on one cheek, before pulling away and gesturing to the new babysitter.

"Aunt Sadie, this is Robin Larkin."

"So formal of you, my girl," said Sadie. "But we've already met."

Sadie and Lonnie had been at the playground in the park a couple of weeks ago when Valentina had fallen from the swings. Robin had been standing nearby, watching over a set of twins, and had gotten to her first. During the comforting and patch-up stages—Robin had had a Band-Aid handy—they'd learned that she was looking for a new position, as the twins were moving out of the city, and Valentina had insisted Robin become her baby-sitter. Lonnie had called her references and, after checking with LuAnn, had given her the green light.

Even though Sadie knew it was the smart thing to do—her hours were about to get crazy as the new exhibit crystalized—a part of her harbored the tiniest bit of resentment at the idea of being replaced. Now it was Robin, instead of Aunt Sadie, who stayed over in the basement bedroom when Lonnie worked nights and LuAnn was away.

She studied the girl. Robin, who appeared to be in her mid-twenties, was only a head or so taller than Valentina, and wore a plaid shirt and jeans. They looked like a couple of schoolchildren together.

Valentina pulled at Robin's arm. "Robin said I can buy a shirt like hers, so I can be grungy as well."

"Grunge," said Robin, laughing. "We'll try to avoid getting you grungy."

"Grunge," Valentina repeated. "Aunt Sadie loves old clothes, from the olden days."

"That dress is really pretty," said Robin.

"Thanks. Valentina's coat is vintage as well," said Sadie. "Remember, V? We got it at a thrift shop together."

Robin looked down at her green coat, as if reassessing its value. "Yeah."

Inside the town house, Sadie said a quick hello to Lonnie in the dining room, where his lanky six-foot-three-inch frame sat hunched over a stack of bills, like a parenthesis wearing reading glasses. Upstairs, in the guest room where their mother had taken up residence, Pearl lay in the four-poster bed, dressed in a rose-colored flannel nightgown. At eighty-seven, and weighing about the same in pounds, Pearl had a habit of smiling weakly, as if she were about to go at any moment, before demanding a vanilla milkshake or a different pillow, in a bellow that rattled the walls.

"How are you feeling, Mom?" asked Sadie.

"Fine, just fine." Pearl looked behind Sadie. "Where's the little girl?"

"You mean Valentina, your granddaughter? She's upstairs with Robin, the new babysitter."

Her mother waved a hand. "I knew that."

"Of course you did." Sadie perched on the side of the bed. "I have good news, I got a promotion at the library today. It's temporary, but it's a good sign, I think."

"Lovely, dear." Her mother's fingernails were a bubblegum pink, slightly smudged around the edges, signs that she'd been the recipient of one of Valentina's enthusiastic manicures.

"Hey, Mom. Do you remember when you were Valentina's age, and you lived in the library?"

"What?"

"When you lived in the library, when you were a little girl?" she repeated.

"We don't talk about that."

Sadie wondered who "we" was. Pearl and her mother?

"I brought you something." She pulled out a small box of chocolates from her purse, from her mother's favorite store on Madison Avenue.

Her mother smiled and, with shaky fingers, chose a dark chocolate one. She put it in her mouth and didn't chew, just let it melt away, her eyes half-closed.

"They're good, right?" said Sadie. "These are what Phillip would bring me every anniversary."

Her mother swallowed the chocolate with a grimace. "Oh, for God's sake."

"What?"

"Sadie, that was years ago. You must move on, my girl."

The sudden burst of lucidity from Pearl was like a foghorn splicing through the mist. Sadie knew it was a good sign, that she was recovering from the shock of being in the intensive care unit for three weeks, but her attack still stung.

"I was just saying something nice, that's all."

"No. You live in the past. Look at those clothes, you read old books for a living. Move on before it's too late."

Pearl had always been something of a benevolent bully, telling everyone how they should live their lives, especially her daughter, but the comment hurt. "That sounds rather ominous."

"Trust me. When your father died, I moved on. Don't you remember? I did that for your sake, and for mine. What's your problem, missy?"

Sadie inhaled sharply and felt an ache deep in her belly. She rose and went to the window, where the sky was erasing itself into darkness.

How easy it had been for Pearl to move on. After Sadie's father passed away, her mother had dated in a tornado of repressed grief before partnering up with a man named Don who bragged about being as different from Sadie's father as "an Alfa Romeo is from a Crosley Hotshot," whatever that meant. His black business suits and shiny briefcase were a stark contrast to her musician father's short-sleeve shirts and battered instrument cases.

Sadie had listened wordlessly as Don expounded on the route of the Grand Prix in Monaco at the dinner table while Pearl beamed. But when Sadie tried out some of the French she'd learned in school that week, he'd stared at her, uncomprehending, unamused.

He brought Sadie a wrist corsage of white roses for Valentine's Day, along with a dozen red roses for her mother, which was followed by a quick marriage ceremony at City Hall. After that, any mention that Sadie made about her father in passing was quickly shushed by her mother and shot down with a sharp look from Don.

One Sunday, Don put a record on the stereo that Sadie recognized as a waltz, and held out a hand for her to join in. When she placed her feet on top of his shoes, as she'd always done with her father, Don shoved her away, hard. "What on earth are you doing?" he yelled. "I just polished these."

She barely managed to stay standing. "It's how we dance," she explained. "Danced. Me and my dad."

Don knelt down, licked his thumb, and rubbed at an invisible scratch in the leather. "Stupid kid."

She'd retreated to her room, too stunned to cry.

Don had lasted a few years before the marriage fizzled and Pearl went back to her maiden name, Lyons. By the time Sadie left for college in New Jersey, her mother had had a series of long-term boyfriends, some better than others but no one special.

Sadie's hard stop to her dalliance with Claude had been the right decision. Between her mother's disastrous choices and Lonnie's growing family, Sadie didn't need to take any romantic risks post-divorce. She was loved and loved back, and that was enough.

Valentina burst in, holding a large, flat box in her hand, Robin trailing not far behind. "Let's play a game, all of us."

"Sure. Set it up on Grandma's bed. What game is it?"

"Operation." Valentina arranged the game on a tray propped

over Pearl's lap. Sadie tucked herself in behind the girl, breathing in the scent of Johnson's Baby Shampoo from her hair.

"Robin goes first," ordered Valentina.

Robin deftly retrieved the spare rib from the torso, the easiest one. Valentina cheered when she pulled it clear.

"It's my turn," announced Pearl. "Or is it Harry's?" She'd turned cloudy again, staring off into the corner of the room.

Sadie spoke slowly, loudly. "Harry is your brother, Mom. He's not here, remember?"

Valentina looked up. "What happened to Harry, again?"

"He died a long time ago."

As if on cue, Pearl began to cry.

The evening was beginning to crack wide-open. "Mom, it's your turn," said Sadie quickly.

"It's my turn!" Pearl smiled through her tears.

Sadie could barely keep up with Pearl's mood changes, the waves of confusion followed by moments of clarity. She and Lonnie sometimes joked that their mother was perfectly sane and just enjoyed keeping everyone off-center. That particular brand of dark humor saw them through the early days of her hospitalization, when they weren't sure whether she'd recover. Once, when Sadie thought they'd taken their joking too far, Lonnie had pointed out they'd learned that particular coping mechanism from Pearl herself, a fact that Sadie couldn't deny.

The buzzer always went off for their mother, whose hand shook with age, and every time she'd yip with surprise. Sadie braced herself for another round of tears.

This time, though, the buzzer didn't sound, and Pearl held up the wishbone with a triumphant "Hah!"

"Something's wrong," said Sadie, pulling the game toward her.

"No, it's not, I did it," said Pearl, an indignant edge in her voice.

Robin patted Pearl's leg over the blanket. "You were amazing."

Sadie touched the tweezers to the metal border of the heart cavity. Not a peep. "The battery must be dead."

"But I didn't get a turn," whimpered Valentina.

"I'll put in new batteries," said Sadie. "Don't worry, you'll get a turn."

Pearl crossed her arms, sulking, as the tension in the room spiked. "No. I don't want to play anymore."

"Me, neither," said Valentina.

From downstairs, Lonnie called out, "Is everything all right up there?"

By now, Pearl and Valentina were competing for who could complain the loudest.

Sadie lifted the game off her mother's lap, fed up with the racket. "Game time's over. I think maybe we're all a little overtired."

Valentina looked up at Sadie, indignant.

"Come on, Valentina," said Robin, giving Sadie a quiet nod of agreement. "Let's get you ready for bed."

They disappeared into the hallway as Sadie replaced the cardboard lid, her mother watching her every move.

"Why are you wearing that, Sadie? You look silly."

The same two sentences had been a common refrain of Pearl's after Sadie launched into her vintage-dress kick. "Lucky that you don't have to wear it, then," snapped Sadie. "But thank you for sharing your opinion."

Her mother closed her eyes for a moment. Sadie waited, preparing herself for the next volley. Somehow, she was always on her back foot with Pearl. Same as she'd been with Phillip. The day he'd loaded his belongings into her apartment, it had been only temporary, at first. His roommate was moving to Texas, and Phillip couldn't afford the rent on his own, nor bother to find a new place while the semester was in session. But whenever Sadie got home before he did, she'd unpack a box of his books and integrate them into her shelves, or hang up his winter coats in the closet. He didn't seem to notice the vanishing tower of cardboard boxes, but it wasn't until the fall came around and he showed no sign of moving out that she breathed a sigh of relief. He was hers.

The move out, on the other hand, came fast. He took a suitcase with him that Christmas Eve, and by the second week of January, everything else was gone. She'd waited in the diner, reading the American Library Association's newsletter but absorbing nothing, as Phillip and some movers combed through the apartment for his belongings, leaving behind gaps in the bookshelves and empty hangers in the closets.

"Don't burn it. Whatever you do, don't burn it."

This was a new one. "What are you talking about, Mom?"

"The book!"

Sadie held up the cardboard box. "No, it's a game. I'm just going to put it away."

"Don't do it!"

Sadie ignored her, placing the game on the bookshelf. She'd check for batteries later.

"Mom, you rest. I'll get you a glass of water, okay?"

In the kitchen, Sadie leaned against the counter. She could have handled this evening better, she knew. She had no excuse for being so short with her family, not when Lonnie was the one who lived with this, day in and day out. Lonnie had always been the golden child, going to med school, having a family. Sadie was the loony librarian who wore weird clothes.

"You okay?"

Robin stood in the doorway.

"Yeah, I'm fine. It's just hard, seeing my mom like that. I didn't mean to be short with everyone."

"Are you kidding? If you hadn't stopped the game, it would have dissolved into two generations of temper tantrums, I'm pretty sure."

"Mom is still a force of nature," said Sadie. "Even lying in bed, she's busy directing traffic."

"Valentina's devoted to her. My own grandmother died before I was born, so I guess V's lucky to have time with her, even if it's hard right now."

"I'm sorry about that. My grandmother died before I was born as well."

"It's hard to miss what you never knew, though, right? Like those high pitches that only dogs can hear, and humans can't." She bit back a smile. "Besides, apparently my grandma was a witch of a woman."

Sadie laughed. "Hey, thanks for helping out. I'm glad you're here."

"You bet."

Lonnie entered, chasing a giggling Valentina in her pink whale pajamas, crisis averted.

The next morning, Sadie's phone rang the minute she sat down at her desk.

"Sadie, it's Marlene."

Sadie smiled at the sound of her former boss's voice, relieved that Claude was in the main room with a patron and she could speak freely. They talked for a good ten minutes, Marlene apologizing for her sudden departure. "They insisted it be a clean break, and I knew it wouldn't help if I lingered about. I will miss you terribly, though. And I'm thrilled that you'll be heading up *Evergreen*. I put in a good word to Dr. Hooper about that, you know."

Sadie thanked her profusely and they said goodbye, promising to stay in touch. She checked her watch and headed down to the stacks, to the section that was devoted to overflow from the Berg, two aisles encased in chain-link fencing and secured with a lock. She fished the key out and opened the door, closing it tightly behind her. Today, she would be going through Virginia Woolf's diaries, which were a requisite for inclusion in the exhibit. The diaries consisted of twenty-eight volumes dated from 1915 to 1941, the year Woolf committed suicide. Marlene had wanted to include the last volume, the final entry of which was written four days before Woolf filled her pockets with rocks and walked into the River Ouse. Sadie always wondered what it was Woolf couldn't bear to write down during those four days.

Sadie put on her white gloves and pulled out the gray box at the bottom of the stack, the one holding the diaries from the year 1941. Opening it up, she took out the stationer's notebooks that Woolf had filled with her thoughts, both mundane and agonizing.

There should be five in each box. She counted and then recounted. Only four.

The missing one was the one she wanted. She put the box aside and went through the next one on the shelf. Five notebooks, all accounted for. Same with all the other boxes of Woolf's diaries. By the time she checked the final one, her heart was pounding. She looked around, as if it might be lying out on a shelf somewhere. But no one else had access to this room other than Marlene and Claude. And they would never have done such a thing.

A couple of pages walked by, not even noticing her as she stood frozen.

The final Woolf diary was gone.

"When was the last time you saw the diary?"

Sadie pulled Claude aside to a corner of the Berg and kept her voice low. The rules stated that an employee of the library had to be in the main room at all times when a patron was present, and currently three researchers sat at the tables. Which meant this conversation couldn't be held in their offices. For all she knew, there was a plausible answer to where the book was, but without Marlene to turn to, she was at a loss for who to ask other than Claude.

Claude rubbed his chin, considering Sadie's question. "The diary notebook? Marlene and I brought it up here a few weeks ago. Then I returned it to the cage."

"You're sure you didn't leave it out somewhere, or put it in the wrong box?"

"Of course not. I'd never do that."

The patrons looked over, curious at the fuss.

"You know what we need to do, don't you?" She couldn't bear to say the words out loud.

A shelf read, where the librarians worked their way along every shelf of the collection, studying the call numbers one by one to make sure the books were in the right position. More often than not, a missing book had simply been put away in the wrong place. With the diary, it could have been returned to the wrong box. Which meant they also needed to go through each box in the Berg Collection and make sure the contents matched the label. A shelf read was exhausting and boring, but it was the only way to track down a missing book and determine if it was truly missing or simply misplaced.

"I do understand what we have to do." Claude didn't say the words out loud, either. "But I have plans tonight. Can it wait until tomorrow?"

She didn't answer, just waited for him to wise up. If he was the last person who touched it, the onus was on him to find it.

He relented with a loud sigh. "Fine."

"We'll start up here while the library is open, and then move to the cage after closing time. It's going to be a long night."

She had plans as well, but she called Lonnie to say that she wouldn't be able to make dinner at his place.

Late at night, the library vibrated with a quiet hum, but the lack of pages' footsteps and chattering made her uneasy. Claude had taken one aisle and Sadie the other, and by three in the morning the call letters and numbers began swimming before her eyes. One by one, they placed each box on a library cart and checked the contents before putting it back and moving on to the next. As she neared the end of her last shelf, the reality of what had happened began to sink in.

Virginia Woolf's final notebook, with its last entry dated March 24, 1941, was nowhere to be found. Sadie had first read the Woolf diaries in college, as if they held the answer to her own deep-seated grief at the loss of her father so many years ago. One entry, "I will go down with my colours flying," was followed by another about what to cook for dinner—haddock and sausage meat.

So heartbreakingly mundane.

The library had been entrusted with the diaries, to keep them safe and in good condition so that future scholars could see the actual pages, the words as they were written, not as a typed copy. The documents were crucial to examining the state of mind of the artist. Nothing else came close.

And the final volume was gone.

She reached the very bottom of the last row. From where Claude stood, he must be close to the end as well.

Sadie had been in charge less than a week, and already there was a crisis brewing. However much she wanted to put it off, she had to tell the director right away.

She and Claude finished up, discouraged. He headed home, while she caught some sleep on the sofa in the back office. She kept a long cardigan in the closet, and she could wear that over her dress today and not be so obvious about not having gone home. She woke, groggy and confused, and hit the deli on Thirty-Ninth Street for coffee. Claude showed up barely looking human at nine on the dot, and together they trudged into the director's office.

Dr. Hooper arrived a few minutes later, the newspaper tucked under his arm, and stopped cold when he saw them. She could only imagine how unprofessional she looked, with bags under her eyes, her wrinkled skirt and messy hair.

"Who's watching your room?" he asked.

"I've put up a notice that we'll be back at nine thirty," replied Sadie. "We have an issue."

He ushered them in to his office and closed the door. "What is it?"

For a moment, Sadie wished Claude had gotten the curator's job so he would have to deal with the director's wrath. "Yesterday, I went to look at one of the items for the exhibit, and it's gone."

"Which is it?"

"The last Virginia Woolf diary."

Dr. Hooper expelled a breath. "Are you sure it's not misplaced?"

"We did a shelf read overnight. It wasn't anywhere."

"When was it last seen?"

Claude spoke up. "I examined it with Marlene a couple of weeks ago. We brought it up from the cage, and I replaced it back a few hours later. I know I put it back in the right box, I'm sure of it."

"I see."

The unspoken accusation hung in the air. Marlene, who'd left all of a sudden, had been one of the last people to handle it.

"Shall I reach out to Marlene?" asked Sadie.

"No. I'll make that call." Dr. Hooper cleared his throat. "In the meantime, I'll ask the head librarians to keep an eye out for it. Do not tell anyone else."

Claude nodded his assent.

Sadie did not. "If we do discover it's gone, it might be smart to enlist the press. If it is a theft, the more publicity, the better the chance that bookshop owners and other experts will spot it."

"That's not a good idea for two reasons," said Dr. Hooper. "If the thief knows we know, he's less likely to try to sell it out in the open. Also, the fewer donors who know of the theft, the better— no one wants to invest in an insecure institution. So let's not get ahead of ourselves. We must find it quietly. In the meantime, I'll have the lock in the cage changed today. Was there anything else amiss?"

"Not that we could see. Everything else was intact."

"This is a terrible loss, if it has indeed been stolen."

At least Sadie had some good news to share. She fanned out the old newsletters on Dr. Hooper's desk with a flourish. "I do have some good news, though. I found the earliest examples of the work of Laura Lyons, right here under our very noses. It turns out she wrote a column about life in the library for the staff newsletter."

"Well, I'll be damned." Dr. Hooper never swore, which meant she'd thoroughly impressed him. "This is marvelous. Well done, Sadie."

"So we can include these in the exhibit?"

"Certainly. But let's not stop here. I'd still like to see something in her own hand. We are one of the top literary collections in one of the top libraries in the world. If there's something out there, we should have it. We need this. Especially with the Woolf diary gone missing."

It wasn't enough. Of course it wasn't enough. "I'll reach out to her estate, and let you know as soon as I hear back."

"Good, good."

As she and Claude walked away, they heard Dr. Hooper barking orders to his secretary to get Marlene on the phone. Sadie hoped they'd soon find an answer. The diary had been sent off to a restorer, perhaps, and Marlene had forgotten to mention it. Although that seemed far-fetched.

When she got back to her desk, her phone was ringing.

"Sadie, it's Lonnie."

Her desk was piled with papers, and she still had to contact the executor to Laura Lyons's estate. Now was not a good time for a brother-sister talk.

But before she could reply, he rushed ahead.

"It's Mom. She's died. She's gone."

CHAPTER SIX

New York City, 1993

The day after Pearl's death, a few of her friends stopped by Lonnie's town house to pay their respects and seemed to be in no hurry to leave, so Sadie ordered Chinese takeout, waiting for it to be delivered as the ladies talked among themselves around the kitchen table about canasta and hip replacements. As soon as the food came, Sadie grabbed one of the plastic containers and motioned for Valentina to join her at the dining room table, where they slurped up sesame noodles, while back in the kitchen LuAnn and Lonnie patiently answered the ladies' questions about final arrangements.

It was nice to have LuAnn back, the rudder to their family ship. When Sadie first met LuAnn, she'd been intimidated by Lonnie's elegant new girlfriend, but LuAnn never failed to draw Sadie out, asking about her job, or her favorite books, and then, once Valentina was born, they'd shared the intimate joy of loving the little creature before them. LuAnn always looked glamorous, even to-day, pairing jeans with a bright silk scarf, a tennis bracelet glistening on one wrist. Once Lonnie and LuAnn had married and taken over the family residence, his new wife had accessorized Pearl's leftover furniture with the same panache, adding bright pillows in the living room and hanging French movie posters on the walls.

Sadie put down her chopsticks. The peanut sauce suddenly tasted like glue and she couldn't eat another bite. "Valentina, I'm sorry I was short with you yesterday, when we were playing the game."

"What do you mean?" asked Valentina.

"I got upset when the game didn't buzz, and was a little short with everyone. I'm sorry about that."

"I don't remember. You're silly, Aunt Sadie."

Relief flushed through her. She'd been feeling terrible about sullying Valentina's last moments with her grandmother, when in fact Valentina hadn't even registered it. Funny what kids noticed and what they didn't.

As Sadie waited for Valentina to finish up, she inspected the display of silver-framed photos of the family on the wall: her mother sitting on a park bench, holding baby Valentina in her lap and smiling broadly; LuAnn and Lonnie on their wedding day; Sadie and Lonnie standing stiffly in front of a Christmas tree, next to their mother. Sadie's awkward stage had come and never left, unfortunately. She still had the same thick eyebrows and too-small mouth. She stepped closer to the photo and studied it carefully, noticing that on top of all that, one of her eyes was slightly larger than the other, making her look loopy. She glanced in the mirror to check. Still loopy-looking.

Before, when she was married, there had been a wedding photo of her and Phillip on the wall, one of her favorite shots of herself. She was smiling up at her new husband in profile—she'd always liked the curve of her nose from that angle, and her hair had been perfect that day, falling down her back in waves. Too bad she couldn't have just cut Phillip out. Although he had looked rather sweet in it as well, a shy smile on his face, blushing as if he'd landed a princess. They had loved each other, once.

Sadie moved in closer to the one photo of their grandmother, taken in London before the war. She was standing by a rosebush, with a faint smile on her face. Laura Lyons didn't seem like the jolliest of types. Her eyes were guarded, suspicious. The photo would have been taken around the time Virginia Woolf started writing her diaries. Maybe they'd bumped into each other, had tea together. Why had one woman saved her diaries for future generations, while the other demanded all her personal effects be destroyed after her death?

The missing diary. Where on earth could it be?

Sadie caught herself. She should be mourning the death of her mother, but instead the missing diary weighed more heavily. Or was she focusing on work to avoid dealing with the most recent family tragedy? If her mother were alive, she'd have been in the kitchen baking scones or some kind of fruit-filled pastry as a balm to their pain. The realization that she wasn't here to do that smashed into Sadie's solar plexus with a thud. She let out a sound that was half coughing, half choking, and suddenly it was as if a hole had opened up in her chest, leaving a void where her heart would be.

LuAnn stepped into the room, one hand on the doorway. "Everyone all right in here?"

"Sure, Mom," answered Valentina. "Are there fortune cookies?"

"In the kitchen. Go for it."

LuAnn came up behind Sadie as Valentina ran off. "The family photos." She picked up one of Lonnie at his college graduation. "His best years. Look at all that hair."

Sadie tried to match her breeziness, although her voice was shaky. "Ah, now, he's still a charmer. How's the geriatric gang doing?"

"I think they'll be wrapping up soon." She looked up as Lonnie joined them.

Sadie turned to her brother. "I'm sorry I wasn't here for Mom's death. I feel bad about that."

Lonnie shrugged. "It was pretty uneventful, she just passed away quietly, in her sleep."

"We thought she was doing well, though, right? We thought she was getting better."

"She was recovering from the pneumonia, but in the night her heart stopped. She was eighty-seven, remember."

"It just seems so sudden."

But it wasn't. Lonnie was right. Sudden was waking up in the middle of the night as an eight-year-old, confused, not sure of what she'd heard. It had been a loud thumping sound, like someone had dropped a bag of potatoes. So Sadie had gotten up, drawn to the light of the bathroom, and gently pushed open the door to find her father on the cold tile, his legs askew, hands palms up, the long fingers slightly curved, like he was playing his bass. She'd rushed to her mother and then waited, kneeling on the floor of the hallway as the paramedics came. She still remembered the scratchiness of the carpet runner on her bare legs.

Their father had been a session musician, playing for advertisements and television shows before embracing the new rock 'n' roll, one of the few older players who welcomed the new sound. He'd taken Sadie to the Brill Building a little north of Times Square a couple of times to listen in, and she'd been surprised at how much like a classroom the studio looked, a dozen folding chairs scattered across a linoleum floor. But her classroom didn't have wires snaking around chair legs and curling up microphone stands, or a dozen men smoking cigarettes during the breaks and teasing each other. When her father played his double bass, his body swayed like a tree in the wind, like he was dancing with a partner, Fred Astaire holding a maple-and-spruce Ginger in his arms. When he was hired by the rock bands, he'd switched to a shiny electric Rickenbacker, the chunky strings no hindrance at all to his quick fingering. How Sadie missed him, still. Especially today.

She supposed a death in the family did that, made you dredge up the silt from the bottom of your life.

They stood quietly for a moment. "What was the last thing you said to her?" asked Sadie.

"I think I told her to take her pills. She seemed out of sorts, confused." Lonnie had a strange look on his face. "She mentioned the library, of all things."

"She did?"

"She looked at me like she was really looking at me, you know? Like she was completely lucid. Then she said something about how she had to leave the library because of the burning book."

Their mother had said something similar as Sadie was putting away the game. Telling her not to burn a book.

"A burning book was the reason they had to leave the library?" asked Sadie. "What did she mean?"

"No idea. It was eerie. Like she was terrified." Lonnie brushed away tears. "I comforted her, and she quieted down until, finally, she fell asleep."

Sadie's *Surviving Spinsterhood* book recommended every single girl find a hobby to keep her busy and interesting to others. Suggestions included collecting snuffboxes and antiquing, neither of which appealed. Instead, inspired by happy memories of her father, Sadie had begun seeking out music whenever she could. From the soaring voices of an oratorio in Carnegie Hall to the wild improvisations of a jazz club set in an old perfume factory, there was nothing better after a day of answering questions than to sit quietly in a room and let the melody transport her.

The Saturday after Phillip had left for good, desperate to get out of the apartment, she'd checked the listings in the *New Yorker* and settled on a small club in the West Village where a trio would be playing. She'd sat at the bar, feeling awkward and alone, but during the first set a woman at a table right up front caught her eye. She had long gray hair and bright red lipstick and wore a fur stole from another era. She moved in time with the music, her shoulders swaying. *That's what I'll be*, decided Sadie. Unashamed, unafraid.

Tonight, though, two days after her mother's death, jazz wouldn't do. The stress that crawled up Sadie's spine and tangled in her brain required stronger fare.

The band onstage at CBGB screamed out lyrics that she couldn't catch, but that didn't matter. It wasn't the point. She had taken her usual spot at the end of the bar closest to the door, where she could observe the room but not feel quite part of it. Tonight's band was a young punk trio without much flair but a ton of anger. The thick beating of the bass drum blasted itself into Sadie's head, almost hurting her ears but not quite.

The bartender pointed to her beer, but Sadie declined another round, and he gave a slight sneer before turning way, as he always did when she showed up.

The walls and ceiling were covered with a sordid mass of stickers and graffiti, the floor gummy and the beer warm. Bands with names like the Cramps called the club home, and the harsh sounds reflected the harsher realities outside its doors. The city was on edge, still uneasy after a bomb had exploded inside the World Trade Center's parking garage a couple of months ago. Sometimes she imagined her father playing at CBGB, if he'd lived, delighting in the way the guitarists bent the sound with such ferociousness.

When the club had opened its doors in the seventies, it had been a mecca for a new kind of sound, one that veered sharply away from the shimmery disco beats that were all the rage. Twenty years later, it still thrummed with dark energy. Sadie loved to watch the dancing that wasn't really dancing, just limbs flailing about. Every few weeks, she'd stop by and recharge her batteries, and then she could go back out in the world and act like a fussy librarian again, sort through questions and supply answers, sink back into the logic and order of the Library of Congress Classification system.

Her desire to keep busy had drawn her back to work earlier that day, even though it was a Saturday and she was technically still on bereavement leave. Lonnie and LuAnn had taken care of the arrangements, which meant there was really nothing much for Sadie to do. At her desk in the quiet of the Berg, she'd left a phone

message for Miss Quinn, Laura Lyons's former secretary and executor in London, before going back to the archives and wading
through her grandfather's boxes again, hoping to find some crumb
related to Laura Lyons that she'd missed the first time around.
She soon became sidetracked by Jack Lyons's daily calendars. So
many appointments and reminders—the man was certainly me-
ticulous, just as Sadie was with her Filofax. She admired his attention to detail, list upon list of upcoming projects, weekly service
appointments, coal prices.

Then she'd reached the very last entry, dated the twenty-third
of May 1914. The same month as the letter from the library detective saying that the family was under watch. Jack Lyons had written a short list, consisting of only three items: *stepladder, rope, note.*
A tidy check mark was placed next to each one.

Three words, innocent by themselves but thick with meaning
together.

She'd never known what happened to her grandfather, only
that he'd died suddenly and the family had left the library. Could
he have killed himself?

Yet it seemed strange that he'd write a to-do list, so clinical,
unemotional.

What had happened back in May 1914 to Laura Lyons and her
husband? And what about Pearl's deathbed utterances about burning books being the reason they had to leave? The past seemed
murkier than ever, and Sadie worried over how the events from
eighty years ago might reflect on her role of curator today. And
not in a good way.

Sitting at the bar at CBGB, letting the music wash over her, she
mulled over what she'd learned. *Stepladder, rope, note.* If her grandfather had indeed killed himself, then Sadie's own father's death

might have been even harder on Pearl than Sadie had imagined, even if it had been from natural causes. It also explained Pearl's reluctance to linger on the past.

A young woman with piercings in her nose and a shaved head threw Sadie a smile as she passed by. That was nice, thought Sadie. She was a semi-regular by now, she supposed, and stood out from the other patrons in her tartan shirtwaist dress, circa 1940. Grunge fashion had nothing on her.

She gathered her tote bag and went to the bathroom, waiting in the cramped space for an open stall.

"Who's the grandma?"

The voice came from one of the stalls, and was answered by another.

"The one at the end of the bar? That's just some old bird who sits like a stone and pretends to be part of the scene. Pathetic, really. Gus hates it because she takes up space and never orders more than one beer. God help me if I'm like that when I'm old."

Old? Sadie was only forty-three, she wanted to answer. But maybe they were talking about someone else, not her.

The stall opened, and the woman who'd acknowledged Sadie earlier stood frozen. "Um, hi."

Sadie turned, blinking back tears, and walked out, back into the noise and mayhem.

Monday morning, in the basement level of the library, Sadie pushed open the door marked BINDING AND PROCESSING. She could have used up more of her bereavement leave, but she preferred to stay busy, and also didn't want Claude to swoop in and take her place in her absence.

Inside, the room was set up like a mini-factory, with long tables where various tools were laid out, empty save one man, who rose creakily to his feet as she neared, his gray beard almost white in the bright fluorescent lighting.

"Mr. Babenko."

He greeted her warmly, as he had long ago when she'd first inquired about the hidden apartment. Mr. Babenko wasn't used to visitors, and had been delighted at Sadie's interest in the history of the building, as well as his work in the bindery, showing her how incoming books were measured and fitted with Mylar dust jackets, then run through a paste machine before being sent off to the stacks for shelving. She'd shown the appropriate admiration for the chunky metal oversewing machine that stood, no longer used, in one corner, and they'd been friends ever since.

"What's going on, young lady?"

Young lady. The cruel remarks by the women at CBGB dissipated into thin air. It all came down to perspective, really.

"I don't know if you've heard, but we've had something go missing from the Berg Collection."

"Your curator?"

Of course, Marlene. The news had spread fast. "Right. She took a job in Boston. Chief of collections."

"Good for her."

"But this is something else."

He let out a whistle when she told him about the missing Virginia Woolf diary. "That's terrible news, just terrible."

"It certainly is. I have to ask you to keep this between us. Dr. Hooper doesn't want it leaking out."

"You have my assurances," said Mr. Babenko. "Was the diary marked?"

The more valuable books at the New York Public Library were stamped with an identifying mark on page ninety-seven, as a way to prevent thefts. But even Sadie knew that some of the more nefarious bookshop owners were known to buy library books regardless, and would remove the mark by either mutilating that page or using chemicals to fade it. Every library with rare books and maps faced the same quandary: whether to "deface" a book, which made it difficult to sell on the black market, or retain the book's purity and leave a tempting morsel for thieves.

"The Woolf wasn't marked, I know that for certain. I want to help find it, if I can, but I'm not sure where to start."

"For the most part, the people who have access to the books are the most likely suspects. Past thieves who have done the most serious damage to the collection are the same scholars who come to study the books, respected patrons who become so enamored with their own expertise they believe they should be the custodians of the material as well. Or want to sell them for profit."

Sadie, Claude, and Marlene had always kept a close eye on the Berg's visitors, who, after all, had to go through a strict approval process before even gaining entry. The intimacy of the room helped in that regard as well. "The librarians' desks are only a few feet away from the tables where our visitors sit. We're practically on top of each other."

"You can't trust anyone. I remember reading about a case twenty or so years ago, where two Byzantine priests were caught smuggling a rare Dutch atlas out of the Yale library. Turns out they'd taken hundreds of books, not only from Yale, but also from Dartmouth, Harvard, and Notre Dame."

"What happened to them?"

"They were defrocked and sentenced to a year and a half in prison."

"A year and half? That's all?" She must have misheard him.

"That's all. An absolute shame."

"Okay, so I'll be on the lookout for men in robes." She paused. "On a different note, I have a strange question. Do you remember hearing about anyone who committed suicide in the library, say a really long time ago?"

"Not that I know of. Why do you ask?"

She had to come clean. Well, almost clean. "I discovered a letter that said that the superintendent of the building, the one who lived in the apartment, was a suspected book thief back in 1914. And I think he may have committed suicide."

"I can't help you there, but we do have a couple of ghosts who like to wander about."

"You mean the worker who fell off the scaffolding in the Reading Room when it was being built?" She smiled. The ghost was a common legend among the staff, although no one she'd known had ever seen it firsthand.

"The very one." Mr. Babenko picked at the dry skin on his hands. "I meant what I said, you know. About the people closest to the Berg Collection being the prime suspects."

"You mean Claude and Marlene?" The timing of Marlene's new job had to be a coincidence. Marlene was devoted to the collection, to its preservation. As for Claude, Sadie had been keeping a close eye on him ever since the theft.

"Not just Claude and Marlene," Mr. Babenko replied. "You, too, Sadie. You, too."

CHAPTER SEVEN

New York City, 1913

I said give the bag here!"

Laura stepped back, deeper into the tenement apartment, even though every instinct told her to make a run for the door, get away from the menacing creature standing before her.

But doing so meant going past him, and he'd easily block her way with his bulk.

"Look, I'm a student reporter from Columbia, just visiting, really. Your son"—she looked over at the boy—"asked me to come up. There must've been some kind of mistake?" She hated the way her voice rose at the end of the sentence.

The mother of the family cowered while her husband roared at Laura. "What? You're a reporter? What kind of reporting do you think you're doing? Going to write up a sob story about our sad little family, hungry and cold?" He leered at his wife. "I say we toss this one out the window."

"No one will be tossing anyone."

The statement came from somewhere near the front door, behind the man, whose head swiveled like an owl's at the sound.

"Mr. Marino, stand down. Now."

A woman, tall and commanding, pushed past him, giving him a good shove as she did so. Her shoulders were wide, her brown hair parted in the middle and pulled back in a bun so tight Laura wondered if she didn't get headaches. A necktie was secured around her neck by a stiff collar, and she wore round spectacles that lent her an owlish air. Something about her seemed familiar, but in Laura's relief at the rescue, she was unable to figure out what.

"Everyone leave except me, the mother, and the babe."

The boy handed over the baby to the newcomer, and the gang of children skipped out, delighted at the reprieve from work. The larger ones jostled the younger ones, who barely stayed on their feet as they all funneled through the doorframe. The father, grudgingly, disappeared into the back room off the kitchen after looking Laura up and down like she was a side of beef swinging on a butcher's hook.

Once he was gone, the woman surveyed the space, nodding. "You've kept the window open, well done, Mrs. Marino."

"I'm sorry, I should go," said Laura. The other students would be heading back to Columbia now, armed with quotes and stories, while she'd almost gotten killed.

"You say you're a reporter?"

"Well, a student reporter. From Columbia."

"Then you stay, take notes. Write the story. No one else is interested."

Laura didn't dare say no. She'd never seen a woman take charge like this, with no hesitation, ordering everyone about as if she were the captain of a sea liner.

"Sit there."

Laura dutifully took a seat at the head of the table.

"The baby isn't eating much," offered Mrs. Marino, who slumped in the chair opposite Laura. Now that her family was gone, she seemed smaller, sadder. Lost.

"Since when?"

"Since yesterday."

The woman placed the baby in Mrs. Marino's arms. "Talk to her."

Mrs. Marino guffawed. "Why? She can't talk back."

"Go ahead, say something. Anything."

Mrs. Marino looked out into space, like she was trying to come up with a phrase. She shrugged and then finally obeyed. "Are you sleepy?"

In response, the child smiled.

The mother looked up, pleased.

"Well done, Mrs. Marino."

"I'm sorry, may I ask your name?" Laura said, pulling her notebook out of the satchel.

"Dr. Potter. I work for the city." Dr. Potter took the baby from Mrs. Marino and placed her carefully on the tabletop. With a practiced efficiency, she undid the child's swaddling and performed a physical examination. "We're executing a new program, where newborns are visited within a day of delivery, with regular follow-ups." The baby let out a giggle and Dr. Potter giggled back. "Mrs. Marino, can you let this reporter know what I've been yammering on about these past few months?"

The woman leaned forward, suddenly eager to win the doctor's approval. Dr. Potter had that effect. She took up space without apologizing for it, like a huge pine among saplings.

Mrs. Marino counted on her fingers. "Let fresh air into the rooms. Bathe her every few days. Don't give the baby beer. And I told the others to stop playing in the gutter, like you said."

"Well done. You're my star pupil today, I have to say."

The mother beamed.

"Do you pick her up when she cries?" asked Dr. Potter.

The mother threw the child a guilty glance. "I never did with the others. My own mother said you have to ignore them, or they'll grow up to be weak."

"Human contact is essential for a child's development." Dr. Potter's answer was swift and emphatic, as if she'd said it a hundred times before. "Comforting your baby is perfectly fine." She finished up and handed the baby back to her mother. "Try nursing her now."

"What is this new program all about?" asked Laura.

"We're trying to reduce child mortality. Starting in this district. I'm a medical inspector."

"Never seen an inspector before you lot showed up," offered Mrs. Marino.

Dr. Potter didn't seem surprised. "The ones I've met—all men, by the way—had a habit of faking records of their home visits. Never mind that last summer, fifteen hundred babies died, either from tainted milk or overswaddling. The basics of childcare can save thousands of lives. I lead a group of inspectors who have been doing home visits, actual home visits."

"Have you seen an improvement?" Laura asked.

"This past summer the number of infant deaths dropped to three hundred."

"Down from fifteen hundred?" Laura sat back, stunned. "How?"

"What you see me doing here. Talking sense to women who understand logic. Like you, Mrs. Marino."

By now the baby was in her mother's lap, sucking at one breast, gazing up in that love-drunk way that Laura had observed with both of her children.

She'd read nothing about this remarkable program in the newspapers. Not a word. She said as much as they walked back out into the street.

"Maternal health, the health of the babies of poor immigrant women, is not a priority in this city at this time," said Dr. Potter. She pulled a pocket watch out from her shirtwaist. "I must move on."

She held out a hand to shake Laura's, and in that gesture Laura realized how she knew her. From Vassar. Amelia Potter had been a student at the college a few years ahead of Laura. At the time, she'd looked quite different, with a softer hairstyle and no spectacles.

"I know you, from college," Laura said. As she spoke, the image of Amelia sitting in the grass, surrounded by other girls, came to mind. Laura had joined, sitting slightly apart, nervous about her young age compared to the rest. Amelia sat not in the proper way, with her legs folded neatly under her to one side, but like a man might, her legs cross-legged underneath her, not caring that one knee was exposed. She was reading aloud from a book that was all the rage, *The Awakening*, by Kate Chopin. Home from break, Laura had mentioned it at the dinner table, but her father had cut her off, saying that it was about a woman who puts her own needs ahead of those of her children and husband, ultimately meeting a tragic end. "An abomination," her father called it. She'd wondered when he'd read it but knew better than to ask.

Amelia, on that sunny fall day, had read loudly, proudly, from the text, while the girls around her tittered and shared knowing glances. At the time, Laura couldn't help but stare at Amelia, whose confidence was so much greater than her own. *One day, I'll be like that*, she'd vowed.

Well, she wasn't quite that confident, as her interaction with the Marinos had demonstrated. But with each test she would become a little braver, she was certain. That was why she'd enrolled in the journalism school in the first place, to be challenged.

Dr. Potter regarded Laura. "I don't remember you. When were you there?"

"Nineteen hundred. I was younger than the rest, and finished earlier. To get married. I'm Laura Lyons now."

By now, they'd reached the el train. "Well, Laura Lyons, I wish you luck in your current studies."

"Thank you. And you with your program."

Laura turned to climb the stairs.

"I say, Mrs. Lyons, you might be interested in coming to the Heterodoxy Club next week, if you're free."

"The what?" Laura had never heard the term before, and wasn't sure what it even meant.

"It's a luncheon club held in Greenwich Village every other Saturday, for women who aren't afraid to speak their minds. You might enjoy it." She pulled out a card from her satchel and scribbled an address, date, and time on the back. "Do come."

Laura began writing her article on the train back to Columbia, so that once she reached the city room all she had to do was type it up, her fingers flying, making small fixes as she went. After everyone's copy was handed in, Professor Wakeman read through them out loud, offering suggestions as he spoke, placing ones he felt worthy of being on the front page in a separate pile. Finally, he got to Laura's piece. He stopped after the first paragraph and looked over at her.

"You met this Dr. Potter in person?"

"Yes, I happened to be there during a home visit."

He carried on reading, making no corrections or suggestions. "Did you make this up?"

Laura stiffened. "Of course not. It's all true. They've saved hundreds of babies' lives in a year."

"Then why haven't I read about this elsewhere?"

Dr. Potter's words came back to Laura. "Because no one cares about immigrants' babies."

He regarded Laura. "This is front page, no doubt."

She grinned as her story was placed on the top of the pile. Even if it wouldn't be read by anyone other than her professor and the other students for now, once she'd graduated she'd make this her first pitch to her editor, and get the word out about the remarkable efforts of Dr. Amelia Potter.

She couldn't wait.

After his initial disapproval, Professor Wakeman had warmed up to Laura, and allowed her to dig into the "women's assignments" from whatever quirky angle she came up with. When they were assigned to cover a suffragist parade in Brooklyn, she hung back at the end of the march with the anti-suffragists, dressed in red and black, who grabbed banners and tore them in half. Some of her articles for the student newspaper fell flat, but she continued to find a way to make each one her own. With each passing week, her writing improved, and she ended up on the front page more often than not.

"You're thinking of your next article, aren't you?" said Jack with a sly smile as they walked up Fifth Avenue on Christmas Eve. The children skipped ahead, eager to arrive at their grandparents' house and open their gifts right off.

"We're on break. Until next month, there's nothing to think on." She nudged him with her elbow. "Well, all right, yes. How could you tell?"

"I recognize it in myself. When I'm lost in thought, I'm sure I get the same look in my eyes. Far away."

He'd been staying up later and later working on his manuscript. The dark circles under his eyes worried her, but he seemed happier than ever. Giddy, some evenings, when he crawled next to her in bed, reaching for her under her nightgown and pressing close. That giddiness had made him the center of attention back when they first met, when he was a young, soon-to-be-famous author who liked nothing better than to exchange quips in a room full of other soon-to-be-famous types. Before the hard work of writing a book had chipped away at his confidence.

"I know you've enjoyed school immensely so far." Jack turned serious, looking down at her with pity. The scholarship that Dr. Anderson had arranged wouldn't cover next term, and she'd approached the provost of the school, hoping for some financial assistance, but apparently, there were no more funds available. Her story ideas meant nothing if she couldn't attend classes.

"Don't worry, I'm sure it will all work out," she said.

"I'm sure it will. But if it doesn't, can you defer a year?"

"No. That's not the way it works." She offered up what she

hoped was a brave smile. "Our only chance lies in this evening's festivities. Don't let my father get to you. Not tonight."

"Best behavior, I promise."

Harry glanced back at his parents. "You already told us that. I said I would behave."

"Not you, my love. Your father."

Relief flooded Harry's face before he broke into a grin. "Father's in trouble?"

"He will be, if he doesn't say 'please' and 'thank you' at the table and be careful not to make a spill."

"I never spill." Jack waved his arms about like a windmill, making Harry double over with glee. Pearl, meanwhile, carried on, refusing to acknowledge the ridiculous antics of the male members of her family.

They had so much to be grateful for this holiday season. Harry had started making friends, finally, even if he didn't get the same glowing reports from his teachers that his sister did. Jack was happy at work, and Laura adored graduate school. Now if she could only stay on.

The Christmas tree in the parlor dripped with garlands and ornaments, a contrast to the empty bookshelves where valuable vases had once been displayed and the bare spot where the grand piano had stood. The glass bulbs on the tree couldn't be sold off, or at least weren't worth the effort, but the lavish decorations only made the gloomy room—electric lights dimmed to save a few extra cents—feel off-balance.

Laura hated to bring up the subject of money with her mother and father. At the same time, they were her last hope. Her mother hugged the children in turn while her father greeted them stiffly, glaring at the unseemly show of emotion. His eyebrows rose up into black arches when he was disappointed or dismayed, and became an angry slash when crossed. A man pickled in misery.

The maid brought out sherry for the grown-ups and chocolate for the children, who took one sip before racing to the tree and plucking out the gifts with their names. Laura sat on the settee with Jack and exclaimed politely as the presents were opened, although their contents barely registered in her mind.

"How is your journalism course, my dear?" her mother asked as the maid cleared away the wrapping paper and ribbons.

She'd hoped to put off the conversation until later, at least during dinner. But Jack gave her a quick nod that she knew meant it was better to address the situation right off. He was right. Doing so gave them time to warm up to the idea.

"It's brilliant. Everything I expected. By May, I'll be able to find a well-paying job with the connections I'm making."

"Women ought not to be working." Her father gestured to where Pearl and Harry were engrossed in a game of jacks on the floor. "Your children need you."

So many rebuttals came to Laura's mind. That if her mother had found a job so that the sole burden didn't fall upon her husband, the tension and blame in the household might have been lessened considerably. That if her mother had followed her heart—

Her mother sat, smiling, perched on the end of her chair. She'd been a handsome young woman once, before the lines crinkled her white skin and her hair turned gray. Now she was brittle, though she still retained some of the bubbliness of her youth. When Laura was a little girl, she would often sneak into her mother's dressing chamber and sit at the vanity, where the jewelry box was kept.

She'd load up her arms with thick bracelets and place diamond-encrusted pins in her hair, like an empress. One day she'd reached for a brooch and discovered the box had a false bottom. Underneath lay a locket containing a lock of strawberry-blond hair.

"He was my first beau," her mother had said when Laura had softly inquired that evening at bedtime. "I loved him more than anything, but we weren't deemed a good match."

"Why not?"

"He didn't have the resources to take care of me." She'd leaned in close. "I promise you I won't let you make the same mistake."

"Mistake?"

"I want you to marry whomever you love."

She'd stayed true to her word, forcing the issue with her husband when Jack had asked for Laura's hand in marriage. The impending baby, of course, had a great deal of influence in that matter. But where her father had sulked through the wedding, Laura's mother had beamed with happiness. Laura wore a locket with Jack's hair around her neck now. It wouldn't be hidden away, ever.

"Are you listening to me? I said your children need you." Laura's father, his cheeks red, gestured like a conductor from where he sat in a leather wingback chair.

"They're both fine, I assure you. Mother has been helping out when I'm at class." Laura took a sip of sherry and placed it on the side table. "There is one problem, however."

"Is there?" The eyebrows lifted.

"I received a scholarship for the first term, but I'm afraid I'm slightly short on the coming one."

She sensed her mother stiffen.

"How much?" asked her father.

"A hundred dollars. But I'll repay you as soon as I start working."

Jack leaned forward. "With luck, my book will sell next year, in which case we could repay you sooner."

Laura had told him to keep quiet, and now he'd gone and said something sure to make her father turn against the request. The eyebrows turned into two nasty arrows, practically touching in the middle of her father's forehead. "Another novelist, just what the city needs." He turned to Laura. "And yet another journalist, raking the muck."

"The things I'm learning at journalism school are important, and will make a difference in the world. For example, I've done a story on a doctor, a woman doctor, who's saved the lives of thousands of babies in the slums. The professor said the story was worthy of being in a real paper, like the *New York Times*."

"A woman doctor?" Her mother nodded encouragingly, her eyes darting to her husband and back to Laura. "That's lovely."

"Her name is Dr. Potter. I went to school with her at Vassar," added Laura.

Her father scowled, unimpressed. He addressed his wife as if they were the only people in the room. "Exactly. Laura's already been to Vassar. Not sure why she needs more schooling."

"Darling, I remember you saying that she'd meet the best of the best at university."

"I did?"

"You certainly did. And you were right about that."

His eyebrows settled into a neutral line. Progress.

"I've come this far. It's only for another five months. Please." She thought of her father turning up day after day to an office where his was the only desk, all the clerks having been let go years before. Having lunch exactly at noon, going over the figures again and again. Watching the balance decline. "You always said one shouldn't quit."

Laura caught a quick glance between her parents, full of worry and fear, and her guilt at having placed them in this position increased. If there was any other way to procure the funds, she would have taken it instead of adding to their woes. But they were her last hope. Her father's pride meant that he wouldn't dare admit how much a loan would cost him. Her mother's love, neither.

"No, Laura," said her father. "We simply cannot help you."

Her mother turned to the children. "I have some sweets for you, if you like."

The children cheered and followed her into the living room. The conversation was over.

An hour later, as they gathered their coats and made to leave, Laura's mother pulled her aside and pressed something hard into Laura's palm.

"Take this. Sell it. Don't tell your father. I'll say that I lost it." She pushed Laura out the door, waving a manic goodbye.

Laura opened her hand when they were a block away, although she already knew what lay there: her mother's engagement ring, a deep-navy sapphire surrounded by a halo of diamonds. As they neared the library, she whispered to Jack what had happened. "I didn't have a chance to give it back, to say anything, Father was right there."

"Why would you give it back?" Jack held the door open for her as they entered the library. "Looks like you might have another term of school after all. Brilliant, my love."

She didn't feel brilliant.

Dr. Anderson stood in the center of the library foyer, speaking to a gaunt man with small black eyes. It was Christmas Eve, when the employees should have been home with their families. Something was amiss. Laura sent the children upstairs.

Dr. Anderson greeted Laura and Jack and introduced the man as the library detective, Mr. Gaillard. "I'm afraid we've had more trouble."

They drew close.

"There's been another theft of a rare book. *Tamerlane.*"

Laura couldn't help but gasp. She'd seen the book before, soon after the library had opened and a few of the highlights of the collection had been put on display: the Gutenberg Bible, the Shakespeare First Folio, and *Tamerlane.* She'd peered in through the glass of the vitrine and wished desperately she could touch the small, thin volume with an olive cover, written by Edgar Allan Poe, one of her favorites. One of only a few left in the world, stated the card beside it. And now it was missing.

Laura and Jack discussed the theft in hushed tones as they climbed the stairs to the apartment. In the parlor, Harry and Pearl were bickering over how best to hang their stockings on the fireplace but stopped mid-argument, studying their parents' faces.

"What's wrong?" asked Pearl. "Are we in trouble?"

"Not at all, my love," said Jack. "It's my work. A very important book called *Tamerlane* has gone missing."

Laura refused to allow Jack's work to cast a damper on their holiday festivities. "Luckily, they have smart men looking for it, so I have no doubt it'll turn up by New Year's. Now let's get a hammer and a couple of nails and get your stockings ready for Santa's visit."

As the children's cheers and excitement filled the air, Laura's unease at the news was quickly erased, lost in the pandemonium of the holiday season.

The day after Christmas, Laura had hoped she might be able to go up to Columbia University's library to check out the books mentioned in next semester's syllabus, but Pearl and Harry were fighting over their Christmas presents, and Jack, who'd earlier that morning promised to stay with them, had disappeared with Mr. Gaillard right after breakfast.

Finally, around two o'clock, he returned, his face weary.

"Any luck with the missing books?" Laura asked.

"Nothing yet."

"Why don't I fix you something to eat?" Once he was settled, she could grab her satchel and head uptown, fit in a couple of hours at least.

But Jack shook off the offer. "I'm worried about all this, how this reflects on me as superintendent."

"You don't think they suspect you, do you?"

"Not exactly, but I know this place so well, better than anyone. You would think I'd be able to determine how the thief is getting in and out, but I don't have a clue. How about you come down to the stacks with me? Without Gaillard breathing down my neck, I'll be able to see it more clearly."

Laura suppressed a sigh. "Of course, my love."

She tucked away her satchel.

Deep in the basement, Laura breathed in the acrid odor from the bindery, where the library's books were repaired. They went down a long hall into the shipping room, where Jack unlocked a door that led right into the stacks.

"We can't figure out how the thief got inside the cages."

"What cages?" Laura had had a quick tour of the stacks—seven stories of shelving located directly below the Main Reading Room—when they'd first arrived. "I don't remember seeing cages."

"I'll show you."

Natural light for the stacks spilled in through a series of long, narrow windows that ran down the length of the building. From Bryant Park, the effect was striking and modern. Inside, the design provided airiness to what was basically a book repository. The cast-iron shelves were painted white, with each row assigned a number. Metal stairways offered access between each section.

They passed by brass pneumatic tubes that glistened like snakes. "This is where the call slips from the Catalog Room and the Main Reading Room end up, and are handed to whatever page is assigned to that section," said Jack.

She imagined the stacks during library hours, with pages traversing back and forth, piling up books in the dumbwaiters for quick retrieval. "How do you know that it isn't a librarian or a page, since they're the ones with the most access?"

"The keys to the cages are limited to the head librarians and me."

She studied the space. "Do the windows open?"

"No."

"Where are these cages?"

"Follow me."

As they walked, she couldn't help herself. "How's the manuscript coming along?"

"I find I'm slowing down as I reach the end, like I do when I'm reading a book that I love."

Slowing down? She knew she should stay quiet, but she couldn't help herself. "Boy, I wish we had that luxury in class. With a dead-line, it's amazing how fast you get things done. Journalists don't get paid if they don't write, so it becomes less precious."

Her enthusiastic delivery did nothing to hide the snippiness of her words. Part of her didn't care, though. *Just get on with it already.*

"You're a student journalist, not a journalist. Yet."

She wouldn't back down. "Maybe if you gave yourself a dead-line, you'd reach the end faster. Easter, or something like that."

"Fiction is a creative process, you can't compare the two. It can't be rushed."

One section of the stacks, in the northeast corner, was set off from the rest by a wire cage that encircled two bookcases, around twenty feet in length. As Jack fiddled with the lock, Laura clutched the wire with her fingers and gave it a shake. "Seems pretty solid."

"You'd need wire cutters to get through these."

She peered inside. "It's like a rare book zoo. Do you remember when we took the children to the Bronx Zoo? How Pearl growled back at the tiger?"

"Fearless, our Pearl." The lock finally clicked, and he held open the wire door for her to step inside. "Harry could use some of her gumption."

He pointed to the shelf that held the oversized books, some of which were in labeled gray boxes. "This is the Gutenberg Bible, one of forty-eight copies that survive from the mid-1400s. And over here is one of Shakespeare's First Folios."

These books had suffered through hundreds of years of han-dling without falling apart, without being lost or damaged. They were each a piece of history. Invaluable and precious. She stepped back, glancing along the shelves. "So this is the section where the *Leaves of Grass* and *Tamerlane* were kept?"

"Yes."

"Were they checked out by anyone? Did you figure out who last asked to see them?"

He sighed. Of course they had. But she was just trying to be helpful.

"Sorry," she said. "I'm sure you've been over this a million times with Mr. Gaillard."

"Not quite a million, but close."

He locked the cage door carefully, checking it twice to make sure the lock was secure. His hands, so large around the key, reminded her just how strong he was, how faithfully he'd taken care of their family and provided them with everything they needed. She remembered how much she'd enjoyed watching him up at the estate, taking his place alongside the other men to help mend a stone wall, heaving rocks into place as if they were made of air. She shouldn't have made him feel bad about his book earlier. He was doing the best he could.

She wrapped her hands around his waist and reached up to kiss the back of his neck.

"Careful. We've added another night watchman, we don't want to cause trouble." He smiled. "Well, not here, anyway."

Laura followed him along the row to the staircase. "What else is kept in the cage?"

"Manuscripts, letters, maps."

"Maybe one day your book will be in there. Imagine that. In a hundred years, when you're a famous author, they'll have all your first drafts lined up on the shelf next to Shakespeare."

He nodded gamely, and she immediately regretted saying any-thing, as it only added to his pressure.

But it was probably just temporary, a part of a creative writer's natural cadence. She shouldn't blame herself for that.

It wasn't her fault.

CHAPTER EIGHT

New York City, 1914

Greenwich Village was very different from Laura's Fifth Avenue neighborhood, all narrow streets at odd angles, the buildings a mix of livery stables, tenements, cafés, and saloons. Recently, the low rents had attracted a new set of residents who called themselves bohemians and didn't mind the fact that the apartments tended to be small and dingy. All part of the charm, Laura supposed. Even in winter, Village streets thrummed with energy, men and women spilling out of restaurants or animatedly chatting in front of a bakery, the windows slick with steam.

She turned down MacDougal Street and found the address for Polly Holladay's restaurant. Inside, she paused, her nerves catching up with her. Men and women sat at long wooden trestle tables, drinking together. Her father would have had a fit if he knew his daughter was indulging in such scandalous behavior. Near the back, she caught sight of Amelia speaking with a woman with bobbed hair and wearing what looked like a meal sack and leather sandals. In February.

As Amelia greeted Laura, the woman was swept up the stairs by another group.

Laura couldn't help herself. "What is she wearing?"

"That's nothing. If you visit Henrietta at home, you'll often find her in her birthday suit. A practicing feminist and nudist, our girl Henny."

Laura memorized the phrase. What a quote. Since the new semester had begun, she'd been struggling to come up with an idea for her thesis assignment: nine thousand words on a single topic, with Professor Wakeman as her advisor. While Dr. Potter's invitation had initially slipped her mind in the craziness of the holidays, the biweekly meetings of the Heterodoxy Club now seemed like a timely opportunity.

She followed Amelia upstairs to a large meeting room, where avant-garde artwork competed for attention with an assortment of sofas and chairs, all upholstered in bright citrus colors. They scrunched into a love seat near the front as a woman called for attention and recited the day's agenda. Laura was just reaching into her satchel for her notebook when the woman's words stopped her mid-reach.

"As we've said in the past, the comments and discussions that take place at the Heterodoxy Club are considered off the record, so members may speak their minds freely. Some of us have experienced firsthand how our words may be twisted by those who wish to demean and deride the causes we delve into over these three hours. This afternoon, you need not fear that."

No note taking. She straightened up, curious to see what this was all about.

Margaret Sanger spoke first, about fighting the obscenity laws that prevented her from publishing and disseminating information regarding contraception to the women who most needed it. She used words that Laura had never heard spoken out loud, like "pessary" and "condom," "coitus interruptus," and talked of douching with carbolic acid or Lysol as a preventive measure. The room was brought to tears with her story of a young Jewish immigrant woman who begged her doctor for birth control, was refused, and then died in childbirth of septicemia. "In that moment, I resolved that women should have knowledge of contraception," Sanger told them. "They have every right to know about their own bodies. I would scream from the housetops. I would tell the world what was going on in the lives of these poor women. I *would* be heard. No matter the cost, I *would* be heard."

Amelia clapped with fervor. How brave, to be on the front lines of change, the way these women around Laura were. There was a sizzle of anger in the room but not in the way that the newspapers usually described, equating the New Woman with rabid, anti-establishment radicalism. The ideas being bandied about were radical, yes, but opposition arose with frequency and everyone got a say. When the talk turned to the suffrage movement, equal time was spent discussing whether gaining the right to vote in what was an inherently male, corrupt electoral system was even worth the effort, a perspective Laura hadn't ever considered.

By the time the three hours were up, Laura had enough material to write ninety thousand words, never mind nine thousand. The Heterodoxy Club made a perfect subject for her thesis. It fulfilled Professor Wakeman's requirement that she cover a "women's topic," but unlike most of his assignments, this one actually mattered, and Laura found herself intrigued by the ideas of the New

Woman. She felt a twinge of guilt when she remembered that it was supposed to remain off the record before setting aside the mandate. Since the thesis was just practice and not for publication, she wouldn't be breaking any rules. Maybe later, after she'd graduated and gotten to know these women better, she'd approach them for permission. But for now, she was just a student learning her craft.

The group broke up, and Laura joined Amelia and a few of the others downstairs in the restaurant. She wasn't ready to leave, not yet.

Their table was made up of a lawyer, an actress, and a couple of authors. Not one woman spoke of her children, if they had any, nor their spouses. Laura realized with a shock that all had achieved financial independence.

Her thoughts were interrupted by the woman sitting across from her. "You're not a monotonist, are you?"

"I'm sorry, a what?"

Amelia put her hand on Laura's arm, a protective gesture that Laura appreciated. She wasn't part of this group, really. The causes—women's suffrage, birth control—she supported, of course, but she was only a student reporter, and didn't want to get too caught up. Still, part of her wanted to impress Amelia, or at the very least not embarrass her. She had lost touch with the few women friends she'd made when she and Jack had lived in the country, and the isolation of residing in a library hadn't helped matters. A thin, invisible thread stretched between her and Amelia, a result of their shared alma mater, and she didn't want to see it dissolve because she was deemed to be too conservative for this downtown crowd.

"A monotonist is a woman who marries young, has children, and remains mated," the woman explained.

"I suppose I am. For now." Laura wasn't sure why she tacked on the last two words. She had no intention of leaving Jack, but her life appeared so stodgy compared to the others. She lived in a marble mausoleum right on Fifth Avenue, for goodness' sake, a far cry from a charming Village flat with flower boxes in the windows. "What's the alternative?"

"A varietist. Exactly what the name implies." The woman introduced herself as Florence. "Varietists try many different iterations of relationships. Men, women. All the combinations you can think of. Open marriage, for example. Why do you think we want to legalize birth control? So we can love freely, without fear."

Amelia jumped in. "Don't try to shock our new member, Flo."

"I'm not shocked," said Laura. "But you won't sell your cause with such talk. The rest of society associates free love with prostitution, with the corruption of the family dynamic. It's all wrapped up together."

"The very phrase 'the corruption of the family dynamic' is another way of keeping women downtrodden," said Amelia. "The family dynamic only works if there's someone—the woman—who is tasked with the drudgery of child-rearing and housekeeping. If her mind and energy are freed up to take on more pressing concerns, the world will turn on its head."

Even though she partly agreed, Laura couldn't help but push back. "I object to the use of 'drudgery' in the same sentence as 'child-rearing.' My children are a delight, a wonder." Their laundry, not so much, she thought to herself.

"We have many mothers in the club," said Amelia. "The two

ideas aren't exclusive. We're more concerned with making sure that mothers can dictate how many children they wish to have, and how far apart to give birth. A measure of control that frees up their economic power."

The conversation veered off in a new direction, ideas and phrases bandied about in a whirl: social and moral repression, liberation, feminism.

Already, the thesis was practically writing itself in her head.

"If you're interested in writing about public health, I have the perfect book for you," said Amelia, digging through a desk piled high with letters and notebooks. "Here it is."

At Amelia's urging, Laura had walked back with her to her apartment on Patchin Place, an alley off Tenth Street. She knew she should head home and start making dinner, but part of her wanted to find out how Amelia lived her life, as it was so different from her own.

The rooms were small but comfortable, with a rocking chair near the fireplace, and filled with color, much like the meeting hall for the club had been.

Laura had tried to make her own apartment in the library cozy, but the strange layout—part public space, part private—had stymied her efforts, and compared to this charming flat, she'd failed dismally. Yet she couldn't help but notice that Patchin Place had yet to be modernized, with the hand pump at the sink and metered gas flares providing heat and light. At least they had an indoor commode at the library. While Laura's decorating skills could be improved upon, an outhouse certainly could not.

She took the book that Amelia gave her and tucked it under the notebook in her lap. She'd hinted that she was interested in covering Amelia's work as part of her studies, which was true, even though she saw it more as a part of the thesis, an inside look at the ladies of the club.

"What made you decide to study medicine?" asked Laura.

Amelia sat beside her on the couch, her arm resting along the back. Her hair was naturally curly, the swirls beginning to release from the hold of the pomade in the dry heat of the room. She'd taken off the stiff collar she wore and loosened her necktie, much in the way that Jack did when he came home. Yet her obviously ample cleavage swelled under the shirtwaist like a Gibson Girl's. A strange mix of feminine and masculine.

"I decided to become a doctor when my father and brother both died of typhoid within six months of each other," said Amelia. "Not because I had some silly notion that I could have saved them—the only thing that could've saved them is if sewage hadn't been dumped in the Hudson River—but I was left to take care of my mother, and I needed a profession that paid."

"I'm so sorry. That must've been awful." They sat in silence for a moment. "That day we met, in that tenement. Are most of your appointments like that?"

"Oh, that was nothing. I remember as an intern going to tend to a birth in a tenement in Hell's Kitchen. The woman's back was blistered, she was in terrible pain, because apparently her husband had come home drunk and thrown hot water at her. As soon as she told me that, he appeared, drunk off his rocker. He tried to come at me, but I sidestepped him out into the hallway, where I gave him a huge push. Down the stairs."

Laura gasped. She waited, uncertain. "What happened?"

"I went back and delivered his child. On my way out, I kicked him in the leg and he swore at me, so it turns out I didn't kill him. Not that it would've bothered me much."

"Really?"

Amelia suddenly looked exhausted. "No. That's not true. I would've been inconsolable if I'd killed him, to be honest. I'm a doctor, after all."

The melancholy in Amelia's voice made Laura want to offer what comfort she could. "You must see so much despair."

"I can't get sentimental about it. You see these mothers with their sick babies, and they have such fatalism in their eyes. They know they'll probably lose that child, as well as the one after. When my nurses and I first show up, they're suspicious of our motives, but as their babies remain healthy, gain weight, and grow, their trust in us grows as well. They become eager to please, happy to brag of their progress."

"Can I ask why you dress the way you do? Is it so that the men in the tenements don't bother you while you work?"

Amelia laughed. "No. It's so the other doctors don't bother me, and not in the way you're inferring. If I show up wearing lace and ruffles, they'll talk down to me, dismiss me and my ideas. So I dress as much like them as possible without being indecent. Just recently one of the doctors—a good fellow, this one—was complaining to me about the nurses for their vile feminine ways and I had to stop him and ask, 'What kind of creature do you think I am?' His eyes went wide and, I swear, it suddenly dawned on him that he had been speaking to me as one of his own gender. I couldn't have been happier. Besides, it's more comfortable." She lifted her skirt and straightened out one leg. "If I could wear trousers, I'd do that."

"Or a sack, like Henrietta."

"That, too. But I imagine it's itchy."

"Probably."

From outside came the faint cries of children playing in the alley, reminding Laura that she really should go home.

"What about you?" asked Amelia.

"What do I like to wear?" she couldn't help joking.

"Very funny. What do you want to do with your degree?"

"Write about things like this. Your work, the changes the city is going through. The changes that women are going through."

"This is the place, then. You won't get a more progressive crowd than here in Greenwich Village. Although you're already too late. I hear that someone's started giving paid tours of an 'artist's gar-ret' off of Washington Square, aimed at attracting visitors to the city and the uptown crowd. He's set up an artist's studio in one room, an actress's bedroom in another, and hired appropriately bohemian-looking people to pretend to paint or act. I suppose they each get a percentage of the take."

"That would make a great article."

"I can't help get the feeling I'm being used, as an insider source," said Amelia lightly. "Tell me about your family."

Laura closed her notebook and tucked it back into the satchel, along with Amelia's book. "I have a girl and a boy. My husband's working on a manuscript but also works for the public library, where we live." She quickly explained their situation, and was pleased to see Amelia's face break out into a big grin.

"You live in that monstrous beast of a library? Simply marvel-ous. I'd love to see it someday."

"Of course, any time."

A noise arose from above, presumably the bedroom, followed by a clumping down the stairs, before a pretty but disheveled young woman appeared, wrapped in a blanket. She regarded Amelia with heavy-lidded eyes. "You're back so late."

Amelia nodded. "And you've been fast asleep the whole time."

"What else am I supposed to do?" She drew close and planted a soft kiss on Amelia's lips.

Laura had known that women loved other women, of course, and heard that the new bohemians were rife with such couples, including men who loved men. Back in college, there had been a couple of girls in her dormitory who were rumored to be lovers, and while the other students exclaimed revulsion at the very idea, Laura had found herself staring at the pair during her American literature class, wondering what it was like, to love a woman.

That kiss, though. The stays of Laura's corset dug into her torso as she absorbed the encounter. She'd never kissed Jack in front of others, wouldn't dream of it. Then again, not long ago she had allowed Jack to take her in the library, albeit after hours, where the thrill of being caught heightened their every touch. She was no prude, she reminded herself.

Yet these were two women, which made it both stranger and more familiar than she'd expected.

She jumped to her feet. "I really must be going."

"Would you like a cup of tea before you go?" asked Amelia. "Jessie here will make it for you."

Jessie's pout indicated otherwise.

"No, I'm fine. Thank you."

"Jessie, put on the kettle for me, please."

Jessie straightened and left. Laura was out of her element downtown. She had to remember she was a reporter, not a participant.

"Are you shocked?" asked Amelia once Jessie had cleared the room.

"A little, I suppose."

She rose and accompanied Laura to the door. "I do wish to have children one day, though. I admit, I envy you that. What are your children's names?"

"The boy is Harry. He's eleven. Pearl is seven. Jack's manuscript of late has been more difficult than he expected, so he's up so late working on it. Then he has to be up at six for work, it's all too much." She stammered on about nothing and everything, her mouth forming words before she could even consider the thought behind them. Amelia shot her a direct, knowing gaze.

Burning with embarrassment, Laura finally left.

CHAPTER NINE

New York City, 1993

I need to find out where in the Antarctic has the largest population of penguins. Can you help me?"

The question sent a surge of adrenaline through Sadie. An hour ago, she'd gotten a call at her desk in the Berg asking if she would cover for a reference librarian who'd fallen ill, and had jumped at the chance. Claude had been annoying her all day with his overly solicitous questions about the exhibit, and she'd told him to cover the room while she manned the reference desk. Here, in the Catalog Room of the library, she was like a dolphin in water. Or perhaps a penguin.

The patron asking about penguins was a writer of geography books who often worked out of the library, and Sadie was happy to help. Behind him, another patron in an officious-looking dark suit began to speak, but Sadie cut him off with a curt "I'll be with you in a moment." She came out from around the desk and led the penguin patron to one of the many card catalogs that stood on the perimeter of the wall. The drawer gave an efficient swoosh as she opened it, and she worked her way through the index cards, speaking aloud the pertinent call numbers and titles as he wrote them down on call slips.

Back at the desk, she fed the call slips into the pneumatic tube. "You can pick the books up in the Reading Room," she said. "My guess is that the correct answer is the Danger Islands. I believe approximately one and a half million penguins reside there, and are kept safe from human interference by heavy ice floes that make landing boats a dangerous undertaking."

With a hearty "Thanks," he was on his way.

"Wow." The man who'd been waiting in line stepped up to the desk. "How do you know all that stuff about the penguins?" He spoke out of the side of his mouth, like he was being sarcastic.

"It's my job."

"Now I know who to turn to if I see a penguin waddling around."

"I assure you they prefer to stay south of Fourteenth Street."

He laughed, which drew nasty stares from the other patrons but gave Sadie a small thrill. She wasn't known around the library for her sense of humor. "Now, what can I help you with?"

"I'm Nick Adriano. Dr. Hooper brought me in as a consultant regarding the theft."

She knew that the director was hiring more security, but she hadn't realized it would involve a consultant. He looked to be in his early fifties, his hair completely gone on the top of his head, thinning around the sides but cut close, like he didn't dispute the fact that battle was almost over. The curve of his pate was balanced by a square jaw.

She caught his eye and realized he was probably sizing her up the same way. Not that it mattered, but she'd put on her favorite dress today, featuring giant magnolia blooms over a bright pink background, knowing that she'd be stopping by the donor cocktail party at five o'clock. She glanced up at her watch. It was quarter after—she really should be there by now. She lowered her voice. "I assume you're investigating the theft of the diary?"

"I am. Do you have a moment?" he asked.

"I'm done here, but on my way downstairs. If you like, we can talk as we walk." She joined Mr. Adriano on the other side of the desk.

"I heard you were called 'No Stumpin' Sadie,' and now I see why."

She hated that name, like something from an old Broadway musical. "It's just a matter of knowing where to start, which I assume is very similar to what you do in your job."

"Like right now, where I'm starting with you."

"As you should. What questions can I answer for you?"

"This book, it was in the cage in the stacks?"

"It was a notebook, not a book. And yes, that's where we keep a majority of the Berg Collection, as we've outgrown our current space and new locked bookcases aren't to be installed in the third-floor space until later this year. I'll be very relieved once it's all under our aegis, as obviously the stacks are not safe."

"Obviously. But first, we have to look closely at those who have access to the collection, as you can imagine. When did you discover it missing?"

"Exactly one week ago. On the thirtieth of March."

"What made you go look for it?"

"It was to be included in our upcoming exhibit, *Evergreen*. I was planning to begin working on the description of the diary for the catalog. My job, as temporary curator, is to ensure that the preparations go smoothly, and make sure there are no surprises."

"What kind of surprises?"

"Any damage, anything out of place. But it was nowhere to be found." The memory of not finding it in its box brought back a muted panic.

"When did anyone from the Berg last see it?"

"My coworker Claude had taken it out a few weeks before it went missing. He says he put it back right after."

"And you and Claude were the only ones who had access to the locked cage?"

"Along with Marlene and the director, yes. Have you talked to Claude yet?"

"I did, earlier today."

So he hadn't started with her, as he'd stated previously. She waited, but he didn't elaborate. What if Claude had thrown some kind of suspicion on her? She wouldn't put it past him, especially after he'd been skipped over for the curator position. "What did he say?"

"He was helpful."

She hated not knowing what was going on. "I'm assuming that in cases like these, the staff has a tendency to turn on each other. I assure you that I will do no such thing. Claude is a fine man, but I hope you take whatever he says with a grain or two of salt."

Had she said too much? It had been some time since a man had looked at her so intently—since Claude and, before that, Phillip— and Mr. Adriano's interest, even if it was professional, unnerved her.

"And why is that, exactly?"

"We dated, briefly. Well, not really. No. Never mind." The words came out with a faint English accent, much to Sadie's horror.

Her mother used to do the same whenever she was nervous, and the affectation always irritated Sadie. Yet here she was doing the same thing.

She'd never hear Pearl's voice again. The thought made her eyes burn.

"Ms. Donovan, are you all right?"

She pulled herself together. "Last week, I got a promotion—although it's only temporary—and he did not, and I would not be surprised if he were less than generous in his description of me. I assure you, the library is paramount to me. I would never harm it in any way."

God, she sounded like an idiot. Protesting too much, and all of that.

They'd reached the door to the room where the cocktail party was being held. Dr. Hooper was probably wondering where she was. "I've arrived at my destination, Mr. Adriano, and I'm afraid I have other business to attend to. Of course, if you need anything else, you can find me in the Berg during business hours."

"Are you trying to get rid of me?" The side of his mouth rose up again, like he was amused. Like this was all a joke.

"Not at all, but I must make an appearance. It's a cocktail party for donors and trustees, and I promised Dr. Hooper I'd attend."

"I'll join you, then."

She hesitated a moment before stepping back and allowing him to open the door for her. "Very well."

Inside, the room was crowded and hot. A waiter came by with glasses of wine on a tray, and they each took one, sipped, and looked about the room.

"See any suspects?" she asked.

"At this point, I suppose everyone is a suspect. How long have you worked at the library?"

"Eight years. How long have you been a security consultant?"

His smile spread slowly, like he was trying to hold it back. "Five years. Before that, I was a cop, at the Twenty-Third precinct. When I retired, I started my own security firm. We're brought in when something goes wrong."

"May I ask, who are your typical clients?"

"Auction houses like Sotheby's, high-end private families. That sort of thing."

She nodded her approval. "So you're discreet."

"I am."

"That will be helpful in this case. Often, libraries that are robbed prefer to keep the incident quiet so that donors and trustees"—she motioned with her glass around the room—"don't pull their support. Which runs counter to the possibility of recovering the stolen object, unfortunately."

"So you're saying it's a choice between protecting the institution or locating the artifact? Can't we do both?"

Before she could answer, Dr. Hooper came barreling over, trailed by Claude.

"Mr. Adriano, Sadie," said Dr. Hooper. "We have a problem." He pointed to the door, and they all followed him outside, into the hallway. He looked around, as if checking to make sure they had privacy. "There's been another theft."

"What was stolen, and from where?" asked Mr. Adriano. He straightened up, his eyes bright.

Claude responded, staring right at Sadie. "A first edition of *The Scarlet Letter*. From the cage."

Dr. Hooper leaned in to their small circle.

"It was taken from the cage for the Berg Collection?" Sadie repeated, her mind whirling.

Claude was gray. "Yes."

"But it wasn't missing when we did the shelf read."

"No, it wasn't." Claude spoke fast, trying to explain, his voice rising. "I brought it up from the cage to my desk yesterday, to review it for the exhibit. I locked it back up before I headed home for the evening, I swear, but when I went back down this afternoon, it was gone."

"Didn't we have the locks changed?" asked Dr. Hooper.

"We did," said Mr. Adriano.

Which ruled out Marlene.

Dr. Hooper turned to Claude. "I'm afraid, Claude, since you were the last person to have handled it, we'll have to restrict your access. For now. Please hand over your key."

Claude, looking sick, pulled it out of his pocket and did so.

Sadie was now the only person left standing, other than Dr. Hooper, who had access to the collection in the cage. Ultimately, she was responsible, as the book thefts occurred on her watch as curator. This was personal, as if someone had broken into her home and rifled through her own belongings.

"What's the resale possibility for the edition?" asked Dr. Hooper.

Sadie jumped in to answer. "It's probably much easier to sell than the Virginia Woolf diary, which is one of a kind. There are several first editions of *The Scarlet Letter* out there."

"How much do you estimate it's worth?" asked Mr. Adriano.

"Somewhere around ten thousand dollars." The words stuck on Sadie's tongue.

Dr. Hooper dismissed them and headed back in to the party,

his mouth a grim line. Claude slunk off, hands in his pockets, leaving behind Mr. Adriano and Sadie.

"How much experience do you have dealing with rare book thefts?" she asked.

"We've run into a couple of incidents, but usually we deal with art or sculpture."

"It's not the same."

"Obviously not."

"Do you think Claude's involved?"

He shrugged. "I couldn't say at this point. Nor would I, to you."

"I want to recover our property as much as you do."

"Whose property?"

He'd caught her there.

"The library's, of course."

She had to make him see that a book could be as important as a Picasso. To not only *know* that, but to be emotionally invested in it as well. "If you don't mind, I'd like to introduce you to the Berg Collection. Would that be all right?"

He agreed, and not reluctantly, which was a good sign. As they walked down the hallway, she asked, "What sort of books do you like to read?"

"I like nonfiction. And poetry."

Now, that was a surprise. She'd been expecting to hear the name of the latest thriller. "What kind of poetry?"

"John Ashbery, Walt Whitman. 'Resist much, obey little.'"

She paused just outside the door, smiling. "Come with me."

In the Berg, she pulled out her key chain and stuck the key into one of the locks in the glass cabinets. She took out a box and placed it on the empty table, put on her gloves, and then carefully sifted through its contents until she found what she was looking for. "Do you know this one by Whitman? 'You Lingering Sparse Leaves of Me.'"

"It was in the annex to *Leaves of Grass.*"

"Here's an early draft, written in his own hand." She slid it out of its protective shield and laid it on the table, stepping aside so he could see.

The paper was stained brown in places, like coffee had been spilled across it.

He leaned in closer. "But this is different from the one I've read."

"Exactly. That's what makes it special. We can see Whitman's thought process, how the poem evolved. Look at the pencil marks." She pointed without touching the page. "He's written 'final version' on the top right corner, then crossed it out. Some of the lines are quite different in several places from the one that was eventually published. Like here, the phrase 'You meagre little banners' is changed to 'pallid banner-staves.'"

"And the final line here reads, 'My hardiest and my last.'" He looked at her. "What's the real version again?"

"The one that was published reads, 'The faithfulest—hardiest—last.'"

"I like that better," he said.

"So do I."

"To think he wrote this as he was sitting around, drinking his coffee, all those years ago." Mr. Adriano shook his head. "Imagine that."

"You could say that it's an active representation of the human act of creation. These stains, rips, and cross-outs are visual records of the work as it was first put on paper and then revised. On some manuscripts, you can tell when the author became angry or frustrated, from changes in the penmanship. One of my favorite mentors in college, Professor Ashton, used to say that it's a bridge from the reader to the author, one that provides far more than just the mechanical representation of the content."

"A bridge. I like that."

"So you see why this is so valuable." She carefully placed it back into the protective sleeve. "We can understand how he got from there to here, why he chose each word, after considering and discarding others."

He looked around. "So everything in the Berg Collection is like the Whitman draft?"

"Some are more interesting than others. For example." She reached down to the bottom shelf and pulled out the infamous cat-paw letter opener.

"What the—"

She explained the provenance and was pleased when Mr. Adriano grinned.

"These archival manuscripts are important," she added. "Even the administrative records from the library when it was first built are vital to understanding its history. History is made by people in power making decisions, and their notes and writings reveal the decision-making process." She thought of Laura Lyons, who hid her life away. How ironic that Laura's granddaughter had made a career of the very ephemera that she'd had destroyed upon her death. "Records should be saved."

The next morning, Sadie took a break from her work in the Berg to bring a couple of Danishes to Mr. Babenko in the bindery. As she turned down the hallway, she spotted a familiar figure outside the door, knocking.

Mr. Adriano.

"You can just go in." She indicated the doorknob with her elbow, her hands full. "It's open. He listens to jazz on his Walkman while he works, so he can't hear you."

Mr. Babenko looked up from his work, delighted, as they entered, and took off his headphones. "Sadie! With delicacies, no less." He smiled at Mr. Adriano. "I was talking about the pastries, of course."

"Of course," Mr. Adriano replied cheerfully.

"To what do I owe this pleasure?"

"I'm just here for a social visit," said Sadie. "Mr. Adriano's probably here on business." She sat down at the table and nibbled at a Danish. Mr. Adriano looked at her as if he were deciding whether to dismiss her, but then returned his attention to Mr. Babenko, reaching out to shake hands. He stopped, mid-reach, as Mr. Babenko held out his palm, an apologetic look on his face. Layers of skin were in various stages of peeling off his fingers, like translucent wood shavings.

"Hazard of the job," said the older man.

"I'm sorry. What job do you do?" asked Mr. Adriano.

"Bookbinding. In 1965 I developed an allergy that stuck with me. Can't seem to stop what I'm doing, though."

Sadie smiled. Mr. Adriano didn't know that Mr. Babenko loved to boast about his hands, that they were a point of pride with him, and that long ago he had refused gloves, saying they stymied his sense of touch. "Mr. Babenko is in charge of processing the new books when they come in, and restoring any that are damaged," she said.

"I see." Mr. Adriano raised his eyebrows at her before turning back to the bookbinder. "I understand you've been here a long time, and I thought I might ask you some questions."

"Is this about the book thefts?"

Mr. Adriano shot Sadie a look, but continued. "Dr. Hooper said you were the building's unofficial historian, and that you'd even written a book on the place."

"You've written a book?" Now it was Sadie's turn to be surprised. "You never told me that."

"A coffee-table book, back in the sixties. Out of print now. Out of date as well, what with the new stacks added under Bryant Park. How can I help you, Mr. Adriano?"

"I was inspired by Ms. Donovan here, who gave me a lesson in the value of archival records yesterday, and decided to do some digging of my own. I was surprised to learn that the library had an on-site detective, back when the library first opened."

"A Mr. Gaillard, I presume?" said Mr. Babenko.

Mr. Adriano took out a notebook and flipped through it until he found the correct page. "Yes. I've spent the morning investigating the paper trail to any earlier book thefts here at the library, in case we can learn from the past, and luckily Mr. Gaillard left a trove of information behind. I've been compiling a list of prior thefts: what was taken, from where, whether or not they were recovered."

Sadie's heart thumped in her chest. "What did you learn?" she asked, her mouth dry.

"The worst was a spate of them beginning in 1913."

Mr. Babenko gestured toward Sadie. "That's when your superintendent was around, right?"

She smiled weakly. "I guess."

"Who's that?" asked Mr. Adriano.

"I had done some digging myself, you see. In the director's archives, for a project." She went on to explain what she'd mentioned to Mr. Babenko yesterday, about the superintendent being a suspect.

"What was the super's name?" asked Mr. Adriano.

"Jack. Jack Lyons."

"Married to Laura Lyons, the essayist," supplied Mr. Babenko.

Mr. Adriano nodded. "I've heard of her, sure."

Sadie struggled to divert his attention. "I also found a note in the director's file, written by the detective, saying that it was as if the thief had 'dropped from the sky.'"

"Interesting." Mr. Adriano scribbled something in his notebook, then flipped the page. "Apparently, one of the first items stolen from the library was a book called *Tamerlane*, by Poe."

"One of only ten copies in the world," Mr. Babenko said. "Never recovered. A terrible loss."

"How much would that be worth today?" he asked.

"One recently went at auction for four hundred thousand dollars," volunteered Sadie.

Mr. Adriano let out a long whistle. "Quite the racket. Mr. Gaillard's notes mention a Book Row. Where is that?"

"From around 1890 to the 1960s, there was a collection of bookstores, called Book Row, on Fourth Avenue just below Union Square," said Mr. Babenko. "These days bookstores that handle rare books are scattered around Manhattan. There might be one or two left on Book Row, and one of the most famous, the Strand, is just around the corner on Broadway and Twelfth, but most were forced out by rising rents."

"I've also assembled a list of bookstores that have been flagged for purchasing stolen items in the past; would you mind taking a look?" He showed Mr. Babenko the page in his notebook. "I'm curious if anything jumps out at you, as a place to start."

Mr. Babenko studied it, and checked off the names of five bookstores. "It's all rumor, of course, but the book world is a small one, and word gets around."

"Thank you," said Mr. Adriano. "I'll look into it."

As he left, Sadie pushed away the plate with the Danish, no longer hungry.

CHAPTER TEN

New York City, 1993

Sadie sat in the middle of the floor of Lonnie's spare bedroom—the one her mother had stayed in—surrounded by clothes, looking for something fancy to wear. She'd let herself in with her key when no one answered the doorbell, knowing that several boxes of their mother's belongings sat piled up in one corner, packed up for the Salvation Army after she'd died. But Sadie's quest had come to a screeching halt after she'd come upon her mother's wedding dresses, wrapped in plastic, at the very bottom of the last box.

The first one was a cream dress suit with a peplum jacket. That was from her wedding to Sadie and Lonnie's father. The second, from her wedding with the hateful Don, was a fifties-style white silk dress that hit just above the knee. At the small celebratory dinner after, she and Lonnie had watched as their new stepfather accidentally spilled red wine down the bodice while giving a boisterous toast. Sadie ran her finger down the stain, which had faded to a dull pink.

How funny that Pearl had saved them, after all these years. It went against her own advice to Sadie, that she hand her own wedding dress over to a consignment shop the same day she signed the divorce papers. "I don't want you looking at it in your closet every time you open it, Sadie," Pearl had said. "Buy yourself something pretty instead."

She had, finding a turquoise cocktail dress with a tight bodice that flared into a full skirt, perfect for twirling on the dance floor. Not that she'd ever twirled, but wearing it made her feel that she might become the kind of woman who did. That dress had sent her down the thrift store rabbit hole, a quest that took up entire Saturdays that otherwise would have been filled with wondering what Phillip was up to, and with whom. Whenever she wore her latest find, people asked about her outfit instead of asking about her life. It was a kind of armor, she supposed.

Pearl hadn't saved much over the years. There were no letters or scrapbooks filled with photos. Just some clothes, including the wedding dresses, but nothing was right for what Sadie had in mind.

"So pretty!"

She hadn't heard Valentina and Robin enter the town house. Valentina gave her a hug as Robin watched from the doorway.

"Lonnie and LuAnn have the Salvation Army coming later today to pick this all up," said Robin. "Is that okay, or do you want me to delay it?"

"No, no need to delay." She smiled as Valentina fingered a black shawl with a long fringe. "Your grandmother used to wear that all the time."

Valentina shrugged it over her thin shoulders, giggling.

"Not quite what I was hoping for, though." Sadie sighed.

Robin sat on the bed. "What is it you're looking for?"

"Something fancy, that makes me look like I'm rich."

Sadie had convinced Mr. Adriano to let her hit the flagged bookstores on his list and see if she could sniff out *The Scarlet Letter*. Mr. Adriano had dismissed the idea at first, but she convinced him that her knowledge of rare books was imperative in this instance. Besides, he looked too much like an ex-cop, she'd pointed out, and he hadn't been able to refute that. When he still hesitated, she'd threatened to do it with or without his support, because she couldn't stand the thought of sitting around and not taking action in some way. Reluctantly, Mr. Adriano had agreed to give it a shot. As long as they got permission from Dr. Hooper.

She needed to look like a rare book collector if she was going to pull this off, and none of her own clothes would do. Her hope had been that her mother's boxes might hold a silk blouse or nice jacket that she could wear.

"I know!" Valentina jumped up and disappeared. A minute later she returned, holding a cache of clothes on hangers, across two arms like she was carrying a bride over a threshold. "Try on these."

She tossed them on the bed.

"Valentina, these are your mother's clothes," said Robin.

"She's away on business. She won't care. Go on, try this one." She held up a crimson double-breasted blazer that came with a chunky black belt.

For a child, Valentina had a good eye. The blazer was cut long and settled nicely over Sadie's hips, and the fabric and stitching were of excellent quality. She held herself straight and stared into the full-length mirror on the back of the closet door. Not bad at all.

"I need something to layer on top. Is there anything that might work?"

Valentina put her finger to her chin as if she were a saleslady at Saks. "What about a scarf? She has a ton of them."

Together, she and Valentina found a patterned silk scarf that picked up the color of the blazer. When Sadie draped it around her neck, Valentina laughed and clapped her hands.

"You just need some pretty earrings and a necklace and you'll be good to go," said Robin.

"I know, follow me!" Valentina shrieked.

They did so into the master bedroom, where Valentina rummaged through her mother's jewelry box.

"Take care, Valentina." Robin got up and gently extricated a pearl necklace and matching earrings. "How about these?" She walked over to Sadie and placed the earrings in her hand before lowering the necklace over her shoulders.

Sadie put on the earrings and turned around, offering a silly curtsy to her beaming audience.

"You look super fancy," said Valentina.

"Very nice," echoed Robin.

"What on earth is going on in here?"

Lonnie stood in the doorway, wearing scrubs. LuAnn was right behind him, a shiny carry-on bag slung over one shoulder.

"Mommy's home!" said Valentina, running to her mother.

Sadie looked around, seeing the room as Lonnie and LuAnn did: the closet, empty of a slew of clothes, the open jewelry box, and, in the middle of it, herself, wearing LuAnn's blazer and pearls.

Lonnie and LuAnn exchanged a look; then Lonnie glanced irritably at the closet. "Where are LuAnn's clothes? What are you guys all doing in here?"

"I'm so sorry," volunteered Sadie. "I was going through Mom's things because I needed a classy outfit, but they were all from forty years ago, and somehow we ended up in here."

Valentina rushed to explain, picking up on her dad's distress. "Mommy's clothes are in Grandma's room 'cause we started off in there. Doesn't Aunt Sadie look nice?"

LuAnn smiled, but there was a weariness in her eyes. Then again, she'd been traveling the past few days and was probably looking forward to a long soak in the tub. "She sure does. And it's fine. You guys can rifle through my closet anytime."

"Come on, Valentina, let's put everything back," offered Robin. Valentina sprang up, and LuAnn followed them out of the room.

Sadie took off the blazer and hung it back up, straightening the collar as she did so. She looped the scarf around the hanger and placed the jewelry back in the jewelry box. Lonnie had taken LuAnn's carry-on from her and began unpacking it. The simple act of kindness on his wife's behalf made Sadie's heart melt.

"Sorry about all this, Lonnie. I meant to just go through Mom's stuff."

"Is there anything you want to keep of hers? I meant to ask you the other day."

"Are you kidding? That goes against everything she stands for. Remember how she tossed out Dad's clothes a week after he died?"

Pearl had done so the day after she'd caught Sadie weeping on the floor of his closet, enveloped in his favorite leather jacket. Pearl had gotten rid of the clothes not to punish Sadie, she knew, but to take away any conduit to sadness. She'd only wanted her children to be happy, which left no room for grief.

"I do. Remember what she baked the day after Dad's funeral?" said Lonnie.

The image of a towering cake sitting on the kitchen counter came back to Sadie in a flash. "Of course. It was like a crazy seven-layer chocolate cake that normally you'd make for a birthday party or something."

Lonnie started to laugh. "Double chocolate. I ate three pieces and then threw up. Haven't touched one since."

"She always said she liked to bake because it was scientific, that if you added the right ingredients at the right time, in the right order, you'd never go wrong." She sighed. "I miss her."

Lonnie's shoulders slumped.

"You okay, big brother?"

"Yeah. I miss her, too. And it was a long day at work."

She sat on the edge of the bed and sighed. "Same here."

This made him laugh.

"Don't laugh, librarians can have bad days. Maybe not that someone died during your shift, but still."

"So someone talked too loudly?" He was grinning again; she liked it when he teased her.

"Actually, someone stole another rare book from the Berg Collection."

He stored LuAnn's carry-on in the closet and sat beside Sadie on the bed. "Another? How?"

"We don't know yet."

"I'm so sorry to hear that."

"They've hired this security consultant, so hopefully he'll get to the bottom of it."

"Between the two of you, I have no doubt you will. How did the newsletters you found go over with the director?"

After everything that had happened the past week, the fact that Lonnie had remembered the small details of Sadie's work life made her want to cry. "He's interested, but he wants something more."

"And he still doesn't know you're related to Laura Lyons?"

"To a suspected book thief? No. And I don't plan on telling him. I've been rereading the few interviews Laura Lyons gave, and she blatantly refuses to talk about her time in New York. Something happened. I want to find out what, just as I want to find my missing books."

LuAnn returned with an armful of her own clothes, having sent Robin and Valentina off to the park. Sadie explained what she needed the outfit for, and made sure to mention the detective's involvement, to make it more official.

LuAnn nodded. "Of course. That blazer suits you, by the way. Literally." She laughed at her own joke, which made Sadie laugh, too. "Lonnie, will you go and make us some tea?"

After he left, Sadie and LuAnn began rehanging everything back in the closet.

"How's Valentina doing?" asked Sadie. "With my mom's death, and all."

"I've been away the past couple of days, but when I've called her around bedtime, she's weepier than usual, asking questions about where Grandma went, wanting to talk about the morning when we realized she was gone. It was a shock, but she's doing okay." LuAnn paused, a faraway look on her face. "I remember when I was a little kid, my parents told us that they'd have to put our dog to sleep. Max was a big old hound, arthritic and slobbery, but had the sweetest disposition. They took him to the vet and came back and were upset, and I couldn't really figure out why."

"You thought they meant Max was just sleeping?"

"Exactly. But even after it had been explained, the loss didn't resonate with me the way it did with them. I'd never seen my father cry before that. Of course, looking back now, I can see that the dog was part of their early life together, he represented so much. And since I'd never had a loss, I didn't realize what it entailed."

Sadie understood exactly what LuAnn meant. "After the first experience of the death of someone you love, each later one is exponentially more painful, because you know how hard it will be to recover from the loss."

"Yes. I was trying to explain this to Lonnie last weekend, but he didn't get it. I knew you would."

Not for the first time, Sadie was grateful that Valentina had a mother like LuAnn, one who was willing to do the deep emotional dive, to examine what lay beneath the surface. Pearl had always refused. Yet she'd always been capable, tough, a survivor. But of what?

"How are you doing?" LuAnn asked, breaking into her thoughts.

"I'm fine. But I'm worried about what's going on at the library, with the missing books."

"How's Claude with all this? Still sulking at his rejection?"

"I swear, you bring him up every chance you get," said Sadie, swatting LuAnn with her hand. LuAnn had been so excited when Sadie had confessed to the stolen kiss, it had been slightly unnerving. Like maybe she considered Sadie's presence in their lives an intrusion, the lonely aunt who stuck her nose into everything—including their wardrobes—and who would now go off and get a life of her own. "It wasn't a big deal, and it's over anyway. Thank goodness, as now I'm his boss. It's awkward enough."

LuAnn's expression was warm, her mouth flickered up in a smile. "If you say so."

"I keep telling you he's got the reputation at the library of being a playboy; I dodged a bullet there. Besides, I'm going to be like my grandmother, an independent woman of letters."

"That's a fine choice to make," said LuAnn, gently. "As long as you're not throwing yourself into work as a way of avoiding something else."

"Like what?" Sadie felt her defenses rising.

"Like the fact that your mother just passed away."

Sadie patted her knee and rose from the bed. She really should be going. "Don't worry, I'm fine."

As Sadie made her way down the steps of the brownstone, she spied Robin and Valentina in the small park across the street. Valentina was playing with three other girls on the monkey bars and gave a cheerful wave. Instead of heading home, Sadie joined Robin on a bench in the shade of an elm tree.

Sadie nodded in Valentina's direction. "She looks happy. Is she okay?"

Robin nodded. "She was a little worried she'd done something wrong, but I explained to her that no one was mad at her and it was fine."

They watched the children playing. "How long have you been in New York?" Sadie asked.

"I moved to the city late last year, from Massachusetts. I figured I'd do some nannying before deciding what else I might do with my life."

"What are you considering?"

"I don't know. Maybe fashion. Did you always want to be a librarian?"

"I did. I loved my high school librarian, looked up to her immensely."

Robin pointed to the shopping bag at Sadie's feet. "You got out with the loot?"

"I sure did."

"Watch me!" Valentina kicked up her legs and held a handstand, before bending her back as if she had no spine and landing on her feet, finishing with her hands held high. "It's a walkover."

"Amazing." Sadie clapped her hands. "One more time, bendy girl."

Valentina took a moment to prepare before launching into the move.

"Be sure to look at the ground as you go over," advised Robin. "Nicely done. Do you want some carrots?"

Robin dug into her handbag and pulled out a plastic bag of carrot sticks. Valentina gnawed on one while leaning on Sadie, one arm thrown around her neck. "Robin said all the grown-ups are acting weird because of Grandma's death," she said.

Sadie shot Robin a look of gratitude and pulled Valentina closer. "I suppose we are. Sometimes after someone dies, the people left behind can act funny, because they miss her."

"Your mother was very sweet," said Robin.

Sadie raised one eyebrow. "I don't know if I'd use that exact word. That last night, I do wish I'd been kinder to her, though."

"Don't worry, Aunt Sadie." Valentina leaned in, putting her forehead against Sadie's. She smelled of clean laundry. "I came back to say good night. Grandma was upset, but then I told her it was okay and she smiled and said she knew the truth about the stolen tambourine, and hadn't told a soul. She said she was good with secrets."

Sadie pulled back, studying her niece. "The truth about what?"

"The stolen tambourine."

The girl wasn't making sense. Pearl hadn't played any instruments; Sadie's father was the only one with musical talent in the family. And Sadie didn't remember any tambourines lying around.

"Did you hear any of this?" Sadie turned to Robin, who shook her head.

"I was cleaning up in the kitchen. Does it mean something to you?"

Sadie shook her head and locked eyes with Valentina. "A tambourine? Are you sure Grandma said a tambourine?"

Repeating the word, the meaning clicked in. It wasn't a musical instrument her mother had been talking about. "I think she meant to say '*Tamerlane*.' Does that sound right?"

"Sure," said Valentina.

"Did she say who stole the *Tamerlane*?"

Valentina blew her bangs out of her eyes. "Her father."

CHAPTER ELEVEN

New York City, 1914

B ut Father promised!"

Harry's wail pierced the air inside the apartment. It was all Laura could do to not strangle him.

"Harry. Enough."

"But I want to play catch."

He'd at least lowered his voice to a reasonable level, so she took a breath and tried again.

"Your father is busy at work, and I have a meeting with my advisor at the university. You'll have to wait."

"The boys will make fun of me if I can't throw well."

"Who? Who will?"

"The boys."

He'd been doing so well, she hated to see him lose his precarious social standing at school. "Fine, I have twenty minutes. Shall we play a quick game of catch together?"

He agreed, grudgingly. He preferred his father in all matters to do with sport—that was clear enough.

When Harry had been a small child, he'd needed his mother much more than Pearl had. Harry had sought out Laura's attention, asking her question after question. They talked so much that she often found her own voice ragged by the end of the day. The subjects changed as he grew older, but the inquiries were no less frequent: Why did they move to New York from the country? How many people live in New York? Could he build a tree house in the park behind the library? Why was the woman begging on the stairs of the library?

Whenever Laura and Jack argued, Harry would ramp up his interruptions, as if trying to save them from each other. It was maddening, and oftentimes Jack would end up yelling for Harry to be quiet and send him to his room. She'd stop in after to check on him, and find him hiding under his bedcovers, sucking his thumb. "He's a sensitive boy," she'd tell Jack. "We must be careful."

Laura and Harry made their way outside, where a fine mist had settled over Bryant Park, coating the benches and walkways and turning the bark of the trees black. Empty of the usual pedestrians, the space felt slightly sinister. Jack had told them that the land underneath the library had been a graveyard for the poor during the first half of the last century. After the bones were moved to Ward Island across the Harlem River, a giant reservoir had been erected over the same spot. He'd pointed out how some of the old reservoir's stone walls had been incorporated into the library's foundation down in the basement, and Laura had wondered if the stones had been excavated from the graveyard, amazed at the way the layers of history settled upon each other over time. One day, would the white marble walls of the library support an even grander building? It was hard to imagine one grander than the New York Public Library.

As she and Harry tossed a ball back and forth, her mind returned to what she'd witnessed at Patchin Place. For some reason, the physical interaction between Jessie and Amelia consumed her more than the radical causes and viewpoints discussed in the meeting above Polly Holladay's restaurant. The words and sentences, spoken in voluble, passionate cadences, were nothing compared to the quick touch of lips of the two women. That was unnervingly physical, tactile, in a way that Laura couldn't quite comprehend.

She fumbled a throw from Harry, who teased her. "You have to hold your hands like this, Mother. Here, try again."

She did, purposefully flubbing it this time. Her son's physical skills took after her side of the family, unfortunately, instead of Jack's, and she wanted to encourage him. "You're much better suited to this than I am," she said. "Try once more, let me see if I can get it right."

This time, she did, and he cheered her success as if she'd swum the English Channel. She loved her boy. His gradual transformation out of his shy awkwardness was everything she had wished for. Lately, he could match Pearl friend for friend as they recounted their day at the dinner table, although, every so often, Pearl surprised Laura by retreating into a sullen moodiness. Laura knew she missed having her mother around, even if she wasn't able to express it. Laura's own mother was no substitute, no matter how she spoiled them. But didn't Laura get to have a life outside of the library walls? She was in her prime, brimming with energy. Wasn't that only fair?

The temperature was dropping with the sun, and she shuttled

Harry back inside. Upstairs, she offered the children bread and butter and then headed uptown to Columbia.

Professor Wakeman was waiting behind his desk. "You're late." He checked his timepiece with obvious disdain.

Laura apologized but then got right down to business. "For my thesis, I was thinking it might be interesting to write an in-depth profile of Max Eastman, who edits the downtown magazine *The Masses*, and his wife, Ida. You may remember they got into some hot water when they married and she decided to keep her maiden name. Put it on their mailbox, even."

Professor Wakeman regarded her as if she'd pulled a bomb out of her satchel. "I remember that. Caused quite a stir."

"The press mocked them, said that she regarded the title of 'Mrs.' as a badge of slavery. Even the letters to the editor were nasty and abusive." Laura pulled some of the pieces she'd dug up in the morgue on the first floor. "They're all written by men, saying that such a notion will unleash a slew of divorces and other scandalous behavior. I want to do a follow-up."

"It's old news. Nothing there." Still, he picked up his pen and scratched something on a notepad near his elbow. She caught sight of the words just as he placed a piece of blotting paper over them: *Eastman—potential story idea.*

So far, so good.

Laura had noticed over the course of the first semester that students' story ideas that had been summarily dismissed by Professor Wakeman sometimes turned up under his byline in the press. To ensure she got the thesis subject she'd wanted, she'd decided to pitch a throw-away idea first, to divert his attention. She waited.

"Anything else?" Professor Wakeman asked.

"Well, how about something on the Heterodoxy Club?"

He yawned. "What a horror of a name."

"They're a group of women who meet in Greenwich Village every two weeks and debate progressive causes."

"It's a ridiculous name for a women's club. Heterodoxy? Sound like they're trying too hard to be intellectual, if you ask me."

"I think it's a valuable story to cover."

"Well, all right," he said finally. "You may write on this subject. Do not try to shock me with any vulgarities, though."

Two weeks later, Laura attended her second meeting. This time, instead of formal speakers, each woman was asked to stand and give a brief summary of her background and why she was drawn to be a member. The stories were so varied, the family origins fascinating—from an isolated farmhouse in Maine to a decrepit mansion overlooking the Hudson River, from barely having enough to eat to a childhood of rich indulgence—yet somehow they'd all ended up in this one place, united not for a common cause, but simply to be able to speak their minds freely, without the disapproval of husbands and fathers. The women were vastly different from each other, yet united by their desire to achieve, to overcome discrimination against their sex. During a break, Laura ducked into an empty meeting room and scribbled some notes, which she then hid in the very bottom of her satchel.

Amelia invited her back for tea at Patchin Place, and again Laura accepted, but this time she didn't get flustered when Jessie appeared from the back room and placed another kiss on Amelia's lips, wrapping her arms loosely around Amelia's neck. She understood that down here in Greenwich Village the old traditions were being subverted and altered, and that the two men standing closely on the corner might be friends, or they might be lovers, and that was fine.

Jack asked her about the Heterodoxy Club meeting after he crawled into bed late that night. All she wanted to do was go back to sleep, but they hadn't had any time to check in with each other lately. She rubbed her eyes, fighting the urge to snuggle back under the quilt.

"It's strange, going downtown," she answered. "I feel like I'm visiting some European city, if that makes any sense. Different customs, different issues, it's all so unfamiliar."

"Did you see your school friend, the one you'd mentioned at your parents'?"

"Dr. Potter. Yes, she was there."

"Funny, I don't remember you ever mentioning her before."

Part of her wanted to tell Jack all about Amelia, as she'd told him about Professor Wakeman and some of the other larger-than-life characters from her outside life, but it would be too difficult. There were too many angles to the woman that Jack would find contradictory, and if she tried, she'd end up missing something important, or stressing the wrong thing. She didn't want to talk about Amelia.

"She was a few years ahead of me, I barely knew her." She pulled Jack close. "I'm sorry you have to deal with all of the craziness here. The thefts, I mean."

"It's fine. You seem happy, I must say." There was a hitch in his voice, but she was too tired to inquire further.

"I guess I am."

She turned over, exhausted, and fell fast asleep.

"Mrs. Lyons."

Laura stopped short as Mr. Gaillard approached her on the

THE LIONS OF FIFTH AVENUE   149

steps to the library. She'd been lost in thought trying to come up with a good lede for the book review she'd been assigned and hadn't noticed him standing right next to one of the lions. She looked about quickly for the beggar, but the woman was nowhere to be seen, which was probably for the best. "Yes, Mr. Gaillard?"

"May I have a word?"

It was almost as if he'd been waiting for her.

"Do you need to see me with my husband?" she asked. It was a Wednesday, so he'd be meeting with the chief engineer. "I'm heading inside and I'm sure I can round him up for you."

"No, ma'am. I was hoping to have a quiet word with just you. This way."

He led her inside and up to the Trustees Room on the second floor. A long table, one end piled high with papers, sat directly beneath a bronze chandelier, which had been decorated with a series of vaguely malevolent-looking satyrs. A bust of a notable figure took up each corner of the room: Alexander Hamilton, Washington Irving, John Jacob Astor, and, finally, Joseph Green Cogswell. When Laura had asked Jack who on earth the last was, he'd proudly informed her that Cogswell was the first superintendent of the Astor Library, back in the middle of the last century.

It was an awfully grand room to work out of, intended for meetings of the trustees. "Do you not have a proper office?" she asked Mr. Gaillard. "I'm sure my husband can secure you one if you prefer it."

"They're in the midst of appointing one for me. This is temporary, although I certainly could get used to it." He waved a hand at the focal point of the room, a massive cream-colored marble fireplace, with a quote from Thomas Jefferson inscribed above the mantel.

"The entire library is a remarkable place. I tell the children that constantly, that they shouldn't take any of this for granted."

"I couldn't agree more."

He gestured to a chair next to the one at the head of the table. "Unfortunately, there are well-organized book-thief rings here in New York, drawn to our city's treasure. I'm doing everything I can to figure out why our books are going missing. I'm guessing that this particular thief is educated and has access to the stacks, in some way. Someone who has a rudimentary knowledge as to how to value a book."

"Why rudimentary?"

"Because he's chosen one that's too valuable to be able to easily sell."

"The *Tamerlane*?"

He nodded. "Unless some collector only wants it for his private collection. That does happen, unfortunately, and when it does, the books are lost forever." He leaned forward. "The only people who have a key to where the *Tamerlane* was kept are the rare book librarian, myself, and your husband."

Laura swallowed.

"May I ask you a rather delicate question, Mrs. Lyons?"

"You may, I am happy to assist in any way I can. But I do need to get up soon to the apartment, the children will be getting hungry."

"This won't take long. I wonder, is your family having any financial trouble?"

The conversation was taking a strange turn. "Absolutely not. We're perfectly fine. It's helpful that the residence comes with the job. We consider ourselves quite lucky."

"Is that right?"

Better to be straightforward, she decided. Get whatever this was out in the open. "Are you wondering if my husband is responsible for the stolen books?"

He didn't answer, just stared, until the silence became intolerable.

"I must say, I resent the inference. Mr. Lyons reveres books and would never take one out of turn. He's writing a book of his own, even."

"What sort of book is Mr. Lyons writing?" Mr. Gaillard asked.

Jack had been working on it for so long that she wasn't quite sure what it was about anymore. "Fiction. Really, I find your line of questioning unreasonable. My husband's character is sterling."

"We have four books missing, Mrs. Lyons. I have to go down every path, at this point."

Four books? Jack had only mentioned two, *Leaves of Grass* and *Tamerlane.*

Mr. Gaillard continued. "The library has guards stationed at every exit who check the bags of anyone coming in or out. The rare books are locked away, and two librarians staff the Rare Book Room at all times. Yet still the books are being taken. I must find out why."

"Of course you must."

"That is why we are currently searching your apartment."

"What?" She remembered the way he'd been stationed outside the library, as if to stop her from entering. "Where are my children? And Jack?"

"Harry and Pearl are down in the children's library, with the clerk there. Mr. Lyons is at the apartment."

She swished out of the room, the detective following behind her, down to the first floor and back up the small stairway to the mezzanine. Jack stood leaning against the banister, looking bored. He straightened when he saw her ascending, the detective behind her.

"Sorry about this, love," he said. "They're almost done."

He and Mr. Gaillard shook hands like they were bridge partners, not suspect and policeman. The detective glanced over to a uniformed cop, who gave a slight shake of the head.

"We found nothing, sir," the man said.

"I thank you for your patience and cooperation." With that, Mr. Gaillard and his crew took their leave.

Only after they'd entered their apartment and shut the door behind them did Laura speak.

"Tell me now. What is going on, Jack? The truth this time."

CHAPTER TWELVE

New York City, 1914

Laura straightened up their apartment, moving from room to room, making the place hers again after the intrusive search by the detective's men. The children had already scampered back in, disappearing into their bedrooms.

Jack followed close behind her. "I don't get it. Now you're demanding that I tell you what's going on? If you were here more often, perhaps you'd already know."

She shoved his desk chair back into place and whirled around. "Mr. Gaillard brought me to his office, asked me questions, and then told me they were searching our home. It was humiliating."

"I gave him full permission as I have nothing to hide. They're just doing their jobs."

"He said that four books have been stolen. You'd said two."

"Again, if you'd been around more, I might have mentioned it."

"What was stolen?"

"Two more first editions. Nothing as valuable as the *Tamerlane*. The thief learned from his mistake, it appears." Jack crossed his arms. "They've taken my key away, which is fine with me, as then they'll see I've done nothing wrong. And now, if you're done with your interrogation, I'd like to get back to my writing."

"So you're angry with me for being away, while you spend hours at a time on your book. Do you see how this isn't fair?"

"You're a mother. What did you expect?"

"You're a father, doesn't that count?" She remembered that cold day playing catch with Harry, how she'd created a fond memory for their boy instead of yet another disappointment. "You've been down in that basement more than up here these days."

"It's the only place I can write without all these distractions."

Harry poked his head out from his bedroom. "I'll be quiet, I promise. I won't be loud anymore."

"Harry, no, it's not you," Laura assured him.

"Laura?"

Her mother's voice rang out from the bottom of the stairs.

"Distractions," whispered Jack. "Everywhere I look. *You* should be here, not her."

Laura ignored him. "Mother, please come on up."

Her mother paused on the top stair, one hand on the banister, unsure. She wore a Persian lamb's wool coat with a thick bow at the waist, a reminder of the cold that had encased the city the past few days. "Is everything all right?"

"Of course. The children are in their rooms, dinner is in the icebox. Jack was just on his way out." She avoided looking at him.

After he'd left, Laura's mother shrugged off her coat. "You look tired, my dear." She brushed Laura's cheek with her fingers.

Laura took her mother's hand and gently kissed it, the ring

finger adorned with only a gold wedding band. They hadn't spoken of her sacrifice; Laura couldn't bear it.

"Things may be difficult right now," her mother said. "But I
want you to know that I admire what you're trying to do."

"'Trying' is the key word. So far, barely succeeding."

"He's a good man. You know that, don't you? He loves you so
much."

Laura couldn't help wondering what might have been if she
hadn't been so awestruck by Jack's dapper bearing and charm back
when they met. He did love her, it was true, but their competing
demands for self-fulfillment didn't fit well together, like two bal-
loons stuffed into a small box.

Her mother only wanted love out of life, and even if she hadn't
achieved it for herself, she'd made sure Laura attained that goal.
But at what cost? Even worse, would Laura pass on a similar blind
spot to her own daughter? She was simply too entrenched in quo-
tidian concerns to be able to step back and view her own biases as
a parent clearly.

After settling the children with her mother, Laura began writing the first draft of her thesis. The first paragraph had taken a
good half hour, but the subsequent pages came more rapidly, albeit
roughly. She'd edit and smooth out the prose later, like a sculptor
working with words instead of clay. As long as she had something
down on the page, she'd be able to make it work. There was so
much to cover, so much going on that wasn't even mentioned in
the big newspapers. She'd prove to Professor Wakeman that a
"woman's story," as he liked to call it, could impact history.

Two hours later, Laura slid her arm into Amelia's as they
climbed the front stairs of a handsome brownstone on the corner
of Fifth Avenue and Ninth Street. She'd been invited by Amelia to

a salon at what she'd said was the premier gathering place for bohemians. Inside the town house, the entire parlor was done in white—a white marble mantel, white painted woodwork, white velvet chairs and silk curtains, a white bearskin rug on the floor. The effect was both pristine and shocking.

"Who lives here?" Laura asked. "It's like being in a blizzard."

Amelia laughed. "Mabel Dodge came to the city a couple of years ago from Europe and decided to pull together the people necessary to 'dynamite New York,' as she put it. Every week, she holds a salon for a hundred that brings together those willing to shake things up." The room pulsed with energy and laughter, a contrast to the dinner parties Laura's parents had given uptown when they were still flush, where dulcet, moderated tones were the only ones tolerated.

Amelia subtly pointed out the guests. "You've seen some of the women already at the Heterodoxy Club meetings, like Elizabeth Gurley Flynn and Emma Goldman. Near the fireplace is Alfred Stieglitz. Max Eastman, editor of *The Masses*, is over there, next to his wife, Ida."

Laura had to smile.

"I know exactly what you're thinking," said Amelia.

"What am I thinking?"

"That they look so normal."

Laura laughed. After all that terrible uproar in the press, there they were, standing side by side, sipping cocktails like any other young married couple, as if nothing had happened. As if it just didn't matter. "I guess I look pretty normal as well," said Laura with a shrug.

"Don't sell yourself short, you're running with the new bohemians these days."

"I'm here as a reporter. To report, not to run."

"I see." Amelia playfully bumped Laura's shoulder with her own. "You have a mission."

"That's the truth. I want to write about so much, I can hardly stand it. The world is changing, and I want to be out there, taking it all down."

"I love your enthusiasm, Laura. You remind me of me when I first went into medicine."

"You're much tougher than I am, though. I know I have a lot to learn."

"Don't be so hard on yourself. You're here, aren't you?"

"What? Sipping cocktails?"

"If you want to get dangerous, I can make that happen." Amelia held Laura's gaze.

"Of that I have no doubt."

Nearby, a woman spilled her champagne, breaking the moment. The man she was with tossed a handkerchief over the spill before leading the woman away.

"Now tell me, what exactly is your angle?" said Amelia. "It sounds like something bigger than some daily story for the *Blotto*."

"Very funny. Our pseudo-newspaper is called the *Blot*. And yes, I have to admit that I think this movement, what's going on down here, might be better as a long feature article. 'The New Woman.' There's so much to encompass."

"Be careful about writing about the club, though. Remember, what's said there is strictly off the record."

"Of course."

The fact that Amelia had accomplished all she had by breaking rules, by pushing boundaries, made Laura a little less concerned about writing about the club, especially as it wasn't for publication.

Laura didn't mention that she'd met some members for coffee, to ask them questions about the views and passions expressed during the meetings. Since she couldn't openly take notes, it helped her round out the competing viewpoints.

One of which was being loudly discussed by a group standing next to the bartender, where Amelia and Laura waited for their drinks to be stirred.

"Don't let men fool you." The speaker, ironically, was a tall man, verging on gangly, with thick curly hair that spilled over his forehead and a jaw that jutted just beyond the point of handsome. As he spoke, he waved his arms, threatening the drinks of those gathered around him. "They love the idea of the New Woman, one who'll raise their children, clean their house, and then make themselves available to all."

A couple of women around him gasped.

Amelia stepped forward. "Then these 'men,' as you call them, notwithstanding that you're one yourself, have the idea of a New Woman wrong. The New Women will make themselves available to whomever they choose, not necessarily to all. And what's more, they will not only demand sexual power, they will also seize economic power."

The man squared his shoulders. "Is that so?"

"Yes. And men are threatened by this. You see, while there is more than enough sexual power to go around, economic power is fixed. If we take more, you get less."

"Your logic holds true. It's a pleasure to meet an equal adversary." He held out his hand. "I'm Frank Tannenbaum. Don't believe a word I say. I'm only acting as devil's advocate. We must be prepared to counterattack."

"Dr. Amelia Potter." Amelia had a glint in her eye.

"Dr. Potter, of course. Delighted." Mr. Tannenbaum lifted his glass. "Let me put on my devil's horns again: Women, the uptowners will say, are the guardians of what's morally right. They keep the rest of us on the straight and narrow. If women throw off those shackles, won't civilization be doomed?"

"Having a husband and child does not make one morally right. There are more ways of living than a man, a wife, and a brood," said Amelia. "It's time to expand our view of the household, and throw off the shackles of gender oppression. I can work, I can have a child, and I can love whomever I like. Just as you can."

Laura, along with some of the others, nodded encouragingly. That was what she wanted also. Well, not the love-whomever part. But the work-and-raise-a-child part, certainly.

"We are restless, energized, and will not back down," said Amelia, building momentum. "Whether for the right to vote, or access to birth control, or the right to make love outside of the bonds of marriage."

Mr. Tannenbaum threw back his head and laughed. "I adore this woman."

The discussion broke up as more guests arrived.

"Who *is* that?" asked Laura.

"Frank Tannenbaum emigrated from Austria when he was young, went to Columbia. This winter he's been organizing protests for the poor."

Laura had read about the nightly protests in the newspaper, five or six hundred men marching through the streets before approaching a church to demand food and beds. "What exactly are they trying to prove?"

"When they're turned away? That the clergy don't really care about the unemployed, that they are heartless."

"He seems awfully young to be leading protests."

"He's twenty-one."

Interesting that Amelia knew his exact age. "You seem impressed."

"He's a natural leader. And smart, you've seen that. While we've been tucked away in our beds during this particularly harsh winter, he's out marching, calling attention to injustice."

"Why don't I see you marching out there with him?" Laura teased.

"I'll march tonight if you will." Amelia's eyes shimmered. "We can go together. They're meeting at Rutgers Square and heading to St. Alphonsus Church on West Broadway. You can write about it for the *Blotto*."

It *would* make a good item for tomorrow's reporting and writing class, Laura had to admit. None of the other students would be out on a cold winter's evening if they could help it. That would certainly prove to Professor Wakeman that she was as good as the men. Furthermore, she wasn't quite ready to quit Amelia's company.

She threw back her drink, wishing she'd worn long underwear beneath her skirts.

"Let's do it."

What looked to be over five hundred men had gathered in the wedge-shaped area off of East Broadway on the Lower East Side by the time Amelia and Laura arrived at the protest. The winds whipped their skirts as Amelia guided Laura across the street, where they took shelter in a doorway.

"Are you sure this is safe?" asked Laura. She'd never been out after dark like this without Jack; two women walking together attracted more attention than she would have liked.

"Walk tall, don't make eye contact. Here he comes." Amelia pointed to Frank, who strode through the crowd and pulled himself up onto the base of a streetlamp, hanging on to it with one hand for support. The light shone on him like a spotlight, glinting off his dark hair. Why he wasn't wearing a hat on a night like this was beyond Laura. He began shouting for everyone's attention, and soon all heads swiveled up at him.

A hush came over the crowd.

"I know that many of you are out of work," he said. "Over three hundred thousand men are out of work, so you are not alone."

The men cheered.

"This makes ten consecutive days that we've come out and raised a commotion. You deserve better, you want to work, to feed your family, and the city, the country, has failed you. This is the era of progressive policies, where the greed of capitalism will be replaced with a safety net for all. You, me, all of us, demand more from our taxes. More from our politicians. More from our government."

The crowd was whipped up into a frenzy that matched the violent gusts of wind, some men leaping into the air. Laura looked around for other reporters covering the story but saw nothing, no men with notebooks nor photographers lugging their cameras. It was day ten of the protests, after all, and frigid. They probably figured there was nothing new to report. She could already hear in her head the professor's disappointment at her lack of imagination, covering a story that had come and gone in the press.

Frank asked for the men to quiet down, and they obeyed. "Tonight, we'll approach the Catholic church and ask for help. For beds, for food. If they refuse, we will expose their hypocrisy, as we have the other churches who refused us. For putting their own riches before the riches of their flock. This nation's working class deserves more!"

In a graceful leap, Frank jumped to the ground and led the men to a church a few blocks away, reaching it just as the priest slammed the door to the church shut, locking it against them. A couple of men tried the side door, but no luck there, either. By then, Laura and Amelia had become swallowed up by the crowd and were being pulled toward the front steps of the church, where men pounded on the doors, cursing and screaming.

"The police!"

The two words sliced through the air. The mob heaved into itself as panic began to spread.

Sirens blared as a group of policemen came from behind, slamming their truncheons down hard on whoever stood in their way. Just to Laura's left, the sickening sound of wood on bone, followed by a howl of pain, made her clutch Amelia closer. There was no way out, not against the bulk of so many.

"I'm so sorry, we have to get out of here, I'm so sorry." Amelia wrapped her arm around Laura, and together they blindly shoved their way north, or maybe west. Laura had lost all sense of direction.

Laura lost grip of Amelia's hand twice, and twice she flailed about like a drowning swimmer before reconnecting with her friend. Finally, they reached an alley where they could catch their breath in the safety of darkness.

On any other night, Laura wouldn't have been caught dead in an alley in this part of town, where rats and drunks scrambled and thieves lurked, hoping for an easy mark. But tonight, she didn't care that she couldn't tell what muck she was stepping on, nor the source of the foul smell that emanated from the ground. The dark alley provided safety, for now.

"We can stay here until it quiets down," said Amelia. "Then we'll get a taxicab and get out of here." Amelia held both of Laura's arms just above the elbow, and stared hard at her. In the darkness, Laura could tell that her mouth was partly open, her gaze fierce. "Are you all right?"

"I'm fine."

"Thank God."

As the mob began breaking up, the two women ran north until they came upon a taxicab. Inside, they sat close together. Laura felt Amelia shaking beneath her skirts, just as she was. She moved closer, drawing a renewed sense of strength and safety from being nestled together in the back seat.

"Well, that was exciting," Laura said quietly.

Amelia let out an unladylike snort. "Your capacity for understatement never ceases to amaze."

"I suppose I'm the one who got us into this mess by daring you. From now on, we will stick to cocktail party chatter."

"I'm glad you dared me. I feel alive. Don't you?"

Laura did. Her lips were raw from the wind and the cold, and her skin tingled with electricity.

When they reached Patchin Place, Amelia gave Laura a long hug. Laura clutched her friend close, unwilling to let her go. Finally, they parted and Laura headed uptown, where the library loomed like a tomb in the darkness.

Even though it was late, she sat down at Jack's desk, eager to get started before the events of the evening faded away. Being a reporter was much like being a bloodhound: just as the dogs picked up a scent and tracked it from one spot to the next, reporters gathered up clues, moving from source to source, following the narrative to completion. She worried that if she waited until morning, the trail of inspiration might go cold.

She wrote of what had happened, moment by moment, but also of how the clash spoke to the hopes of the future and the failures of the past. She wanted to get down the whole picture, just as she wanted to provide a well-rounded thesis on the women of the Heterodoxy Club, and how their words and actions would affect their daughters and the daughters who came after that. She'd picked up the scent of change, of revolution, and wanted to see where it took them all.

The next day in class, she staggered to Professor Wakeman's desk, bleary with exhaustion, and watched as he read it through.

"My, my, Mrs. Lyons. A protest, with police, even. When did all this happen?"

"Last night."

"You didn't make any of this up, did you?"

She wished he'd stop asking her that. "No, of course not."

"Quite the intrepid reporter, aren't you? What did your husband make of this?"

Jack had been sullen that morning, but that was nothing new. "My husband is fine with my studies, Professor."

"Quite the modern man, then." Professor Wakeman gave her top marks. She knew she deserved no less.

She also knew exactly who she wanted to share the good news with.

Downtown, she turned onto Patchin Place and stopped cold. Amelia's door was wide-open. She stood on the stone step, her head tipped forward in a kiss, Jessie's arms wrapped around her waist. The two women remained locked together, unconcerned by the bold display of affection.

Laura hung back, out of view. Here she was, bringing high-minded uptown morals downtown again. It was fine for two women to love each other. So why did she feel sick?

No, not sick. Angry. She had felt so connected with Amelia last night during their terrible adventure, racing through the rabble, maneuvering this way and that without signals or words, as if they were a pair of birds in the sky. Seeing her share a close moment with someone else this morning felt like a betrayal. It was *their* story, not Amelia and Jessie's.

But that wasn't it, either.

She was jealous.

Because she wanted to be the one kissing Amelia's lips.

Jack was her husband, and made her so happy, or had made her happy. She loved being in his arms, his very maleness. But with Amelia, she could talk of her fears and worries without censoring herself or worrying that she'd take it personally and grow cold. They'd laughed more in these past couple of months than she and Jack had this past year. Part of that was the stress of his work and his book, of course, and her going to back to school. There simply wasn't enough time.

In fact, it wasn't fair to compare the two desires. Family life was far more complicated than this idea of free love could possibly encompass. She and Jack had children together, a household. A shared life.

Yet sometimes, when she and Amelia walked down the street and Amelia linked arms with her, Laura's arm accidentally brushed Amelia's breast and neither woman would pull away, not immediately. Even after, the ghost of the sensation lingered.

Maybe her jealousy was simply a reaction to being thrust into a new, dangerous, and exciting world. How could life in a library even come close?

She peered back around the corner as Jessie and Amelia kissed again, long and deep. She thought of Pearl and Harry, what would happen to them if she ever acted on her own desires. Women like her weren't tolerated north of Fourteenth Street. This could not be.

Amelia was her friend; that was all.

CHAPTER THIRTEEN

New York City, 1993

I have to go with him, in order to identify the stolen goods."

Sadie sat next to Mr. Adriano in Dr. Hooper's office, where the antique grandfather clock had just rung nine thirty. To Sadie, the logic couldn't be clearer. Time was of the essence. They had to case the downtown bookstores as soon as possible, at the very least to rule them out.

"And that's why you're all dressed up? Like normal, I mean," Dr. Hooper asked.

She fingered the pearls at her neck, momentarily embarrassed. "I have to come across as a wealthy book buyer, I figured."

"I see." He didn't seem convinced. He turned to Mr. Adriano. "You're all right with this?"

"It makes sense. I couldn't pull it off alone. And I'll be there every step of the way."

Sadie caught a glance between them, a knowing look. This was a setup, possibly, to catch her in the act. No doubt Mr. Adriano would be watching her closely, but that was fine. She had nothing to hide.

Other than her family's past. Valentina's comment in the park about the "tambourine" had been whirling around in Sadie's head since yesterday.

"I suppose it's worth a shot," Dr. Hooper finally said.

The downtown train reeked of sweat and greasy metal, the passengers packed together with a physical intimacy that would have been overbearing if they didn't all refuse to look each other in the eye, an unspoken agreement that made city living possible. A pole separated Sadie from Mr. Adriano, their hands grasping it a few inches apart. This close, she realized he was taller than her by several inches, taller than she'd first thought. She didn't look at him, instead focusing on the small ketchup stain on one sleeve of his raincoat.

"What's the plan for today?" she asked. "How do you want to play it?"

He raised an eyebrow. "Quite the lingo. We go in, you say you're looking for rare books for your collection, that you're willing to pay for items that are truly valuable. I'll hang back, pretending to be a random browser, and listen in." He paused. "We'll see what they offer up." He stifled a yawn.

"Out gallivanting last night?"

"Gallivanting." He seemed to be considering the idea, the word. Maybe he didn't understand what it meant.

"Out with the boys."

"I know what 'gallivanting' means. No. I was up all night with a sick kid."

She glanced at his left hand—no ring—and he followed her gaze. "Divorced. My kids live in Westchester. I went up last night to cover the night shift so my ex could get some sleep."

Something about being three inches away from each other with only one more stop to go made Sadie bold. "How long were you married?"

"Fifteen years. Long enough."

His answer was so matter-of-fact. "What happened?"

"The usual. What about you?"

"Divorced as well. A while ago." The train screeched to a halt. "This is our stop."

Together, they made their way to two of the three downtown bookstores from Mr. Babenko's list. Both times, Sadie stumbled through her inquiry, nerves getting the best of her. If the bookstore owners had the stolen items hidden away, they didn't show their hand. The volumes they did offer lacked the distinction of the Hawthorne and the Woolf diary. Sadie hoped she wasn't blowing it.

The last stop, before they headed north to case the uptown shops, was called J&M Books, one of the remaining stores on the former Book Row on Fourth Avenue. The place was empty of customers, and Sadie strode to the clerk's desk at the back of the shop. This time, she'd try a different tack. "Hello, is the owner available?"

She affected an English accent this time, which was met by a muffled guffaw from Mr. Adriano, who stood somewhere behind her, doing his browsing thing. The clerk, a tall, thin man wearing a bolo tie, sat behind the counter.

"I'm the owner, name's Chuck." He held out his hand, which was manicured and smooth. "How can I help you?"

She shook it. "I'm looking for something valuable, something rare, as a gift to my husband. It's his birthday in a month, and I promised him something whopping."

"Whopping?"

"I want to give him a gift that will knock his socks off." She lifted her heels slightly at the end of the sentence. She needed to appear foolish enough to not understand the trade, and wealthy enough to afford the best. "It's his fiftieth, so the sky's the limit. Although I probably shouldn't tell you that."

The man loosened the tie around his neck. "I see."

"For his fortieth, I purchased an antique globe by Blaeu, from the early 1600s." She made a point of looking down at the counter, where a couple of letters from famous authors were kept under glass, so as to give Chuck time to size her up. "Paid forty grand, but was worth every penny to see the look of surprise on Cyril's face." She pointed to one of the letters. "Is this really from Dorothy Parker?"

"Sure is. Would you like to see it?"

"No. That's not what I want." She looked up, fixing him with a steady gaze. "I want something fabulous, that no one else has. Do you have anything like that?"

"Right. I think there's something here, just in." He disappeared behind a door marked EMPLOYEES ONLY. Sadie looked around at Mr. Adriano, who raised his eyebrows before turning away as the man returned, clutching an oversized, ragged atlas.

"There's this." He laid it down on the counter. "An antique atlas, from the seventeenth century. Quite an addition to any collection."

Sadie lifted the cover and examined it. She could tell already that the binding had been replaced. Some of the maps had suspicious markings, where an identifying mark had been either removed or painted over. How horrible, to mutilate what had been intact. Then again, it said something about the shop, that they would try to fob this off on an unsuspecting buyer.

"It's great, but I want something with words this time. Not pictures."

"Huh. Hold on." He disappeared again, coming back a few minutes later with a small stack of books. "These were just about to go in the safe. Take a look and if you see something you like, I can check with the seller."

"Check with the seller?"

"These are quite rare. Just arrived from London."

Sadie sorted through the books. The top two were first editions but not by noted authors.

Then she got to the third and froze. *The Scarlet Letter.*

Willing herself to remain calm, she lifted the cover and flipped through it, pausing slightly on page ninety-seven. There it was, the mark for the New York Public Library. Whoever had taken it either hadn't known about the mark or hadn't yet had a chance to remove it.

This was the first edition, the one stolen from the Berg Collection. In her hands.

"Never read this one," she said. "It's pretty, with the cover." She put it to one side and went through the other two. She immediately recognized the familiar stationer's ring-back notebook. She opened it up, carefully, and her heart leaped at the sight of Woolf's scrawled cursive, the lines rising up to the right, the date written in the margin.

"How much for these three?" She included one of the lesser books, to throw off the scent.

The man scratched his cheek. "I'll have to ask the seller. What did you say your name was again?"

"Elaine, is that you?" For some inexplicable reason, Mr. Adriano chose now to come forward, arms wide, pulling Sadie into a hug.

"Sure is." She went along with the charade, giving him a hard look at the same time. Why was he getting in the way?

"It's been too long. Of course I'd run into you today. I have something fabulous to show you, come here for a moment."

"Will you excuse me, please?" Sadie gave an apologetic smile to the clerk and let Mr. Adriano drag her to the front of the shop, out of sight of the desk.

"What are you doing?" she whispered.

"Say you'll come back tomorrow to make the sale."

It would be like leaving her children behind, if she had children. They were in her hand; it was just a matter of taking them. And wouldn't Dr. Hooper be pleased? She'd be sure to get the permanent curator job at that point, no question. She'd be a hero, all problems solved. "I can't leave the books behind."

Mr. Adriano practically snapped at her. "You have to. The bookstore owner will want cash, since they're hot. Do you have enough on you?"

She hadn't thought of that. "Then what do we do?"

"Say you'll come back tomorrow. We'll bring some cops and make an arrest."

"We have to wait a whole day?"

"Yes. Now go and let the man know."

Still, it had been worth it. At the very least, they knew where the books were.

She walked back, chin lifted. "Chuck, I'll be back tomorrow. Can you let the seller know that I'm interested in these three books?" She pointed to them, her finger lingering on the Woolf diary. "My name is Elaine Edmundson, and I simply must have them."

"I will, but I must ask you a favor."

She waited, worried.

"My regular customers would be very upset to learn that I didn't let them in on my latest acquisitions. Which means you'll need to be discreet about where you found them."

"Oh, I can be discreet, Chuck. Don't you worry about a thing."

She watched, itching with irritation, as he gathered up the stack in his hands.

So close. She was so close.

"How long do we have to wait?"

Although the day was cool, Sadie was sweating in one of Lu-Ann's cashmere sweaters, her chosen outfit for the sting operation. She and Mr. Adriano had met in a coffee shop across from the bookstore, and together they watched from the window, looking out for the unmarked car that meant that backup had arrived and they could go meet Chuck and rescue the books from captivity.

"However long it takes," said Mr. Adriano. "It's not as if recovering stolen books is on the top of their to-do list."

"It should be." Sadie took a sip of coffee. The bitter taste made her stomach churn, or maybe that was just her nerves. "Once we do recover the books, what next?" They'd already alerted Dr. Hooper to the success of the operation, and she could tell he was as excited as she was at the possibility of recovery.

"We'll find out from this Chuck guy who the seller is, and follow the trail from there."

"Do you think it's an employee of the library?"

She was trying to be vague, but Mr. Adriano picked up on her inference. "You mean Claude Racine?"

"I suppose so. He was the only other person with access. Until they revoked it, of course." In fact, Sadie had deliberately kept the news of the sting from Claude, per the director's instructions, which made him even more of a suspect, in Sadie's opinion.

"How well do you know this Claude guy?"

"Too well." The coffee had started working its way into her bloodstream, and she felt a bolt of energy. "As I mentioned, we dated, briefly, earlier this year."

"Huh." Mr. Adriano raised one eyebrow, like he didn't believe her. The nerve.

"It was a brief affair. I called it off. It's too difficult when you're working together."

She still remembered their kiss, at that Christmas party. They'd stood in a small hallway off of the room where the festivities were raging inside. That evening, Claude had put his hand on the back of her neck and drawn her to him, and she'd closed her eyes and enjoyed the sensation of his mouth on hers. It was a little too wet for her liking, but that was fine. It felt so good to be wanted again, after so many years. He'd laughed then, and she'd pulled back, ready to be offended, but he'd pulled her close again, this time sending his hand roving up to her breast.

"Lovely," he'd said.

A group from the genealogy division had spilled out of the room and they'd pulled apart. Even though she and Claude hadn't spoken of the kiss after he returned from his vacation, she was certain that every comment between them, under Marlene's watchful eye, had been fraught. But then she'd spotted him in the hallway with the young page and, soon after, come upon the *Surviving Spinsterhood* book, which reminded her that her life was just fine as it was.

But she didn't want to think about all that. "Mr. Adriano, what made you decide to start your own firm, after retiring?"

"You can call me Nick. I figured my working days were over, but then my wife invested her part of the divorce proceedings with a scam artist, and lost it all."

"So you're helping her out?"

"Sure. She's the mother of my kids. Besides, I enjoy it. Otherwise, what would I be doing? I hate sitting around." He spoke without any hint of resentment. "Although, at the library, there's a little more action going on than I expected. A hotbed of intrigue, that place."

"Well, it's not usually like that, I assure you. Hopefully, by tomorrow we'll be back to normal. Which will be a big relief to me."

Nick's radio squawked. He looked outside and rose. "Let's go."

Inside the shop, Sadie headed straight to the back, where Chuck was waiting, wearing a different bolo tie and a crisp white shirt.

She held out her hand. "Hullo. I'm back to buy the books I set aside yesterday."

"Right. Mrs. Edmundson."

"Please, call me Elaine."

Chuck eyed her up and down again, and she was glad she'd put some time into her hair and makeup. For a moment, she was also glad that Nick had seen her at her best.

The front door squeaked. That would be Nick, who'd said he'd hover within earshot and out of sight. She didn't want to let him down.

Chuck disappeared for a moment and came out carrying all three books.

She took her time perusing each one, studying the inscription page and quality of the binding on the Hawthorne, then checked that the last diary entry was intact on the Woolf. "Lovely," she murmured.

"One hundred thousand," Chuck said in a low voice.

Should she bargain with him? No. Better to get it over with. "Done."

"You can wire the money into an account. Once I get it, you can retrieve the books. No receipts."

"Of course, just send me the details. By the way, where did you find them?"

She heard Nick cough. Probably a sign to her to not try to drive the investigation on her own. But she had to know.

"A client came upon them in his grandmother's attic, in London."

She almost laughed. Grandmother's attic? Pathetic that he couldn't come up with something more original.

The bell to the shop clanged hard as the cops burst in, wearing plain clothes, badges dangling from around their necks. "Stop what you're doing and stand back."

Sadie flattened herself against the wall as the cops went straight for Chuck, who stood frozen in place, hands up in the air.

Then, Nick was by Sadie's side, and together he and Sadie

watched as Chuck was placed in handcuffs and read his Miranda rights before being led off, protesting the entire way.

As the police carefully placed the books into evidence bags, it was all she could do not to hug Nick.

The books were safe again, hers again. Finally.

CHAPTER FOURTEEN

New York City, 1993

A few weeks after Sadie's successful sting downtown, she was still giddy. Dr. Hooper had personally brought the books to the Berg Collection and handed them over, thanking her and Nick for their detective work. Nick had kept his eyes on the books through the whole speech, as if he was scared they'd escape from their clutches again if he glanced away. After Dr. Hooper left, Nick had watched as Sadie secured them in the small safe that was lodged in the wall of her office. It was too small to hold much, but until the exhibit was up, she didn't want to risk their being out of her purview.

Then she'd turned and given Nick a hug.

She hadn't meant to; it was just he was standing right behind her and she was so happy and his bulk seemed so huggable. He'd patted her back a couple of times and then disengaged, and she'd looked up expecting to see horror in his eyes. But it wasn't that.

He seemed sort of stunned, blinking hard, like he'd been hit up-side the head instead of given a friendly squeeze.

Since then, he'd stopped in to check on the Berg every couple of days and give her an update on the investigation. When she heard his confident knock on the door—a very different sound from the discreet rap of the regular scholars—she had to stop herself from rushing to open it. It was nice to have a friend.

After her divorce, most of Sadie and Phillip's friends had stayed close with Phillip, who was much more a social animal than Sadie; he was the life of the party. She had to admit she'd turned maudlin after being dumped, not much fun to be around and unapologetic about that fact, before Valentina's birth had provided a welcome distraction. Until now, though, she hadn't realized how isolated from her few friends she'd become. Maybe it was just because she and Nick had a common enemy in the book thief, or a mutual dis-trust of Claude, but she liked the camaraderie.

If Claude *was* the thief, he showed no sign of concern at the turn of events. Whenever a knock on the Berg Collection door revealed Nick, Claude muttered under his breath something about Inspector Clouseau having arrived. Claude's impertinence galled her, not the least because he wasn't out of the clear. The thefts had stopped after his key was revoked, which, to her, meant all signs pointed to him as the culprit. Today, Nick came by while Claude was out at a dentist appointment, and she took the opportunity to ask him about it point-blank.

"What if he is the thief and we never find out the truth?" She spoke quietly, as two patrons were in the room and she needed to stay put and keep watch over them.

"We may not. Not if our boy Chuck keeps his mouth shut. He's hired an expensive attorney to fight the charges."

"Can't Chuck go to jail for having stolen property?"

"Eventually, but his lawyer is going to play this out very slowly. In the big, bad world of New York, a couple of stolen books is at the bottom of the court's to-do list."

"That's not right." She hadn't meant to raise her voice. The two scholars looked up from their work, and she nodded serenely back at them, just as Claude entered, whistling the theme from *The Pink Panther* under his breath.

The Lincoln Center concert hall where the New York Philharmonic performed wasn't Sadie's favorite venue in the city—Carnegie Hall was more beautiful and had better acoustics—but there was nothing that compared to the trio of buildings that made up the heart of the Lincoln Center campus. Alone, each one might have seemed stark, but arranged in a horseshoe shape around a burbling fountain, they became a kind of Brutalist town center, reminding Sadie of the Italian village plazas that she and Phillip had visited on their honeymoon.

She perched on the lip of the fountain, watching the zigzag of audience members heading home after an evening of Wagner at the Metropolitan Opera House, or having caught the latest Wendy Wasserstein play. She'd just spent a blissful evening listening to an Elgar concerto at Avery Fisher Hall, and wasn't ready to leave.

The blast of a trumpet caught her attention, then another joining the first in harmony. A set of drums kicked in, and finally an entire orchestra erupted in a swinging beat. Curious, she followed the sound to an open plaza just to the south of the opera house, where an outdoor stage had been set up. A hundred people were gathered on the dance floor, doing some kind of step that Sadie didn't recognize. A fox-trot? Not a tango—she knew that much. She watched in amazement at the mix of music and motion, hypnotized, the orchestra performance forgotten.

"Sadie?"

She turned to see Nick beside her, an amused smile on his face. Unsure, she gave a little wave just as he held out his hand to shake hers, which meant he only grasped the tips of her fingers, like one would greet the queen of England. All the connection from their bond over Whitman and the stolen artifacts seemed to have disappeared, replaced by discomfort.

"You a dancer?" he asked.

She shook her head. "No. I just got out of the Philharmonic. But isn't this incredible?"

"Sure is."

"What are you here to see?" He didn't seem like an opera-lover type. Then again, he did enjoy poetry.

"I'm not here to see anything, I'm here to swing." He gestured to the dance floor.

"You?" She hadn't meant to sound so dubious.

He shrugged. "My wife made me take lessons for our wedding, and after we divorced, I thought I'd take it up again."

He had a hobby. Just as her *Surviving Spinsterhood* book advised. The thought made her smile.

The band finished, followed by applause from the crowd. A redhaired woman, with matching lipstick and a short pink skirt, took the microphone. She was all sharp angles from her nose to her knees, like a spindly coral reef. She called for everyone's attention in a raspy voice that was gritty and overly sweet at the same time, as if fueled by strawberry Quik.

"It's salsa time! Beginners, welcome. Take the floor, my dancers."

Nick, to Sadie's horror, held out his hand. "Shall we?"

While Lonnie had inherited the quick coordination of their father—something Valentina shared—Sadie had missed out on that particular family trait and was about as flexible as an eighty-year-old man. She preferred walks in the park to anything active. Once, after a New Year's resolution, she'd joined a neighborhood gym and tried out a step class. Her foot had slipped after only five minutes and she'd landed with a thud on the floor. The instructor kept on shouting instructions as Sadie quickly collected her things and scrambled out the door, embarrassed and bruised.

"I don't dance."

"Neither do half the people here."

"Maybe we can just grab a drink instead?"

But it was too late. He gently pulled her to the middle of the dance floor. Sadie looked around, her heart pounding with fear, like she was about to jump out of an airplane. All the women were wearing dance shoes with a heel, while Sadie was in beat-up leather ballet flats, which, on her size-ten feet, resembled black flippers.

"It's easier to follow up near the front," he said. She pretended she hadn't heard him.

The music began, and she watched as the woman onstage—working with a partner—demonstrated the basic step and then encouraged them to give it a try. That part wasn't so difficult, moving on every count but four and eight, backward first and then forward. Nick held Sadie's hand in his, lightly, while the other rested on her shoulder blade. Not her waist, but up higher, and she liked that as he wouldn't be anywhere near the roll of flesh right above her waistband. Then the band began to play. To her surprise, she picked it up quickly, partly because the music made it so clear—beat, beat, beat, pause; beat, beat, beat, pause—and also because Nick signaled with the lightest of touches which side she was to focus on. A squeeze of the fingers for the right, a push of his hand on her shoulder for the left.

But when they moved on to turns and cross-body leads, she grew frustrated, confused about which way to go, and so for the rest of the song they simply did the basic steps, as he moved her across the floor and then back the other way, gently, smoothly.

It felt nice to be in someone's arms.

Nick offered up an encouraging smile and laughed when they stepped on each other's toes. He was comfortable, in his element, which helped her to relax and enjoy the music and the sensation of gliding across the floor together. They continued on for three more songs, and as the final notes sounded, she couldn't help but imagine what it would be like to kiss him. Reaching over, touching his chin, and bringing her face to his. She wondered what his lips would feel like, what his tongue might feel like.

The fact that they stood less than a foot apart, without ever touching torsos, made it even more agonizing. It was as if an invisible force ran between their chests, their stomachs, keeping them tantalizingly apart from each other. She hadn't felt this fiercely about a man in a while. Hadn't known she still had it in her.

After, he suggested they hit a nearby diner for coffee and pie. They slid into opposite sides of a booth and she was glad they had a table between them so she could pull herself back together. Her equilibrium had shifted out of whack as they danced—she felt like one of those levels used to hang pictures on a wall, the bubble drifting outside of its marks.

"You like music, then?" he asked.

"My father was a musician, a session musician, played bass. So we always had music playing in the apartment. I love finding it wherever I can."

"Lots of opportunities in this city."

"Where you least expect it, like today."

"It's neat that your dad was a musician. Is he still around?"

She took a deep breath. "My father passed away when I was eight. That was a tough year."

"I'm sorry." He rubbed his chin with his hand. "I know all about tough years. In the span of twelve months, Sue and I separated, then she got swindled, and then my spaniel died."

"So many *S*'s."

He began to laugh, his eyes watering. "That's amazing."

"What?"

"My dog, what do you think his name was?"

"Oh no." She started to giggle as well.

"Sebastian."

"No!"

"Yes. Leave it to a librarian to point out the alliteration in my life's tragedies."

They talked of everything but the thefts, about his children and Sadie's niece. Nick asked where she liked to go to hear music, and she rattled off her favorites, relishing the shock on his face when she mentioned CBGB. Then the waitress came with the check, and there was the pulling out of wallets and Nick saying that he'd cover it and figuring out the tip.

A giant wave of uncertainty washed over Sadie. What next? What if she'd said too much and made a fool of herself? She sat frozen, unsure. She looked out the window, down at the table, anywhere but at Nick's face. She had no confidence anymore, and wasn't sure what to do or say.

Outside on the street, they parted with a hug, like two friends. Perhaps she was overthinking all this and they were just colleagues. Or maybe he still considered her a suspect. It was all too draining.

Which was why the next day she found herself in the stacks, waiting until there were no pages around, to reread some of the *Spinster* book. Fortify herself with its timelessness.

"Sadie?"

Nick's voice rang out. She slid the book into her tote bag and stepped outside the cage, locking the door behind her.

"Yes? What are you doing down here?"

"Claude said you were here. I came to find you." He shifted from one foot to the other. "Um, did you just put a book in your bag?"

"A book?"

The rules for anyone working in the stacks were clear. No placing books from the stacks into outside containers or bags. They were supposed to stay in plain sight at all times.

"What's inside your tote bag?"

She took a deep breath. This was awful. She hadn't meant to take the book, just gotten distracted when she'd heard his voice and tucked it away, out of sight.

She pulled it out and handed it to him, looking off to the side as she did.

He read the title out loud. "*Surviving Spinsterhood: The Joys of Living Alone*. Oh."

She squirmed as the words hung in the air. It might as well have been a pair of her underwear, out there for everyone to see. All because she was stupid enough to think that an old book could fix what was wrong with her life.

"I accidentally put it inside my bag. So silly. I'll put it back."

She grabbed the book from him and turned back to the cage, fumbling with the lock.

Maybe he had been watching her, following her. Maybe this whole charade was just a way to catch her in the act.

And she'd fallen right into it.

CHAPTER FIFTEEN

New York City, 1914

Laura lifted her head up to the late March sun as she walked through Bryant Park on the way home from class, taking in the tantalizing hint of spring through the bare branches of the trees. Two more months and she'd be done. The time had gone by so quickly.

"Laura."

She turned to see Amelia seated on one of the benches, a book in her lap. Today, her usual uniform had been replaced with a blue plaid tunic and a brown velvet skirt that fell softly over her long legs. Amelia rose and greeted her with a light kiss on the cheek. The warmth of her lips on Laura's cheek lingered after she pulled away, smiling.

Laura instinctively looked up at the imposing facade of the library, as if Jack might be in one of the windows, looking down.

"What are you doing here?" Together, they walked along the promenade toward Fifth Avenue.

"I haven't seen you in a while. I'm feeling quite bereft, not having my cub reporter by my side."

Ever since the morning after the protest, Laura had meant to stop by Amelia's—she'd been downtown several times to finish up details on her thesis—but hadn't been able to. She didn't want to see Jessie lounging in the parlor, or hear her banging around in the kitchen as she and Amelia tried to talk. So instead, she'd avoided the street altogether. Besides, there was so much to do.

"It's been busy, at school. But really, what brings you to the library?"

"I was in the neighborhood and figured I'd linger, in case you came by. And you did."

Amelia had come for her. Laura didn't know how to answer. "What are you reading?"

Amelia held up her book. "*The Awakening,* one of my favorites."

"You were reading that book the first time I ever saw you, at Vassar." Laura blushed at having shared such a vivid detail.

"Always good to return to the favorites, I say." Amelia paused. "Everyone at the club has been asking about you. It's been three weeks."

She'd kept count. Laura's stomach flipped.

"Did you hear about what happened to Frank Tannenbaum?"

According to the papers, Mr. Tannenbaum had been one of 190 men arrested the night of the protest. "I did, it's terrible."

"That's one of the reasons I wanted to speak with you."

Laura had hoped Amelia had come by because she missed her. Obviously not.

"The patrons of Mabel Dodge's salon arranged a fund to bail the protestors out, but we just learned today that Frank's sentence is a year."

"A year? That's ridiculous." They turned right just before Fifth Avenue, heading toward the front entrance.

"I know. We're asking for everyone's help to get the word out about this injustice, about how the protest was squashed."

So that was why she'd come. "I'm not a real reporter. It's all just for practice. The *Blotto*, remember?"

"You'll be one soon enough, and maybe there's something you can do now."

"Like what?"

"I don't know, talk to your professors, something like that. Maybe they have colleagues at the papers who can take up the cause."

"Reporters aren't supposed to take up causes. Besides, I can barely catch my breath these days, I'm hanging on by a thread." Laura knew she was being unnecessarily obstinate. She was a terrible person, awful.

Amelia came to a stop beside one of the lions and looked at her curiously. "Are you sure there's nothing wrong? Between us? Was it something I did or said?"

"No, of course not." Laura shouldn't behave this way with her friend, pushing her away. She tried to explain. "I'll pass on the information about Frank to the other students, and mention it to my professor. I'm sure someone will jump at the chance to cover it."

"I appreciate it."

She couldn't help herself. "How's Jessie?"

"We broke up."

Laura tried to rearrange her features into that of a caring friend, one for whom the news was just that—news—not a soaring relief, a gift. "You did? When?"

"The day after the protest. I didn't want to be with her anymore, and I'd felt that way for a while, just hadn't reckoned with it until then. She was sad, but understood. She was so much younger, and it began to fray my nerves."

The kiss Laura had witnessed was one of parting, not passion.

But her joy quickly curdled. How easy it was for Amelia to discard a lover who no longer pleased. A bitter envy welled up inside Laura, and she hated herself for it. She wanted to be free to love like that, even just for a day.

"On to the next girlfriend, then?"

Amelia studied her. "Maybe. Maybe not. To be honest, I find your question rather patronizing."

Laura had meant it to be flippant, but instead, she came off churlish and stern, just like her father. "Patronizing"—what a horrible word.

She was too close to her subjects for this thesis, too caught up in the Heterodoxy Club's mystique and revolutionary ideas, the members' pleas for equality. She'd lost her impartiality, a dangerous thing for a reporter. Even worse, she'd fallen in love with her source. She imagined leaning in and kissing Amelia right here on the steps of the library, in front of the whole world.

She looked around, as if waking from a trance, horrified at the thought.

No, this wasn't love.

It was a crush. Amelia was everything Laura wished to be: brash, outspoken, taking what she wanted. And so Laura had somehow projected her own desires on the embodiment of them, Dr. Amelia Potter, the New Woman of bohemia.

She'd taken it too far, and regretted getting so caught up. Amelia's world was so different from her own, an exotic country with its own rules and laws. Laura could never fit in. For all of her mother's urging to follow her passions, this was not what she'd meant, not in the least.

"I'm sorry, you're right, Amelia. I guess I just worry for you. That's all."

"I'm the last person you need to worry about, my dear." She leaned against the lion's pedestal. "Which one is this?"

"I'm sorry?"

"Which lion, Lenox or Astor?"

Amelia looked up at the sculptured feline. "Astor. The one to the south is Lenox."

"I love that you know that."

Amelia flashed a warm smile, and Laura couldn't help but return it. Then they both laughed, the sound breaking through the awkwardness. They were dear friends after all.

"Will we see you at the meeting on Saturday?"

She could use a little more color for her thesis, which was due in two weeks. Now that she'd thought through her complicated feelings and come out the other side, she felt more in balance, more in control. Amelia was her friend, that was all, and that was enough. "Of course. I'll see you there, thank you for coming uptown."

Inside the library, Laura encountered Jack on the narrow stairway that led to their apartment.

"There you are!" He pulled her upstairs to the landing and lifted her into the air.

"Jack. What on earth is going on?"

"I came up to tell you some good news."

"They've caught the thief?"

Her guess was off, judging from the dismayed look on his face. She couldn't seem to read him anymore, to say the right thing.

"No, I'm afraid not. In fact, another two books were picked off this week."

"That's terrible." Again, why hadn't he told her? It was as if he'd held back the information on purpose.

"Certainly. However, since I don't have access to the collection anymore, it means I am no longer a suspect. This has to do with my own book. An agent has asked to read it."

"You finished it?"

"Yes. I finished it. Your patience with me has been wonderful, Laura. I don't tell you that enough, and I'm sorry. After I finished it, I felt oddly forlorn, which is why I didn't mention it. I haven't been a good father, a good husband, as this manuscript has had me by the horns."

"You have seemed removed lately, that's true. But so have I. We've both been through a tough year." Saying it out loud was such a relief, she threw her arms around his neck. "I'm so proud of you. You've finished the book. That's an incredible accomplishment." They stood there, rocking each other gently, the motion refilling the reserves of love Laura felt for her husband. "Tell me all about the agent."

"I saw him in the Main Reading Room, when we were conducting an inspection of the pneumatic tubes. He knew my friend Billy, from back in the day, and came up to say hello. I wasn't sure if it was too forward of me, but I knew this might be my only chance, my only connection, so I gave him a pitch, told him all about it.

He said he'd like to read it, and I'm dropping it off at his office tomorrow, in person."

"That's wonderful."

"Follow me." He led her to his study, where a thick ream of papers sat in the very center of his desk, tied with string. "There she is. Would you like to read it before I send it out?"

"I've love to." She checked the clock. "But let me first get dinner started. So the children aren't hungry."

"I'll do that. You sit by the fire and have a read, and I'll put together something for us."

"You?" The thought made her giggle.

"You'd be surprised at my culinary skill. Back when I was an eligible young bachelor, I was quite handy."

She did as she was told, and a half hour later was called into the kitchen for scrambled eggs on toast.

"What on earth?" she said, laughing.

"Dad says today's an upside-down day," announced Pearl, clutching her fingers together with excitement. "Breakfast is for dinner."

Harry brought the plates to the table, arranging them carefully in between the forks and knives. The last one he dropped, and it clattered to the floor, eggs scattering across the tiles.

"I'm sorry." Tears welled up in his eyes.

"But that's perfect," said Jack. "It's upside-down day, so dinner's on the floor, not the table."

"Really?" Harry looked over at Laura for confirmation.

"Exactly right," she said.

"I know," said Pearl. "We should eat sitting on the floor. Don't worry, Harry, I'll get you a new plate."

They left the mess and settled on the rug in the living room,

like a group of picnickers in Central Park. Pearl spoke of her favorite teacher, going on and on at length, until finally Laura interrupted and asked Harry about his.

"You're my favorite teacher," he answered.

Jack reached over and put his large hand over the boy's bony
shoulder. "Good answer, my child. Mine, too."

That evening, Laura dove into Jack's manuscript, the only
sound the low murmur of Jack reading aloud to the children from
the other room.

The next day, he woke her from the easy chair where she'd
fallen asleep, the last few pages on her lap.

"How was it?"

She yawned and smiled up at him. Losing a night of sleep had
been well worth it. "Wonderful. Brilliant."

"You're not saying that because you're married to me, are you?"

"It's one of the best books I've read in ages." She wasn't lying.
He'd captured the internal and external journey of a young man
coming to New York at the turn of the century with an acuity that
took her breath away. "It's splendid, and I couldn't be prouder
of you."

At the Saturday meeting of the Heterodoxy Club, Laura was
greeted like a returning hero—or, more aptly, heroine—for having braved the protest with Amelia, for being part of the revolution. She tried to downplay her role in the demonstration, since
she was truly there just as an observer, but that didn't matter.
Jessie approached Amelia, the two of them sharing a friendly chat
before the opening remarks, but it didn't bother Laura at all. What

she'd experienced earlier in the month was simply leftover anxiety from being so close to violence, most likely. Needing a comrade to deal with the aftershocks, and that comrade naturally being Amelia, who took charge and offered safety. They were just friends, and that was perfectly fine, perfectly normal. She and Jack had weathered the storms of the past few months and come out the other end, now that he'd completed his book.

A hat was passed around for a collection for Frank Tannenbaum's defense, and she handed over the money she'd put aside for her lunch. In the near future, she'd have a steady stream of income of her own. That day couldn't come soon enough.

Her master's thesis was almost finished, but she'd been worrying about how to wrap it all up. Inspiration, once again, came from the day's speaker, a woman named Inez Haynes Gillmore, who read from a series of articles she'd published in *Harper's Bazaar*, titled "Confessions of an Alien."

"'It seems to me,'" began Inez, "'I hang in a void midway between two spheres—the man's sphere and the woman's sphere. The duties and pleasure of the average woman bore and irritate. The duties and pleasures of the average man interest and allure. I soon found that it was a feeling which I shared with the majority of my kind. I have never met a man who at any time wanted to be a woman. I have met few women who have not at some time or other wanted to be men.'"

At this, the members in the audience broke out in applause. For the first time, Laura wondered if she wouldn't be happier as a journalist who went beyond mere reporting and actually stated an opinion, like Inez. Inez's words struck a chord in every woman present, more than if she'd simply reported on the increase in the number of women working outside the home, reflecting the facts back to the public in the hopes that they understood the implications.

What if she wrote specifically to further a cause, in order to change minds?

She wasn't ready for that, not yet. For now, she had to stick to the facts if she wanted to graduate. Professor Wakeman would have a fit otherwise. Luckily, when she'd shown the rough draft of her master's thesis to him, he'd told her it was impressive. "But it's a mess," he'd added. "Tighten it up and get the sections to flow together better. Your transitions need work. However, I could see a book in this."

A book! She'd almost fainted. Of course, it couldn't be a book, as the club had its rules. But maybe after Amelia saw the finished thesis, she'd be just as impressed as Professor Wakeman, and convince the others to give their consent. To think that both she and Jack could have books of their own. In fact, once they were situated in their new careers, he could quit his job at the library and maybe they'd find a pretty apartment in the Village. Professor Wakeman had handed the pages back to her. "It's better than the other women's work I've seen so far, I'll give you that. Tighten it up and turn it in. I want it perfect."

She knew his idea of perfection was higher than any other advisor's. No spelling errors, no dangling prepositions. Not only did the story have to be solid, but the presentation did, too.

Sunday evening, she retreated to Jack's desk in the study to finish up the conclusion of her thesis. Now that he'd finished his book, she didn't feel so obtrusive when she placed his many to-do lists in a neat pile in one corner (the best way to approach a challenge is methodically, he'd always say), before spreading out her own notes across the leather blotter. He walked in and gave her a kiss on the head. "How's it going?"

"I have a new appreciation for what you've been through the past several years. How do I distill everything I've learned into a final section that's powerful, but not repetitive?"

"Remember what made you want to write this in the first place, where that first spark of an idea came from. You can do it, I know you can."

After he left, she remained in place, staring out the window.

She'd wanted to demonstrate what women were thinking, what the New Woman was thinking, specifically. The women she respected most were those who followed their passion and weren't afraid to speak the truth out loud, like Amelia. Like her mother, although it was a more muted passion, she being of an older generation. If her mother had been born later, Laura had no doubt she'd be out there marching, instead of dependent on her husband for every little thing.

Laura picked up her pen and began scribbling over the typewritten words on the final pages of the latest draft, editing each paragraph one by one. She'd end this on a sharp note, she decided. She'd take a position, make a stand, and show how much this story meant to her, instead of hiding behind dry facts and quotes. It was a risk, she knew, but wasn't that what Amelia had done when she'd performed health inspections when every other doctor faked the reports? When Frank Tannenbaum led hundreds in protest? By comparison, this act of rebellion was a minor one. Professor Wakeman had believed she might eventually write a book—why not show him how much she could do with words?

Thank goodness she'd gone back to the club, to get this last dose of inspiration before the final push. After she finished editing, she put a fresh piece of paper into the typewriter and retyped the last few pages, incorporating the new sections. After a thorough proofread, she placed the new pages at the bottom of the stack and sat back, smiling. Her thesis was complete.

Three weeks later, she sat next to Gretchen outside Professor Wakeman's office on the seventh floor of the journalism school, waiting their turns for his critique. After this hurdle came final exams, and then graduation, which was to be held on the lawn in front of the university's library. She imagined her father's face in the crowd, finally proud. Her mother, crying and flapping her arms about like a pigeon.

"Last year, only a third of the class graduated," said Gretchen. "That's only nine of us."

"I know. But we've both turned in consistently good work." As the semester had progressed, Laura and Gretchen had relied on each other, figuring out ways to circumvent the professors' sexism and comparing notes, and formed a respectful camaraderie. They'd come a long way from that first, tense week.

"Miss Reynolds?"

Gretchen gave Laura a quick smile and disappeared into the office.

Laura thought of the stack of paper that was her thesis, now sitting on Professor Wakeman's desk. She'd created that from nothing, and even if he didn't like it and gave her a low grade, she knew in her heart it was a valuable piece of reporting and writing. The school had taught her well, and had given her a confidence that would serve her for years to come.

Around fifteen minutes later, Gretchen emerged, a huge smile on her face.

"It went well?" asked Laura, relieved.

"Yes. He thought my profile of the mayor's wife was 'elucidating.' I'm over the moon!"

"Good for you."

Laura had to wait another few minutes before Professor Wakeman intoned her name.

"Mrs. Lyons. You may enter."

CHAPTER SIXTEEN

New York City, 1914

Professor Wakeman's office window offered a lovely view over an oval patch of grass where several of Laura's classmates lolled in the April sun. Laura peered out before taking a seat in the battered wooden chair beside his desk and waiting for him to speak. She wasn't nearly as nervous as she'd been at their first meeting, when he'd initially scoffed at her idea of profiling a women's club for her master's thesis.

He leafed through a couple of pages before looking up at her over his spectacles. "You took my advice and tightened up the middle, which I approve of. I like what you've done there, and the women's points of view are much stronger than I expected. You brought them to life."

"Thank you, Professor."

"I don't agree with all of their ideas, of course. But you've presented the issues clearly and thoughtfully. The narration flows."

"I'm glad you think so."

"I also admire the way you included a section that gives the reader some historical perspective on the club."

"I thought that might help. You see, what these women think and say is quite different from their mothers' ideas, or their grand-mothers'. With the surge of interest in the life and rights of the common man, the worker, there's been a similar surge in the rights of women, as an oppressed class."

He shuffled the stack of paper until the edges were perfectly even. "Unfortunately, Mrs. Lyons, your grade is an F."

She must have heard wrong. "I'm sorry?"

"As I've said since the first day of class, a journalism degree is not one to be handed over lightly. Just as the law school students must pass the bar, we demand that any graduates of the journal-ism school pass a similar bar. You, sadly, have not."

For a moment she wondered if he had mistaken her for another student, or mixed up her thesis with someone else's. But no, the pages in front of him were the very ones she'd typed up in Jack's office. "I'm sorry? How? You've said only kind things, and I made the changes you asked for."

"Your conclusion reads like an editorial in one of Hearst's slimy broadsheets. It's shrill, and even though it's just words on a page, it hurt my ears. This is not what we teach at this institution. You are not here to tell me what to think. Has that not been hammered into you in every class?" As he spoke, splotches of pink emerged on his cheeks.

Laura thought of Amelia and the pushback she got for standing up for herself and her work. This was no different, and she refused to step down. "You mean it offends your sensibilities? You don't like what you've read, and it doesn't agree with your morals, and so you fail me? That's not fair."

If Laura received a failing grade on her thesis, she wouldn't graduate. She wouldn't be one of the students standing out on that fine lawn; she wouldn't get a degree; there would be no job. The whole point of going to graduate school was to be able to land a decent job right off, not fetch tea for the top brass for five years and hope to land a scoop that impressed them. She sat back and clasped her hands on her lap, a ladylike gesture that seemed to mollify him slightly. "Professor Wakeman, you've seen that I can report and write and edit just as well as the men. You know I can. Just because I showed some feeling at the very end of my thesis, I'm being punished?"

Professor Wakeman tugged at his collar. "Believe me, it hurts to do this, as you've been a promising student up to now. I know this is upsetting, but the school must maintain its high standards."

She laughed out loud, not caring about her rudeness. She'd been stupid, taking this risk. She'd known about the low graduation rate but had figured it wouldn't be her. Couldn't be her. All that money, gone. Wasted. She thought of her mother's engagement ring; of Dr. Anderson at the library, who'd gone out of his way to secure her a scholarship. She'd disappointed all of them, including Harry and Pearl. Pearl, who she'd hoped would see that women deserved satisfying careers, just as men did. Jack, who'd be overly kind and understanding in a way that would make her squirm.

She tried again, leaning forward slightly in her chair. "You've said my work's been good and consistent. I've been out in the trenches with the best of the boys. Please."

He gathered up her master's thesis and placed it on the desk in front of her. "I'm afraid not."

"Let me ask you, how many other women who are under your tutelage did you fail?"

"That has no bearing on your case."

"Tell me. Otherwise, I have the investigative chops to find out myself, you see. I know Gretchen passed. How many others besides me did not?"

He tensed up. "All except Gretchen failed. She did a lovely profile on the mayor's wife. There was no reason to fail her, none at all. No private agenda. It was factual, straightforward, and well written. Delightful. I'll have you know that last year, none of the women whom I advised for their master's theses passed. So you see, there's been an improvement, Mrs. Lyons."

She didn't bother to hide her incredulity. "Have the men been allowed to express their opinions in their writing?"

He paused. "It's different for them because their topics are more complicated. Politics, wars, economics."

"So they've been allowed to editorialize?" She waited. "Keep in mind, the master's theses are on file in the library, so I can see for myself."

He lowered his eyes, staring down at the sheaf of papers in front of her. "Some do, yes. But it's not the same."

"How?"

He sputtered, then fell silent.

"You must change my grade, then."

"I see your point, I do." He shook his head. "It's too late to change the grade, though. It's been entered with the registrar."

"Then my first article out of school will be on the sex discrimination rampant at the Columbia Journalism School." She snatched her thesis off the desk.

"Rampant? No need for hyperbole, there's no need for that, Mrs. Lyons." He touched his desk where the thesis had been, his fingertips splayed like spider legs. "I'm sorry, I can't change it. But I do appreciate you bringing this to my attention. I will certainly keep it in mind for next year. Will that do?"

With that, she swept out the door, slamming it shut behind her.

Without classes to attend, without a goal to achieve, Laura would be back to square one. Reading to the children at night, cooking meals, ironing and mending clothes. It was all she could do not to burst into tears when Jack opened his office door to her.

"Darling, how grand to see you." He closed the door behind her and gestured to the chair. She'd hoped he would take her into his arms, but he seemed unaware of her distress.

"I have great news." He took his seat behind the desk and finally looked up at her. "What is it? Is something wrong, the children?" He half rose from his chair, but she motioned him to sit.

"No, they're fine. It's me. I failed my master's thesis. Professor Wakeman failed me."

"What? I read it, and it was wonderful."

"He's known to be tough—last year he failed a top student for a mere spelling error. School of hard knocks and all that, I suppose. He liked everything except the very end."

"I loved the way you summarized it. He's bonkers."

"I changed it before handing it in. I added in my own opinions and thoughts. He didn't approve."

Jack frowned. "What made you do that?"

She wanted to scream. "Because I had them," she cried. "Because I felt they mattered."

"Of course, that makes sense." He rose and came to her, leaning down to give her a hug, as if it might erase his stupid question.

She accepted the embrace but pulled away first. "What's your good news, then? We sure could use it."

"The agent loved my manuscript." He reached into a drawer and pulled it out, placing it on top of his desk. "There are some changes to be made, of course. But I agree with them all, they're going to make it even better."

"That's terrific. I'm so proud of you. What's the next step?"

"I edit the book, then turn it back in. He's given me a couple of months. It'll be tight, but I think I can manage. After that, he'll send it out to publishers. He said he's already mentioned it to several and they're all excited to see it. 'A bidding war' is what he said to me. 'They'll get into a bidding war for your book.'"

He was like a child on Christmas Eve, beaming and giddy, and his excitement was infectious. She reached her arm across the desk and took his hand. "Well done, my dear. You're going to be a literary sensation, of that I have no doubt."

"I couldn't have done it without you, Laura-love. Don't you worry, we'll find something interesting for you to do, something other than that journalism school."

The black cloud settled back over her. "Like what? I even sold my mother's engagement ring, and now it's all for nothing. What have I done?"

"Don't fret, the book advance will make it easy to pay her back. She can buy a new one." He snapped his fingers. "Hey, I have an idea. What about if you type up my edits for me?"

Her heart sank. "No, thank you. I don't want to be your assistant or your secretary. I want to write on my own, do something on my own."

"Don't get upset, it was just a thought."

That he would voice that thought out loud disturbed her to no end. He didn't seem to understand, after all this time, that she wanted a passion like he had. She would never have imagined asking him, if the agent had taken a pass, if he would like to type up her master's thesis for her instead. As if that might make him feel useful. It would never have crossed her mind.

She excused herself and went up to the apartment, where her mother and Pearl were sitting at the kitchen table, sewing clothes for Pearl's doll.

"What are you doing home so early?" asked her mother.

"I failed. It's over. Where's Harry?"

"What?" Her mother rose and held out her arms, but Laura waved her away; she didn't want to cry in front of Pearl. "Harry's off with friends. You had your master's thesis review today, right?"

"I did. The professor failed me, for a senseless reason. We got into an argument about it, and to be honest, I think I won. But it doesn't matter, it's too late for him to change it." She sat at the table, next to Pearl. "I'm sorry, Mother, but we will find a way to make it up to you. Jack got good news about the book, and in a couple of months things will be brighter."

"For him. What about for you?"

"Why did they fail you?" Pearl asked. She sat very still.

Her concern took Laura out of herself, finally. She put an arm over her daughter's shoulders and pulled her close, placing her forehead against Pearl's. "I took a risk and it didn't work out. It was a foolish mistake."

"That's nonsense," said her mother. "There's nothing wrong with taking a risk. I highly recommend it, whenever possible. Pearl, your mother is strong and will be fine. Taking risks is what life is all about."

Pearl looked from her grandmother to her mother. "But Mother seems unhappy."

"Maybe for now," said Laura. "But I assure you I'll be fine. That we'll all be fine. Grandmother is right."

The buoyancy of Laura's mother's faith in her future sustained her through the evening, but the next morning, Laura found herself standing dejectedly at the kitchen sink. She threw down the dish towel, took off her apron, and headed to the Village, to Patchin Place.

Over the past several months, whenever Laura had discussed the thesis with Amelia, she'd provided a watered-down summary, one that lacked any specific references to the Heterodoxy Club. She didn't bother to elucidate further today, as it really didn't matter anymore. Amelia listened quietly as Laura told her what Professor Wakeman had done.

"The professor knew he was wrong," said Laura, her fists clenched in anger. "He *knew* it."

"You should do what you threatened—compare the number of women who've failed to the men."

"It would be a very small sample, and probably wouldn't prove anything. I suppose the good news is that, going forward, Professor Wakeman will consider women students in a new light, and think before he dismisses and fails them for something that he allows, encourages even, in the men. I had the bad luck of the draw."

"I'm so sorry." Amelia reached over and gave her a hug, holding her close, before getting up to put another log on the fire and rejoining her on the sofa. They sat, side by side, staring at the burning log without speaking for a minute, and Laura's mind spun. How would her life change once Jack's book came out? Would they move from the library? Would he agree to move downtown? Every possibility nagged at her, and in every one, her wishes were secondary to her husband's. If she'd graduated, she might have landed a job and held some economic weight. The right to have an opinion. Without a salary or income of her own, Jack's desires were more important, even if he insisted otherwise. It wasn't fair.

Her head ached. "I feel like with every year, my brain is a sponge that soaks up painful experiences like water, so by the time I'm fifty, I won't be able to hold it upright."

Amelia laughed and turned to her. "What on earth are you talking about? You're raving mad."

"You're probably right."

"But I know exactly what you mean."

"I knew you would."

They looked at each other; Amelia's brown eyes were soft and kind. Laura was glad she'd come.

"So what now, Mrs. Lyons?" Amelia asked.

"Jack wants me to be his typist."

"God, no."

"Don't worry, I said pretty much the same thing. But I'm not sure what else to do."

"You don't need a journalism degree to be a journalist."

"It's going to be harder starting from the ground up. I have no experience, no published pieces, nothing to offer an employer."

"You've got all of us. The club. We've got a lot of connections in newspapers, magazines."

"I suppose so." She hadn't realized until just now how wide her social circle had become. Maybe Amelia was right.

"Hell, write a book about the women's movement. I'd buy it."

Amelia considered the world as if it were full of possibilities, not closed doors. Laura studied her friend's features in the firelight. The way her mouth moved, the curve of her chin. What Laura wanted, more than anything, was to sit across from Amelia all day, listen to her speak, and stare at her features, just take in her very being. The last time she'd felt this way was when the children were newborns—a rush of love, of devotion, that was unstoppable.

"You are part of our family, now," Amelia said. "You can count on us."

"Thank you."

Amelia closed her eyes and leaned back again, smiling.

The temptation was too much. It was as if an invisible wave propelled Laura slowly forward, leaning closer and closer.

Until their lips met.

She pulled back immediately, the shock of the softness too much, but Amelia stayed still, placing a hand on Laura's arm, the gentle pressure leaving no question about her own desire.

Laura kissed her again, and this time Amelia's lips parted and then there was tongue and breath. A fire raced through Laura's body, from her stomach to between her legs. She shifted her hand from where it rested on Amelia's waist up to her breast, which was full and heavy. She'd dreamed of touching Amelia this way the last time she and Jack had made love. While her hands had stroked his body, her mind had imagined another silhouette, a woman's.

Amelia's.

Laura's love for Amelia, their friendship, the way their bodies moved, defied any kind of categorization. Over the past few weeks, the minute they found themselves alone, it was as if a magnet pulled them close, and before long their skirts and petticoats were mixed in with the sheets and pillows, two pairs of stockings lumped down at the very foot of the bed.

They spoke quickly and easily around each other, interrupting and correcting, reevaluating their own positions and opinions. Laura had never seen anything of the sort between her mother and her father—her father's desires always overruled her mother's—nor really between her and Jack. Jack was a traditional husband, in many ways, and made the lion's share of the decisions for their family. She hadn't noticed until now how much she deferred to his wishes, even if they came from a place of benevolence. They weren't equals, as much as she'd pretended they were.

But that was no excuse for what she was doing. Every time she turned the corner into Patchin Place, Laura's guilt peaked into a sick panic. But then Amelia would draw Laura into her arms, and their inevitable dance of desire would unfold as naturally as a summer rain.

Amelia stretched out on her stomach on her bed and ran her finger along the inside of Laura's arm, rattling off possible interview subjects for Laura's book. "Marie Jenney Howe, of course. I'm sure we can get Emma Goldman, if we approach her the right way."

"I'm still not sure. I've written articles, but an entire book?"

"You have to stop doubting yourself," Amelia said, taking her hand and kissing each finger lightly on the tip. "It'll be good for you to write this book," she said, after. "Get you out in the real world."

"I am out in the real world."

"It's way bigger than New York City, my girl."

Something in the way Amelia spoke caught Laura's attention. "What do you mean?"

"You should come with me."

"Where?"

"London." Amelia's lips twitched.

"London?"

"I've been asked to move there in the fall, once my study here is complete. They want to try to re-create the conditions and programs I've set up here, in the East End, where they're battling similar issues with regard to infant mortality."

"That's wonderful news. What an opportunity. I'm so happy for you."

"No, you're not."

Amelia knew her so well. She didn't need to explain, but tried anyway. "I am happy that you've been given such an opportunity. To travel, to have this recognition of your accomplishments. But I'll miss you."

"Why don't you come along?"

Laura laughed. "Because I have a husband and children. Or am I supposed to bring them, too?"

"I don't want to be without you."

This was madness. "Exactly how do I explain to Jack that we must follow you across the ocean? He'd know something was going on."

"There is something going on. I love you, Laura."

The words she'd been desperately hoping to hear landed hard. "You know I can't."

"Consider it, please?"

She shouldn't do any of this. She should return to her family and assume the role of dutiful wife and mother.

She stood and looked out the window as if searching for an answer, but the cloudless sky overwhelmed her. She was exposed down here in the Village. Or perhaps she was truly herself down here. Both thoughts frightened her.

The horn from a passing automobile made her jump. Amelia came up behind her and wrapped her arms around Laura's waist. "You don't have to decide right away."

More than anything, Laura wanted to lose herself in Amelia's scent, one that hinted of cinnamon and the sea, and not think about what the future held.

Together, they retreated to the warmth of the bed and each other's arms.

CHAPTER SEVENTEEN

New York City, 1993

Wait."

Sadie turned away from the cage door, where she had been fumbling with the lock. Nick stood where she'd left him, hands at his sides. "Yes?"

"What's the book about?"

She looked down at the worn cover of the *Surviving Spinster-hood* book, wondering what on earth she was thinking, finding comfort in this ancient volume. The world had changed, and here she was, stepping back in time instead of moving forward. Studying the appropriate tipping etiquette for a lone woman traveler in the late 1800s, learning how best to budget on sixty dollars a month. Useless knowledge, all of it. Her mother had been right all along.

She handed it over to him, cringing inside. How pathetic she must seem. There was no explanation as to why she'd have the book in her bag other than the fact that she was deficient, a loser who couldn't hold a man.

Or the book thief.

"Any good advice inside?"

He had the tiniest of smiles on his face. But not like he was making fun of her, like he was curious.

"The author, Abigail Duckworth, says to find a passionate interest."

"I like to dance. Check. What else?"

Sadie rose to the bait. "That every lady should have the makings of a manhattan at hand."

"Rye, bitters, and vermouth. Yup."

She wasn't called "No Stumpin' Sadie" for nothing. "Miss Duckworth suggests owning at least four bed jackets, including one of quilted silk and another in velvet."

He didn't even hesitate. "Check and check."

The incongruous image of Nick reclining in bed in a quilted bed jacket made her laugh. She regarded the battered volume. "I'm fond of this book. It's a quirky slice of history, published in 1896, part of the original donation from the Berg brothers. Certainly not the most valuable, but still." She paused, breathing hard, like she'd run a mile. "I really must go."

His face grew serious. "Actually, I came down here to find you. Claude said you had headed to the stacks."

"What is it?"

"Something else is missing."

God, no. "From the Berg? Another book?"

"Not quite. A page from a book."

"Which one?"

"Shakespeare's folio."

Up in the Berg, Claude and one of their regular scholars, a rabbity fellow named Mr. Blount, stood staring down at an oversized volume laid out on one of the tables.

Mr. Blount had been studying it for over six months now, part of a project with Harvard University, and he looked up with huge eyes as Sadie and Nick approached.

"The title page. It's gone."

She could see it clearly in her mind's eye. A portrait of Shakespeare, high forehead and lashless eyes, above which were the words *Mr. William Shakespeare's Comedies, Histories, & Tragedies.* Dated 1623. So very long ago.

The page had been cleanly cut out, only a narrow column remaining.

"When did you last request this, Mr. Blount?" she asked, her voice faint.

"Before this morning? Two days ago. You retrieved it for me."

This was more than an act of vandalism. This was war.

Nick spoke up. "Tell me more about it."

"The First Folios," said Mr. Blount, "were published by Shakespeare's friends seven years after his death in 1616. They're the closest thing that scholars have to his original works, since no handwritten copies survive. There are two hundred thirty-three in existence."

Sadie addressed Claude. "How could this have happened?"

"One of us has been in the room consistently," said Claude with a hint of aggression. "I haven't seen anyone pull out a knife or a razor. Have you?"

They were turning on each other, and she welcomed the challenge. "Certainly not."

Nick broke in. "In this case, someone didn't take the whole book, just the page. Why would they do that?"

"I'm not sure," said Sadie. "It's not like a rare map, which can be resold after it's been cut from an atlas. This is just destruction, like the thief wanted to make a point. It's almost as if someone is trying to sabotage the exhibit. The folio was to be part of it. Open to this exact page."

Nick considered her reply before turning to the patron. "Mr. Blount, I'm a security consultant, working for the library. Would you mind emptying your pockets and briefcase?"

"Of course not."

Mr. Blount opened his briefcase and stepped back as Nick went through it, item by item, flipping through several legal pads filled with notes. Sadie wished more than anything that the missing page would flutter out, anything to have it back. Mr. Blount also handed over his coat and emptied out his pockets. Nothing.

"Thank you for your help, Mr. Blount. Please keep this to yourself, and I'll be in touch if we have any more questions."

After Mr. Blount collected his things and left, Sadie locked the door behind him. She caught Nick's eye and tipped her head. "How about Claude?"

"How about me?" Claude's neck turned red with indignation. "How about you?"

"I'll need to look at each of your desks," said Nick. In the back office, he started with Sadie's and, of course, found nothing out of order. Then Claude's, with both Claude and Sadie peering from behind his shoulder. When he pulled out the skinny drawer at the top, the one that held pencils and pens, Sadie let out a bellow. "Look!"

Nick sifted through the detritus of erasers and nubby pencils. "What?"

She plucked out a small plastic holder. "This!"

"You're mad," said Claude, checking in with Nick to make sure he understood how mad she was. "It's dental floss."

"Dental floss is a traditional tool of rare map thieves." She addressed Nick. "They put it in their mouths and get it wet; then, when the librarian isn't looking, they lay it down on the page they want, right against the binding, and close it back up. After a few minutes, the page slips out easily, and voilà, the job is done. Our map department bans dental floss specifically."

Claude slammed the drawer shut. "I had work done on my teeth, and the dentist recommended I use it after every meal. I can have him attest to that personally, if need be."

They glared at each other, at a standoff.

"Why would I try to sabotage the exhibit?" Claude pointed a finger in her direction. "You've been out to get me for the past few months. Don't deny it."

"I have not." She didn't want to get into it, not in front of Nick.

But Claude was incensed, unstoppable. "We kissed once, at a fucking holiday party. Ever since then, you've been acting all weird, first happy and then mad, like it was some kind of big deal. It was a stupid, drunken kiss, that's all."

She stared at him, mouth open. His male vanity had been shot down when she'd rejected him, and now he was trying to pretend she was some kind of giddy schoolgirl. That was unacceptable. And mean. Her mind raced through responses, but it was as if she'd been rendered mute in front of Nick. Nothing came out.

Claude's eyes were hard, cruel. "That's what holiday parties are for, letting your hair down. Although it was obvious you'd never done anything like that in your life."

He paused, letting the words sink in. "You're the crazy one, not me. Don't be putting this on me, no way."

Sadie grabbed her jacket from the coat stand in the corner, breathing hard. If she didn't get out of here, she'd fall apart. Her brain was spinning, shocked by Claude's disdain and the terrible embarrassment of having had that discussion in front of Nick. Then there was the vandalized book, on top of everything.

But the appearance of Dr. Hooper in the Berg Collection's main room prevented her from fleeing.

She nonchalantly draped her coat over the nearest chair, as if she hadn't been running for her life. Nick and Claude joined her as soon as Dr. Hooper's voice rang out.

"I cannot believe we're dealing with another theft," said Dr. Hooper. "This is terrible. Sadie, you were the last one to handle this?"

"I retrieved it from the cage this morning, yes."

"Did you notice the title page gone?"

"I didn't check." It would be lunacy if the librarians had to check every page of every volume requested.

Nick tapped his finger on the desk. His face was a neutral mask, giving no indication of what he'd thought of Claude's outburst. "What if Mr. Blount stole it and then pretended to find it missing?"

"Either Claude or I have been here, we would have seen it," said Sadie. "It's a small room. Any noise or odd movement would have attracted our notice. Especially after the earlier thefts. We've been on the lookout, I assure you."

Even Claude nodded in agreement on that.

"Look." She addressed Dr. Hooper. "I strongly suggest that we get this out in the world. If you like, I can write up a press release."

"No." The syllable erupted from Dr. Hooper, short and sharp. "We're about to launch a massive capital campaign. The board does not want the fact that we're losing valuable items getting out, as it might give potential donors pause. It would mar the objective."

"'Mar the objective'?" Sadie couldn't help herself. "Our objective is to be stewards of history, and if things are being stolen, we're not doing our jobs."

"*You're* not doing your job." Dr. Hooper stared hard at Sadie, then Claude, then Nick, like they were misbehaving students, before turning on his heel and leaving.

That was enough. Sadie grabbed her coat and left as well, not looking at Claude or Nick. Claude, because she already knew he had a smirk on his face. Nick, because she couldn't bear to see the look of pity that must be there. Pity at what an ass she'd made of herself, between the *Surviving Spinsterhood* book, her failure at her job, and that awful showdown with Claude.

She mulled it all over as she headed downtown on the subway, staring at the filthy floor and strangers' shoes. She hadn't misread Claude's signals: he'd wanted to pursue the relationship with her after that kiss, right until she'd shut him down, hard, without an explanation. And even though her reasons for doing so had been sound—he *was* a big flirt, and other than work, they really didn't have much in common—the mature thing would have been to have a private chat with him. Either way, she knew deep down that she'd made her choices out of fear. Because after Phillip, she simply hadn't had the courage to take any risks. The thought of loving someone again and then losing them cut her to pieces inside.

She entered CBGB, asked the bartender to hold her purse and NPR tote bag behind the bar, and pushed her way into the crowd. Even though it was early, some kind of band marathon was already in full swing.

The kids on the floor didn't bother to make room for her, but that was fine. She wanted to have to force her way in, to be pushed by shoulders and elbows and arms, knowing that tomorrow's bruises would be the price of admission. The band members onstage were five tattooed, skinny boys who screamed unintelligible lyrics to the appreciative crowd. Being inside the mob made her feel part of something, never mind the danger. She found her footing and bounced up and down in time with the bass drum, eyes closed, her senses on fire, filled with energy. The air smelled like cigarette smoke and sweat. She'd open her eyes for a moment and catch a glimpse of a nose ring, a tattoo on a neck, a bead of sweat rolling down the side of a cheek. It was as if the crowd were providing the electricity for the amps and guitars with its wild gyrations, not the other way around.

Finally, after a few songs, she retreated to the bar.

Nick was sitting there, waiting.

She asked for her bags from the bartender and walked by him without saying anything, but he followed her outside. She whirled around, the cool air evaporating the sweat on her skin. She must look a treat, with her hair a mess, smelling of smoke and beer.

"If you think I'm the thief, stop trailing me around and just arrest me or whatever you're supposed to do," she said.

"I followed you because I knew you were upset." He gestured toward the club door with his thumb. "You letting off steam?"

"Exactly right, Mr. Tango."

"Mr. Salsa, to you. I think it's great."

She paused. "You do?"

"Sure. It's anarchy in there. I like the contrast. Prim librarian during the day, punk rocker at night."

"They think I'm a joke in there." Tears came to her eyes. Why was she telling him this? "Just like with Claude." She paused. "This is all so embarrassing."

With Nick last night, first dancing and then talking in the diner, Sadie had opened herself up to the possibility of taking a risk. She loved how his brow furrowed when he was really concentrating, and the fact that he enjoyed poetry as much as he enjoyed tracking down thieves. She could continue guarding against betrayal and hurt by shutting herself off from even the idea of love, but in many ways, that was no different from protecting the folio from vandals by locking it away in a sealed vault, or attempting to protect her job by hiding information from the past that might be relevant to the present.

It was time to come clean. No more secrets.

"Can we go somewhere?" Sadie said. "I have something to tell you."

CHAPTER EIGHTEEN

New York City, 1993

Sadie and Nick walked up Lafayette Street and sat on the steps of the Public Theater. If she didn't figure out who was behind the thefts, if her reputation as a librarian was sullied, it would be hard to find work elsewhere, and then what would she do?

"I'm related to Laura Lyons, the essayist, whose husband, Jack Lyons, was a superintendent for the New York Public Library back in the early 1910s. They were my grandparents."

"Is that so?"

"Yes. Lyons was my mother's maiden name. She spent a few years living in the library as a young girl. When I first came to work at the library, I was curious about the old apartment they'd lived in, what their lives were like. I did some research and didn't like what I found."

"What was that?"

"That Jack and Laura Lyons were under suspicion for book thefts when they lived there. At the time, Laura Lyons wasn't the big deal she is now, so I didn't feel the need to mention it. But I recently found out information that was more disturbing."

"How do you mean?"

"Apparently, before my mother passed away, she hinted that her father—Jack Lyons—stole a 'tambourine.' I only just heard about this. From my six-year-old niece, so it's not exactly veri-fiable."

"A tambourine . . . the *Tamerlane*?" Nick considered it. "So you think that your grandfather stole that book back in 1913? The one that's never been recovered?"

"To be honest, it's all really murky. My mother also said some-thing about how they had to leave the library because of a burning book. I have no idea what that means."

Nick looked at her closely. "What happened to your grand-father?"

"He died in 1914. There's a chance he committed suicide." She explained about the last entry in his diary: *stepladder, rope, note.*

Nick looked out into the street. "It's likely not related, but I need to pursue every angle I can, so you should have told me from the start. If there's anything useful there, I need to know it." He paused. "You should inform Dr. Hooper of your connection to the Lyons family, I would think."

"I will. First thing Monday morning, I promise."

Nick stood. The conversation was over. She got up as well.

It felt good, to have this out in the open, finally.

"I want you to show me everything you've found in the ar-chives," he said.

"That's fine. I'll meet you in the Rare Book Room tomorrow at four. Will that work?"

"Tomorrow at four. And no more secrets."

"No more secrets."

On Saturday, Sadie and Nick set up a workstation at one of the corner tables in the Rare Book Room. She showed him the note the library detective wrote to the director, the one that said that it was as if the thief had "dropped from the sky."

As he studied it, she asked if he'd heard any news from the bookseller.

"The owner of J&M insists the books were sent by messenger to him, that he never met the seller. His instructions were to send the money by wire to an overseas account."

They fell silent as they made their way through years' worth of files and notes.

Sadie gave a sharp intake of breath.

"What is it?" Nick leaned over to see.

"I've been going through the 1915 correspondence from the director, in case anything had been mislaid." Something had. She handed it over to him. "The detective's file, from 1914, ended up there."

The very first document was a note, signed by Sadie's grandfather. It consisted of only a few lines, in careful cursive:

I'm sorry for the trouble I caused the library. The fault is mine, as is the shame. Please tell my family I love them.—Jack Lyons

Sadie sat back. "It's a suicide note."

Nick came up behind her and read it, then touched her arm lightly. "I'm sorry, Sadie."

"So this means my grandfather was definitely the thief?"

It was more a rhetorical question, but Nick answered. "Looks like it."

That explained Laura Lyons's intense privacy, coming off of a scandal like this. A family, broken. And Sadie's mother, Pearl, knew about it all along.

She sifted through the file. "It looks like the books from the 1914 theft were also stolen from a caged-off area."

"Where does it say that?"

"Here." She pointed to the page. "It lists the original locations of the missing books. Including the *Tamerlane* and a first edition of *Leaves of Grass*." She looked out across the room, lost in thought. "'Dropped from the sky.'"

Nick looked over at her. "What?"

"Such a strange phrase. That it was as if the thief 'dropped from the sky.' If we can solve that, maybe we can figure out how our own thief is getting access." She stood up, letting the answer wash over her. "I have an idea."

After returning the archives, she and Nick headed to the Art and Architecture Room, on the south side of the building. Sadie approached the desk and asked for any architectural plans of the library, waiting impatiently while the clerk fetched them.

Sadie rolled them out on one of the tables. "No good. These are too recent, you can see the stacks under Bryant Park are included." She turned back to the clerk. "Are there any of the original floor plans? From when it first opened?"

The clerk checked the records. "There are, but you'll have to come back Monday." He pointed at his watch. Closing time.

They filed out, standing in the hallway as the exiting patrons streamed around them. "I'm sorry about what we've learned today," said Nick. "I hope that isn't too difficult for you."

"The signs were all there, so I'm not surprised. It ripped apart the family, and I can see how it affected my mother for the rest of her life. I'm just sorry that I wasn't able to talk to her about it, that she died before I figured this out."

Nick gazed down at her. "I have to go. But I look forward to straightening this all out."

"Me, too. I think we're close, I think there's a connection with the past. And I'm going to do everything in my power to catch the thief."

"Oh, I have no doubt of that. I don't know what I would've done without your help this past month, so thank you."

His acknowledgment of their partnership gave her a strange rush; she wanted to burst into tears and laughter at the same time. Instead, she offered up a sober nod. "My pleasure."

After he left, she finished up some paperwork at her desk, still thinking about the detective's letter. *Dropped from the sky*. If the thief didn't have the key, maybe there was something in the ceiling, some kind of hatch that he could access from the floor above the Berg's cage. She tried to picture the ceiling, but couldn't. It hadn't ever occurred to her to look up.

The stacks, after hours, loomed large in the dim light from the windows, each aisle a narrow canyon of books. Sadie turned on the light and was about thirty feet into the stacks when she heard a strange scraping sound, like someone was raking cement. She froze, listening, scanning the space for any movement, but all was still. Probably just the library's ventilation system acting up.

"Anyone here?"

Her voice echoed around the stacks, with no reply.

She walked as quietly as she could toward the Berg section and peered around the corner. It was empty. Her nerves were just getting to her. She unlocked the cage and looked up, studying the ceiling. Solid steel. As she stepped back, still looking up, she almost tripped.

The cover to one of the gray storage boxes stuck out partway from the bottom shelf, and she'd kicked it with her heel. She knelt down. Beside it lay the bottom half of the box.

The label read, *JANE EYRE by Currer Bell (Charlotte Brontë), first edition (1847); three volumes.*

Yet only two of the small volumes were nestled inside.

She glanced around, scanning the shelves, the floor. Nothing.

The thief had been here. And might still be. Slowly, she rose to her feet, listening intently for any sign that she wasn't alone.

She exited the cage, locking it quietly behind her. As she did so, the sound of a door slamming shut rang out.

He was getting away.

Sadie took off running down the aisle and back out the door she'd come in. She took the stairs two at a time, listening hard as the footfalls of the thief above her crossed the landing of the second floor and kept on, up to the third. As she reached the landing, she almost tripped over something.

The missing *Jane Eyre* volume lay splayed on the marble floor, like a broken bird.

She scooped it up, tucking it into the top of her dress for safe-keeping, before flying up the final set of stairs to the third floor.

At the very top step, her foot caught the riser and she was suddenly in midair before falling hard, her knee slamming down first and her hands taking the rest of the hit. The book flew out of her dress and skidded across the floor.

It came to a stop before two pairs of black, polished oxford shoes.

"Sadie?"

Dr. Hooper and Nick stared down at her in surprise. Nick helped her up as Dr. Hooper gingerly picked up the fallen book.

"What are you doing?"

She couldn't speak; the wind had been completely knocked out of her by her awkward splat. She finally caught her breath. "I was down in the cage. The thief was there. I ran after him. He's up here."

Dr. Hooper looked curiously at her. "Are you sure? We didn't see anyone go by."

She nodded, still panting. "Yes. Here, somewhere." She ran to the door at the end of the hall that led to the Art and Architecture Room. Locked. She tried the others on the hall, and Nick, following her lead, did the same on the other side. All locked. Only the women's room was open, and Sadie dashed inside, ready to corner her prey, but every stall was empty.

She walked out, deflated and confused. "He had a good lead on me, but you must have seen him. We had him cornered, between the three of us. Where did he go?"

Dr. Hooper didn't seem concerned about the thief; instead, he stared at Sadie, his jaw tense.

In a rush, she realized what this must look like. A crazed woman in possession of a rare book, chasing an imaginary quarry.

Alone, in the library, after hours. The thief.

CHAPTER NINETEEN

New York City, 1914

Laura cut through the Catalog Room both heart-happy and heart-sick. Amelia wanted her to go to London, but it could never happen. In fact, Laura had vowed, only half joking, to do everything in her power to get Amelia to stay in New York. This coming summer was all she had to convince Amelia not to go away, not to leave her behind. At least once a day, while riding the el or sweeping the apartment floor, Laura would disappear into a dreamworld where she could act on her wildest impulses, where she and Amelia would create a life together, Harry and Pearl in tow. Jack would be upset at first but would easily find a new wife— one who was eager to fill that role in a way that Laura simply wasn't—and they'd all remain friends.

But that was only a dream.

Laura's mother had always encouraged her to follow her passion. With Jack, that had yielded wonders, including the children.

Well, this was a new passion, one that she hadn't expected but wanted to explore further. Why not? Men did so all the time, with other women, with their work. Last night, Jack had explained over dinner that he needed to spend every extra moment working on the manuscript edits if he was to meet the deadline. That was his passion, his mistress. And Amelia was hers.

Then again, how would Laura feel if Jack had an actual mistress? Another question she preferred not to delve into. He was a good man, and he would be devastated if he knew she'd found physical love elsewhere. She had to take time and figure this out, for the sake of her children, her family.

Amelia had suggested Laura speak at Saturday's Heterodoxy Club meeting, on the issue of suffrage, as a way to impress the members with her writing skills. Laura was excited to see what she could come up with. It was also a way to keep her mind from whirling away with thoughts of Amelia, and how destroyed she'd be if their love fell apart.

She filled out several call slips, waited for the books to be retrieved from the stacks, and took a seat at one of the long tables, eager to lose herself in her research. Three hours later, her eyes burning with fatigue, she headed to the Periodical Room on the first floor. The *New York Times* had recently published an interview with one of the leaders of the New York suffrage movement, Mrs. Alva Belmont, and Laura wanted to refer to it in her talk.

Jack had admonished her when she'd first stepped inside the Periodical Room and joked that it resembled the lair of a gout-ridden monopolist, with its dark French walnut walls and opulent doorway. On closer inspection, she'd discovered subtle surprises scattered throughout, like the pair of dolphins carved into the table pedestal and the ceiling panels that featured roosters and eagles. Since then, she never ceased to be amazed at the way the building's architects, John Merven Carrère and Thomas Hastings, had injected a refreshing air of whimsy into their stately edifice. You just had to know where to look.

She took the remaining vacant chair, where the *New York World*, Joseph Pulitzer's newspaper, lay open on the tabletop. The same man who'd founded the journalism school. The reminder of her failure made her wince.

As she went to fold it up and move it out of her way, a headline caught her eye.

THE SECRET CLUB OF THE MODERN WOMAN, REVEALED.

No, it couldn't be.

Laura recognized the first paragraph as her own words, then the next, and the next. The entire article took up three columns, far less than her master's thesis but longer than any others on the page. Her work had been edited down to include all the more sala-cious comments of the women, and anything that put their words and statements into context had been cut. The end result sug-gested the Heterodoxy Club was a den of insatiable vixens, deter-mined to overturn the patriarchal world order by force.

At the very bottom ran the byline: *An exclusive to The New York World written by Mr. George Wakeman, professor at the Columbia University School of Journalism.*

The vile man had published her story as his own. If the mem-bers of the club saw this, they'd know she was behind it, or, at the very least, had supplied the information. She'd be cut off, reviled. She sank down in one of the chairs, not trusting her legs, her hands curled into fists. Amelia would hate her after this, think that she'd been using her the entire time, all in the hopes of getting a scoop.

"It wasn't meant for publication."

Her voice sounded far off, like it wasn't her own, and was quickly answered with the librarian's loud shush.

She gathered her things and fled.

Laura arrived late to the Saturday meeting of the Heterodoxy Club, exactly what she didn't want to do, but Harry had complained of a tummy ache, so she'd given him a couple of digestive tablets before she'd left and tucked him back in bed. Jack would be working in his study in the apartment all day, and promised to keep an eye on the boy.

Her hope had been to get there early and pull Amelia and the other members she knew well aside and explain what had happened. Instead, she walked in just as the meeting was commencing, everyone in their seats and Marie Jenney Howe, the club's founder, up front.

To her dismay, Marie held a copy of the *New York World* in her hand.

Laura had admired Marie for her calm demeanor during the meetings she'd attended—no matter how heated the discussions became—but now she turned to Laura with scorn. "The perpetrator has arrived."

Laura spotted Amelia in the front row but couldn't meet her gaze, her shame was so complete. Legs shaking, she walked to the front of the room, leaving a good five feet between her and Marie.

"I'm so sorry, it was a misunderstanding," Laura began, but a woman in the back interrupted her.

"Get out. Or are you going to run back to your typewriter and write about *this* now?"

Marie held out one hand. "Enough. Mrs. Lyons, the rules were made clear to you from the beginning, that any discussion within this room is off the record. We did that so that our members could feel free to talk and explore radical ideas without having it skewed by the press. According to the members quoted, the information in this article can only have been provided by you, regardless of whose name is on it. You have misrepresented everything we stand for, everything we've said. What do you have to say about this?"

Laura took a deep breath. "My deepest apologies, to you and to the rest of the membership. I wrote a story about the club for a class at Columbia, it's true, but it was never to be published, I swear. Without my knowledge, my advisor edited it dramatically and then submitted to the *New York World* under his own byline. I had no idea that this would happen. I respect everything that you're doing and fighting for and would have never allowed it, had I known."

Laura stood there, waiting for her judgment like a criminal on trial. The exposure seared her every nerve, like she was on fire.

"The damage you've inflicted on our reputations and our efforts is immeasurable," said Marie, finally. "You are expelled from the club. You must leave at once."

Laura did so, not looking at any of the members but feeling every glare as if it were an arrow. She made it to the stairs and out the front door and paused, clutching the railing. What a mess she made of things, no matter what she tried to do.

She'd burned all her sources and contacts for the book, for any future articles, in one fell swoop. She'd set herself up for this failure by falling for the allure of the forbidden, and had no one to blame but herself. Out on the street, a woman passing by looked up at Laura with concern, and she realized she was crying fat tears of self-pity. Laura brushed them away and tried to collect herself.

The loss of the community of women stung hardest, as she had no similar role models in her life. They were taking a completely different tack from the other women she knew, and she'd desperately wanted to be part of that sea change. Not anymore. All ruined. The loss of Amelia stung hardest. How she'd let her down, betrayed her, in front of all her colleagues and friends. Laura would never forgive herself for having caused Amelia pain.

She started up the street, figuring she'd walk all the way home as punishment for her crimes.

"Laura!"

Laura waited for Amelia to catch up. The fact that she'd left the meeting to come after her, a courageous thing to do, didn't surprise Laura. That was how Amelia carved her path through the world, by never being afraid of what others thought or said. If only Laura were that strong.

"You were brave to come, Laura."

"I had to. I owed them that much, although I knew it wouldn't amount to anything. But you believe me, right? That I didn't know it would be published? I swear, I just found out yesterday. The professor stole my article, without my permission. Worse than that, he edited it to make it sound negative. Remember, I told you that he'd stolen the ideas of other students?"

"I remember."

Laura let out a sigh of relief. "Thank God."

"I don't forgive you, though." Her voice was cold, ferocious.

"But I never meant for it to happen."

Amelia looked down at the ground, then back up at Laura, as if she were trying to compose herself. "You never should have written about the club in the first place." Laura tried to respond, but Amelia held up her hand. "You used me, you used all of us, to impress your professor. Well, nicely done, that worked like a charm. He loved your idea so much he stole it. But it's still your fault, all your fault, that we're being vilified in the press. You set this in motion, not him. And what about the future of the club? What woman will join us and believe she can speak openly, going forward? I'm so mad I could spit, Laura."

"I'm sorry. I hate the fact that I disappointed you."

"Me? What about all of them?"

"Yes, of course. But you most of all. Please, Amelia, you have to forgive me."

"Why?"

The answer didn't come. Laura couldn't form the words because she knew it was all over from the way Amelia was looking at her, as if she was worthless, an utter disappointment. There would be no more conversations in front of the fire, no more kisses. She tried to remember their last kiss, but couldn't. How could that be? If she'd known it was the last, she would have lingered, drawing Amelia's breath into her own lungs.

Shame enveloped her. For the past year, Laura had been searching for fulfillment and found it in Amelia and in her own work.

Now both were gone, destroyed by her own hand.

She turned to go, knowing that if she stayed a moment longer, her heart would blister and break.

CHAPTER TWENTY

New York City, 1914

Laura entered the library apartment, steeling herself to not fall apart amid the bustle of family life, and was taken aback by the silence. Maybe Jack had brought the children to the park, in which case Harry must be feeling better. In the kitchen, she was pulling items out of the icebox for dinner when Pearl appeared in the doorway.

Laura blanched when she saw her daughter's tear-streaked face. "Pearl? What's wrong?"

"You're finally home. Where have you been?"

"I was downtown." She knelt down in front of the girl. "What's happened? Where are your father and Harry?"

Laura couldn't make out her response as Pearl sobbed into her shoulder. "Where?"

Pearl lifted her head. "The hospital. Bellevue."

Laura rose abruptly. "What happened?"

"Harry was sick, he went into a spell. Father raced out with him and told me to wait for you."

"How long ago was that?"

"I don't know."

Laura took her hand. "We must go now."

After a slog through traffic in a cab and a dizzying run through the halls of the hospital, practically dragging Pearl behind her, Laura spotted Jack sitting outside a door. The look of relief on his face as she approached only added to the brick of guilt building inside her.

"Is Harry inside?" She put her hand on the knob, but Jack stopped her.

"We can't go in. It's not safe."

"Why not?" Through the glass, she could see rows of beds filled with children, with only a few nurses flitting around.

"He's very sick. Here, sit with me."

"No, I must see him."

"They won't let you in. I tried. Besides, it's locked."

She turned the handle to confirm it herself. "Tell me everything."

"It's typhoid."

She shook her head. "That can't be. It doesn't make sense." The drinking water for the library was brought down via an aqueduct from the reservoirs upstate, and safe.

A doctor in a white coat approached. Jack lurched toward him, grabbing his elbow. "Doctor, if you have a moment."

The doctor pulled his arm away, annoyed, and knocked on the door. "I can't talk right now, sir." He nodded to one of the nurses inside, who unlocked it.

"Can we please see our son?" Laura asked.

The doctor barely glanced their way. "No, you may not. Not yet, anyway."

As Laura began to cry, the doctor let out an exasperated sigh. "Which one is yours?"

"Harry Lyons," Jack replied.

"Right. Just brought in. How long has he had a dry cough?"

Laura thought back, relieved to have something specific to concentrate on. It'd been before she'd failed out of Columbia. She'd been consumed with her thesis, and when Harry had approached complaining about a sore throat, she'd felt his forehead and turned back to work, determined to meet her deadline. She whispered her answer. "About two weeks."

"It slowly became worse and worse?"

"I guess so. Yes." She should have never left him today. She'd been so selfish.

"Did you notice any small red spots on his shoulders and chest?"

Jack jumped in. "This morning, he came to me, feeling miserable, and showed them to me. Then he went back to bed, and when I went to check on him, he wouldn't respond."

"He's fallen into what's called the typhoid state. We'll do what we can to take care of him, but he should have been brought to us sooner. Meanwhile, you should get the vaccine. Don't listen to the idiots who say that it causes tuberculosis. It's perfectly safe."

"Of course. How long until we can see our son?" asked Laura.

"When he gets better. If he gets better. In the meantime, be sure to tell the teachers at his school that he has it. We don't want an outbreak."

The doctor closed the door behind him with a thud. Laura pressed her face to the glass, searching for Harry. She spotted his profile, with that familiar snub of a nose, in the bed farthest from the door, his eyes closed. His cheeks were red, as if he'd been slapped. How had she not known?

Typhoid. The same illness that had killed Amelia's father and brother. She whirled around to Jack. "We have to fetch Amelia. She knows typhoid well, she'll be able to help."

"Yes. If you think so." Jack frowned. "I thought you'd be home a few hours ago, after you'd said your piece at the meeting."

"I know, I'm so sorry. I ended up walking home." What an utter waste of time, bemoaning her sorry state when she should have been by her son's side.

Through the window, Harry opened his mouth and shut it again. Had he called out for her? None of the nurses responded. This was torture, watching him suffer and not being able to hold his hand or comfort him in any way. She wanted to break through the glass, open the door, and gather him up in her arms.

She arranged for her mother to come and take Pearl home, and then Jack and Laura spent the rest of the day like sentries outside the ward, asking questions of anyone, nurse or doctor, who came in or out. One nurse had kindly offered to encourage Harry to look over at them, and to Laura's delight, he had, his eyes focusing on her own and a slight smile on his lips. It had felt like a victory, that interaction. He knew they were there; he knew he was being looked after.

As the city darkened outside the window at the end of the hallway, Laura heard a familiar step, the even, solid strides of Amelia. She'd received her note. Amelia asked Laura and Jack some questions, speaking in clipped tones, laying her hand once on Laura's arm in comfort. The touch was kind, reassuring, but that was all. She requested that a nurse fetch the doctor, and the nurse blinked with recognition before disappearing down the hall.

The doctor appeared, the scorn in his voice replaced with cheery bonhomie. "Dr. Potter, I'm Dr. Bell. We're thrilled to have you visit our ward."

"Thank you. I'm concerned about one of your patients, Harry Lyons. I'm a dear friend of his mother, you see." She glanced at Laura.

"Of course. Would you like to join me in examining the patient?"

Amelia checked with Laura, who emphatically approved.

She and Jack watched again through the window as the two doctors spoke to Harry, who giggled at something Amelia said.

Finally, they reemerged. "Harry's doing quite well," said Amelia. "Dr. Bell has assured me he will keep me informed, and you also. We predict a full recovery."

The doctor smiled widely at them before taking his leave.

"Thank you, Amelia, for coming uptown." Laura swallowed. "I know you're busy."

"Of course. I'm happy to help in whatever way I can."

Jack stepped in closer and held out his hand. "Dr. Potter, as my wife said, it was kind of you to put in a good word with Dr. Bell. Our family appreciates it, very much."

"You're welcome, Mr. Lyons."

A silence rose. Seeing Amelia again was strange, like meeting a confidante and a stranger all at once. Laura knew everything about her—that she liked her tea with two sugars and had a birthmark on her lower back—yet her face at this moment was a fortress, impenetrable. Once again, Amelia had done Laura an enormous favor, and Laura had nothing to offer in return. She probably couldn't wait to get away fast enough. "You must need to get back. Thank you again."

With that, Amelia turned and left, meeting Laura's eyes only briefly.

By Monday, Harry was sitting up in bed and eating again. The kind nurse read a letter to Harry from Laura and Jack, saying they loved him and to focus on getting well. Harry had even managed a small wave.

"You might as well go about your business," said Dr. Bell on Monday morning. "You can't do any good sitting around here."

Laura sat back down on the bench, like a passenger waiting for a train that would never arrive. Jack joined her but soon became twitchy, alternating between standing and sitting, pacing and staring through the window. After a half hour he turned to Laura. "I might as well go back, since the doctor says we should. I can get some work done on the book."

She didn't reply.

Around four o'clock, remembering the doctor's warning, Laura stopped by the school. She was promptly shown to the principal's office, where a long, thin man sat behind a desk drumming his fingers at her. "Mrs. Lyons."

"Yes." Laura explained the situation, that the other students should be sure to be vaccinated, as she, Jack, and Pearl all had been.

"Typhoid?" The principal stopped drumming. "We'll warn the parents. When exactly did he fall ill?"

"A couple of weeks ago. I didn't notice at first, thought it was a cold. There was just a cough, you see. That's how it began, and I never suspected it could be so serious."

He waved away her explanation. "It's fine, then. There's no danger."

"I'm sorry?" She couldn't figure out what he meant. That because Harry was recovering, the other students couldn't be infected? She wasn't sure how it all worked, but this didn't make much sense.

"None of the students could have been infected if he only came down with it two weeks ago," said the principal.

"Why is that?"

He consulted a leather notebook filled with names and X's, an attendance record. "Here it is. Yes, I'm correct."

She buzzed with fury. The man was being cagey, and she wasn't sure why. Harry's illness brought her impatience to a sharp point. "Correct about what?"

"Harry hasn't been in school for two months now."

"Harry? Harry Lyons? Of course he has."

"I'm afraid not, Mrs. Lyons." He licked his finger and turned the page. "Two months. We sent home a note with your daughter after the first week, but didn't get a reply. Between that and his illness, which of course is quite unfortunate, he'll have to repeat the same grade next year."

Part of her wanted to laugh. The thought of Harry being held back was much less important today than it might have been a few days earlier, before he'd fallen ill. At least he was alive.

But why hadn't he come to school for two months?

And where had he been?

The note that the principal had given Pearl sat beneath a pile of books on Jack's desk. Laura had a feeling that Pearl hadn't wanted to get her brother into trouble and had tucked it away where there was a good chance it would be overlooked. If Laura had been home instead of at school or out reporting, Pearl probably would have handed it right over. Laura blamed herself, not her daughter, for the lapse. Upon questioning, Pearl had insisted that Harry walked into school with her and was always waiting at the end of the school day in the playground, ready to walk her home. As far as she knew, he'd been inside the whole time, like her.

The next day, Laura checked in with Harry at the hospital and was thrilled to learn he'd been moved out of quarantine and into a children's ward, where she could sit with him in the mornings. He was still subdued, sleeping most of the time, but the fever had subsided and his prognosis was good. She wanted to pepper him with questions but held back. She certainly didn't want to upset him while he was still fragile.

That afternoon, she showed up early to the children's school for dismissal. As she waited for Pearl to appear, she scanned the crowd until she found a boy who looked familiar. Sam was his name, she recalled. He'd come home with Harry once or twice early in the school year. Jack had caught them playing baseball in the Stuart Room, using books as bases, and let them off lightly, much to Laura's relief. It wasn't easy growing up in a revered institution like the library.

"Sam?"

The boy turned.

"I'm Harry's mother. You visited us at the library." She moved closer and bent down, so they were face-to-face. "I understand Harry hasn't been in school recently. Do you happen to know where he's been going?"

Sam shrugged.

"It's fine for you to tell me. You see, he's gotten very sick, which might have gotten the people around him very sick. You'd be a hero if you let me know anything at all."

At the word "hero," the boy came to life, standing a little taller and looking her in the eye. "He started to go downtown to Fourth Avenue, with some boys."

"Where, exactly?"

"Around Union Square."

"Would I know any of the boys? How might I recognize them?"

"One used to go to school here. Red Paddy."

"That's his name?"

"He has ginger hair, you see."

"You are incredibly helpful, Sam. You say he used to go to school here?"

"I haven't seen him in a while. He doesn't come to school anymore."

"Is he your age?"

"No. Older, around fifteen."

What was Harry doing being friends with an older boy like that, one who dropped out of school? She should have known all this. If she'd been home, she might have noticed. Surely she would have.

She thanked Sam and, after escorting Pearl home and getting her started on her homework, put her coat back on.

"Are you leaving again?" Pearl watched her from the doorway to the kitchen.

Laura kissed her on the forehead. "I'm sorry, love. I have to find out where Harry's been all this time. I'll be back for dinner."

Union Square was bustling with cars and pedestrians but no redheaded boys, as far as Laura could tell. She walked down Fourth Avenue a few blocks, peering into alleyways. No luck.

Back in the square, she wandered the perimeter, imagining her son here, doing . . . what? Nothing that the principal or Sam had told her made any sense. Harry wasn't the sort of boy to cut school and lie to her and Jack. He was sensitive, empathetic, listening closely when she and Jack had an argument, his eyes darting back and forth between his parents. These days, with the tension between her and Jack so high, he had probably needed more reassurance than she'd given.

Somehow, she'd always believed that if she just loved everyone enough, all would be well, that love would be the snowfall that blanketed the crevasses and jagged edges of their world, smoothing them out into a gentle field of white. Maybe she was wrong.

A flash of color caught her eye. A group of boys were gathered under the statue of George Washington on a horse, and the tallest one had a crop of ginger-colored hair under his cap.

She waited until she was only a few yards away to call out, and didn't shout. She didn't want to scare them off and watch them scatter. "Red Paddy?"

The boy sauntered right up to her, with an insouciance she would otherwise never have tolerated in a child that age. "Who wants to know?"

"I'm the mother of Harry Lyons."

The boy's eyes didn't flicker. "So?"

"He's sick. With typhoid. I wanted to warn you to be careful, in case he passed it on to you."

Red Paddy surveyed his audience with a crooked grin. "What do you think, boys, are we sick? Anyone about to faint? Let me know and I'll catch you." The last sentence was directed at Laura with a leer.

"You must be serious about this. It's a terrible disease. Harry has been very ill."

"Don't know anyone named that."

"You aren't in any trouble, I promise. I just want to know what he's been doing these past couple of months. We know he didn't go to school. Did you meet at school, is that what happened? And then decided to cut class?" She babbled on, desperate to connect. "I don't blame you, of course, but I need to know."

"I told you, woman, I don't know a Harry."

The other boys snickered.

She tried one more time. "Please, I'll pay you some money, if that's what you want. My husband and I, we just want to know why."

"We don't want your money. We don't know you, don't know him." Red Paddy spit on the ground near her feet.

"If any of you feel ill, please go to a doctor right away."

"We don't get sick, not us toughies. It's the soft uptown boys that get sick."

He was referring to Harry, Laura was certain. "So you know my son, right? Is that true?"

But already the boys had withdrawn, heading south, Red Paddy the last to follow. He touched Laura on the arm, and she had to stop herself from yanking it away. "I don't know anyone. But I'd like to know you better. What do you say we get together some time?"

"You're very rude. I'm sure your mother and father wouldn't be happy about what you're up to, getting young boys into trouble. He nearly died, I'll have you know."

Red Paddy just laughed, giving her arm a squeeze before stepping back, looking her up and down. "You tell him to get well soon from me, then, Mum."

She watched them dash across Fourteenth Street, nearly getting run down by a carriage before disappearing into the crowd.

Poor Harry. What had happened for him to seek out these boys?

Laura should have been home instead of out reporting on violent protests and radical women's clubs for her studies. Her family had almost sunk without her sure hand on the tiller. Her choices had been all wrong. The fact that she'd so enjoyed the past seven months only made her failure more damning.

There was nothing more for her to do here, downtown. It was time to go home and put right what had gone wrong. Hopefully, by tomorrow, Harry would be well enough to speak, and she could beg his forgiveness for having neglected him.

She would make her family whole again.

CHAPTER TWENTY-ONE

New York City, 1993

Sadie spent what felt like the longest weekend of her life holed up in her apartment. Outside, she heard the cries of the children on the playground across the street, a reminder that she really should return Lonnie's check-in call and have a chat with Valentina, but she didn't feel like it. He'd detect her nervousness and ask why, and she didn't want to have to explain that she'd been banished from the library by Dr. Hooper. Even worse would be pretending to be happy for Valentina's sake. She didn't have it in her.

Instead, she reworked the draft of the catalog for the exhibit, making the essay as taut and instructive as possible, cutting down any extraneousness prose. All the previous week, the workers had been toiling in the exhibit hall next door to the Berg Collection, placing the cases where she'd instructed them. They were so close to the finish line.

It was all she could do not to return to the library, carry on as she had before. But Nick and Dr. Hooper had made it clear that, at least for the weekend, she was not to appear, and had confiscated her key. Which was ridiculous, as now Dr. Hooper was the only one with a key, and unless he planned on running the library and mounting the exhibit as well, there was no one left to make *Evergreen* happen. Monday at nine o'clock sharp, she had an appointment at Dr. Hooper's office. She hated not being able to explain what she'd seen before then.

Now that she'd had a chance to collect herself, she felt it more important than ever to be able to describe to Dr. Hooper and Nick what she'd heard—or, more specifically, not heard: that there was no slamming of the door to the cage. Whoever was in there hadn't used the door to get in and out.

As soon as she explained that to Dr. Hooper, she'd hightail it to the Art and Architecture Room to take a close look at the original floor plan of the library. There had to be something that they were missing, a way for the thief to get access so easily and then escape into thin air. That scraping noise she'd heard before the thief fled—if she could get back into the stacks, she might be able to figure out what had caused it. There was so much to do.

She tried calling Nick at home, but his answering machine picked up, his voice growling for the caller to leave a message. She'd hung up without doing so. Whatever it was that had been blossoming between them was in terrible jeopardy. Right when she'd been ready to take a chance, everything had fallen apart.

By the time her Monday morning meeting rolled around, Sadie's nerves were at a breaking point. Nick stood, refusing to take the chair next to her, as Dr. Hooper loomed behind his walnut desk like a Supreme Court justice. Which, in her case, he was, really.

"Please, Sadie, we'd like to hear what happened on Saturday

night." Dr. Hooper placed his elbows on the desk and put his hands together, index fingers pointed out like the silly game she used to play as a child. *Here's the church, here's the steeple.* The nursery rhyme buzzed through her head.

"Sadie?"

She gave her head a shake. "Sorry. You see, I was in the stacks when I heard something. Although I wasn't able to see the thief, I think we can figure out how he got down there. I have an appointment with the Art and Architecture division right after this—"

"Sadie, stop."

She did so, surprised by Dr. Hooper's harsh interruption.

"Let me explain the way I see this. You are the only employee, other than me, with access to the Berg Collection in the stacks. On a Saturday evening, after the library had closed, we came upon you with one of the rare books hidden on your person."

She had to clear things up, fast. "It wasn't hidden. The thief had dropped it, and I wanted to keep it safe as I ran up the stairs after him."

"Did you see the thief?"

"I told you, no. But I could hear him running away from me."

"Yet we were right there and we didn't see or hear anyone. You can see why we're worried. About you, and about the collection."

"I'm fine." She pulled out the essay from her tote bag, desperate to discuss logistics, get things back on track. "Here's the essay for the catalog, all ready to go. The exhibit cases are almost ready. In the meantime, I need to see the library's original floor plan. The answer's there, I'm certain."

Dr. Hooper took the essay and placed it on the corner of his desk without looking at it. "Mr. Adriano has informed me of something else."

She looked over at Nick, who refused to meet her eye.

"He said that you're related to Laura Lyons. I find it curious that you never mentioned the family connection when we spoke of her. I don't like secrets, and it makes me wonder what else you've been keeping from me." He paused. "I'm afraid we have to ask you to take a leave of absence. Until we determine our next steps."

She hadn't even gotten to tell her own story. "Leave of absence?" Sadie shook her head. "But I can help. Don't you see?"

"For now, no. We will not need your assistance. Nick will escort you to your office so you can take any personal effects with you."

"But the floor plan. The exhibit."

"Sorry, Sadie. It hurts me to do this, but we must."

She didn't speak to Nick until they were walking down the hallway toward the Berg Collection. "I know the way it looks, but we're so close to figuring this out. There's something we're missing."

"You'll have to stay out of the building until the board of trustees can be informed and I can do more investigating."

She stopped and made him face her. "You think it might be me, don't you?"

He didn't answer right away, but the way he avoided her eyes said it all. "You've been under a lot of pressure lately. Your mother's death, this exhibit. Maybe you need some time to rest."

"Exactly what I don't need is rest. What I need is to figure out what's going on." Her heart thudded in her chest.

She reached out and touched the sleeve of his shirt.

"Sadie, no."

He pulled away, and she let her hand hang there, in midair.

He didn't trust her anymore. She'd lost him. But it was worse than that. "I know what you're thinking, Nick. And you're wrong."

"What's that?"

"That maybe I manufactured this thing between us, our friendship, whatever it is, so I could get away with stealing books. Is that what you believe?"

"I don't know. I've gotten confused, too close, and that's not good. I have to keep a clear head."

She'd brought the whole world crashing down around her.

Sadie wiped her tears away before they entered the Berg, where Claude looked up, victorious, from his desk. A couple of scholars were there, which made any further discussion impossible and for which she was grateful.

She collected her things and let Nick escort her downstairs.

She was on her own.

"So are you fired? Or is it a leave of absence?"

Lonnie poured out two glasses of wine and set one in front of Sadie. Valentina and Robin were doing homework together in the other room—LuAnn was off on another business trip—and Sadie wished she could escape her brother's questions and just sit there, listening to the singsong cadences of Valentina reading out loud.

"I really don't know," said Sadie. "I'm not allowed back until they've done their investigation." The exhibit was due to open in three weeks, and Claude was now in charge. All of her hard work and she had nothing to show for it. She was an outcast, a pariah.

"We should get a lawyer for you, someone who can defend you."

"From what? There aren't any charges against me."

"A lawyer might help you clear your name."

"The only way that's going to happen is if the thief shows up and confesses, which isn't likely."

Lonnie swirled the wine in his glass, his eyes on Sadie. Usually, talking things through with Lonnie made her feel better, but this wasn't solvable. "I thought the missing books had been found," he said.

"They had. But someone got into the cage and stole another one, and I chased him, but then Dr. Hooper and the security consultant showed up and there I was, holding the book he'd dropped, with no thief in sight."

"So they think it might be you?"

"Yes, they figure it was me. Plus, only the director and I had keys."

"Do you think the director did it?"

She considered it and shook her head. "No. I don't think so. There's something we're missing, or else this thief is some kind of a ghost." It certainly seemed as if a ghost was slipping in and out of the cage, the angry ghost of her grandfather coming back to seek vengeance on whatever it was that went wrong way back then.

"Maybe one of our ancestors?" He was teasing her, but gently.

"I'll be honest, I do think there might be a connection. If only I could figure out what."

She wished she'd dug further when her mother was alive, hadn't allowed her to skirt her questions about life in the library way back when, though she could see why Pearl might have wanted to avoid talking about those years. Until recently, Sadie hadn't really considered what it must have been like for Pearl, as a young girl, to lose both her brother and her father. Then, later, her husband. But now it was too late.

Lonnie set down his glass. "Are you okay?" He'd slipped into doctor mode, his delivery steady and reassuring.

"No, I'm not." Her voice came out raspy. "I can't seem to do anything right."

"Now, Sadie."

"Mom was so resilient, and I don't think I ever appreciated it. She suffered so much loss, and still carried on, baking her fancy cakes, living her life."

"Maybe it's time for you to bake some cakes yourself."

"Are you serious?" She burst out laughing. "That's quite the euphemism. What on earth are you talking about?"

He gave a sheepish grin. "Explore your options. You've been through a lot, and maybe it's time to take a break."

"There's nothing to take a break from."

"Your job. Mom's death. Which I'm sure reminds you of Dad's."

"You lost Dad as well, and you haven't taken a break."

"I was eighteen and off to college when Dad died. You were just eight, and you were there." He swallowed. "You found him."

Valentina burst into the room, holding something pearly in her hand. "Look! I lost a tooth."

Robin followed behind her. "First one. She'll be all grown up before you know it."

Sadie glanced over at Lonnie, whose face was brimming with fatherly pride, as if Valentina had just won a gold medal at the Olympics. "Let's see it, my love." Lonnie held out his hand and cupped the tooth gently, as Valentina smiled up at him with a gap-toothed grin.

After her divorce, Sadie had thrown herself into her work at the library, embraced her new life as best she could. She'd distracted herself with facts, convinced that knowledge and logic could solve all the world's problems, and cut a part of herself off in the process. Now she had a choice: she could continue doing so, waiting patiently for Nick and Dr. Hooper's determination of her guilt or innocence, knowing that she'd done nothing wrong, or she could take action. The thrill she got from investigating the book thefts and her family's history made her want to keep on moving forward, following the clues, despite her banishment from the library, and no matter what she discovered.

She'd never known her grandmother, who seemed to be the linchpin of both her work life and her family. The one woman who had all the answers had died during World War II, killed during the German Blitz on London. It was too late.

Or was it?

She turned to Lonnie. "Maybe you're right, about taking a break. Maybe I should go to London."

England. The home of Virginia Woolf. Of Charlotte Brontë. Of so many of the Berg's authors. Including Laura Lyons.

"You mean where the bridge is?" Valentina launched into an off-key version of the children's song.

"Yes."

Lonnie studied her. "Why London?"

"Well, there's nothing going on here for me, for the time being. And I've never been before. On top of that, it was part of our mother's life, even if she didn't talk about it much. Now that I've been outed as Laura Lyons's granddaughter at work, why not go there and see what I can discover?" She didn't say out loud the thought that maybe she could take advantage of the connection and secure something for the *Evergreen* exhibit. Get back into Dr. Hooper's good graces. It was a long shot, to be sure.

"I figure, why not?"

CHAPTER TWENTY-TWO

London, 1993

Why anyone traveled more than two time zones away was beyond Sadie's comprehension. She'd woken up drooling and groggy as the flight attendants passed around breakfast trays with a deafening clatter. The slow trudge off the plane was followed by a long wait in line at customs.

The travel agent had found her a cheap fare that departed three days after she'd first brought up the idea with Lonnie, along with a reasonable rate at a bed-and-breakfast. Once there, she lay down for what was meant to be a twenty-minute nap and woke up six hours later, starving and confused. A restless night in her room attempting to sleep followed, before the lady who owned the B&B knocked on her door the next morning carrying a tea tray, chatting away in a singsong voice about rising and shining, when all Sadie wanted to do was go back to bed.

She'd wasted most of her first day asleep, and there were only four left, so Sadie pulled herself out of bed and took a long bath, washing her hair using the unwieldy spray nozzle and trying not to wet the lime-green floral wallpaper as she did so. Not an easy task.

The tube wasn't at all like the subway in New York, where tokens were swallowed up by the turnstiles and off you went. Here, you had to prove you hadn't traveled any farther than the zone you'd paid for, or so explained the irritable tube agent as Sadie bumbled her way through the turnstile, having misplaced her ticket. It was embarrassing, getting so much wrong, when she usually prided herself on getting things right.

She tried her best, eating sandwiches consisting of only a bit of cheese and a drippy tomato, drinking tea, figuring out which coins to leave for a tip. If she were with Nick, they might have had a good laugh at the myriad of differences between the two cultures. She missed him. She missed the library, the smell of old books, and her squeaky desk chair. The days when everything was in order, and she knew what to expect.

She was discombobulated—what a perfectly onomatopoeic word to describe her current state, all jumpy, confused, and tired. The city of London was discombobulated as well, the IRA having blown up a bomb-filled truck in the city's financial district two weeks ago, killing one and injuring more than forty. It hadn't deterred Sadie from coming, though, just as the bombing in the parking garage of the World Trade Center hadn't changed the way she went about her day in New York. Although she had to admit she quickened her step as she passed by trucks—they were called lorries here—idling by the side of the road.

But Sadie's shoulders began to drop and her mood lifted as she followed the map along the hilly streets of Highgate to the address that was on all of the correspondence from Laura Lyons's estate. The air felt lighter here than the air in New York City, softer. She ended up in front of a redbrick town house with a manic rose garden out front, a crazy riot of white blossoms and thorny vines that looked vaguely sinister, like flowery barbed wire. She realized with a start that it was the exact location where Laura Lyons was standing in the photograph in Lonnie's dining room.

Sadie knocked on the door. After a short wait, an older woman with high cheekbones and huge blue eyes opened the door.

"Hello, I'm looking for Miss Hilary Quinn," said Sadie.

The woman didn't answer right away, just stared. "That's me. Who are you?" She spoke with a throaty croak.

"I'm Sadie Donovan. Laura Lyons's granddaughter. I've been calling, trying to reach you, from New York. I thought I'd stop by during my trip abroad and introduce myself."

Miss Quinn squinted at her suspiciously; then her eyes softened. "You look so much like her. Forgive me, I've been a little under the weather, and seeing you is something of a shock. Come in."

The apartment took up the first two floors of the building, the lower one opening up to a large kitchen with a long wooden table in the center and a living room behind it that looked out onto another jungle-like garden. This was where Laura Lyons had written her essays. This was where she'd come up with her radical ideas and put them into words that had inspired generations.

And this was where Sadie's mom, Pearl, had spent several years before returning to New York for college. Once again, Sadie felt a pang of guilt for not asking more questions. Then again, what child cares about their parent's life before they were born?

It's not until it's too late that the resonance of the earlier times, and how they echo through the next generation, are deemed valuable.

"Would you like some tea?" Miss Quinn moved stiffly toward the stove.

"Can I help? Please don't if it's a bother."

"No bother at all."

Sadie settled into one of the wooden chairs at the table. "When did you first come to work for my grandmother?"

"Back in 1935. Eons ago."

"Did you know my mother, Pearl?" Even as she asked, she realized the math didn't add up for their paths to cross.

"No. Laura sometimes talked about her daughter in the States but never went to see her, and the girl never came here."

"Did she ever say why? Was there a falling-out?"

Miss Quinn shrugged. "I'm not sure."

Sadie waited, but the woman didn't seem inclined to elaborate. Maybe Sadie was being too direct, too American. She tried a softer approach. "It's been wonderful, the way Laura Lyons is finally being appreciated for her work."

"These days, I get legions of Lyons fans wanting to know more about her, about her life," sniffed Miss Quinn. "Knocking on my door first thing in the morning, asking for a tour." That explained her reticence.

"I'm a fan, but I hope you realized it's more than that. Although I do have questions."

Miss Quinn poured the tea into teacups and sat across from Sadie. "Hoping for something for your exhibit? Is that why you've really come?"

So she'd listened to Sadie's telephone messages. But Miss Quinn's words were in no way an invitation. They were a warning.

"It's my field. So of course I'm interested in anything that might have been left behind." There was no point in mentioning that an early draft of a Laura Lyons essay might be the only thing to save what was left of Sadie's reputation. "But honestly, as her granddaughter, I'd love to know more about what she was like."

"It was a long time ago."

"I assure you, I don't want to be a bother. My mom was close-lipped about her mother, and Laura Lyons was such an iconic figure. You can understand, can't you?"

Miss Quinn seemed to gather her thoughts. "She was quiet, not a chatty sort. Careful, but generous."

That was a start. "I'm sorry I never knew her."

"You look just like her, almost gave me a heart attack at first. That hair. But it's more than that, it's your eyes, too."

"And we both love literature, of course. I quite like the idea of taking after her. We both were married, and then embraced an independent life." She pushed aside thoughts of Nick. "Forging ahead alone."

Miss Quinn's lips pursed, like she was going to say something but thought better of it.

The look in her eyes brought Sadie up short. "Did Laura fall in love again later?"

"No. What a silly question." Displeasure dripped from Miss Quinn's words. The woman was hiding something.

"No beaus or mad affairs?" Sadie couldn't help but dig further.

"Of course not."

"Huh. I mean, I would think it would be natural for a talented, successful woman like her to find someone later in life." Sadie waited, but Miss Quinn didn't elaborate. "Can I ask, why didn't she want to leave any of her papers behind?"

"Why should she?" Now she really had Miss Quinn's back up. The interview was going downhill, fast.

"As a curator, what writers leave behind in the way of early drafts, diaries, or notes interests me greatly. I'm curious as to why Laura Lyons refused to leave anything for posterity."

"She said she wanted the work to stand on its own, and not have it watered down by rough drafts or snippets scrawled on envelopes. The work, she said, had been distilled to its essence, so nothing further was necessary."

"So her directive was to destroy everything after her death?"

Miss Quinn pointed to the hearth in the living room. "I did it right there, the day after."

Sadie stared into the hearth, horrified. Her entire professional life she'd collected, preserved, and revered notes and letters. To think of all those clues to a life gone, up the chimney, turned into ash.

What a terrible loss. Sadie wanted to shake this woman and make her understand that it was nothing to be proud of, what she'd done.

"You're judging me, I can see that," Miss Quinn said.

"No, of course not." But the words rang false, even to Sadie's ears. In her eagerness, she'd pushed too far.

"I think you better leave."

"I'm sorry. I really am. Please, I've come all this way. My mother recently passed away, and I've been under pressure at work . . ." She trailed off, uncertain of what more to say. "Could we start again? Please?"

But the woman remained unmoved by Sadie's pleas. The interview was over.

Sadie returned the next morning. And the next. She knew Miss Quinn was there, lurking just behind the front door, and figured she'd show her that she wasn't about to give up.

At night, she sought out the London music venues she'd only read about: the Blue Note for some acid jazz, the sonorous voice of Leonard Cohen echoing through the Royal Albert Hall, and the pounding beats and pulsing lights of the Four Aces. But the energy that normally coursed through her body as she ventured out into the night wasn't there anymore. She felt tired, yes, but also spent. Like the beat of a bass drum would no longer serve its purpose as a way of losing herself, hiding from herself.

On her final day, she stopped by Miss Quinn's place again. The front curtain fluttered as she stepped around the rose brambles that encroached upon the front walk, but again, there was no response to the bell. This was madness, really. What had her grandmother been thinking, to put such a selfish ninny in charge of her estate?

Then again, she probably hadn't counted on dying so young.

She rapped hard on the door, waited a beat, then knocked again. "Miss Quinn, it's Sadie again. Sadie Donovan. I would love to talk to you."

Outside the gate, a woman pushing one of those old-fashioned prams walked past, pursing her lips at Sadie's racket.

Sadie gave her a fake smile and kept on. "Miss Quinn, are you in there? I'm fairly certain you're in there."

Still, nothing. She'd be heading back to New York with nothing to show other than a T-shirt with the Union Jack on it for Valentina. She put her back against the door and slid down to the stoop, watching the fog roll by like a parade of ghosts. It felt good to just sit and be and not have to think.

"Here's the deal, Miss Quinn." She spoke out to the air, to the garden, to no one in particular. "I'm going to be honest with you. I do want something out of you, it's true. I'd love to get my hands on something, anything, of Laura Lyons's that I can show my boss and we can put up in the exhibit. You see, my job is on the line, for a number of reasons—none of them to do with my qualifications, I assure you, I'm the best librarian in the institution, by far—but my people skills, you might say, could use some polishing. Really, we have a lot more in common than you'd think. My grandmother, our ability to successfully tune other people out and go about our business. Hats off to you, I say."

She heard a bump on the other side of the door. Miss Quinn was there listening to every word. She straightened up. "There's been a series of thefts of books at the library, and I have to find out who did it and fix that situation. It turns out that there were thefts during Laura's time there as well, and I want to know if there's a connection, any connection. Or if she said anything about them to you."

The door opened unexpectedly, and Sadie almost fell into the foyer. She twisted around and looked up at Miss Quinn, who from this angle seemed fierce, staring down at her with those frosty blue eyes. "Come in."

More tea, more sitting at the kitchen table, but this time Miss Quinn took some biscuits with jam centers from a tin and put them on a plate. "Where are you staying?"

"In Bloomsbury." Sadie nibbled on a biscuit. "Delicious. My mother used to make these."

"Laura used to brag about her daughter's skill in the kitchen."
Progress.

"My mother was an excellent baker. She passed away in late March."

"I'm very sorry to hear that."

"I'd read in the biographies that my grandmother died during a German raid on London, a bombing during World War II, but not much more. Did it happen nearby?"

For a moment, it seemed as if Miss Quinn was going to shut down again. But then she gave a slight shake of her head, as if rousing herself. "She'd gone into town, to visit her friend Amelia."

Something about the way Miss Quinn said the name gave Sadie pause. There was a softness to it. She'd been fond of her.

"Amelia?"

"Yes. Dr. Amelia Potter, the public health advocate. She was quite famous, in her time."

"What did she do?"

"She made sure the poor received decent medical care. Saved thousands of lives, improved thousands of others."

"And she and Laura were close?"

"Very close."

It all clicked. Amelia and Laura had been more than friends, Sadie was certain of it. It explained Miss Quinn's defensiveness to Sadie's earlier questions about Laura's love life. She took a deep breath. "Can I ask, were they lovers?"

Miss Quinn looked down at her hands.

"If they were, I think it's a fine thing," commented Sadie.

"It's not to be discussed."

"Maybe back then, but times have changed. Or at least, they're changing. If they were close, I think it's wonderful."

Miss Quinn regarded her with a raised eyebrow, as if she were assessing Sadie's worthiness. When she finally spoke, the words tumbled out, her relief at disclosing a long-held secret palpable. "It was wonderful. They were a beautiful pair. They first met in New York, and although they kept separate residences, they rarely spent a night apart."

All this time, Sadie had imagined she was modeling her life after Laura's, keeping her focus on her work, when in fact Laura had been in a relationship for decades, one that easily could have imperiled her reputation and livelihood if the truth were discovered. Yet Laura had pursued who she loved regardless, while Sadie had refused even the possibility of love after her divorce.

Sadie leaned forward. "It means so much that you protected them. I can understand why you would, as you wanted her legacy to be about her work. Were they together, at the end?"

"I'd told her not to go to Amelia's, that it wasn't safe, but she insisted. She always had a strong will." Miss Quinn stared out the window into the front yard. "She stayed late, as she sometimes used to. A German bomb dropped, and the building toppled over onto both of them."

"How awful. For you as well."

Miss Quinn looked over at Sadie. "Thank you for saying that."

Sadie saw the situation from the older woman's point of view. She'd done as she'd been instructed, protecting her employer's legacy, and then, once Laura Lyons became a household name, been scorned for it. "Thank you for taking care of her estate. My brother and I appreciate it."

"I wish she'd been alive to see how far she's come."

"To see how far ahead of her time she was, you mean."

"That's right." Miss Quinn gave Sadie a slight nod. "I'll tell you something I haven't told anyone else, since you've been asking about her writings. And I'm only telling you this because you're her granddaughter. A few months before she died, when the entire city was on edge and no one knew what the future held, she told me that she'd written one essay to be saved for after her death, and that she'd give it to me one day, but not yet. She said it told the truth, and that for now she always carried it with her."

"The truth?" repeated Sadie. "It wasn't on her when she was found?"

Miss Quinn waved a hand. "I went through all her belongings. Combed all the pockets of all her coats, her dresses. There was nothing tucked away in a secret lining."

"Did she ever mention her husband, my grandfather?"

"She never spoke of him, and rarely spoke of her children, but it wasn't from lack of emotion. I got the impression that it was too much emotion that stopped her. She was focused on whatever she was working on. Laura was at times joyful, always quick-witted. But she didn't talk about her life in America."

"So she never talked about a robbery at the library in New York?"

"No." But Miss Quinn's answer was careful, measured. "What was stolen?"

"A number of rare books. Probably the most important work was Poe's *Tamerlane.* It was really valuable, and one of the first things that went missing, back when Laura and the family lived there."

"Poe. Her favorite."

"She told you that?" Sadie put down the cookie she'd just picked up.

"One time, I remember we were at a Christmas party given by

the family down the street. A husband, wife, two children, a boy and a girl. Laura had gotten quite drunk, which was not like her, and was staring up at this bookcase that covered one entire wall. In her hand was a volume of Poe's collected poetry, and she turned to me and said she loved Poe best." Miss Quinn paused, as if deciding whether to continue. "She grew very mysterious, sort of playful, and she said she knew one that was hidden away, in a place where no one would find it."

"One—meaning a book by Poe?"

"She laughed. She told me that the book was exactly where it should be, yet exactly where it should not. I asked her what she meant by that, but she got teary and changed the subject. I remember this well because I'd never seen her cry before. She was a controlled woman."

Where it should be, yet where it should not.

In a library, was the answer to the first part. What if the answer to the second was somewhere inside the old apartment, where they had lived? What if Laura Lyons knew her husband had stashed the stolen book somewhere close by, somewhere safe? That would be the most obvious, and easiest, hiding place. Maybe under an old floorboard or in some old cupboard. With all the boxes and detritus piled up since the rooms had been turned into storage, it was possible that anything hidden had remained undisturbed in the intervening years.

Miss Quinn finished her tea. "I'm sorry I can't be more help to you."

"No, it's nice to hear about her."

"I hope you're able to secure your job."

"Me, too."

They parted with Sadie promising to keep in touch.

Back at the bed-and-breakfast, she remembered with a start that it was Lonnie's birthday, and gave him a call to wish him well, filling him in on what she'd learned. "I'm eager to get back into the old apartment and see what I can find," she said.

"You're dealing with recollections from many years ago, but I hope it leads to something. I take it you're ready to come home?" he asked.

"I am. It was good to get away, I'm glad I went. I feel like I can handle whatever's coming down the pike now."

"I've got your back."

"Thank you. And happy birthday, big brother."

After a long flight home, Sadie threw down her luggage and fell into bed, dreaming of sirens blaring, of bombs going off, and of fire. She woke to the sound of her phone ringing and answered with a groggy "Hello?"

"Sadie, it's LuAnn."

She checked the clock, seven in the morning. "LuAnn? What is it?"

"Is Valentina with you?"

Sadie shot upright. "No. Why?"

She waited for LuAnn to say more, but the only sound was a strange inhalation, like she was unable to catch her breath. Like she was underwater.

"What is it? What's happened?" Sadie demanded.

"She's missing." A pause, another choked cry. "Valentina's gone."

CHAPTER TWENTY-THREE

New York City, 1914

"Tell me where you went to, when you weren't in school."

Harry was nestled beside Laura in his bed at home, where he'd been slowly recuperating the past few weeks, getting a little stronger every day. Laura gave a silent thanks. Harry was alive, they were well, and eventually everything would get back to normal, now that her energies were no longer diffused.

Harry avoided her gaze.

"I know you went downtown, with someone named Red Paddy, from school."

Now she had his attention. In a strange way, the investigative skills she'd learned in journalism school were paying off, she supposed. She could follow a trail and wasn't afraid to ask questions, which had led her to Red Paddy and his cohorts. She hadn't told Jack what she'd learned, partly because she wanted to speak with Harry alone first but also because no doubt he'd blame her for not being around enough to know their boy had been skipping school, week after week.

"Tell me why, Harry."

He shrugged. "I hate school. I was going to fail, so what was the point?"

"Why would you fail?"

"I don't know. I can't get anything right. The teachers would hit my hands with a ruler when I didn't know the answers." He clutched a stuffed animal that she'd bought for him after he'd returned home, a fluffy lamb with a small bell around its neck.

"Why didn't you tell me or your father? We could have helped you."

"You weren't here."

That was true. Jack had been busy either working or with his manuscript, and she'd been immersed in school and the club. And Amelia.

"I'm sorry, my love. But we'll figure this out together now, all right? You know that I also failed out of school this year, don't you?"

He gave a solemn nod. "Because you couldn't understand?"

"Well, more because they couldn't understand. But you see, I'm fine, and will figure out my next steps, just as we'll figure out yours, too. We're in this together, all right?"

He squeezed the lamb tighter, and the bell gave off a faint ring. "Will you read to me?" he asked.

She picked up *Maritime Heroes* but handed it over to him instead. "I think you should read to me."

He sighed and turned to the bookmarked page. Holding the book only a few inches away from his face, he began reading, stumbling over word after word. After a paragraph, he threw the book down on the bedclothes in frustration.

"I can't, I tell you. Please, will you read to me?" The plaintive cry broke her heart.

"Harry, can you not see unless you hold the book so close?" She picked it back up and placed it open on his lap. "What does it look like when it's here?"

He pointed to his lamb. "Like him. Fuzzy."

"The letters look fuzzy?"

"And the words. All of it."

She almost laughed out of sheer relief, but caught herself. "You need glasses, Harry. That's all this is. I'm sure of it. Once you're well, we'll get you a pair of spectacles, and you'll be able to see, able to read, just like the other students."

"You mean this isn't what you see?"

"No. It's clearer to me. Not fuzzy at all. No wonder you've been frustrated. You're not seeing the same thing the rest of us are." She held him close. "I'm sorry you've been through a terrible time of it. I promise I'll be here from now on."

"How's my boy doing?" Jack stood in the doorway, beaming, and didn't wait for an answer. "I'm almost finished with the editing. I'll work all night tonight, and then the manuscript will be ready to go back to the agent. From there, it's out into the world."

His self-centeredness irritated her, but she supposed he had every right to be proud. She rose and let him envelop her in a bear hug, trying not to note how different it was to be hugged by Jack than Amelia, thick limbs and whiskers versus soft skin and a quiet lightness.

All that was over with.

Her family came first, from now on.

Dr. Anderson had been surprisingly compassionate when she'd told him she'd not finished school, and even asked if she would contribute to the next staff newsletter. She'd turned him down. If Jack needed a typist, she'd do it. If Harry needed spectacles, she'd take care of it. No one could manage these three people better than she could. Her own mother had been a dear to help out, but no one could take Laura's place and no one else should have to. Her failure at Columbia only proved that there was no point trying to get ahead in a career unless a woman was unshackled, like Amelia, like so many of the other members of the Heterodoxy Club. Otherwise, the obstacles were insurmountable. She'd been reckless to imagine she could manage so much at once, and her failure to her family only proved that. If she'd been home, she might have noticed Harry's problems with reading and taken care of it before he got punished and ran off with Red Paddy in frustration. This was her job, now. The children and Jack.

She tried not to think about Amelia, tried to forget their silly jokes and the way Amelia looked at Laura as she spoke, as if every word were a gumdrop to savor. Laura's life had settled back to the way it was supposed to be. But she still missed Amelia terribly, missed the frisson that passed between them when they grew close, the physical joy of having the person she loved most sitting right next to her, the emotional connection with someone who knew exactly who she was, and loved her for all the right reasons. The person who wanted her to stretch, to reach, to challenge herself.

But it was too much to ask for.

She pulled out of Jack's embrace. "I must be getting dinner on the table. We have so much to celebrate, don't we?" She turned to her husband. "I have a strong hunch that our boy here needs glasses, which will make it easier for him in school."

"Glasses?" Jack chucked him under the chin. "You'll catch all the girls if you start wearing glasses, you know. It'll make you look quite grown up and serious."

"Really?" Harry blushed.

"Trust me, my boy. I know these things."

Jack was a good father, a good provider. Now that his book was nearly finished, they could move on to the next phase of their lives. Maybe move out of the library, somewhere farther uptown nearer to her parents. Not downtown. That dream had died.

For a moment, she wondered who she'd be once the children had moved into homes of their own, with families of their own. The empty days stretching long as Jack wrote another book or toured the country giving readings. Would she regret her choice then?

No, no more aspirations for her. Let Jack be the dreamer.

Once Harry had fully recovered, she took him to the eye doctor, his first trip out since coming home from the hospital. The doctor told him he looked quite "scholarly" with his new glasses, and Harry stood a little taller on the way home. Laura gave a quiet prayer of thanks for the healthy color of his cheeks, which had finally replaced the flush of illness. On the way home, he read out loud all the signs and posters they passed, eager to show off his revived skills. She couldn't have been prouder.

Pearl was curled up in a miserable ball in the armchair in the parlor when they arrived home. No doubt Harry's illness had taken its own toll on her. "Pearl, what's wrong?"

"Father is upset. He threw a book at the wall."

Had the agent rescinded his offer? Did that kind of thing happen in the publishing world? Poor Jack. Laura looked around, searching for a blizzard of loose paper, finding none.

"What happened, exactly?"

"We were walking into the library and there was a lady standing at the information desk that he knew. She was bringing a book for you, and Father offered to deliver it."

"What lady? What did she look like?"

"She wore a tie, like a man."

Amelia.

Pearl bit her lip. "The lady didn't seem to want to give him the book, at first, but Father insisted."

"Where is it?"

She pointed to the corner behind the other chair. "He unwrapped it and looked at it, and then threw it over there and left."

She told Harry and Pearl to go to their rooms, and only after they'd left did she reach down behind the chair and pick up the book, its pages bent and the binding broken.

The Awakening, by Kate Chopin.

Amelia was sending some kind of a message. That she missed her, perhaps. A heat spread across Laura's body.

She leafed through it and noticed an inscription in pen on the title page.

XXVII—A.

She turned to page twenty-seven, and the warmth disappeared. Her eye went to the second paragraph of the page, where the heroine admits to being charmed by the sensuous beauty and candor of another woman: *Who can tell what metals the gods use in forging the subtle bond which we call sympathy, which we might as well call love.*

Jack had seen Amelia and intercepted her delivery. He'd read the inscription and known. Known that it was a love note, bound in leather.

At the bottom of the page, one more word was written, in ink. *London?*

Laura said hello with a tight smile to the workers she encountered as she made her way to the basement. She was relieved to find Jack in his office, where they could talk in private, away from the children. She had a chance, here, to explain.

"I saw your gift from that doctor." He didn't bother to wait until she'd closed the door behind her to speak. "I read the inscription."

She groped for what would be the right words, but all were inadequate. She felt wholly incapable of explaining her feelings for Amelia and what had happened between them in a way Jack would understand.

"Is that where you've been spending all your time? With that woman, doing what? Were you not happy with me?"

"It wasn't about not being happy with you. I'm very happy with you." But she was happier with Amelia.

He grimaced. "I've heard of such things, of course, but my wife? What does 'London' mean? Does she want you to run away with her to London?"

"I never considered it, I wouldn't do that, and told her so."

"Don't think for a moment that I'd let you leave with my children. I will never allow that."

While she understood his shock, she couldn't help but observe that—once again—she was being dictated to, being told what she could do and where she could go. His fury made him ugly.

She sat in one of the chairs and waited for his face to soften. They'd been together for so long, she'd forgotten to see him as a man, as a partner. Instead, he'd become someone else to have to take care of, another shirt to wash, another meal to cook. That wasn't fair to him.

She reached her hand across the desk, but he didn't take it. "I'm not going anywhere, it was a moment, I got caught up. I love you, I love the children. I've learned a lot about myself this past year, and now, with Harry getting sick, I understand that I don't need all that."

"All what?"

"To work, to do anything other than take care of you and the children. When I was downtown, it was a different world in so many ways, and I was dazzled by it all."

"Dazzled? What are you, a showgirl?" Contempt dripped from the word.

"No, that's not the right word. I'm not making much sense, I know. But it was a crush, let's say, like schoolgirls get on each other. I love you. I love our family, what we've created."

He took a quiet breath.

"I feel awful, Jack. I do. I'm sorry."

"I should have never let you go back to school. That was a terrible idea."

"I wanted to have something like you did, like your book, that took me out of myself. That's all. That was why I wanted to study journalism. Amelia was something else, I can't explain it properly."

"Don't say her name."

Another edict. She should expect this, of course, but it still rankled. "You were wrapped up in your book, I wanted something like that for me, something that challenged me."

"So you took a lover. A woman lover?"

To hear Jack name her relationship with Amelia so directly

after they'd skirted around saying the words was like a slap in the face. It was finally out in the open. She had been having an affair, betraying her husband and their family. Her cheeks flushed with shame. "No. I'm talking about journalism school. They're two separate things. Please don't confuse them. She was just a friend who—"

He held up his hand. "Don't say it. I don't want to hear it. If this gets out, I'll be a laughingstock. My book will never be published. I can't believe you jeopardized all I've worked for."

If only he would understand. "You had that book, which was all you could talk about for the past many years. You were away nights, working and working, leaving me alone. I didn't mean to hurt you, but that damned book."

"That damned book is going to put food on our table. But let me tell you, no agent will touch me if it gets out about your unnatural tendencies."

The phrase "unnatural tendencies" was grotesque. Laura's guilt tilted toward anger. As if Jack were such the model husband and father. "You love that book more than any of us. Even when Harry was sick, you still crept away to edit."

"I was under a deadline."

"Harry nearly died!"

She stood to go and he did as well, grabbing her arm. "I'm not done talking to you yet."

"That hurts. Ouch, Jack!"

A movement near the door caught her eye. While she was sure she'd closed it behind her, now it stood slightly ajar. She stood and looked out just in time to see Harry's back retreating down the hallway.

She turned to Jack. "Harry was listening. He must have followed me. My God."

Jack took off after Harry, and she followed, up the stairs, up to the mezzanine. They couldn't run; there were too many other people about; it would be unseemly.

Finally, they reached the apartment. As Laura opened the door, she heard Pearl crying out.

"Stop, you can't do that."

In the sitting room, Harry sat staring intently at the fireplace, where bright yellow flames flickered and flared. But Laura hadn't lit a fire that morning; it was far too warm for that.

Harry held a poker in his hand and didn't look up at them as they drew closer. The fierceness and sheer glee in his face reminded her of the boys downtown, that day when they'd mocked and taunted her.

"Harry, my boy, we should talk," said Jack.

"He's burning it." Pearl was crying, pointing to the fire.

"Burning what?" asked Laura, but in an instant she knew the answer.

Jack raced to his study and back. "Where's my manuscript? It was on the desk."

Harry didn't answer, just stared into the flames, as if hypnotized, where a stack of white pages curled into ash.

CHAPTER TWENTY-FOUR

New York City, 1914

Jack stood frozen, but only for a moment. Within seconds, he had crossed the room to the fireplace and shoved Harry out of the way, reaching for the burning manuscript with his bare hand before pulling it back with a sharp cry. "We have to save it. Pearl, get water."

Jack grabbed the poker and tried to drag the charred manuscript out as Pearl entered from the kitchen with a pitcher of water. Laura poured the water into the fireplace, but nothing could be saved; it was too late. The three of them stared into the soggy, charred mess.

There was nothing left of Jack's masterpiece, his life's work.

Jack slowly turned his head in a way that reminded Laura of a wolf. Deliberate, focused on his prey.

Focused on Harry.

The boy stood with one palm planted on the dumbwaiter door, the other clenched at his side.

"Harry, how could you?" Laura spoke to break the intolerable silence, but as she did, Jack was up and across the room.

He slapped the boy, once, hard. Harry fell against the door of the dumbwaiter and Laura cried out, imagining the door giving way and her son falling to his death. Laura ran to Jack and grabbed his arm, holding on tight. "Jack, don't!"

Jack turned to her, other hand raised, ready to come down on her own cheek. She flinched, stunned at the fact that she was in combat with her own husband. How had it come to this? She'd never seen such a dark side to Jack, but then she never would have imagined her son could do such a terrible deed. Had they been like this all along, or had she missed it, focused on the happy family she imagined they were?

The sudden violence in the room was like an infection, contaminating Laura as well. She was desperate to lash out, to punish. She shoved Jack, hard, with both hands, the blood in her veins at the boil.

In the brief moment that Laura and Jack wrestled, Harry slipped away, down the stairs.

Jack whirled around and disappeared down the stairs after him as Pearl wrapped her hands around her mother's waist. "Don't leave me, don't go."

Laura turned to her daughter. "I won't. Go to your room, all right? Everything will be fine, we just need everyone to calm down."

"But Father's book . . ." Pearl pointed to the fireplace, but Laura didn't look. She couldn't.

"Stay in your room. I'm here, I won't leave you."

Pearl did as she was told, and Laura, not knowing what to do next, went into Harry's bedroom, where his stuffed lamb sat on the bed, looking desolate. Harry had always been closer to Laura than to Jack, it was just his way, and he'd seen Jack go after Laura in the basement. But to have burned the manuscript in retribution? It was unthinkable, something she couldn't fathom doing even after what Jack had said about her relationship with Amelia and their "unnatural tendencies." But Harry was so young, and Laura was beginning to grasp now how neglected and misunderstood he must feel. To skip school for months and have neither parent even notice? Not to mention the behaviors Harry might have witnessed with Red Paddy and this gang before he became ill.

She returned to the staircase and leaned against the banister. These rooms had held such happy memories, the fireplace mantel where Pearl had carefully arranged pine boughs in December, the kitchen where Harry had presented his tooth last year.

Her eye went to the place Harry had last stood, watching them as they tried to salvage the manuscript, as if by staring hard enough she could summon him to reappear. Something about the memory was strange, though. The way he'd positioned himself, with one hand flat against the dumbwaiter door, like he was holding it shut.

She stepped forward, examining the apparatus closer. A small piece of paper, hardly noticeable, jutted out from the crack at the bottom.

They'd never used the dumbwaiter; there was no need. In fact, Jack had warned the children soon after they moved in that they weren't allowed to play with it, that it was too dangerous.

She rose and opened the small latch. As the door swung wide, something fluttered to the ground.

She reached down and picked it up. A ten-dollar bill.

The dumbwaiter car was out of position, a few inches from the top of the opening. Laura pulled on one of the ropes, and it slowly cranked into place.

Inside the car sat a wooden box, which she recognized as the one where Harry stored his keepsakes. Why was it here and not in his room? But when she opened it, she knew why. Ten- and twenty-dollar bills, dozens of them, covered a book. The *Tamerlane*.

The front door opened and she heard Jack's heavy tread, but not a second one. Harry had escaped. For now.

Jack stopped at the top of the stairway. She held up the *Tamerlane* for him to see. "It was here all the time. In the dumbwaiter."

He moved closer, breathing hard, and looked down at the contents of the box. "What is all this money?" He held up a couple of the bills.

None of this made sense. Stolen books and hidden money—nothing in front of her paired up with the sweet boy she loved so very much. She had to come clean, tell Jack what she knew. "When Harry wasn't at school, he was hanging with a gang of boys, down near Union Square. My guess is he stole the other books as well, and sold them."

Jack stood frozen for a moment, taking it in. "Our own son. The book thief. When were you planning to tell me this, Laura?"

"I found these just now, I didn't know he was the thief. But the books are locked away. How would he get to them?"

"He had plenty of opportunity at night, while we slept, to figure that out. We should hand it over to Dr. Anderson."

Laura shook her head. "Do you know what they'll do to Harry if we turn him in? He'll be sent away. We don't know the whole story yet."

Jack leaned against the stairway banister, his face white. "If we turn this in without Harry, I'll lose my job. I don't have the manuscript anymore, so there's no advance, no income. We've lost everything."

Again, Jack's only care in the world seemed to be for his precious manuscript. But if they were going to figure this out, they would have to come together. For the sake of her children, Laura knew she had to slow her anger and treat her husband like an ally.

"What if we say we found the *Tamerlane* but don't know how it got here?" she suggested.

It was a ridiculous idea, and Jack didn't even bother answering.

"We have to find Harry and see if there's another explanation," she finally said. "Maybe the other boys forced him into it." She moved to get her coat, but Jack stopped her.

"No. Let him spend the evening out on the streets and see how that feels. Maybe it'll teach him something."

"But he's still recovering."

"I'm not listening to you anymore, Laura." Jack didn't bother concealing his impatience. "You can blame yourself for this."

"You put your hands on me, that's what set him off. It was your beastly actions that made him angry."

At that, Jack's eyes grew wet. "My book. It's gone. My son is a thief. My wife is . . ." He trailed off.

Laura blinked at him. Did it matter to him at all that their family had collapsed around him? "We destroy it, then. The *Tamerlane*." Laura couldn't believe she was saying this. "We don't tell a soul. Then, when Harry returns, we put this family back together again."

Jack regarded the book as if it were poisonous. "I need to think. I'm going downstairs."

She encouraged him, knowing that it would be better for him not to be there when Harry returned.

She sat down in the big chair by the fire and cried. She cried for her boy, for her husband, for the life she'd imagined she'd be leading. For her arrogance at thinking she deserved more than she had. For the fact that she was willing to destroy a treasured piece of history if it helped keep her family together. She rose and carried the box to the fireplace, placing it on top of the detritus of her husband's writings.

But she couldn't light the match. Her fingers shook, the match wouldn't take, and after a couple of tries she gave up, returning the box to its hiding place. A gentle tug on the rope lifted the box up and out of sight, into the darkness.

Laura woke with a start, unsure of where she was, before realizing she'd fallen asleep in the chair by the fire. Her neck and shoulders ached.

Harry.

She checked his room, but the bed was still neatly made; there was no sign he'd returned in the night. Pearl, one room over, was fast asleep, her head buried facedown in the pillow so that only a messy swath of hair was visible.

Yesterday's events—the argument with Jack, the futile effort to save the manuscript, the dumbwaiter's secret contents—washed over her in a painful wave. But the few hours of sleep had brought a renewed energy, a sense that she could fix this, make it right. She must think clearly, and her first goal was to protect her children. Harry shouldn't be punished for something that was completely out of character for him. He was only a young boy and had been through a tough year, had made stupid mistakes. She wished they'd never moved into the library, that they'd stayed upstate, where life was simpler and none of them would have fallen victim to the temptations of the big city. Temptations like a career of her own, like Amelia. Like the rare books.

Jack was nowhere to be found; he'd probably spent the night downstairs on the sofa in his office. She'd talk with him, convince him to forgive his son.

Harry would return today, and they'd have a long discussion, without anger or tears. Without blaming each other. They'd find out why he'd done it, and how. The thought of him out on the streets all night made her ill, but at least he had Red Paddy and the gang to run to, which was an odd comfort. A terrible comfort. What if the gang had forced him to steal the books for them? If Harry explained to Dr. Anderson everything he knew, and turned in the awful boys who forced him to steal, wouldn't he be offered some leniency? Of course he would; he was only eleven years old.

It wasn't lost on her that he'd be turning in the sons of other women, mothers whose own boys had lost their way. But her own family must come first, from now on. She didn't have any compassion to spare.

A solid knock on the downstairs door stopped her ruminations. She placed one hand on the door to the dumbwaiter, checking that it was firmly shut, before making her way down the narrow stairs. Mr. Gaillard stood in the hallway, two men in uniform lurking just behind him. She looked around for Harry, but the boy wasn't there.

"Can I help you?"

"Mrs. Lyons, may we speak with you a moment? Would you please come with me?"

Jack must've said something, mentioned Harry's crime. Turned him in as vengeance for his terrible misdeed. She imagined stepping into Mr. Gaillard's office, seeing Jack sitting in one chair, tiny Harry in the other. Having to choose.

What would an innocent party say to this? She wasn't sure how to respond. "It's awfully early. Is something wrong?"

"We need to talk."

Every fiber of her being resisted being led away. "I can't leave the apartment just now."

"An officer will stay with the children."

Children. He didn't know that Harry had run off. Which meant Harry was safe, for now.

She followed him and the other officer out into the hallway, where two librarians walked by, staring at her before quickly averting their eyes. Around the corner Mr. Benson, the janitor, stood frozen with his mop and bucket as they passed. What was going on?

Mr. Gaillard's office was vacant, thank goodness. He asked the police officer to wait outside and gestured for her to take a seat.

"Mrs. Lyons, I'm afraid I have some terrible news."

Harry. They must have found him. What if he'd been attacked in the middle of the night? She imagined his limp body lying under one of the lions, where he'd taken refuge in the dark, too scared to come home. He'd been so ill—to have made it through typhoid fever for this? She'd kill Jack for this, she would.

"What?" She needed Mr. Gaillard to tell her quickly, get it over with. Yet another part of her wanted to go back to the apartment, back to the chair, back before she knew her life was going to tilt precariously into danger.

"It's your husband."

"Jack? What about him?"

"The coal passer found him in the boiler room not long ago." Somewhere, a clock chimed. "I'm sorry. I'm afraid he's hanged himself. From the pipes."

They must have it wrong. Jack would never do such a thing. She said as much, her voice trembling.

"I'm so sorry."

"I don't believe you. I must see him."

"I don't think that's a good idea."

He was wrong, and she'd prove it to him. "Show me."

Mr. Gaillard held her arm as they walked down to the basement, as the workers scurried out of sight. Now she knew the reason for their discomfort. News must have spread fast. Still, they were wrong.

A body lay on the floor, the face covered by a small cloth. She knelt down beside it as Mr. Gaillard lifted the cloth. Bloodshot eyes stared up at the ceiling; a tongue, thick and swollen, protruded from the open mouth. None of these strangled features were familiar, not really Jack's at all. The stuck-out ears were his, though. She pushed a lock of hair off his forehead. "What have you done?" she whispered, the words coming out as barely a hiss of breath. "What have you done?"

The rope he'd used was still looped around his neck, the frayed end curled beside his head like a serpent. His cheek was cold.

This Jack wasn't her Jack, who'd walk into the room at any moment and laugh at all this silliness. The husband who'd cried when they'd exchanged vows. No, this was the body of a stranger.

Mr. Gaillard took her by the arms and led her away, out of the room and into Jack's office, where they'd had that terrible argument. Had that been only a day ago? It seemed like years. She let him place her in a chair.

All because of a lost manuscript. She wanted to fix things, make it all fine again. The book could be rewritten; she'd type as he dictated. They'd find Harry and bring him home.

But it was too late.

"Mrs. Lyons, I'm so sorry for your loss," he said. "I can't imagine the pain you must be in, but I must ask you about a note we found near the body."

She looked up. "A note?"

He took a piece of paper out of his pocket and unfolded it. "It appears to be a confession. For the thefts."

"No. Jack didn't do that."

He handed it to her, and she read it, her hands shaking.

I'm sorry for the trouble I caused the library. The fault is mine, as is the shame. Please tell my family I love them.—Jack Lyons

Mr. Gaillard cleared his throat. "I must ask you, and I'm sorry but I must. Do you know anything about this?"

"I do not." The lie was delivered smoothly, easily, over the turbulence of all these new emotions. Loss, disbelief, shock. They came to her in waves, one after the other. Pearl. How could she tell Pearl her father had killed himself? And Harry. What a horrible burden for any young child to have. How could Jack have inflicted this on them all?

To save his son. He'd done it for Harry's sake.

The door opened, and the other officer came in, a groggy Pearl by his side. Laura rushed to the girl and held her as Mr. Gaillard and the officer exchanged whispers.

Mr. Gaillard offered a sympathetic look. "Mrs. Lyons, I'm afraid we have to search your apartment again. You and your daughter can wait in here. I'm told your son isn't present."

"He's with my parents." Another lie.

She sat with Pearl on her lap, holding her head to her shoulder, singing softly under her breath. Harry was somewhere out there in the alleys and streets, scared and alone. Jack had left her behind, the loss of his manuscript, the unfaithfulness of his wife, and the shameful acts of his son too much to bear.

This building had crushed their family, just as if it had crumbled to the ground right on top of them all.

CHAPTER TWENTY-FIVE

New York City, 1993

W hat do you mean, Valentina's missing? What happened?"
Sadie tried to make sense of what LuAnn was telling her. She was still half-asleep and caught up in that terrible dream.

"I caught the red-eye back last night, and when I arrived home, Lonnie was still out on his shift. Valentina is supposed to be here, with Robin, getting ready for school. I checked her bed and she hasn't slept in it." Her voice was ragged with panic. "She's not with you?"

"No. Where's Robin?"

"Same thing, gone. My God, if something happened to them while I was away, I'll never forgive myself."

"Slow down, let's talk this through. Did anyone see them leave?"

"The police are here now and are reaching out to the doormen on the street to find out. Lonnie's on his way home. He's the one who suggested I try you."

The police. The seriousness of the situation hit Sadie hard. Her niece and the babysitter had vanished in the night.

She tried to come up with ideas of where to find them as she ran the five blocks to the brownstone, frantically wondering who could have taken them. And why?

It was New York—anything was possible.

Robin was too small to be a caretaker. Sadie had known that right away, and should have told Lonnie so. How could a tiny person like that protect another tiny person? If they had been kidnapped, they would've been easy pickings.

When she arrived, Lonnie and LuAnn were sitting on the couch, ashen-faced, as two policemen asked them questions.

Lonnie rose and hugged Sadie. "I'm so glad you're here."

"Any news?"

He shook his head. "The cops have been through both Valentina's and Robin's rooms, and found no sign of foul play. It's like they just disappeared."

"Have you checked the hospitals?"

"We have." A policeman introduced himself—Sadie didn't catch his name—and started asking questions about Valentina, if she had difficulties at home, if she might have run away.

"She's only six," said LuAnn. "Of course not."

Lonnie put a hand on her knee. "They have to ask."

Sadie spoke up. "What about Robin? Is there family of hers you should call?"

"I looked through her things for an address book or something like that, but no luck," said LuAnn. "She said she was from somewhere in Massachusetts, I remember."

Another policeman appeared at the front door. "One of the doormen down the street who worked a double shift said he saw them last night, around five thirty. He's worked there for years, knew Valentina by name. He said Robin walked by first, and the little girl followed a little later and waved at him. He didn't notice them return, but he could have been busy helping residents if they did."

"Hold on, they didn't leave together?" asked Lonnie.

"The doorman figured they were, even though the girl passed by a few moments later. Like she was hurrying to catch up."

Strange. Lonnie and LuAnn exchanged a look.

"Was anyone else with them?" asked Sadie.

"Not that he recalls. He also said that they weren't carrying suitcases or anything."

"Maybe they went out for ice cream and something happened," LuAnn suggested tearfully.

Out there, anything could have happened. Two young kids, so easily picked up, picked off.

Sadie couldn't sit still. She asked the cop for permission to go into Valentina's room.

Valentina had always been neat, with everything in its place. Sadie walked over to the small vanity, where the nail polish bottles were all lined up in a row, in the order of the rainbow. Her heart broke at the thought of this little girl out somewhere strange, lost and alone. They had to find her, make sure she was safe, protect her. Sadie shouldn't have gone to London and left them. Maybe she would have been here when the kidnappers came, and stopped it. And poor LuAnn. How horrible for her to come home to an eerily empty house.

She opened the closet door, where Valentina's clothes hung— mostly varying hues of purple and pink, her favorite colors—her shoes paired up on the floor below. The bookcase was overflowing with books and games and silly knickknacks, including a jewelry box with a ballerina who twirled about when opened. Inside was one of Pearl's rings. A pearl, of course, which brought tears to Sadie's eyes.

Valentina's favorite games were stacked up on the bottom shelf: Connect Four, Clue, a box of Uno cards.

Sadie glanced back at the closet. Up on the top shelf, high above the clothes, sat the box for Operation, Valentina's favorite game of all time. The last time they'd played it was with Pearl, when the game had descended into tears and chaos. Sadie had promised to get new batteries, but then forgotten.

Odd that it was on the top shelf. Valentina was too short to have placed it up there easily, not without having to pull over a chair to stand on.

Sadie lifted it down and placed it on Valentina's bed. Inside, the buzzer still didn't work.

Something was off, though. The cardboard piece where the goofy patient lay on his back, staring at her with alarm, was worn and bent along one side. She didn't remember it looking this beat-up before. Like it had been removed and then replaced. Maybe Valentina had been curious as to how it worked, or tried to replace the batteries herself. But then how did it end up hidden away in the top of the closet?

She pried off the top of the operating table. Underneath lay a folded piece of paper. Old paper, brown and crinkled at the edges.

She unfolded it and dropped it on the bed, like it was on fire.

"Lonnie!"

He and LuAnn came rushing in.

"Look."

They stared down at the page, where Shakespeare's face stared right back.

"Is that the page that was stolen?" asked Lonnie. "The one you told me about?"

"Yes. From Shakespeare's First Folio."

By now, the policemen had joined them. Sadie explained about the missing page, then turned back to Lonnie. "Why on earth would Valentina have this?"

"I have no idea."

In fact, the children's game was the perfect hiding spot. But not for Valentina.

"How much do we know about Robin?"

Lonnie's eyebrows knitted with concern. "That she worked as a nanny for those twins we saw in the park. I called her references and checked them out."

That was easy enough to fake—just ask a friend to make up a story. "Was Robin here last night, when I called from London?"

Lonnie nodded. "I was in the kitchen, I'm not sure where she and Valentina were, exactly, but they were both here in the town house."

Sadie tried to recall what she'd said to Lonnie. She'd definitely filled him in on the details of her conversation with Miss Quinn. About how the *Tamerlane* was somewhere deep in the library. And how she suspected that meant the apartment. "Could Robin have been listening in on the extension?"

"I suppose. But why would she?"

"Lonnie, think back. Is there a chance that she would listen to our weekly check-in calls, when I told you about what was going on at the library?"

"Again, I have no idea. What are you getting at?"

"We have to go to the library. Now. LuAnn, you stay here in case they return in the meantime."

LuAnn rose. "No, I want to come with you."

Lonnie took her hand in his. "Please stay, so one of us is here if they do come back."

Reluctantly, LuAnn relented.

Sadie grabbed her coat and made one call before they left, to Nick. His answering machine picked up, but she left a message telling him it was urgent and to meet them at the library.

She hadn't seen the danger, and it turned out that it had been right in front of her.

"I'm sorry, Ms. Donovan, I can't let you in."

The burly security guard at the library's side entrance put up his hand, but couldn't quite meet her eyes. She'd brought the man a cup of coffee a couple of times a week since she'd begun working there, and almost felt sorry for him, having to keep her out on Dr. Hooper's orders.

"It's important. There's a little girl missing and we think she might be inside."

She'd explained this to the police at Lonnie's, but they'd seemed confused, asking her repeatedly what "antique books" had to do with the case, and finally she and Lonnie had thrown up their hands and taken off, telling LuAnn to call the Berg Collection if they got any news.

"I'm sorry." The guard shook his head.

"It's okay, they're with me."

Sadie turned to see Nick struggling out of the revolving door, heading straight toward them.

"Nick, my niece is missing, I think she's inside the library."

"Right. I got your message." His eyes were wary. He probably thought she was a madwoman, trying to worm her way back into the library to steal more books. She didn't care—Valentina came first—but she had to pull herself together if she wanted to get inside.

"This is my brother, Lonnie. I think my family was somehow involved in the thefts, but not directly. I found the page from the folio in my niece's bedroom, hidden in a game."

His face hardened. She was explaining this all wrong. "You found the missing folio page?" He looked over at Lonnie. "In your brother's home?"

"Yes. But he didn't have anything to do with it."

"Your niece stole the page? I thought she was like seven or something."

"She's six. And no, she didn't steal anything. I think her baby-sitter did." She looked at Lonnie, who didn't nod his head or affirm her statement, still unwilling to admit she was right. Sadie supposed that doing so meant that he'd put his daughter in harm's way, and it was easier to imagine some other person forced them to leave. Either way, the girl was gone. Panic rose up in Sadie's throat—she thought she might be sick.

"The babysitter?"

"Yes. Please, Nick, she may have brought her inside, to find the *Tamerlane*. I think they're still in here. She's only six, and probably terrified. Can you at least alert the staff, tell them to be on the lookout?"

"All right. Let's go."

She almost collapsed from relief. With Nick on board, they had a chance.

He grabbed a walkie-talkie from the information desk. "What do they look like?" Lonnie provided descriptions of Valentina and

Robin, and Nick relayed them over the radio, with instructions to begin searching for the duo.

"Does the babysitter know the library well?" he asked.

"Not that I'm aware of. But I think I know where they might have headed. I went to London to see the executor of my grand-mother's estate, to find out if there were any links between that earlier robbery and ours. She said that Laura Lyons once alluded to the *Tamerlane*, and hinted that she knew where it was."

"Where is that?"

"She said, 'Where it should be, yet where it should not.' Like a riddle. I'm guessing in the old apartment where they lived when my grandfather was superintendent."

"And how does that connect with your niece's babysitter?"

"I told Lonnie about it over the phone yesterday, and I think Robin may have been listening in. In fact, looking back, the thefts track with what I mentioned to Lonnie over the phone, about whatever I was working on for the exhibit."

"So you think this woman rushed here to beat you to it?" He still didn't quite believe her, she could tell.

"Yes. According to a doorman down the street who spotted them, they left with enough time to get into the library right be-fore closing. It's not yet open to the public, so I'm hoping maybe they're still in here."

"Show me."

She led them to the mezzanine level, where the old apartment used to be. When Sadie had first seen it, it had reminded her of that one closet in every house that was jammed with random de-tritus. But this morning, it looked far worse than usual, the boxes' contents spilled out, covering the floors.

Sadie turned to Lonnie and Nick. "Robin was here, looking for the *Tamerlane*."

They waded their way through the litter of paper, checking each room. The farthest one, at the end of the hall, was locked. Sadie banged on the door, called out for Valentina. No answer.

Nick called on the walkie-talkie for someone to bring a key.

"Do you think Robin found the book?" asked Lonnie.

"It's hard to tell," said Sadie.

He let out a soft moan. "Please God, let Valentina be okay. This place is huge, they could be anywhere."

"Don't worry," said Sadie. "We'll find them. I want to go to the Art and Architecture Room to look at the floor plan I requested last week. It might give us a sense of how Robin has been getting around the library or where she might be hiding."

"I'll stay here and wait for the key, and keep on looking," said Nick.

In the Art and Architecture Room, the clerk handed over the old floor plans. Sadie rolled them out on the nearest table, Lonnie peering over her shoulder.

"You can see the mezzanine area clearly here." She pointed to the location of the apartment. "These were the bedrooms, this was the kitchen and living area."

"What's that?" Lonnie pointed to a small square marked with an *X* located inside one of the columns.

Sadie scanned the page, counting almost a dozen similar markings scattered through the library. Including in the center section of the Reading Room.

"It's a dumbwaiter. They're dumbwaiters. Here's the one that runs between the Reading Room and the stacks. There's another here, and here. That's it. That's how Robin's been scurrying around without being detected." She remembered the way the thief disappeared into thin air, after Sadie had chased her to the third floor. Sure enough, there on the plans was another *X*, this time in the women's restroom, which originally had been a study room. "It's like a vertical maze."

"Robin's tiny enough to fit, I suppose," said Lonnie. "Do you think they're hiding out in the dumbwaiter?" His expression turned to horror. "That that's where Valentina is?"

Sadie suppressed a shiver. "I hope not. I didn't see anything like that in the old apartment. It would have been right where we were standing."

Nick was still waiting for the key when they returned, and hadn't found the book, either. Sadie filled him in on what they'd discovered and marked the spot, a few feet from the top of the stairs, where the dumbwaiter should have been. A clean wall presented itself, with no sign of an open shaft.

Nick began knocking on the wall, and the sound changed from solid at the edges to hollow in the middle. "There's definitely an opening here."

Sadie searched the room where the janitors' supplies were kept and found a rusty old toolbox. Nestled inside was a hammer, which she handed to Nick.

He swung at the column, not too hard, but enough to crack through the plaster. It crumbled easily, and together they pulled it off, eventually revealing a paneled door. Lonnie joined in, pulling off the chunks of wall, and soon they had enough of an opening to view the entire dumbwaiter.

The dark wood was smooth and pristine, kept safe from exposure behind the false front, clasped shut with a metal latch. Nick clicked the latch and opened the door. Inside, the interior shaft was dark, ominous, and filthy. The dumbwaiter car wasn't lined up with the opening, the bottom edge resting a few inches below the top of the doorframe. Nick leaned in, looking down.

"Valentina?" he called out.

The sound echoed back up at them.

Lonnie looked like he was about to be sick.

There was no answer. Nothing.

"See if you can lower the dumbwaiter car so it's even," said Sadie.

Nick reached up and tried to pull it down with his hands, but no luck. He grasped one of the two lines of rope that ran down one side of the shaft, and the shelf slowly creaked down.

In the very middle of the car sat a wooden box.

Sadie reached in and lifted it out, carefully, as if it were a religious relic.

Inside were some old bills and, beneath that, a worn-looking book with an olive green cover.

The *Tamerlane*.

They'd found the book.

"What does this mean?" asked Lonnie. "What about Valentina?"

The radio squawked again. Sadie jumped at the sound. What now?

"We've found the little girl." The voice came from the radio, a man's baritone. "Down in the basement, in the bindery. We've found the girl."

Sadie almost tumbled down the stairs. Her legs wouldn't move fast enough. She held on to the railing to keep from falling but really wanted to throw herself down to the bottom level, to the basement.

If something had happened to Valentina here in the library, she would never forgive herself.

Lonnie, beside her, was pale and panting.

At the bottom of the stairs, Nick took off down the long hallway like a high school football player. Sadie and Lonnie followed him along what seemed like an endless passageway. It reminded Sadie of recurring nightmares where she was in a hurry to get somewhere, but the destination was murky and always out of reach.

Inside the bindery, Valentina sat at a table, a book in front of her, with Mr. Babenko standing nearby. She looked up and smiled.

Lonnie ran to her and grabbed her in his arms. "My girl."

Valentina's smile quickly changed to alarm. "I'm sorry."

"What are you sorry for, my love?" asked Lonnie.

"I don't know." At that, Valentina began to sob.

Sadie wrapped her arms around both of them, not sure of what to say. She had so many questions, but didn't want to scare the girl any more than she already was.

"We were just putting a jacket on a new library book," said Mr. Babenko. "She's quite good, I must say. Has a delicate touch."

Valentina broke off her crying and looked up at him. "I do?"

"You do. Here, show them what you've done."

Valentina picked up the book, which was wrapped in shiny clear Mylar. "I put the sticker with the call number on it here, see? Then we do this wrapping, like a Christmas present, but see-through."

"Well done, my girl." Lonnie stood and addressed Mr. Babenko. "Thank you for finding her."

"Oh, she found me, I must say."

Valentina remained seated at the table, not in any hurry to

leave. Sadie took the chair next to her. Valentina was safe—that was what mattered most. "Mr. Babenko, can my brother use your phone to call home, let them know she's safe?"

Mr. Babenko nodded. Lonnie went to his desk and dialed.

As he spoke in a low voice with LuAnn, Sadie turned to Valentina. "How did you end up here, V? Did Robin leave you last night, at home?"

Valentina didn't answer, but she didn't have to. Her eyes grew wide at Robin's name.

Sadie put a hand on Valentina's shoulder. "You can tell us, it's okay."

"I'd lost another tooth, and she said she had to see the tooth fairy, that she'd bring me back a present."

"She left you alone in the town house?"

"She told me I could watch TV until I fell asleep. But I wanted to see the tooth fairy, too, so I followed her, right to the library and up to that big room at the top with all the desks." Valentina would have felt at home in the building, as she'd visited Sadie there multiple times. And with the hordes of tourists coming in and out of the Reading Room, she would have blended right in. "She went into one of the doors."

The Reading Room. Sadie tried to picture where she might have gone. "Where exactly?"

"Inside was a curvy staircase."

Sadie knew immediately what she was referring to. By now, Lonnie had returned, and she directed her reply to him. "It's one of a few doors that line both sides of the Reading Room. The spiral staircase inside leads to a railed walkway that runs above the shelves." When she'd first been hired, the new employees had been given a behind-the-scenes tour, where they'd been taken up the spiral staircase, onto the walkway, and then out to a balcony that led to a sweeping view of Bryant Park. Thank goodness Valentina hadn't gotten that far.

The enclosed spiral staircase would have made the perfect hiding space for Robin until the library shut down for the evening. After everyone was gone, she would have had easy access to the stacks via the dumbwaiter at the delivery desk. How she got inside the Berg's cage, though, was still a question.

"Did you follow her through the door?" Sadie asked.

"It was locked. I walked along the shelves to the very end and sat down to wait for her, and I must have fallen asleep."

A low row of bookshelves, about four feet high, ran just in front of the wall containing the door. If Valentina had tucked herself in there, she would have been out of sight of the librarians closing up. Sadie imagined the dark library at night, with all its creaks and groans. "That must've been very scary, V."

"It was. When I woke up, the door in the wall was unlocked again, but Robin wasn't inside. I wandered around for a while. Then I found this room and there was a couch." She pointed to the corner, where a sofa was pushed against a wall. "So I lay down."

Mr. Babenko took over the story. "When I came in this morning, there she was, fast asleep. I called up to security to say that we had a visitor, and we did some work together in the meantime."

Sadie was grateful for Mr. Babenko's kindness, that he'd done everything he could to keep Valentina calm and safe.

"Security is guarding the exits," said Nick. "If Robin's still here, we'll find her."

The police arrived, and Sadie gave her niece a huge hug before watching Lonnie and Valentina go off with them.

She turned to Nick. "We should loop in Dr. Hooper, bring him the *Tamerlane*."

"Right. I'll wrap up down here. Why don't you take it up, and I'll meet you at Hooper's office?"

She appreciated the opportunity to explain what they'd deduced. Even if they didn't have all the answers. "Will do. Hand it over."

Nick froze. "I don't have the book. You have it, right?"

Sadie thought back. She had had it, but couldn't remember much of anything once they'd heard that Valentina was found. She could have sworn Nick had picked it up. She checked her purse, in case she'd put it away there. Nothing. The hairs on her arms prickled, and the room felt like it was spinning around her. "I don't have it. In all the rush to come down here, it must've been forgotten."

"Then it must still be up in the room."

The thought made Sadie ill. She followed Nick out the door.

CHAPTER TWENTY-SIX

New York City, 1918

Do you need help, Mother?"

Laura smiled at her daughter and handed her one of the bags of groceries. "That would be lovely."

In the four years since Jack's suicide and their eviction from the library, Pearl had turned into Laura's helpmeet, doing exactly what she should, when she should, and going above and beyond to make sure things were just right. As if she could make up for the loss of her father and brother, and Laura's anguish. Laura knew it was unwise to take her good nature for granted, but days like today, when she was beat down with loss and worry for Harry, she welcomed it wholeheartedly.

"I made a lemon sponge cake," said Pearl, pointing to the top of the oven, where it sat cooling. "For Harry's birthday."

Tears sprang into Laura's eyes. "That's so kind of you."

They both stared at the cake for a moment, knowing that

Harry would never taste it. He'd not come back to the library that day, nor come to his grandparents' brownstone after Pearl and Laura had taken refuge there. Refuge that didn't last long, as her father's disapproval and contempt became insufferable. Finally, Laura had packed them up again and headed downtown, Amelia answering the door without a word and ushering them inside her apartment at Patchin Place, where they'd been ever since.

"Do you mind if I run over to Sarah's for a bit?" asked Pearl.

"Of course. And we'll have our cake after dinner. You're a love." Laura watched as she headed out, noting that the hem of her dress needed to be taken down again. At eleven, she'd sprung up several inches.

Pearl seemed to enjoy living in Greenwich Village, and had made friends with the other children who lived on the alley. If she had any resentments, she didn't let them out and Laura chose not to pry. When she'd pried in the past, she discovered answers that ruined everything. Maybe later, when Pearl was grown up, she and Laura would be able to speak on the matter, but not yet.

Amelia had been a good friend and partner the past four years, taking over when Laura had her spells and couldn't get out of bed. Luckily, they were occurring further and further apart these days. Since her own tragedy, the United States had entered and then won a war, and now, after an anxious and precarious time, a sense of optimism finally seemed to be winding its way back into daily life. That same hopefulness had slowly seeped into Laura, and every so often she even experienced short bursts of joy, like the day she deposited her first paycheck into her very own bank account.

She was glad she had the financial freedom she'd always hoped for. But she'd never imagined obtaining it this way. The loss of half her family burned into her like a branding iron, a mark that would never fade. The day after Jack's death, Dr. Anderson had told them they had to leave. She'd stood on the steps of the library, Pearl weeping by her side, holding whatever they could fit into their suitcases. Dr. Anderson had apologized, explaining that he had no choice, and handed her an envelope of money. She'd refused it, but had thanked him for his past kindness. It wasn't his fault. That day, Laura had vowed to never be financially dependent upon another person again.

As the shock of their changed circumstances wore off, Laura began to see her past life in a new light, one that was slightly less filled with self-loathing. With Amelia, the workload of taking care of Pearl and running a household was shared, which meant Laura had more time to spare. What if she and Jack had shared the work of domestic life, been true equals both inside and outside the home? Then her year at Columbia wouldn't have been such a shock to their children and Harry might not have been so vulnerable, not fallen into Red Paddy's clutches. What if, as a rule, husbands helped out more around the house instead of putting their work ahead of family, the way Jack had done?

It wasn't all her fault, and maybe it wasn't so terrible that she'd wanted more out of life.

Once she'd had enough time to gather both her thoughts and her courage, she'd marched into Marie Jenney Howe's parlor, prepared to see a sour expression on the woman's beautiful features. Marie's hand rested on the neck of a guitar she'd been playing, and she motioned for Laura to sit.

"I would like to make a proposal." Laura had run through the speech in her head multiple times, but the compassion in Marie's eyes stopped her cold. She didn't want pity.

"What's that, Mrs. Lyons, and may I say how sorry I am for your loss?"

Laura took a deep breath. "Thank you. I would like to interview a member of the club each week, and write about who they are, what they're doing."

"That's an audacious idea, coming from you." Marie's sympathy went only so far.

But after dealing with Professor Wakeman's resistance, Laura knew how to handle the same from Marie. She owed him thanks for that, at least. "The only way for women to gain equality—true equality, inside and outside of the home—is to showcase the accomplishments of those who are out there changing the world, as a way to inspire others to reach for more as well. I've spoken with Max Eastman at *The Masses*, and he thinks the column is a grand idea. We both know the article that ran in the *World* was edited by a man, and his perspective warped the interpretation. Mr. Eastman has promised me full editorial control over each essay. This will be our story."

"Don't you mean *your* story?"

"My story is intertwined in everyone else's, I see that now. I can't stand apart from the causes that are dear to me as a woman. I failed out of Columbia, and I no longer want to be a reporter. I want to editorialize, convince people that their way of thinking is out of date, and use words as a means to change minds."

Marie, after speaking with Mr. Eastman, had agreed to allow Laura to interview her and use her as the first source. A test, of sorts. Their conversation had run deep into the night, and the resulting essay had stirred controversy with its candor and passion, which pleased Mr. Eastman—and Marie—to no end.

Much to Laura's selfish relief, Amelia's offer to move to London had been suspended as the clouds of war roiled over Europe. For this, she was grateful. At Patchin Place, they loved each other quietly and furtively but without the grand passion as before. This was an arrangement that suited them both, and their natures fit easily together because the relationship was balanced; neither had more power than the other. The members of the Heterodoxy Club had eventually warmed back up to Laura and allowed her to attend meetings, where she came up with more ideas for the column than she could write in a lifetime.

Here she was, living the life she'd dreamed about before everything else fell apart. Living in the Village with the woman she adored more than anyone else in the world, working as a writer, and part of a community that welcomed eccentricity and change.

But she hadn't wanted it in this way, at the expense of Jack and Harry.

At dinner that evening, Pearl lit and blew out the single candle on Harry's cake.

"Happy fifteenth birthday, my boy," said Laura quietly under her breath.

Amelia handed Pearl a knife. "It looks delicious."

So many bland words. How silly they all looked, having a cake for a boy who wanted nothing to do with them.

"Red Paddy's gang is back on Fourth Avenue," said Amelia as Pearl handed her a plate. "I have my inspectors keeping an eye out for you."

Harry had been spotted several times over the years since Laura had taken to making near daily treks through the Lower East Side in the hopes of catching a glimpse of her son. But he had always disappeared into the crowds or around the corner before she could reach him. Over time, she'd gotten to know his routes, but he'd made it clear that he'd run if she got too close. Her sightings, though sporadic, gave her hope. One of these days, she'd reach him again.

"Thank you," said Laura. "To think he's fifteen now."

"Almost a man."

Laura didn't look at Amelia and instead tried a small bite of cake. "It's lovely, Pearl. Well done."

"He's been on his own for four years now, Laura." Amelia wasn't going to let up once she got started. "It might be time."

"I can't leave."

"Pearl would like London, wouldn't you, my girl? We can visit the Tower and Buckingham Palace, now that the war's over and it's safe to travel."

Amelia didn't have to add that her job offer still stood, and that it would be a boon to her career in public health. Laura couldn't leave New York when her boy was still wandering its streets, likely still in pain.

"I would like that." Pearl, always trying to take care of them both. "I could learn to make scones."

"I'm going out," said Laura.

She didn't want to have this discussion, not on this day, and it irritated her to no end that Amelia would bring it up. They'd have a long talk about it later that night, no doubt, and Amelia would apologize and hold her close. But that wouldn't change anything, not in Laura's mind.

The sting of the October air in her lungs was a shock after a warm few days, punctuated with a light drizzle. Soon enough, she'd need to fetch out the gloves and scarves. Where did Harry get his clothes from? Did he steal them, like he had the books? The adorable boy she'd raised, with his bow-shaped lips and sparkling eyes, could not be reconciled with the feral young man, living on the streets, who no longer needed her. She carried his stuffed lamb in her bag when she went out looking for him, although she wasn't sure why. Red Paddy would probably laugh and toss it in the gutter if she dared to pull it out.

Only one of the bookstores on Fourth Avenue was still open at this late hour. She entered to escape from the rain, breathing in the unique smell of the old books, a musty mix of vanilla and wet wood. When she'd lived at the library, she'd sometimes buried her head in one of the books and inhaled, even when the other patrons gave her strange looks. Better than any perfume, Jack had agreed.

"I got something for you." The voice was familiar.

She peeked around a bookshelf to the back of the store, where a cashier stared down at a reedy boy wearing a cap, red curls wrapping around his neck like worms. Red Paddy.

The cashier sighed and put an elbow on the counter. "What now?"

Red Paddy pulled a book out from his coat. So they were still at it. The gang probably had moved on to other libraries, or stole from other bookshops. It was a lucrative business.

The cashier shook his head and returned to his newspaper, ignoring the protestations of Red Paddy, who eventually gave up and sauntered out.

Laura followed at a distance, the red hair like a beacon under the streetlamps, until Red Paddy reached a building on Second Avenue. He scampered down a stairway into a basement entrance. After a moment to gather her courage, Laura followed.

The door opened into a hallway so narrow a burly man would have to shift sideways to get through. To the right was a door, and she could hear Red Paddy swearing from inside.

"Bastard wouldn't take it."

Murmuring from other boys followed. She didn't hear Harry, even though her ear was pressed close.

She could knock, but that would give them time to run.

Instead, she turned the knob, relieved and also terrified when she met no resistance and the door swung open.

She almost reeled back from the stench, a mix of sweat, alcohol, and rubbish. One tiny window near the street offered the only light, and just beneath it three small boys sprawled against an upturned barrel, fast asleep. In the far corners of the room, stuffed mattresses covered rickety-looking lofts, and a table of sorts was pushed against one wall, holding the remains of what looked like last week's breakfast.

"Are you a charity lady?" said Red Paddy, nonplussed. "Going to give us a speech, are you?"

By now, her eyes had adjusted to the darkness.

There, at the table, sat a boy who stared back at her with an electric shock, who lacked the disdain of the others.

Her boy.

Harry.

The first year that they moved into the library, Jack had come up to dinner one evening complaining about the difficulty of fixing a leak in the basement, where a crawl space narrowed almost to nothing. "Can't reach it for the life of me."

Harry had offered to help, but Laura had dismissed the idea as too dangerous. Jack studied his son as if he was seeing him for the first time, sized him up, and announced that it was worth a try. Together, they disappeared after dinner and returned an hour later, both covered in muck and grinning madly. Harry had been able to reach the leak and patched it, following his father's instructions.

The next day, Harry dashed into his room after school, pulled on his overalls, and told Laura he was going to work. She nodded solemnly, not wanting to let on how adorable he appeared. He returned less than fifteen minutes later, in tears.

Jack, caught up in whatever crisis had arisen that day, had roughly dismissed Harry, forgetting that he was only a little boy who just wanted to help. After dinner, Laura tried to explain to Jack why Harry was hurt, but Jack hadn't listened. "The boy's too sensitive," Jack said, before turning away.

In the dankness of the tenement basement, Laura's sensitive boy stared at her with huge eyes. This was her only chance.

"Harry, let me buy you something to eat. That's all I want to do."

She'd guessed correctly. He was hungry. He glanced down at the detritus on the table and then checked in with Red Paddy, who leaned against one of the lofts and raised his eyebrows.

"Please." She locked eyes with Red Paddy.

Red Paddy shrugged. "He can do what he likes. I'm not in charge of him."

As they walked up Second Avenue, Laura kept her arms tight to her side. She reminded herself that she mustn't touch him, mustn't reach out to grasp his hand or his arm, even if not doing so went against her every instinct. It took her a moment to get used to his height—he was now as tall as she was. This was a new Harry, and she'd have to treat him carefully, not baby him or beg him to come home.

They settled in at a Russian restaurant and ordered blintzes. She tried not to stare as he tore into the food. All those boys in that room, growing and needing to eat. What was dinnertime like for them? A fight over whatever scraps they could scrounge together, probably.

"Pearl made a cake for your birthday."

"When was it?"

He didn't even know. "Today. Do you not know the date?"

"No."

Of course he didn't. He must have outgrown the pair of glasses they'd bought together, so long ago. Without them, reading a newspaper would be impossible. "Why don't you come home and have a piece. It's delicious, and we saved you plenty."

"No thanks." He glanced up at her, then back to his food, as if it might be snatched from him if he didn't put it away fast enough. "I don't want to live with you and Father anymore. I don't need to . . ." He trailed off.

Laura's mouth went dry. He didn't know his father was dead. Dr. Anderson and Mr. Gaillard had successfully covered up the suicide, so it hadn't made the news. Of course, they'd been more concerned with protecting the institution's reputation than maintaining discretion for Jack's family. She took a ragged breath, focused on keeping a semblance of composure. Harry didn't seem to notice, engrossed as he was in his meal.

She couldn't tell him, not yet. "We've missed you."

"You wouldn't, not if you knew what I've done."

"The manuscript? That's over with, done. No one is angry with you about that. It was a moment, that's all."

He lifted his chin, a challenge. "I've done worse."

"I know."

The chin wobbled, slightly—almost imperceptibly—but Laura knew what it meant. It was a glint of the old Harry, letting down his defenses. She spoke as tenderly as she could. "I found your hiding place. I found the *Tamerlane* and the money. I'm not angry, you don't have to worry about that."

Relief washed over his face. He was still a boy in so many ways, his reaction no different from when he'd accidentally ripped the dress of one of Pearl's dolls, confiding in a rush of regret as soon as he realized his mother knew it had been him.

"Why did you steal the books, Harry? Was it the gang that forced you to do so?"

"I took *Leaves of Grass* because I thought it would be about the countryside, where we used to live. I brought it to school with me one day, and Red Paddy saw me with it and started talking to me, asking about what it was like to live in a library. We became friends."

Harry, who'd had a terrible time making friends, would have been easy prey for Red Paddy and his gang. Laura remained quiet, listening.

"He said that I could make money if I liked, by nicking books like that for him. I heard you and Father saying that you needed money, so I thought this way I could help out."

He'd done it for her, for them. She wanted to embrace him so badly. "How did you get to the books? They're locked up."

He paused. "You already know."

She thought of the hiding place. "The dumbwaiter."

"I could fit inside the shaft. Couldn't now, of course. But back then, I could crawl in and lower my way up, down, wherever I wanted. Another one brought me right into the stacks. I could pretty much get around the whole building without being detected, late at night, when everyone was asleep."

He was such a scrawny kid—of course that would work. The

dumbwaiters were scattered all over the library, and Harry had turned them into a thoroughfare of sorts, a way of moving from floor to floor undetected.

All along, they'd been looking for an employee, a grown man. It must've seemed like a game, like climbing up a tree. If something had gone wrong, though, if he'd slipped and fallen—

"Weren't you scared, being in the dumbwaiter? What if you got trapped?"

"Nah. It was an adventure. And Red Paddy paid me well for the books I stole. He made me second in command. It was all for you, you see. So you could continue at school and not have to worry. All except the *Tamerlane*."

"What do you mean?"

He waited a beat before replying. "That was to be your Christmas gift."

She sat back and braced her hands on the table. "What?"

"The *Tamerlane*. You always said you loved those poems. But after I'd taken it, I overheard you and Father talking about it and realized that it was too rare, that you'd know I'd stolen it."

The simplicity of his thinking disturbed her. But Harry had always been caught up in a dreamworld, or at least that's what his teachers had said. Staring off into space, not listening. Running free with a gang of boys must have been a refreshing change to being in class. Not to mention stealing books—a way of taking revenge on the very objects that had given him so much trouble that year.

As she listened, she took in the small details, the changes. How he had the beginning of a beard in ragged spots of his chin and cheek, how his hair was matted under the plaid cap. One eye was crusty at the edges. He needed good food, a warm bed, and care.

"Look, Harry. I want you to come home with me. We live in Greenwich Village now. It's a nice apartment, warm and cozy. I needed a fresh start, and I think you do, too."

"I can't go back with you. Not after what I did."

"I don't blame you. Neither does Pearl."

"How is Pearl?" For the first time, his eyes softened.

"She's fine. She misses you."

"I bet Father doesn't. He probably never wants to see me again." The way he said it, with a prickle of hope, made Laura realize that, in fact, he desperately wanted to come back, to be part of the family again. To be forgiven.

She couldn't put off the news any longer. "I'm so sorry, Harry. I'm afraid your father's passed away."

Harry grew pale. "What? How?"

"He was fragile, I didn't realize how much."

"When?"

"The night you left."

"How?"

She scrambled for a way out of this line of questioning. "Harry, it's over now. It's been four years, you must come home."

"Tell me." Harry inhaled deeply, like he'd just swum a mile underwater. The look on his face was raw with need.

"He was upset."

"He killed himself?"

She couldn't answer that question. "What he did, it wasn't your fault."

Harry swallowed. "I killed him."

"I promise you, you did not."

But they both knew that the tragedy had escalated, one misdeed building upon another, until one of them had toppled over.

Harry whimpered softly, but could only hold back his tears so long. His cries eventually built into heaves of despair. Laura switched to the seat next to him and put her arm around him, letting him sob into her shoulder. No one at the neighboring tables looked up. The war had taken its toll on many, and grief was nothing new.

"At night, I dream of Father," said Harry, finally. "Every night in my sleep I see him. He's gasping for breath and calling for you."

His sobs were for all of them, she knew. For the family that was no longer there and the wrenching pain that came with the separation. They had planned on life going one way, and then it had blown to pieces, sending each of them flying up into the air and then crashing down hard. Pearl's tightly wound goodness, Harry's wildness, Jack's despair.

She handed Harry a napkin to blow his nose, and he did so like a child, shaking his head at the finish before handing it back to her. Just as he'd done as a boy.

How she'd missed him. "Please," she said. "Come home with me."

"I have no home. I don't need you anymore." His resistance was rising back into place.

"Of course you do. How will you take care of yourself?"

"We take care of each other. Red Paddy and the boys are my family now."

"But you're living in terrible conditions. You don't look well. Please, come home. It's been four years."

"Which only shows that I am fine on my own." He straightened. "We have plans."

"What, stealing books from one bookshop and selling them to another? How much money can that bring in? How many of you are there, a dozen? More? It's not sustainable. You'll need a real job, eventually."

His eyes hardened, and he shoved his empty plate away. She'd said too much, shown her desperation.

"I don't want your help. Stop looking for me. Leave me alone."

Without another word, he was gone.

That desolate night, she knew for certain that Harry was lost to her forever. He believed he deserved eternal punishment for the death of his father, his own self-sacrifice a stark contrast to Jack's selfishness. Both of their perspectives warped by love and loss. Both gone.

Laura vowed never to love someone that much again.

CHAPTER TWENTY-SEVEN

New York City, 1993

It must be here somewhere."

Sadie twirled around, searching for the missing book in the old apartment.

Nick began rifling through the boxes as she checked the dumbwaiter again. Nothing.

"I know I had it in my hand," she said, "but honestly, once we heard that Valentina had been found, I can't remember what I did with it. I must've put it down somewhere, it has to be here."

"Unless . . ." Nick turned and made his way along the hallway that led to the old bedrooms, checking each one. At the last one, he turned the doorknob and looked back at Sadie, surprised. "It's unlocked now. But we never got the key."

Someone had opened it. They checked the room, but there was no sign of life.

"Do you think Robin was hiding inside here the entire time?

Listening to me?" Sadie didn't wait for a response from Nick. "We basically found the damn book for her. Unbelievable." She sat down hard on one of the boxes as tears came to her eyes. "What an idiot I've been."

"No. You were worried about Valentina, she came first. Family comes first. Remember, it's just a book. The fact that Valentina is safe is everything."

That was exactly right.

They walked out of the apartment together, Sadie lost in thought. "Who is Robin?" she said, half to herself. "And why did she go to such lengths to ruin my life?"

"Well, we know she had some kind of insight into the library's architecture. We can check to see if she ever requested the floor plans from the library, right? They keep records of that."

"They do," said Sadie. "If she was listening to my conversations with Lonnie on the extension whenever I called, I basically fed her the most important items from the exhibit. I couldn't have made it any easier for her."

"We recovered the Woolf diary and the Hawthorne. The folio page is safe, if unattached."

She groaned in frustration. "What bothers me most is that the *Tamerlane* was here the entire time, safe and sound, until I figured it out and placed it in harm's way. It wasn't in Robin's clutches until I put it there."

At Dr. Hooper's office, his secretary informed them that the entire board was meeting in the Trustees Room, and escorted them over when they explained it was urgent. She entered first, and then motioned Sadie and Nick to follow.

Thirty faces turned their way as Dr. Hooper scowled from the head of the table. It couldn't have been a more daunting setting for

Sadie to have to deliver her news. "I understand there's been some kind of commotion this morning," he said.

Sadie stood at the farthest end of the table, the arrangement like a very narrow firing squad. Nick stayed beside her and, when she faltered, confused as to how to begin or what to say, took over. She was beyond grateful. Together, they filled the board and Dr. Hooper in on the missing child, the suspected library thief's identity, the recovery of the folio title page, and the discovery—and disappearance—of the *Tamerlane*.

"Well, I'm glad the girl is safe," said Dr. Hooper. "She's related to you, Sadie?"

"Yes. She's my niece, and we are quite certain that the thief was her babysitter. A woman named Robin Larkin."

"The police have it in hand and will be following up," added Nick. "I'll be working with them closely, of course."

Dr. Hooper grunted. "So what you're saying is you found a rare book that's been missing since 1914, and then lost it minutes later?"

"Let's not be so harsh, Humphrey."

The speaker was one of the trustees she'd given a tour to a couple of months ago. Mr. Jones-Ebbing.

"Why not?" countered Dr. Hooper.

"Because they've done a remarkable job figuring out what the hell was going on here."

Sadie appreciated his support, and noticed a couple of the other board members nodding their heads.

She knew she should let it go and get out of there. She needed to check in on Lonnie, LuAnn, and Valentina, and Nick was probably itching to consult with the police. But she couldn't help herself. "Sir, if you don't mind."

"Yes, Sadie?"

"I would suggest again we put out the news that the *Tamerlane* is missing, to every bookstore we know that accepts rare books, as well as the Antiquarian Booksellers' Association of America. The booksellers need to be on the lookout, and those that might be tempted need to know that they won't be able to resell it easily, without attracting attention. It's the only way we can possibly get it back."

"Hold on there." Mr. Jones-Ebbing spoke up, addressing the board, not Sadie. "We're due to announce our new capital campaign in two weeks, timed with the opening of the exhibit. I really don't advise letting word of this get out, as the press would have a field day. Especially with the fact that it's been stolen not only once, but twice. I strongly suggest we hold off until right after the announcement. That way we can secure the big donors' commitments before they learn the news."

The men and women around the table murmured in agreement.

"We'll discuss this further," said Dr. Hooper. But by his tone, Sadie knew the alarm would not be sounded. "Thank you for the update."

She paced in the hallway outside Nick's temporary office while he made a couple of phone calls, too worked up to sit still. The shortsightedness of the board made her furious. What was the point of being a library if you didn't put the books first, ahead of the big checks? In three weeks' time, the *Tamerlane* would be in Europe or somewhere else far, far away, lost once again and this time for good.

She thought of how dear everything in the Berg Collection had become to her, of how terribly she'd miss it if she was never allowed back. Not only the books, manuscripts, and letters, but the quirkier pieces, like Jack Kerouac's harmonicas, Vladimir Nabokov's butterfly drawings, that damn cat-paw letter opener.

Wait.

She remembered one of the last times she'd seen the letter opener, and as she did, something in her mind clicked, like a gear snapping into place on a bicycle.

Nick finished up and together they walked outside.

"Thank you for coming to the rescue," said Sadie. "I'm glad you were there today."

"Sure thing." He looked uneasy. "I'm sorry they didn't listen to you."

"Well, no surprise there." She studied him, trying to figure out how to make her next request. "If I ask you to do something really, really strange, would you? I have an idea. But I need your help."

"What is it?"

She looked up at the revolving door. "Oh no, hide!" She grabbed Nick by the arm, pulling him around the far side of one of the lions, where she crouched low to the ground.

"What on earth are you doing?" he said.

She slowly stood back up, looking out toward the street before taking hold of his arm yet again and yanking him down the steps.

"Follow me. Now."

"Where are we going?" asked Nick as Sadie practically shoved him inside a taxi.

"We're following that cab," she said to the driver, before turning to Nick. "I've always wanted to say that."

"Why?"

"Because it's in all the old movies."

"No, I mean, why do you want to follow that particular one?"

"Because Mr. Jones-Ebbing is inside it."

"What do you want with him?"

"Maybe this is crazy, but the way he acted seemed off to me," she said. "He's new to the board, yet jumping in like he's a top dog about not wanting it to leak to the press."

"Isn't that what board members are supposed to do, worry about things like that?"

"When he first joined, I gave him and some others a tour of the library. He reached out and touched everything he could, even when I asked him not to. Like he couldn't help himself." She remembered him sliding his finger along the blade of the letter opener, as if he owned it. "My hunch is that he's involved."

"His reasoning about keeping the theft a secret was sound, if you consider his point of view."

"There's something wrong there, I'm sure of it." Nick started to respond, but she cut him off. "Trust me, okay?"

The cab pulled up to a brownstone in the East Fifties.

"Must be where he lives," said Sadie.

"Or maybe it's where the Stolen-Book Lovers Association is having its annual meeting."

"Very funny."

Jones-Ebbing got out of his cab and walked up the steps, opened the front door, and disappeared.

"Now what?" Sadie let out a sigh of frustration. "We can't just walk in there."

They got out of the taxi and sat on a stoop on the other side of the street, partially hidden from view by some garbage cans.

Across the street, a woman walked quickly, head down. Long brown hair cascaded from underneath a baseball cap. Even so, Sadie recognized her immediately. "Bingo. It's Robin."

"Lonnie said she had short blond hair."

"It's a wig. She's the right size, and come on, who walks around on a cloudy day wearing huge sunglasses and a baseball hat?"

"Celebrities?"

"No. Book thieves. But that doesn't explain how she got past security with the book still on her. They would have checked her bag. How did she get out?" Sadie held her breath and only let it out when the woman turned up the same stairs that Jones-Ebbing had.

"Double bingo," said Nick.

The door opened, and Sadie just made out Jones-Ebbing's profile, ushering Robin inside.

"We have to go in there." Sadie knew it wasn't feasible, or even legal, but still. "What do we do now?"

Nick stood. "Finally, they're on time for once."

Two police cars glided down the street, no sirens sounding, but moving fast.

"What? Is that our backup?" Sadie turned to Nick. "You had the same idea?"

"Sure. Jones-Ebbing was a dead giveaway back there, sweating and jittery. All the signs of deception. In fact, he had recently become a focus of our inquiry."

"That's what you were doing when you made those phone calls?" Sadie didn't wait for him to answer. "Then why did you play dumb behind the lion?"

"For the look on your face now." Nick smirked. "Besides, you wouldn't let me get a word in edgewise."

They met the cops at the foot of the stoop and let them lead the way. Jones-Ebbing opened the door, sputtering with confusion, and tried to protest as they pushed their way in. Down the hallway,

Sadie spotted a figure running to the back of the town house. "It's Robin!"

One of the policemen took off after her, while the other remained nearby.

Jones-Ebbing sat down hard on the couch, staring at the *Tamerlane* on the coffee table in front of him. Nick picked it up and handed it to Sadie. "Let's not lose it this time, please."

She was about to answer as Robin was led out—kicking, screaming, and wigless—to a police car.

This crook, this thief, couldn't possibly be the same woman who'd sat in Lonnie's apartment and comforted Sadie after the loss of her mother. Who'd taken such care with Valentina. It seemed impossible.

"Thank God you got her, she's an absolute criminal for what she's done." Jones-Ebbing rose to his feet. "Can I get you a cup of coffee, or anything stronger? I could sure use a drink."

The gall of this man. "No thanks, I think we have bigger things to discuss," said Sadie.

"I assure you, I had no idea who she was," Jones-Ebbing said. "This woman turned up at my door, showed me the book, and asked if I'd like to purchase it from her. I pretended to be interested so I could secure it for the library. Then you turned up. Well done. Great teamwork."

"Is that how it went down?" asked Nick.

"Of course. I was waiting for her to leave, and my next call was to Dr. Hooper, to give him the good news."

"You're on the board of the library. Why would she approach you?" Sadie wanted to keep him talking, see if he could be forced into a corner.

"I'm quite well-known in the rare book world, of course."

"And what if we go through your own collection?" Nick pointed to the endless bookshelves. "I wonder what else we might find."

"You're welcome to examine my shelves."

"We might also want to show Mr. Jones-Ebbing's photo to the owner of J&M Books," suggested Sadie. "I'm sure he's eager to throw someone else under the bus."

At that, it was as if the man deflated. He sank back on the couch, head in his hands. "She approached me, I swear."

Nick motioned for Sadie and the policeman to hang back, let him handle the questioning. "Robin came to you with the idea to steal the books? It makes a difference, you know, if you weren't the one who initiated the idea."

He gave a tentative nod.

"Did she tell you what books she was going to take?"

Jones-Ebbing looked at the policeman, then back at Nick. When he finally spoke, the words poured out of him in a childish whine. "I never had any idea what she was going to turn up with. Until last night, when she said she was going to try for the *Tamerlane*, but I didn't believe her. I knew it had been missing for decades."

Something about his confession didn't ring true to Sadie. He was underplaying his part in the whole scheme, she was certain.

"What about the folio?" asked Nick. "The torn page?"

Jones-Ebbing went pale. "I would never have condoned ripping a page out. Macabre, to have done that."

"And the others you brought downtown to J&M Books to be sold." It was a statement, not a question.

"I had to."

"Had to?"

"Money trouble. Keeping up appearances was becoming difficult."

The damage he'd done, the stupidity, riled Sadie. All for appearances' sake.

At the police station, Robin sat on a bench, handcuffed, looking as small and waifish as possible, her eyes huge, but all that changed when she spotted Sadie. She practically spit on the floor as they neared, morphing from Little Orphan Annie to Bonnie Parker in one fell swoop. Remarkable, really.

"Who are you?" asked Sadie.

"Wouldn't you like to know."

Nick intervened. "Enough. You can't talk to her right now."

Sadie reluctantly turned away.

A week later, Nick got word that the district attorney had decided against going after Robin for kidnapping. Robin had insisted that Valentina had followed her into the library without her knowledge, that she hadn't held her against her will, which was corroborated by Valentina's story. However, Robin was charged with endangerment of a minor, and accepted that charge as well as those of the book thefts. Part of her agreement was that she explain how she pulled the thefts off.

Sadie met Nick at his company's space in the Grace Building overlooking Bryant Park along Forty-Second Street. A receptionist directed her to his private office, which offered a stunning view of the library. "How convenient," she said, taking the seat he offered. "I'm surprised you didn't have a telescope set up to watch the goings-on through the windows."

"Don't think it didn't occur to me."

"Tell me everything she said."

"Robin's family history is pretty awful," he said. "She was abandoned by both parents and put into the foster care system in northwestern Massachusetts. Then she and her sister were separated from each other. As a teenager, she got involved in a program that placed at-risk youths in local businesses, in part-time jobs, and worked in a bookstore for a few years before heading to a community college."

"And that's where she got to know about rare books?"

"Looks like it. At some point, though, she was caught razoring maps out of rare atlases at Amherst's library. She'd said she needed the money to pay for her tuition and, since it was her first offense, was given probation."

If only Robin had been handed a harsher punishment back then, she might have been thwarted early on.

"How did she meet Jones-Ebbing?"

"Turns out he has a summer home up in western Massachusetts, and it was there that they first connected. Eventually, they began working together, stealing from estate sales and bookstores. It was a low-key racket until Jones-Ebbing was asked to join the board of the library and they hit the mother lode."

Nick had also learned that Robin had specifically targeted Sadie and Lonnie when they first met, the day that Valentina had fallen in the playground. The young twins she said she was with, it turned out, weren't even her charges. She'd been following Lonnie and Sadie for some time, hoping to ingratiate herself into their lives.

"I don't understand the connection, though. Why us?"

"She knew that the *Tamerlane* had been stolen by your family at some point, but she wouldn't say how she got that information. She's protecting someone, I'm sure. In any event, she figured you were the missing link. Once she landed the job as babysitter, she'd listen in on the extension whenever you and Lonnie spoke. That was how she figured what books to take, and what sent her into the old apartment looking for the *Tamerlane*, hoping to find it before you did."

"How exactly did she get around the library, not to mention in and out?" asked Sadie.

"She'd hide out in one of the spiral staircase anterooms in the Reading Room until the library closed, then take the dumbwaiter from there to the stacks in the basement level. She'd exit via the fire escape hatch under Bryant Park, which opens out beneath some shrubs. Apparently, even once, a cop walked by, and she just pretended like she was homeless, sleeping under a bush. He didn't blink an eye."

Unbelievable. "How did she get into the cage once she was in the stacks? There's no way in."

"She'd pull up the bottom and secure it with a bungee cord, then crawl underneath."

That was the scraping sound Sadie had heard, when she'd almost come face-to-face with the thief. Robin's tiny frame had worked in her favor, both in the dumbwaiter and in the stacks.

"If they were looking for books to fence, why did she tear out the page from the folio? That doesn't make any sense, it's just mutilation."

"She said that was just for her own private collection. Wouldn't give a reason."

There were too many loose ends, in Sadie's opinion. But the library was mainly interested in knowing how she pulled off the thefts so that they could prevent anything similar from happening again.

However, there was one question left. The most important one. "The dumbwaiters. I get that it's obvious that the one in the Reading Room led to the stacks. But Robin knew enough about the library to be able to escape through the one in the women's room on the third floor when I was chasing her, which wasn't even in service anymore. How did she know about that in the first place? How did she get down it?"

"She said she shinnied down the shaft, even bragged about pulling that particular escape off. But as for how she knew about them in the first place"—Nick shook his head—"she wouldn't say. Even when we pressed her, she wouldn't say."

CHAPTER TWENTY-EIGHT

New York City, 1993

With only four days until the exhibit opened, Sadie was more nervous than excited. She'd worked so hard on this, yet it wasn't quite right, and she wanted it to be perfect.

She'd been allowed to come back to work right after the arrests of Richard Jones-Ebbing and Robin Larkin. Dr. Hooper wasn't thrilled about Sadie's connection to the thief, but the fact that he'd placed Robin's coconspirator on the board of the library meant that he had to shoulder some of the blame himself. Sadie made sure to push that fact when they met to discuss the terms of her return, and had been reinstated as curator of the exhibit.

Inside the exhibit hall, Sadie stared out over the display cases where the best of the Berg Collection sat opened to their most important pages, like a bunch of literary peacocks. She took the tour as if she were a visitor, new to all this. To start, there was the First Folio. The title page had been carefully laid into the correct position, but not affixed. It couldn't just be glued back; the damage was permanent. Heartbreaking, indeed. The description next to it stated as much.

A 1719 copy of *Robinson Crusoe* included a vivid illustration of the title character, and next to that was her beloved *Tamerlane*. Its label stated that the anonymous author listed on the cover—*By a Bostonian*—was indeed Poe, and mentioned that the volume had been recently rediscovered. If only Sadie had more than six lines to describe the book's journey.

The exhibit itself *was* a journey of sorts, of letters, manuscripts, and books, of poets and writers, Austen and Tennyson and Yeats. To have them all assembled in one room was a dream. It was as if she'd summoned the very ghosts themselves to chatter with each other, compare edits and changes, remark on the elegant bindings. The exhibit almost made up for the ordeal she and her family had gone through the past few months. Almost, but not quite.

The case against Robin was still making its way through the court system. The prosecutor had warned Sadie not to get her hopes up, that judges didn't view valuable books the way they might a painting or other item taken from a museum. In fact, the typical sentence was less than three years in jail.

Sadie had asked to speak at the sentencing, in the hopes of pleading their case, but so far hadn't heard anything back. She made a mental note to bother the prosecutor again tomorrow.

There was still no understanding of how Robin knew about the dumbwaiter system in the library. The original floor plan of the building hadn't been checked out for years. Sadie had called Miss Quinn in London to ask if she knew of the girl, but no luck there, either. It was as if she'd sprung out of nowhere, insinuated herself into Sadie's family, and then taken advantage. Richard Jones-Ebbing had pleaded guilty right away and volunteered all the information he could about Robin, but it didn't add up to much.

Lonnie, LuAnn, and Sadie had brought Valentina back to the library a few weeks after her overnight adventure, hoping to ease any lingering trauma. She'd proudly shown them where she'd hidden out in the nook in the Reading Room; then she'd skipped down the main stairway to the basement, where Mr. Babenko had found her and taken such good care of her.

In the exhibit hall, Sadie stopped in front of Laura Lyons's walking stick, displayed between Dickens's cat-paw letter opener and Charlotte Brontë's writing kit. The nonliterary choices gave the attendees' eyes a rest from the printed page, and also helped humanize the authors as actual people who opened letters and walked and traveled. Souls who'd accomplished amazing things during their lifetimes, and were more than just a litany of names from high school English class.

She unlocked the display case and lifted out the walking stick, wishing again they had an original piece of writing from Laura Lyons to include, not just the old library newsletters. She ran her fingers over the curve of the wood. Her grandmother had put her own hand there, gripped the stick as she made her way across London, to her death. According to Miss Quinn, she'd been found still clutching it, surrounded by debris.

In her most recent call with Miss Quinn, the woman had volunteered that the walking stick, which Laura never left home without, had been a gift from Amelia Potter. By now, Miss Quinn had become a confidante of sorts, and regaled Sadie with stories of Laura and Amelia taking weekend trips to Brighton in the warmer months, of hosting dinner parties that dissolved into laughter and song. Even though they kept separate residences, they were rarely out of each other's sight, staying together in one place or the other. It made Sadie happy to learn that her grandmother had been loved, and she'd changed the label on the case to reflect that new information.

"Laura never left home without it," Miss Quinn had said.

Sadie paused. Wasn't that the same thing that Laura Lyons had said about the essay she mentioned to Miss Quinn before her death? *It told the truth, and . . . for now she always carried it with her.*

She regarded the walking stick again, remembering the ones she'd seen on television or in the movies with flasks or knives hidden inside. Holding it up to the light, she examined its handle, looking for any edges where it might come apart. Nothing. The wood was smooth, with no signs of separation.

She turned it upside down. The very bottom was worn, but in the middle, there appeared to be a kind of stopper made from a similar wood, so that it was hardly noticeable.

What to do? This was a valuable artifact. If she dug her nail in to try to wedge it out, she might damage the stick.

But Sadie couldn't help herself. She had to see if the plug could be removed. She wouldn't do anything drastic, not use a screwdriver on it, for example, but if her fingernail could loosen it a little . . .

It popped off, landing with a click on the floor and rolling to a stop by her shoe. Sadie bent down and picked it up, placing it carefully on top of the display case.

She peered inside the opening of the cane and could barely make out the edges of a piece of paper rolled up inside.

Laura Lyons's final essay. The one she always carried with her.

Sadie knew she shouldn't attempt this alone. She picked up the plug and the cane and went back into the Berg Collection's main room, where Claude looked up with concern. Since Sadie had returned to her job, they'd reached a lukewarm détente, both eager to move forward and focus on mounting a successful exhibit. Their alignment of interests had smoothed over their previous troubles.

"Should you be handling that without gloves?" he asked. "Why is it out of the case?"

"I think I found something strange. I need your help."

She explained about the plug, saying that she'd noticed it was sticking out and that it had fallen off when she lifted the walking stick. Just a white lie. At least she'd stopped herself from examining it alone.

By the time she'd finished speaking, Claude was practically salivating. "What do we do?"

"We should bring it downstairs, to Mr. Babenko. He might have the tools to get it out without damaging the paper or the cane."

As they walked down the three flights of stairs, Sadie gathered up her courage. "Claude, I want to apologize about the way I behaved, after the Christmas party. I was rude to you, and I'm sorry about that."

There, she'd said it. She waited as Claude absorbed the change in the air between them, the sudden intimacy her words had created. He cleared his throat. "And I'm sorry to have lashed out at you like that. We were both worried about the collection, and under pressure. But it wasn't very nice. I'm sorry."

"Can we be friends?" She snuck a glance at him.

"I'd like that very much."

At that, a weight lifted from Sadie that she didn't realize she'd been carrying. How silly she'd been to not have had this conversation back in January, but she was learning. Learning how to be clear, to express what she was thinking without worrying it was wrong or stupid. To take up space and not apologize for it.

In the basement, Mr. Babenko approached the project with a careful enthusiasm, finding a pair of tweezers with rubber tips that wouldn't tear the paper.

"What if it's just an old shopping list?" joked Claude.

"I wouldn't put it past her," said Sadie. "Laura Lyons, getting the last laugh."

The paper slipped out, and as Sadie held her breath, Mr. Babenko gently unrolled it, placing weights at each corner to hold it flat. The paper had turned yellow but wasn't cracked, and Sadie recognized Laura Lyons's signature at the bottom. This was no shopping list.

The note was filled with tiny handwriting, and dated not long before Laura's death.

A valuable book by Poe sits in a dark, unused dumbwaiter in the superintendent's apartment of the New York Public Library. Although my husband took the blame before killing himself, the true thief was my son. I will do anything I can to protect him, so while my boy is alive, I will never tell a soul. Yet I can't bear the thought of it being lost forever, and I write this to try to absolve some of my terrible guilt at keeping such a secret. This has been weighing on me deeply. I hope one day the truth will come out, and the book will be rescued.

So Laura Lyons's son—Sadie's uncle, Harry—had been the culprit back in 1914, not Sadie's grandfather. In the note, Laura explained that it had all begun when Harry burned his father's manuscript, a book that he'd been writing for years, but that it was all ultimately her fault, that her own actions had initiated a cascade of tragedies.

The burning book. Not a rare manuscript, an unpublished one.

While my boy is alive, I will never tell a soul, Laura had written.

But Sadie's uncle Harry had died of typhoid in his teens. At least, that's what Pearl had told Sadie and Lonnie. Or had Laura lied to her daughter in order to make a clean break prior to their move overseas? Sadie's head spun.

"We have to include this in the exhibit," said Claude. "Is it too late?"

"It's definitely too late for the catalog," said Sadie.

"What if we include an insert, like they do in theater playbills when there's an understudy?"

Sadie snapped her fingers. "Great idea. Bring these back upstairs and get them safely in the display case. I'll work on the language for the insert when I'm back."

"Where are you going?"

"To find some answers."

The exhibit opened with a bang, with glowing write-ups in all the national newspapers and even a segment on *60 Minutes*, where Sadie spoke of the importance of the books and, with Dr. Hooper's permission, the backstory of the thefts and Sadie's personal connection to Laura Lyons. It was a juicy story, so juicy that even Dr. Hooper didn't mind the exposure, not with lines out the door to view the exhibit every day, and new donors offering to support the collection every week. Sadie explained to Lesley Stahl that in a way, the robbery had made the books come alive, become part of our current conversation, instead of remaining inanimate, historical archives. Stahl seemed to really like that.

At the opening-night reception, Sadie took a break from accepting congratulations from her colleagues and hung back in a corner, observing the crowd. In the center of the room, Dr. Hooper was guiding several board members through the exhibit, while nearby, Lonnie, LuAnn, and Valentina stared into the case containing Laura Lyons's cane, as Lonnie animatedly explained the story of the secret hiding place to Valentina, whose eyes were huge.

"Hey there."

She turned to see Nick in the doorway, holding two glasses of champagne in his hands. He was dressed in a black suit with a sea-blue tie that matched his eyes. "Care to join me?"

She followed him out into the hallway, where waiters were passing trays of food to the guests who had assembled in the McGraw Rotunda.

Nick handed her a glass and pointed up to the mural on the ceiling. "Who's the tough guy with the sparkler?"

"That would be Prometheus, who stole fire from Zeus and gave it to mankind."

"Brave soul."

"Zeus didn't think so. He punished him big-time. Chained him to a rock, ordered a bird to eat his liver, that kind of thing."

He cringed. "Glad the painter decided to skip that half of the story. Not sure I could stomach it."

"Probably wouldn't go over very well with the library's visitors, either. Not exactly the message we want to get across."

"Although it might deter future book thieves."

"Good point."

Nick cocked his head toward the exhibit hall. "I saw Dr. Hooper earlier and he was practically levitating, he was so giddy. You've done it, Sadie."

"It was a team effort. Including you, of course."

They locked eyes, and neither looked away.

Sadie considered her choices. She could put him off, the way she'd done with Claude, and stay safe from harm. Or she could take a leap and pursue him, allow herself to be pursued, and possibly end up hurt and betrayed. Laura Lyons had taken the risk with Amelia Potter. After losing so much more than Sadie had, she'd been able to open up and love someone again. Sadie was certain she could, too. Her future was in her hands, a book yet to be written. How she chose to fill its pages was entirely up to her.

"Sadie, tomorrow night, at the Village Vanguard, there's a—"

"Yes. I'd love to."

He laughed. "Don't you want to know what it is?"

"Whatever it is, there will be music and you. A winning combination."

"We are a winning combination, Sadie. Don't forget that." His face was lit up from within, boyish, and Sadie's heart swelled. She wished she had a camera to capture his expression. He stepped closer. "We'll have a good time, I promise. By the way, how is your follow-up research going, into Robin's past?"

She'd described, in vague terms, her hunt to uncover Robin's connection to the library, but wasn't ready to disclose anything just yet. She'd fill him in once she had the proof she was seeking. "I'm close, I'm sure."

Just then, Dr. Hooper and the other guests spilled into the rotunda, and a spoon was clinked on a champagne glass. Sadie and Nick stood side by side, arms touching, as the speeches began.

Sadie was granted permission to speak before Robin's sentencing, which the lawyers predicted would be between thirty and thirty-seven months for the crime.

"Don't be nervous, you'll do great," said Nick as they took their seats in the courtroom. He'd come partly to offer her support, and also as a security guard for the large box she kept on her lap, even though there was more than enough space on the bench beside her. This time, she was taking no chances.

They both looked up as Robin was brought into the room, wearing a drab gray suit. Her hair had grown out, and long bangs partially obscured her face.

"All rise."

Judge Kiernan entered through the door behind his bench, took his seat, and signaled to the clerk to proceed. The prosecutor spoke first, followed by Robin's attorneys, and then finally the judge called out Sadie's name.

She clutched the gray box like it was a lifeline, and stared over at Robin so hard that at first she didn't hear the judge's question.

"Ms. Donovan?"

"Right. Yes. I'm here to ask for an upward departure." She'd been told the term by the prosecutor, which meant asking the court to consider granting a harsher sentence than normal. The phrase seemed more suited to first-class seating on an airline flight than a criminal's punishment.

"Proceed."

"While all the items were eventually recovered, I can't help but think it's important to send a message to other thieves out there who might be considering something similar."

"The sentence is determined from the value of the items stolen. Are you saying that's wrong?" asked the judge.

"The problem with that approach is that the value of a rare book is imperfect, fluctuating. These items have been held for years, centuries, and our perspective changes over time. For example, records of sales of slaves from the 1800s were considered extraneous items a hundred years ago. Today, they're rare artifacts from a time that requires further examination, renewed study. Their value has gone up because society's view of them, and the history they describe, has evolved.

"What Miss Larkin stole was not simply a certain number of pages worth a certain amount, but pieces of Western history and culture that have a dramatic impact on scholarly research. The loss of these items is a detriment to all humanity and civilization."

She glanced over at Nick, who had a pained expression on his face. She might have overdone the hyperbole at the end there, but when she looked at the judge, he was leaning forward, listening.

"Continue, Ms. Donovan."

"One solution would be to lock them away permanently, to keep people like Miss Larkin from stealing them. But we depend on the accessibility of these documents so that new ways of thinking can flourish. That means the library's contents must be made available to the good people who seek them out and use them to advance knowledge and scholarship. As much as they need protection, we can't hide them away." She paused. "Can I show you something?"

The clerk motioned for Sadie to place the box on a table in front of the judge's bench. Sadie pulled white gloves out of her purse and made a show of putting them on—Claude's idea, and a smart one—before uncovering the box and lifting out the folio. She slowly opened it to the title page.

"I can't see from here, hold on, I'm going to join you." The judge was by her side a few moments later. Sadie pointed out the page that had been sliced out, how the book would never be the same, and that the title page was now at great risk, having been removed from its rightful place in the binding.

Next, she took out the Woolf diary, and opened it to the final entry. "This tear wasn't here before it was taken. The pages are delicate, and can't be handled roughly. In time, we may lose this entire section."

The judge shook his head. "It's the last thing that she ever wrote down, is it?"

"So we believe, yes."

"Thank you for your information, Ms. Donovan."

She had more to say, but went back to her seat. The court was recessed, and after lunch they gathered again. She'd been too nervous to eat anything.

The judge cleared his throat. "Section 5K2.0 of the legal code permits a departure whenever there exists an aggravating or mitigating circumstance not adequately taken into consideration by the Sentencing Commission in formulating the guidelines. The nonmonetary loss caused by Robin Larkin is such an aggravating factor. Hence, an upward departure is appropriate. Indeed, the case directly supports that conclusion."

The courtroom erupted in cheers, but the clerk called them back to order as the judge continued. "Robin Larkin, you are sentenced to five years in prison, three years of probation, three hundred days of community service in an adult literacy program, and directed to pay full restitution to the New York Public Library."

Nick hugged Sadie close. "Well done."

"We did it."

Robin hadn't moved from her seat, but turned her head in their direction. Sadie expected her to grimace or glare at her, but she didn't, not really. Instead, she looked beyond Sadie, a faraway look on her face.

Strange.

The court officers led her away, and once the judge had exited, people began milling out. Sadie turned around. Who had Robin been staring at?

In the very back row, tucked behind a scrum of reporters, sat an old man with a thick gray beard and round spectacles, like he was out of another time altogether. The rest of the room whirled around in her vision, only the man staying still, in the middle of the frame.

She gave the boxes to Nick and told him she'd meet him uptown. "Do not leave these behind in the cab, please."

"Look who's talking." He kissed her goodbye. "I assure you they'll get back safely. I'll give them directly to Claude."

After he'd left, she approached the old man, slowly, carefully, as if he might disappear into thin air.

"You came." She studied his face. His skin was mottled, the lids of his eyes hanging low. Yet his profile matched hers; they shared the same nose and chin.

He looked up at her, his body trembling slightly. "You were quite good up there. To watch you was"—he paused—"remarkable."

"Thank you, Uncle Harry."

They stared at each other, unsure of what to say or do next. Sadie was both fascinated and terrified. She'd found him.

"You look just like my mother," he said.

"That's what my mother used to say as well. The few times she mentioned her."

His voice cracked. "Our dear Pearl. Thank you for letting me know about her passing." Sadie sat down next to him. For a moment nothing was said, and then he took her hand, the grip surprisingly strong. "I hope she went peacefully, in the end."

"She did. I'm sorry you had to hear it that way, in a letter."

Sadie had mailed the letter to a bookstore tucked deep in the Berkshires of western Massachusetts, unsure if it was the right thing to do or not. She'd included her phone number, and every evening since, she'd eagerly checked her answering machine, to no avail. Over the past few days, she'd decided that if she didn't hear back from him soon, she'd enlist Nick in driving up there with her, just show up in person. But that hadn't been necessary.

"How did you know to look for me?" he asked.

Sadie described finding Laura's hidden note, which implied that Harry was still alive at the time of his mother's death. "According to Laura, you were the only other party involved who knew about the dumbwaiters. You had to be the link to Robin. I tried to locate a Harold Lyons, but it's too common a name, I couldn't track you down that way. And even if I could, turns out you'd changed it."

"Right. To Merrill. When I left the city, I needed a fresh start."

"The answer came to me when I requested the name of the bookstore where Robin had worked as a teenager. It stood out."

Harry smiled. "Lion Books. I suppose I couldn't help but hold on to a vestige of my lineage."

"I sent that letter and hoped for the best, and here you are."

To find Pearl's long-lost brother so soon after losing Pearl broke Sadie's heart. The joy that he was still alive was tempered by the decades that he'd kept away, by choice, which Sadie simply couldn't comprehend. After everything his mother and sister had been through, why had he remained estranged? Sadie couldn't imagine abandoning Lonnie, LuAnn, and Valentina.

"Why did you stay away for so long?" she asked, finally.

As the courtroom emptied, the old man spoke of gangs and stolen books, of a city vastly different from the one they were in now. "Initially, I was too afraid to return home, and by the time I realized I had to face what I had done, Red Paddy—the gang leader—threatened my family if I stopped stealing books for him. He was a charismatic, dangerous sort, who brought me under his wing and then told me lies to keep me under his control. I hated that it tore us all apart, that I couldn't make amends for my actions, but I didn't think I had a choice. The world is a large place when you're just a child, and I didn't have any perspective on what was true and what was not. I only saw danger, and couldn't find my way out. After I learned my father had killed himself, there was no returning to my family. I'll never forget the look on my mother's face. They were better off without me. There was no going back."

Sadie watched, unsure of what to do or say, as he dabbed at his eyes with a handkerchief. "How *did* you eventually get out?" she finally asked.

"At some point a few years later, the police raided our hideout, and we scattered. I knew it might be my only opportunity, and so I hitched a ride out of town. The truck was going north, which was good enough for me, anywhere I couldn't be found. Books were what I knew, so I got a job at a bookstore, working as an assistant, eventually taking over after the owner died."

"And in all that time, you never thought to reach out?"

He shuddered. "No. I was too ashamed. I'd read about my mother's budding literary career in London, and was happy for her. Once, when I was in New York years later for a booksellers' conference, I looked up Pearl in the phone book and stood outside her town house. I saw her leave with you in tow. You both looked happy, safe. That was good enough for me. I couldn't intrude. I figured Pearl hated me.

"I tried to make up for what I'd done by hiring at-risk teenagers to help out in the store. Most of them weren't interested in the books, but Robin was different." The quiet, devoted way he said her name suggested he had a soft spot for the girl. "She'd had a terrible childhood, and lost herself in reading from an early age. She said books had saved her sanity. One day she was sad, missing her sister, which made me miss my own, and I began to regale her with stories of living in a huge library, where we played baseball in the great rooms using books as bases until we got caught and yelled at, of secret elevators that took you to faraway places. Robin didn't believe me, so I showed her an old article written about our family's life that I'd unearthed at my local library.

"We connected, you see. Robin felt guilty at the fact that her younger sister was living in another city with another family, that they'd been split up, and I told her that I understood, having lost my sister as well. No doubt some of my residual bitterness seeped into our conversations, bitterness about being left behind when my mother and Pearl moved to England, bitterness that Pearl never tried to find me when she returned. Every evening as we closed up the shop, Robin would ask me for more stories, and somehow, in the retelling, my bitterness slowly faded away. I realized I also could have reached out, but had chosen not to." He glanced over at the empty defense table. "One time I stupidly told Robin about the

Tamerlane. I told her that it had never been recovered, and was probably now in the care of my sister, Pearl."

Which had sent Robin on a mission to find her. Pearl had gone back to her maiden name after husband number two—Sadie remembered her saying something about how pleased her own mother would've been. With the information gleaned from the newspaper article, it would have been easy enough for Robin to look up Pearl Lyons's address in the phone book, just as Harry had, and begin staking out the family.

"Robin was a good girl, early on," said Harry. "Smart, hungry for knowledge. She was mad for Shakespeare, and I would read the sonnets out loud to her, just as my mother did for me."

Sadie thought of the folio page. It had indeed been some kind of sentimental token. But Sadie felt no sympathy for the woman who'd put Valentina in danger. "Robin wasn't forced to steal, she chose to do it."

He remained silent, as if the storytelling had drained him of words. When he finally spoke, it was in a tearful whisper. "I can't help but think that by telling the stories, I displaced my anguish onto Robin—who also felt forgotten—where it festered and grew into something terrible. We are both to be blamed. It should be me, not Robin, locked away."

She sat for a moment, lost in her own grief. Finally, she put an arm around him. Strange how she was more willing to forgive her uncle than Robin, even though they both had done terrible things. Yet Harry had tried to atone for his actions by fostering a love of reading in customers and kids from tough circumstances, while Robin allowed reading to bring joy to her life, and then embarked on a crime spree that would take that love away from others. They'd made choices at every turn. No one was above reproach.

Harry's face crumpled. "I blame myself, for all of this. For everything."

"You were only a boy." Sadie couldn't believe she was comforting the library's original book thief. But it was true. Unlike Robin, he'd been only a child.

"What a mess it all was." He patted her hand. "But what a marvel you are. Tell me, how is your exhibit going?"

"Quite well." In fact, she'd been named permanent curator just a few days ago, and after, she and Nick had celebrated with a night at the opera, lingering in front of the Lincoln Center fountain for a long, glorious kiss.

"I am sorry for this. I hate that these books were harmed. I've spent my life trying to make up for what I did back then. But it's all been for naught."

"No. This case was important. The judge made a stand, and because of that, any future book thieves will be held accountable. It took a while, but we've made a big difference."

He nodded, still looking bereft.

The pent-up anger that Sadie had been holding in, ever since the first theft, finally began to dissipate as the secrets of generations of the Lyons family unspooled like typewriter ribbon.

"Uncle Harry, have you returned to the library since that day?"

He shook his head. "No. I couldn't bear it."

"Maybe it's time. Since you're in town, I'd love it if you would come by and visit the exhibit. I could give you a personal tour. I know my brother, Lonnie, and his wife and daughter would love to meet you as well."

"Are you sure?" His voice shook with hope.

"Yes, I'm sure. You're the connection that's been missing all this time, the link I've been searching for between my mother and my grandmother. There's so much I want to learn, if that's all right. All the stories that I never knew. Will you share them with us, with me and Lonnie? Say, tomorrow at four?"

"I would, most certainly. It would be my honor. Tomorrow at four it is."

She stood, reluctant to leave this man. Eager to find out more in the coming days.

Yet, no matter what, some questions would remain unanswered. What had it been like for Laura Lyons to leave her son behind, to move to another country and start a new life? Only a tiny sliver of what she'd experienced had been left behind in her note, the anguish and pain pulsing behind each word, behind each carefully chosen phrase. It was a crucial piece of literary history, recovered and now safely tucked away within the library's walls. And a crucial piece of Sadie's personal history, too. She was grateful that she was finally learning about her extraordinary grandmother, who had taken risks and pursued what she cared about, even when society didn't approve. Sadie might not have quite as many obstacles, but she was proud to think that she'd overcome her fear, and was following in her grandmother's footsteps.

Like Laura, Sadie was devoted to her work. And also like Laura, she'd met and fallen in love with someone who was as passionate about their career as she was. After all the uncertainty of the past several months, Sadie had finally set herself free. She was free to love the handsome, burly man who'd approached her in the Reading Room so many months ago, and free to continue as curator, protector, and champion of the Berg Collection. She checked her watch.

It was time to head uptown, back to the library, back home.

AUTHOR'S NOTE

While I enjoy researching the history of each building I write about, the stories and characters are fictional, and with this book, especially, I took great liberties with the security procedures and organizational policies of the New York Public Library. For over a hundred years, this beloved literary mecca has anchored my city and been a haven for its residents, and for that I'm truly grateful. The seven-room apartment inside the library, however, did exist, and for three decades was the home of the library's superintendent, John H. Fedeler Sr., and his wife and three children. The family I write about in this book comes from my imagination, not from the historical record.

Several books helped me during my research, including *The New York Public Library: The Architecture and Decoration of the Stephen A. Schwarzman Building*, by Henry Hope Reed and Francis Morrone; *Pulitzer's School: Columbia University's School of Journalism, 1903–2003*, by James Boylan; *American Moderns: Bohemian New York and the Creation of a New Century*, by Christine Stansell;

The Book Thief and *Thieves of Book Row*, both by Travis McDade; *Fighting for Life* by S. Josephine Baker; *Radical Feminists of Heterodoxy*, by Judith Schwarz; *Brothers: The Origins of the Henry W. and Albert A. Berg Collection*, by Lola L. Szladits; *Top Cats: The Life and Times of the New York Public Library Lions*, by Susan G. Larkin; *The Story Collector*, by Kristin O'Donnell Tubb; and *The Awakening*, by Kate Chopin. The *Surviving Spinsterhood* book was inspired by Marjorie Hillis's *Live Alone and Like It* (I couldn't resist including two of her utterly perfect chapter titles, "Solitary Refinement" and "Pleasures of a Single Bed"), and the article by Inez Haynes Gillmore mentioned in the novel was first published in the April 1912 issue of *Harper's Bazaar.* Laura's experiences at the Columbia Journalism School in 1913, which are true to the prevailing sexism of the time, are far from my own when I attended. The J-school taught me everything I know about writing, editing, and shaping a story, and for that, I'm truly grateful. For further reading on the Columbia University library heist that inspired my story, I recommend "Picking Up the Pieces," by Jean W. Ashton, in *The Strategic Stewardship of Cultural Resources: To Preserve and Protect*, edited by Andrea T. Merrill.

ACKNOWLEDGMENTS

Thank you to Stefanie Lieberman for your keen insights and support, and to Stephanie Kelly for your ingenious editing skills—knowing you're both by my side makes all the difference. Thanks to Kathleen Carter, John Parsley, Christine Ball, Amanda Walker, Alice Dalrymple, Becky Odell, Stephanie Cooper, Natalie Church, Christopher Lin, Lexy Cassola, Nikki Terry, Liz Van Hoose, Adam Hobbins, and Molly Steinblatt.

I'm grateful to everyone who shared their knowledge with me as I researched and wrote this book, including Jean Ashton, Andrew Alpern, Francis Morrone, Hope Tarr, Kristin O'Donnell Tubb, George Bixby, and Marion and Sue Panzer. At the New York Public Library, I'm indebted to Melanie Locay, Matthew Kirby, Carolyn Vega, and Keith Glutting. Greg Wands, I'm so grateful for your love, advice, and encouragement.

Finally, a huge shout-out to my family and friends, as well as my fellow writers and readers, for making this journey such joy.

The

LIONS

of

FIFTH
AVENUE

FIONA DAVIS

Reading Group Guide

An Excerpt from
The Spectacular

READING GROUP GUIDE

1. Laura Lyons, despite her husband's protests, wants to be a wife, a mother, and a dedicated journalism student. Do you think women still face societal pressure today to only fill traditional roles? Do you think it's possible to "have it all"?

2. The New York Public Library is very important to both Laura and Sadie. Is the library important to you? What role do you think your local library plays in your community?

3. How does Sadie's character challenge stereotypes about librarians? Before reading this book, did you know the different roles they play in serving the public?

4. How did going to the Heterodoxy Club change Laura? Do you see similar organizations at work today? What is the importance of having spaces where women can voice their opinions, stories, and plans for the future?

5. What do you think of how Laura handles the situation after she finds out the identity of the book thief?

6. Losing the only copy of his manuscript is a devastating blow to Jack. Do you think the act of burning the manuscript was justified? Why or why not? How do you think technology has changed the value we put on the written word?

7. In her note, Laura writes that "it was all ultimately her fault, that her own actions had initiated a cascade of tragedies." Why do you think Laura believes she is responsible? Do you agree? Would things have been different if so much responsibility in the home didn't fall only to Laura?

TURN THE PAGE FOR AN
EXCERPT FROM FIONA DAVIS'S
THE SPECTACULAR,
COMING SOON FROM DUTTON.

CHAPTER ONE

December 2012

I still dance in my dreams.

But not in my life. In my life, I shuffle around this too-large house, tossing whatever is within reach into the nearest cardboard box, not bothering to wrap anything in newspaper or to make sure the box labeled LIVING ROOM actually contains items from the living room.

The movers are far more worried about my belongings than I am. When you get to the age of seventy-five, the stuff that surrounds you every day loses its charm. Like the clock over the fireplace that hasn't worked in a decade. Or the cast-iron Le Creuset pot that sits in a drawer doing absolutely nothing. I haven't given a dinner party in ages, and I'm not about to start now. Some people end up hoarding their possessions, unable to get rid of the plastic bags that the groceries came in, but that's not me. To be honest, I'm getting a kick out of seeing box after box go out the door, like a snake shedding its skin. Out the door and into the big truck, to be dropped off at the Salvation Army. The few pieces that are left, including my antique bed and my favorite rocker, will be delivered to a sunny studio with high ceilings in Sutton Gardens, an independent living community. Never mind that most of its residents have been living independently for the past fifty years. I said so during my tour, but the young lady just gave me a vague look and opened the door to the crafts room, where several silver-haired ladies were painting with watercolors.

You would think that after independent living comes dependent living, but instead it's "assisted," which brings to mind someone delicately holding your elbow as you cross the street in the best of circumstances, or offering extra leverage as you rise from the commode in the worst. Having been the assistant myself for many years, I know full well what's involved. Finally, there's the memory care floor, which is a laugh because for most folks behind those locked doors, there aren't that many memories left to be careful about.

That's not me, though. Not by a long shot. I have all my memories intact. There are days when I wouldn't mind blocking out the more painful ones, but I have nothing to complain about, not yet. At least at Sutton Gardens someone will be there to pick me up when I tumble. Which seems to happen a lot these days.

My new lodgings are just down the road from this house, so it's not as if I'm venturing very far. Even though Bronxville is only eighteen miles from Midtown Manhattan, it's an oasis of green, renowned for its "stockbroker Tudor" houses, the term coined after the newly rich who snapped them up in the 1920s and '30s. People like my father, who was looking for a home that was close to the city but not too close, a place that showed he had good taste and a good job. My father never got tired of pointing out the slate roof and leaded glass windows to visitors. He may not have been a stockbroker, but he was a company man and proud of it.

I look about my living room, almost expecting to see him drinking a scotch in his favorite armchair, and my throat tightens with sorrow.

"Let me help you with that."

One of the movers, a skinny kid with freckles whom the others have teased all afternoon, puts the box he was carrying on the coffee table and comes toward me, eyes wide. He gently takes the clock from my hands.

"It doesn't work," I say, wiping the dust from my palms. "You can have it, if you like. Maybe it can be fixed."

"We're not allowed to take anything," he says. "But thanks."

He looks like he's barely sixteen and is more tentative in his actions than his cohorts, who move about the house like they own it. "You're new at this," I say.

"It's my first job."

"That's why they're making you do all the hard work, like climbing up into the attic. You better not take that kind of guff from them. They'll never stop."

"I don't mind." He pauses. "I found something in the attic that I thought you might want to see. It seems like the kind of thing you might not want to give away without a last look."

I wave my hand. "No one's been up there in decades—whatever it is, I don't need it. Not for the tiny cell I'm heading to." I know I'm being dramatic but I can't help myself sometimes.

"You're going to jail?" asks the boy with a sly smile.

"Might as well be. Space the size of a closet."

He turns to the large box sitting on the coffee table and opens it. "The bottom of this one broke when I was upstairs." He lifts out a pair of pointe shoes from when I took ballet class as a teenager, the ribbons fluttering loose like silk ringlets. "You were a dancer?"

I wish I had taken a moment, just one moment, back when I was dancing, to stop and appreciate what it feels like to lift your leg effortlessly high, what it's like when your limbs and mind are rich with music and your body snaps into place. When your arms and legs do exactly what you tell them to do. In my dreams, I stretch like a rubber band and my body is nineteen again. And then I wake up stiff and sore and realize it's only getting worse.

He places the shoes carefully on the coffee table, as if they were made of glass. Reaching back into the box, he pulls out a program for the Radio City Music Hall *Christmas Spectacular* of 1956. Then a pair of worn Capezio character shoes. I remember exactly what it felt like to buckle them up and dash out of the dressing room, how they eventually molded to my feet after hours dancing on-stage. When I see those shoes, the voices of the other dancers fill my ears, along with the strains of the orchestra warming up.

But some memories are not as welcome. Screams of fear, the smell of smoke. Blood stains on my dance tights, a lone red ribbon.

A combination of terror and regret wraps around me like a straitjacket.

The boy is about to dig deeper, but I stop him. "Enough."

The doorbell rings and I leave him so I can answer it. He can decide what to do with that box. I don't want it.

A young girl with raindrops in her hair stands on my porch.

"Yes?" I ask.

"Ms. Brooks? It's Piper Cole. I'm here to pick you up."

"For what?"

She blinks. "Um. The anniversary? It starts at seven P.M. Sorry

I'm early, I didn't want us to run into rush-hour traffic." Behind her, a black sedan with a driver sits idling at the curb.

I don't remember ever saying that I'd attend. The Rockette alumni group is always sending me newsletters with chipper reports of grandchildren and moves to Florida. I usually give it a quick scan for any familiar names and then toss it in the bin.

"Do you mind if I come in?" Piper asks. The wind has picked up and the rain is getting both of us wet now.

I let her in, and she follows me to the kitchen. There, on the refrigerator, is the invitation, held in place with a small magnet. *Radio City Music Hall invites you to the 80th Anniversary of the Rockettes.* Right, of course. A couple of weeks ago a woman had called to confirm I was coming. Ann Burris was her name. I'd said I couldn't because I don't drive or take the train anymore. She'd told me she'd take care of that, and apparently Piper was the result.

"Are you a Rockette?" I ask.

"Gosh, no." She says it with a rush of air, as if I'd asked if she was the Queen of England. "I'm an assistant to the events coordinator, Ms. Burris. I was told that you were precious cargo and to make sure you made it to the theater in one piece."

"Precious cargo." What a strange phrase. "I'm sorry to make you come all this way, but it's not a good day. I'm moving, you see."

"Oh." Her face is crestfallen. "Ms. Burris will be very upset. She'll think I did something wrong or said something wrong. Won't you reconsider?"

She looks like she might cry.

"Why? I'm sure you'll have a bevy of current and former dancers in attendance. Why do I have to go?"

"It's because of the book. I hope you won't think me

insensitive—I mean, I still can't believe what you went through—but the book is the reason they want you there. Everyone is so eager to know more about what happened when you were a Rockette."

Right. A recent nonfiction account of the events of 1956, published a couple of months ago, has stirred up interest in a time I'd rather not dwell on. Since it came out, I've had all kinds of former friends and foes resurface, not to mention reporters who looked up my address and stopped by unannounced, hoping for an interview. I prefer not to talk about that time. It was when I was at my best as a dancer, yet the worst happened.

I haven't been in that theater, that beautiful, majestic space, since.

"That was long ago. I don't wish to talk about it. Or think about it."

"Oh. Okay." Her eyes flit to the windowsill, where several family photos sit in silver frames. "Of course." She pulls out a cell phone. "I just need to call and let Ms. Burris know."

As she murmurs into the phone, I go back into the living room, where the young mover has left another box on the coffee table, this one marked with my mother's handwriting. Inside are her treasures, objects that she touched and worried over, pages she leafed through and scribbled on in pencil. But as far as I'm concerned, the programs and diaries might as well be dusted with cyanide.

Piper comes into the room, tucking her phone into her coat pocket. "Ms. Burris is so disappointed. And I'm sorry to have wasted your time. I'll excuse myself now and head back."

Just then, the young mover bounds down the stairs carrying a dress on a hanger across his arms as if it were a sleeping maiden.

"Oh my gosh!" Piper takes the dress from him. She holds the hanger high so it doesn't drag on the floor. It's one of my favorite frocks, sapphire blue with a high neck and long sleeves. I haven't seen it in years, but I know it would still fit.

I wore it one of the last times I saw my first love.

"This is beautiful," Piper says.

"Do you want to keep this, Ms. Brooks?" asks the boy. "Or donate?"

He's only doing his job, but I don't want to engage with these questions—or these objects—anymore. The slow drip-drip of memories feels lethal, or at least dangerous enough to drive me from the house. I've got to get out; it doesn't matter where. I could stay here and have my heart torn open or I could go into the city and lose myself in the bright lights and the constant swirl of people. I could mix in with the crowd and disappear for a while, and when I return, all this detritus will be gone for good. I'll sleep in my house for the last time, and tomorrow, I'll start fresh at Sutton Gardens.

I take the hanger from Piper and swoop up the fabric with my free hand so it doesn't touch the floor.

"I've changed my mind," I reply. "I'm going after all."

FIONA
DAVIS

"The master of the unputdownable novel."

—*Redbook*

For a complete list of titles,
please visit prh.com/FionaDavis